EDEN

A ZOMBIE NOVEL BY TONY MONCHINSKI

Permuted Press
The formula has been changed...
Shifted... Altered... Twisted.
www.permutedpress.com

For Kilgore Trout.

EDEN

A Permuted Press book
published by arrangement with the author

ISBN-10: 1-934861-17-0
ISBN-13: 978-1-934861-17-2
Library of Congress Control Number: 2008932534

Cover art by Chris Kaletka.
Edited by Leah Clarke.

10 9 8 7 6 5 4 3 2 1

The frailty of everything revealed at last
—Cormac McCarthy, *The Road*

"Yeah they're dead. They're all messed up."
—Sheriff McClelland, *Night of the Living Dead* (1968)

So he drove out the man; and he placed at the east of
the garden of Eden Cherubims, and a flaming sword which turned
every way, to keep the way of the tree of life
—*Genesis*, 3:24

"The whole burden of civilization has fallen on us."
"What's that supposed to mean?"
"It means we do not cross against the light."
—*Night of the Comet* (1984)

PREFACE

I **FIRST MET** Tommy Arlin at an open mic night in downtown Raleigh, North Carolina, a monthly event dubbed *The Cypher*. I'd started to attend these as an outlet for pent-up energy and as a way to meet women. I didn't meet many women—to be exact, one lesbian and one certifiable hottie who came up to me *with her boyfriend* in tow after I read to let me know how much she'd liked what I'd read (the boyfriend liked my shit too), but I'm sure my natural shyness didn't help matters (nor, for that matter, did the presence of said boyfriend). So I didn't meet any women, which only added to all that pent up energy, but I did meet the author of this book in your hands.

The Cypher wasn't your usual run-of-the-mill open mic night. This was no Barnes & Noble, and the poets weren't forty-something, cappuccino-sipping, beret-wearing, suburbanite Beatnic-wannabies trying to look anything but. There was something special about *The Cypher*, something I might not be able to articulate in words. A *vibe*. Something *always* went down at *The Cypher*.

Anyway, that night was shaping up to be a memorable one. Shirlette Ammons got up there and tore shit up, Paradox's set had people scratching their heads from the heavy mental he'd dropped, and I'd done my thing about my fictional neo-beat poet and rake Stanislaus Kaerevsky and his sidekick in crime and rhyme Incognito Willy.

Then this guy got up on the microphone, looked like a homeless bum. Turns out he *was* a homeless bum. He reached into a pocket of the raincoat he was wearing—it was a humid summer night outside, I have no idea why he was decked out in a full length raincoat unless he spent his free time as a sex pervert flasher—anyway, this guy reaches into the pocket of his stained musky raincoat and fishes out a crumpled-up, discolored scrap of loose-leaf paper which he precedes to unfold. "They call me Dirtbag Brown," he announced. This was not Tommy Arlin. Taking a swig from the bottle in the paper bag he had on stage with him, drooling half its contents onto the head of the microphone, risking electrocution—how it *didn't* happen I don't know—he proceded to hurl invective and scorn upon all of us in the audience.

There were "bitch-ass" this and "jive-ass honkey" thats, insults aimed at the crowd in general. At least two or three women turned and walked out of the joint when Dirtbag Brown leered at them and stammered some half-discernable lewd comments their way, and a couple of college boys made a big show of having to be held back by their buddies from charging the stage.

Whoever and whatever Dirtbag Brown was, he was *for real.* I found out later his first name was Euripedes. *Euripedes.* I shit you not. After he had managed to offend nearly every race, creed, sexual orientation and color in the joint, Dirtbag Brown poured some of his drink onto the stage—"for the dead homies"—and staggered off into a corner where he dropped trough and pissed his bladder dry. All were aghast and parted for him as he left like the Red Sea around Moses.

"This poem here is about something very special to me, one of my favorite things in the world," a new guy had stepped into the shocked silence and taken the mic. "It's called *The Pussy.*" *This* was Tommy Arlin.

If there could be a polar opposite of Dirtbag Brown this man was it. Arlin was tall, clean, apparently scabies-free, and didn't look homeless. I would later come to learn that he was homeless, though by choice, in his "global nomad" phase. Anyway, Arlin had his shit together and his shit was *tight* that night. He was up there ripping off lines about the vagina—"the P, the U, the double S, *yes!*, the Y, why ask why, the pussy do defy imagination"—but in a nonthreatening, tongue-in-cheek manner that didn't put anyone off. In fact he quickly had the crowd laughing and cheering him on and not a few ladies looked like they might swoon. Arlin's piece ended with the audience laughing and clapping and ignoring the stink of Dirtbag Brown's piss puddled in the corner, a new sense of calm and security having settled back in.

"I want to talk to you about Stanislaus Kaerevsky." Arlin sidled up next to me at the bar where I was trying to imbibe enough liquid courage to get up the nerve to walk over to this hot goth chick and her friend and talk to them. Bars and clubs were never my scene to meet women. I worked best when they could get to know me, be it work situations or a college class. Arlin, I soon found out, had a knack for picking up women anywhere. He turned out to be an insufferable ladies man, and despite poems with titles like *The Pussy,* there was nothing nasty or misogynistic about him. He just liked having sex with women, which I did too. Arlin just got more of it than me. He may not be doing so at the present time however, as he is quite possibly dead. Which helps explain this introduction.

Anyway that night I met Tommy Arlin and almost fell headlong under his spell—they should have his picture in the dictionary under the entry for *charismatic*—but I also immediately started to notice hints that Arlin wasn't everything he was cracked up to be or wanted people to think he was.

The night ended with Arlin and me with two women back in the double wide trailer I shared with my roommate, empty cans of beer and a fifth of Vodka littering the carpet, the girls bent over our knees while we took turns spanking them with a blue rubber whale my roommate's girlfriend had won at the state fair. Arlin had seen something like it on the Howard Stern show and was eager to give it a try. He also thought it was beyond-words great that me and my roommate had a disco ball hanging from the trailer's living room ceiling, but that's besides the point.

Anyway, I started to realize Tommy Arlin's brand of happy horseshit might be just that when early the next morning the women woke me up demanding payment they claimed Arlin had promised them. I had no clue what they were talking about. Arlin took one of the women to my roommate's bedroom in the back while the other, suddenly unfriendly if not downright hostile, sat on the couch under the disco ball alternating glares at me and the rug. Whatever transpired Arlin must have settled it because when they came out his girl told her protesting friend "let's go" and dragged her from there, seemingly satisfied, never mentioning the dough. My roommate, fortunately, was away for the weekend.

Arlin didn't say a word to me about the women, just launched into some mono-logue about Snuffalufagus being the least appreciated resident of Sesame Street while he collected the empty cans from the carpet into a plastic black lawn and leaf bag. He asked me if I could drop him off downtown by the University and I agreed. I was a bit shocked when we spotted Dirtbag Brown pushing his stolen shopping cart down Hillsborough Street, and then dumbfounded further when Arlin bade me farewell, hopped out of the still moving car, ran up to the guy and high-fived him like they'd known each other since forever.

My last image of Arlin that day was in my rear view mirror walking side by side with Dirtbag Brown, the black garbage bag of recyclable cans slung over one shoulder, seemingly not a care in the world.

And we had not discussed zombies at all.

***

I encountered Tommy Arlin again in the West Indies, during his gigolo phase. I was a Peace Corps volunteer on the Third World side of the island nation of St. Vincent, living in an apartment without air conditioning or hot water, and infested with furry spiders the size of my palm, while wealthy honeymooning tourists frolicked amongst the Grenadines' white sand beaches. This was before they filmed the *Pirates of the Caribbean* movies down there.

Off on my own I was hiking through the rainforest up Mount Soufriere, the island's dormant volcano. I was one of fourteen American volunteers on the island—only three of whom were male—and all our females had promptly hooked up with locals. The American women from the Medical School wouldn't look twice in my sweaty, grungy, volunteer-assed direction. I'd dated a few nationals here and there but found it difficult to make conversation with someone who had no more than a fifth grade education. So I found myself alone on a day off doing what I'd done four or five times before: hiking Mount Soufriere.

I'd come to a little clearing where I sat upon a log and drank from one of the three two-liter bottles of water I stowed in my backpack when Tommy Arlin came out of the rainforest like he'd always been there.

Tommy was wearing cargo shorts, a t-shirt with a marijuana leaf printed on it, hiking boots, a camel back over his shoulders and a camouflaged boonie hat. I was surprised to see him but he didn't seem surprised to see me and, in retrospect, I guess he wasn't. A week or two after the night in the trailer I'd gotten a letter from him in the mail which started an on-again, off-again correspondence, he with a string of forwarding addresses from various spots around the world, usually in the name of some woman. Arlin knew I was in the middle of my first year of a two-year stint in the Caribbean and his travels had taken him to the island nation where I was stationed. He explained that he'd blown into port on a Catamaran with a wealthy older Ellen Barkin look-alike.

We hiked to the top of the over four thousand foot high volcano together and looked down from the mists into the crater and the lake of water that had pooled there. Arlin assured me that the volcano had not erupted since 1979 and down we went into the crater, backwards along a seemingly vertical slope clinging to a thick rope that had been secured there long before us for just such purposes. The temperature on top of and inside the volcano was a good twenty degrees cooler than the rest of the island, and it always came as a relief to me. The heat and a lack of seasons would eventually make the Caribbean unbearable for me.

We squatted beside the lake and I shared my lunch with Arlin, who produced a whole pound of skunky weed he'd bought off some Rasta farmers on the other side of the volcano and proceeded to role a series of thin little joints. Of course, like our president at the time, I didn't inhale. Arlin explained to me that when he first came upon the Rastas's secret fields on the side of the volcano they'd looked at him warily, probably high with legitimate CIA paranoia to boot, but once he'd gotten close enough and they'd seen the pot leaf ironed on his t-shirt they'd broken into wide smiles and "all tings were irie." Incidentally, Arlin at a later date would remark to me that he "never appreciated" Russell Banks until he'd been to the West Indies. I also suspect it's why one of the first zombies we see in *Eden* is a Rastafarian.

I asked Arlin what he was really doing in the Caribbean and he said he was scoping out its revolutionary potential. Walter Rodney was long dead, Fidel was a decade away from his intestinal woes, and the revolution, if there ever was going to be one, didn't look like it was going to be televised. Arlin and I shared a passion for left wing political theory and small 'd' democracy, though I'd put myself more along the lines of the libertarian socialist—anarchist—camp while Tommy allied himself with the authoritarian communists (though he wouldn't describe them, or himself, with that adjective). I don't know how or why it came up but looking out onto the lake I mentioned a film I'd seen as a little boy, *Shock Waves*, starring Peter Cushing, about Nazi zombies that rise from the ocean bottom to terrorize a Caribbean island full of vacationers.

Arlin, as it turned out, had seen the movie and it was here we discovered our mutual love of zombie cinema. We talked about zombie movies in general and Italian zombie movies in particular. We discovered our mutual infatuation for Italian actress and scream-queen Anna Falchi (circa the mid-1980s) and agreed to continue to both love her from afar and across time. Arlin told me about a novel he was writing, an action-horror zombie gore-fest with the working title *Dead World*. There was no good zombie fiction of the time and it would be at a later date when we discussed Max Brooks and Brian Keene. For the record, I'm a Brooks fan where Arlin wasn't (for reasons you'll be able to figure out below); I'm not keen on Keene where Arlin (go figure) was; but we both agreed that Jamie Russell's *Book of the Dead: The Complete History of Zombie Cinema*, was a necessity for the zombie cineophile.

Several hours later I asked Arlin if his dowager wouldn't be missing him. He ignored his watch and looked regretfully at the sun and agreed she would. We climbed out of the crater and back down the side of the volcano. I got to meet his doyenne that night when she took us out to eat at the fanciest restaurant on the island, and I have to admit I was jealous: she *did* look like Ellen Barkin. Was Tommy really scouting out the area's likelihood for revolution or merely cadging off the MILF? I suspect some of both. They set sail the following morning.

It wasn't the last time I'd see Tommy Arlin, nor was it the last time we'd discuss zombies.

***

Tommy loved (loves?) zombie films, but he was a purist, a fundamentalist if you will. A Taliban of living dead cinema. Where I could enjoy the lighter-stuff like *Return of the Living Dead* and even Australia's *Undead*—until the aliens come in anyway—and viewed the release of more recent films like *Fido* and *Shaun of the Dead* as positives, as an evolution and extension of the genre, Tommy was disturbed and alarmed. He felt there was *nothing* inherently funny about zombies and there *shouldn't* be anything funny about zombie films. He failed to see the black humor in even his favorite zombie films, including Romero's, though as a socialist he was the first to play up the scant and often thinly-disguised social commentaries.

For Tommy, zombies were terrifying, and a world inhabited by the undead couldn't be anything but a horrifyingly bleak place. "Shopenhauer's wet dream" as he called it, though in retrospect given what I know of Arlin and what little I know of German pessimistic philosophy, I have no idea if Tommy knew what he was talking about of if it just sounded good.

This is why *Eden* reads as dark as it does. Tommy was frank that he'd borrowed the opening conceit—the doomed protagonist—from Rudolph Mate's 1950 film *D.O.A.* (*film noir* being his third favorite genre behind westerns, though my second), but he remained adamant that he socked it to the reader more quickly as to Harris' fate than the original film did to Edmond O'Brien's Frank Bigelow. And indeed, looking back, the reader knows within the first two sentences of *Eden* what end will befall Harris. Yet throughout the novel, Arlin pummels the reader, again and again. I mean, Hasidic zombies? For me the hardest hit is the turn he takes with the character of Bobby Evers, the good natured and sentimental Irishman. I took that as a distinct *fuck you* from Tommy to the reader, just a reminder that less we forget, the world Eden takes place in is Tommy's world, and its one ugly, malevolent place.

But what terrifies me most about Eden are the unanswered questions, the uncertainty. We're never given a clue as to the cause of the outbreak. What reason do the dead come back to life? Radioactive space dust? Peacenik hippies releasing an animal virus across the globe? Microsoft? Arlin won't specify. Further, we never learn the fate of many of the major characters. What happens to Raquel or Mrs. McAllister or Daffy for that matter? I'd guess in a real world, cataclysmic catastrophe uncertainty is the way of things. What happened to that hysterical woman in the crowd, to the firefighter rushing into the building, to the man with blood streaming down his face staggering past? I guess we'd never really know in real life, and I assume that's the effect Tommy was going for here. Closure obviously isn't a cure-all for the pain, but it does lend a sense of finitude to matters from whence we can trudge on. That said, I find it ironic that as to the whereabouts of Tommy Arlin the man, there is no clue today.

***

The last time I saw Tommy Arlin he gave me the manuscript for this book and told me to feel free to try and get it published or throw it out. He was packing his camel back and said he was going to continue walking the earth, which Jules had said in *Pulp Fiction* and Kane before him in *Kung Fu*. I haven't heard from Arlin since. I have heard rumors. That he had assumed another name and was ghost writing a autobiography for Rocket Jackson, the adult industry icon. That he had compiled a group of singers, poets, and performance artists called the New Tribe Collective and that they sojourned from town to town and city to city, performing in coffee houses and student unions on college campuses. That he had joined a band of private contractors and was hunting Osama bin Laden in the badlands of Pakistan. In fact, the last letter I received from him was post-marked Pershawar. That was three years ago.

Why did Arlin entrust this novel to me? I think there are a couple reasons. For one thing, Tommy knew I loved zombies and zombie-movies almost as much as he did. We both kept scratching our heads wondering when some big publishing house was going to drop a major zombie novel. If I tell you that over two dozen major publishers rejected this novel with impersonal form letters I'm not exaggerating.

Tommy also knew I was starting to get published more and more, first in magazines and then academic texts, and he thought that was cool and hoped I'd make some connections that could help him out. Though I've had a few (nonfiction) books published and another in the works, my own novels gather dust in a filing cabinet in my basement. Perhaps Tommy's faith was misplaced. But I refused to let this book die. No, even if it meant publishing it myself through a vanity press, and then the major problem would be distribution. A little research, I found out about Permuted Press, and here we are.

The title *Dead World* already being taken, I thought simply calling it *Eden;* a liberty Tommy wouldn't mind. I find it suitably ironic that the agnostic Arlin named humanity's fictional last redoubt after the biblical epicenter for humankind's everlasting damnation. Why not let the place take front and center stage as the title? I suppose if he is alive he's somewhere in the world trying to bring about that revolution he always dreamt and spoke of. I suppose if he is I will run into him again. I suppose if I should we will talk about zombies.

Tony Monchinski
Peekskill, NY
2008

EDEN

BY TOMMY ARLIN

THE BITE WOKE him up.

"Motherfucker—!"

Harris exploded out of bed, naked—Julie, his woman, startled awake beside him sitting up blinking. He bodily drove the rotten, undead thing that had invaded their bedroom and attacked him in their sleep, propelling it across the room, ramming the creature with his shoulder hard enough to drive it half through the dry wall. Something inside the beast broke audibly on impact, its teeth still gnashing, straining to taste flesh, jagged black finger nails clawing at Harris.

He felt no pain. His senses were nearly overpowered, so much washing over him at once: the low inhuman moans, the stink of necrotic, mottled flesh, the shambling forms stumbling through their bedroom. Harris' last night on earth was behind him for ever.

Weak, pre-dawn trails of sun leaking in through the blinded windows. The stench of putrid flesh everywhere, nauseating. What were once human beings, now dead things, lurching through their bedroom, coming for him, coming for Julie.

"Harris!" Julie yelled.

Bull-fucking-shit! Seeing white, pure rage, his fist balled, aiming three feet past the head of the undead pinned against the wall, the monster struggling to dislodge itself, Harris punched it with everything he had and then some. The soft, decaying skull collapsing under his clenched fist, he wrist deep in its head, pulling back, gore and grey matter clinging to his hand, stuck between his fingers, gobs of it dripping off his hand.

The thing was truly dead now: a death it wouldn't be coming back from.

Julie was fully awake, her revolver retrieved from the bedside—*Boom! Boom!*—the sound deafening, the hammer dropping repeatedly in the confines of the bedroom. What feeble sun light filtering into the room illuminating each blast from the Magnum, a zombie body jerking, headshot, skull contents spraying off into the shadows, the thing dropping, a troupe of them surrounding the bed, reaching for her, she dispatching them one by one, methodically.

The light battling the darkness of the false dawn, so many more black stains on walls already shadowed.

Another undead, this one moving fast, loping, wearing dreadlocks under a tam, charging as Harris yanked the sheet from the bed, draped it over his shoulder, his nudity awkward, uncomfortable, vulnerable. Harris capable of coherent, linear thought again, no longer only reacting to a waking nightmare.

The zombie made noises, clacking what teeth it had, intent on making a meal of him.

A guttural roar from Harris, something human but only just, primal fury unleashed as he launched himself forward to meet it, colliding with the thing in a half tackle, both of them sprawling.

He scrambled around on the floor, got above it, punching down on its head repeatedly, this one's skull solid, refusing to yield.

The undead shifted its weight, dislodging him. It clawed its way around the bedroom floor, losing the tam, ratty dreadlocks splaying around its head, the thing greedily seeking its prey, looking to grab onto a foot, a limb, to sink its teeth into human flesh. Its hunger insatiable, driven by instinct, the beast was without fear.

Looking up it saw the man with the bed sheet about his torso and shoulder like an improvised toga.

Harris with the 12-gauge, the pump always kept barrel up beside the bed. He thumbed the safety, no need to trombone the slide. As the undead creature sprang shrieking from the floor towards his throat Harris squeezed the trigger—

The headless thing flopping onto the floor. Cordite and gunpowder competing with fetid putrescent flesh. Harris pumped the shotgun, vaulting atop the bed where Julie—the revolver emptied, using it as a club to bat at two of the zombies groping for her on the other side—grunting as she kicked and swiped at zombie heads, fighting silently for her life, determined not to—

The shotgun blast devastating in the confines of their bedroom yanking both undead from their feet, slamming one against the wall, the brunt of the buckshot buried in its torso. The second beast dumped on the floor, half its face and the entire jaw missing.

Harris tromboned the shotgun and stepped down from the bed, the empty shell bouncing off the mattress and clattering across the hard wood floor.

"Are you okay?" he asked Julie.

She cool and calm in her actions, quietly reloading the revolver from one of the speed loaders on the nightstand aside their bed. The key to survival is to keep one's head straight at all times in all situations, Julie was aware of this. Only her voice betrayed her, trembling, barely concealing the shock and revulsion gripping her.

"I'm okay," she lied. "I'm fine."

"Okay." Harris breathing deep, working one foot then the other into his low-rise hikers, the Chukkas loosely laced from the night before.

He could hear them coming, more of the zombies beyond the bedroom door. Creeping down the hallway, searching for them. Leveling the shotgun in the direction of the door Harris skirted the bed to the bureau. The chair there toppled in the confusion of the early morning melee, his shoulder holster with the twin nine millimeters somewhere on the floor.

A faint rustling, an undead—its spine severed by the shotgun blast—slapping with one hand at the wall against which it lay. Its eyes followed first Harris, then Julie. The zombie couldn't move any more than to pound the wall with an open palm, a fish out of water, doomed to flop about on solid ground.

Julie flicked on the lamp at her nightstand, Harris spotting his shoulder rig and pistols under a corpse. He pulled the leather strap from beneath the limp body, slinging the holster across one shoulder the way Buddy used to with his saddle bags.

A soft moan from the doorway, the zombie revealed in the light from the lamp. A nurse it had been, stained uniform bearing a smudged nametag. Harris with no inclination to know its name, thinking such a thought a strange one to have anyway. Whatever once constituted its humanity long absent. The thing staggered into the room looking for breakfast.

Julie put it down clean, one between the eyes.

"I'll clear out the rest of the house," Harris told her. He worked as he spoke, retrieving his utility belt with the holstered .45, the extra magazines, the sheathed machete, strapping it onto himself around the bed sheet at his waist. "You stay here. Stay safe. Let me see what the hell is going on downstairs."

"Harris."

He looked at her questioningly.

"Don't go pulling a Richard Simmons on me."

He raised his eyebrow at her.

She gestured.

"Your balls."

He adjusted the sheet.

The paralyzed undead, propped up in the corner, a streak of blood and viscera dripping down the wall above it, eyes darting between them. Though it appeared grievously injured it felt nothing, darting a marbled tongue in and out of its drooling mouth.

Harris espied himself by the light of the lamp in the full length mirror. Another situation, he would have laughed at how he looked now, decked out as he was, bristling with guns, a foot long machete. In another situation.

A bandolier of shotgun shells went over his shoulder, the one covered by the bed sheet.

Harris knew he'd been wounded, bitten. He just didn't want to think about it yet.

Four easy strides took him to the bedroom door. They were out there, a lot of them. He could see two of the undead bouncing against the walls, reeling down the hall towards him. The first wore jeans, an open flannel shirt over nothing, its bloated belly sagging. They would eat until their stomachs burst and then they would keep eating.

The second wore a bathrobe and one slipper. Harris wondered how it'd managed to keep the one slipper all this time.

Behind the two on the landing a third undead spied Harris and howled at the top of its lungs, something evil and intelligent in its gaze.

The first two caught sight of him and also started to make noise, impatient. The sounds they made never ceased to send chills up Harris' spine.

He pumped the 12-gauge, all business. Thumbed another shell into the slide. He looked back at Julie.

"Honey," he said, motioning at the thing on the floor, the zombie impotently palming the wall. "Do me a favor, take care of that one."

"I will," said Julie. Shorts and one of his t-shirts on, she checked the safety of the tricked-out black rifle. Collapsible stock, vertical fore grip, rail mounted flip-up front site, M-7 bayonet, the carbine length free floating rail system lending the AR-15 a ventilated look.

They always slept with their guns next to their bed, fully loaded. It was what one did.

Harris turned back to the hallway, stepping out onto the cool carpet, determined to drive the undead invaders from their home.

His curse had woken her, saved her. Julie had only heard Harris curse once before. She wouldn't describe him as a prude. He claimed his job taught him patience, to temper his tongue. He reserved what he considered strong words for situations that required them.

Julie had heard Harris curse only once before. His curse had accompanied actions she considered out of character for the man she knew better than anyone else.

Julie spread her legs above either side of the felled beast, the thing spastically flapping its one hand against the wall faster than before, excited. She lunged with the AR-15, embedding the fixed bayonet into its braincase under one eye. Julie jiggled it there, feeling the tip of the bayonet scraping the back of the zombie's skull. The hand limp in its lap.

She pulled the bayonet free, the eyeball collapsing farther back into the socket.

Harris walked the house, dispatching undead, clearing rooms. He could hear gunfire from outside as the residents of Eden joined the fray. It seemed like there were dozens of zombies in his house. He wondered how many had breached their walled enclave.

Five of them had Mr. Vittles trapped under the entertainment center in the living room.

"Vittles," Harris called, alarmed, the zombies looking up at him from where they crouched and squatted, swiping at the cat in his hideaway. Vittles hissed from somewhere unseen, presumably safe, still in the fight.

Propping the shotgun against the living room wall and unsheathing the machete, Harris waded into the zombies, their arms outstretched and reaching for him, dropping to the hard wood floor, skulls cleaved.

The zombies moaned outside amid whoops, human sounds, and between the staccato gunfire.

Harris brought the cutting edge down as hard as he could, missing the skull, splitting a zombie from sternum to mid-chest. It was unfazed, wrapping its arms around Harris' knees, threatening to take him to the floor, to grapple him. Harris wrenching free from its embrace, bringing his booted foot down once, twice, again, its head mashed into the floor, an eyeball dislodged from its orbit, the skull cracking, still Harris pummeling it, switching to his other foot now, all sorts of gore adorning the steel toed Chukkas.

Most of its skull contents pooling on the hardwood around it, Harris stepped back, lookied over the scene, bent, wrenched the machete free from where it was lodged in the unmoving nasty's trunk.

Vittles poked his head out from under the entertainment center, and shot like a bolt into the kitchen, out of sight again.

Harris breathing heavy as he scabbarded the blade, taking up the shotgun, reloading it from the bandolier. Two more stumbling over each other to get through the doorway into their house. Harris put them both down, thumbed two more shells into the shotgun, one last look around, made his way outside.

The firefight in the street was intense. The wall had been breached and hundreds of the undead plodded about. Eden's denizens fought back, firing their assault rifles on semi-auto, always aiming for the head, conserving ammo, keeping it together as they set about their grim task.

Julie sat in a window on the second floor, sniping at the undead with the AR-15.

It looked like their house had been the first hit, which meant the break had to be near. Harris stood in his doorway and fired the shotgun, pumped it, fired, pumped and fired until he emptied it. Close enough that each blast scored a head shot.

A scream, and a zombie came at him full speed, Harris raising the shotgun and clubbing it over the head. The thing puddled on the steps to his porch and Harris drew one of the twin nines and sent a single bullet into its head.

Harris closed the door to the house and buttressed the shotgun against it.

He worked his way down the street towards the wall, both nine millimeters filling his hands. Harris waited until he couldn't miss, walking right up to each undead and firing. One thing he had learned fast about shooting a gun: even in close quarters, most of your shots missed. What seemed now like a lifetime of fighting for his survival had steadied Harris' hand and his aim was true.

Pop. One in the temple, the thing down. *Pop.* Another through the mouth, the back of a skull lifting off. *Pop.* In one ear, out the side of its head. And so on.

"Howya, Harris!"

Bobby Evers, his neighbor in Eden. Bobby with a flame thrower, hosing the undead down under a withering stream of fire. Evers, some other men and women in a line, making their way towards Harris and his house, herding the zombies back towards the wall before them. They moved in a staggered enfilade, covering one another as they reloaded, such tactics drilled and practiced.

Harris dropped the mags in the nine millimeters, sliding home fresh ones, nodding in Bobby's direction. Neither Bobby nor any of the others were fully dressed but none of them was wrapped in a bed sheet either.

A steady stream of rifle fire from above. Julie paused only to switch magazines. She concentrated on the zombies outside the shepherding gunfire and blaze, those lurching about wildly, some alight and flailing, screaming in their immolation.

Julie tried to lead one zombie which was lurching wildly, a caterwauling torch. A round from the AR-15 pocked the asphalt, another disappeared into the flaming mass as the thing made the sidewalk, a third bringing up cement dust from the walk. The zombie collapsed burning, draped over a fire hydrant, wailing the whole time until Julie breathed, sighted afresh and placed a fourth round into the flaming head region. It shuddered once and slipped off the hydrant, gobs of its melted self clinging to the casement of the discharge pipe.

One by one they collapsed in the street and on sidewalks to burn silently and smolder.

Harris and Evers found the breach. When the wall around Eden had been con-structed—before Harris or Julie or Bobby had arrived—the residents had failed to build gates. They were more concerned with keeping the dead out and had no intention of risking leaving their haven. When those first inhabitants ran out of food, foraging missions were led through the sewer system. The monsters outside their walls seemed unable or unwilling to navigate the miles of extensive tunnels beneath the city streets. After several unfortunate, jarring incidents, and after much arguing and discussion, the walls of Eden had been rebuilt, revamped to include gateways this time.

The break-in had occurred at one of the doors. The wall itself rose twelve feet above the street. Though some undead remained extremely agile, none could scale it. This particular door was a heavy duty security door taken from a Home Depot. Before the world had gone to shit, people who lived on these blocks in this outer borough neighborhood would have installed such a door to protect themselves from crimes like burglary. That long before anyone had to worry about dead hungry for human flesh.

Harris and Bobby Evers reached the door together, and it was unlocked and wide open. They would have looked at each other but they were preoccupied, Harris squeezing off round after round, Evers dousing the undead with flames. Some undead dropped, others were driven back outside past the gate.

His nine millimeters out, Harris made a mad dash for the door, the machete loosed, hacking at undead heads and outstretched arms, severing limbs and cleaving skulls, firing the .45 in his right hand, allowing for the recoil that jerked his arm up slightly with each shot.

Thrusting the machete like a rapier before him, Harris drove it through the jaws of a particularly rotten undead, the blade lodged, the beast impelled back, through the gate, out into the no man's land beyond where thousands of its kith thronged, Harris slammed the door shut, leaning his full bodyweight against it.

He leaned against the door, waiting while Bobby Evers slipped out of the flamethrower harness. Evers retrieved the cross bar from the cement and a zombie, charred black, reached for him with hands the fingers of which had been fused together in a blistery welding. The Irishman brought the cross bar down on its skull twice. By the time the steaming mass stopped twitching on the street the cross bar was affixed, the door secured.

Evers, his back against the door, sliding down to a seated position, huffing, his asthma catching up to him. Harris stepped back, mopping his brow with a forearm, contemplating the morning's events, their implications.

"Looks like you done lost your machete," Bobby noted.

"Looks like," Harris, panting.

"The fookin' gate, Harris," Bobby said what was on both their minds. "Go way outta that! How in the hell did this happen?"

Harris stooped down and picked something from the ground.

The gunshots within Eden petered out, those alive within its walls finishing off those who were not.

"You're a fookin' mess, Harris. You okay?" A look of genuine concern on Evers' face, Harris looking like something that spent its days crawling around the floor of a slaughterhouse.

Bobby was one of the good guys. Harris never doubted Bobby.

"None of it's mine."

"By the way, grand outfit." Bobby winked.

"Harris!"

Julie was coming down the block, hair drawn back and kerchiefed, cradling the black rifle, the .357 holstered on her hip looking too big for her lithe frame.

Harris hugged her, ignoring the muck and gore, and she hugged him back. "Julie."

In their bathroom, the door locked, Harris set about cleaning and inspecting himself. The plumbing did not work, hadn't since before he moved in. Jugs of rainwater in the bathtub facilitated the clean-up. Communal baths erected on the opposite end of the block had hot water. Julie was there now.

Harris didn't care to be seen as he peeled out of the damp blood-stained bed sheet, letting it fall to the cool tiles.

The bite on his upper right arm, shoulder almost. Not even such a bad bite: the skin was broken, but only just. His kid brother had been attacked by a dog once when they were young, one bite, one way worse-looking than this, but his brother had been fine. A shot from the doctor, a few stitches, a hug from mom, dad tousling his hair, and James was good as new.

Harris understood it wouldn't be this way for him. The rules had changed. He knew what this bite meant.

If I ever get bitten, Buddy once told him, *and I can't do it myself, you do it for me, okay?*

He sighed. He had always figured it would end like this.

If I can't do it myself. The only hint of weakness Buddy had ever let on.

He'd told Buddy to be quiet, not to talk like that. Buddy persisted. Buddy always persisted.

Promise me, Harris. You put one in my head if I can't do it myself. Promise me.

To shut the other man up, get them off the topic, Harris promised he would.

Harris looked at himself in the mirror. It is always strange to gaze at oneself in the glass, to see oneself as others do, and not as we imagine. Hadn't shaved, hadn't cut his hair since… Since it all began. How long ago was that? A year and a half ago? Maybe more? Time no longer meant what it once did.

You don't shave or cut that hair of yours, Buddy had told him, *You're gonna wind up looking like Charlton Heston in* Planet of the Apes.

Harris had taken it as a compliment. Raquel always thought Heston hot in that movie.

Skull fragments entangled in his hair.

Feeling old, forty-four now, perhaps time to feel that way, at least once in awhile. Already feeling a bit unwell, not himself. How much that due the bite versus the circumstances surrounding the bite, of being jolted from sleep, undead cannibals ferociously attacking him and the woman he loved, Harris could not discern.

He knew what would happen, what was bound to happen.

What *had* to happen.

He'd turn into one of those undead things after degenerating, come back as something that would try to eat Julie and Bobby and anyone else it could. No matter how much they begged, no matter how much they implored and cried about what had been, the thing he would become would ignore their words and feast, insatiable.

How would Buddy respond if he were here now. What would the big man say to him in a situation like this? What would Buddy say?

If it'd been Buddy, Harris had no doubt the man would have gone off on his own somewhere, eaten a bullet.

The skin around the bite was discolored, purple.

You da man, Buddy would have clapped him on the shoulder—the other shoulder. They'd have gone for a walk, Buddy's idea, and as much as it might hurt him to do so Buddy would have raised his silenced nine millimeter when he thought Harris unaware and dispatched him to whatever came after this life or the nothingness in its absence.

And Harris would not have blamed him.

For the first and only time, Harris was glad Buddy wasn't around at that particular moment. There was one thing he knew he had to do.

He reached down, picking up the object found outside, next to the door in the wall. Knowing what it was as soon as he saw it, knowing *whose* it was.

The door in the wall had been unlocked. Someone had *let* zombies into Eden. Purposefully. Malignantly. The lock on the door to his and Julie's house broken open. Someone intending them the next human happy meal for the undead parade.

Why, Harris had his ideas. *Who,* he was more solid on. No doubt there.

Harris flicked the wheel on the Zippo lighter he held, watching the blue yellow flame flare up, catch. It was Thompson's Zippo lighter, the one the nineteen-year-old fancied.

This Harris knew.

"JOEY, DON'T FORGET," Joy Noddings reminded the 10th grader as he left her Math 2R class.

"What's that Ms. Noddings?" Joey was a good-looking kid, popular with the girls.

"Do your homework."

Joy knew Joey wouldn't do his homework. Joey didn't do homework.

"For shnizzle," he still good enough to go through the motions, act like he cared. Maybe he did.

Joy Noddings in her first year of teaching high school, fresh from a Masters degree program. The Hillcrest Alternative School took a chance, hired her to teach math.

The school was small, a dozen staff members serving thirty children labeled "emotionally disturbed" and "learning disabled." Though located in the upscale New York City suburb of Bedford Hills, the student body itself was quite diverse. Hillcrest had earned its reputation as the last stop for students who couldn't cut it on the main high school campus across town.

The staff provided a more therapeutic setting than that available to these kids at the regular high school, where over sixteen hundred students packed the halls, an institutional setting where the traditional Hillcrest kid found herself in trouble, more often than not.

Joy was still surprised Hillcrest had taken her on.

Nervous at her interview, she went home doubting herself, wondering how badly she'd bumbled the questions. To this day she wasconvinced she had the job due to the good graces of Hillcrest's principal. He was a couple decades older than Joy in her estimation, attractive, the type of guy women and his peers would describe as distinguished in a few more years. Besides his good looks and his tough but fair demeanor with the often trying students of Hillcrest, Joy admired her principal's professional attitude.

Joy was used to drawing stares, the occasional cat call from the men on the corner waiting for work, relieved that her principal never crossed any lines with her. He was so much unlike the math teacher, she wasalways noting how the eyes of that one went right to her chest in conversations. Joy was relieved that her principal wasn't that way, yet somewhat disappointed.

Ed was the boyfriend she'd been dating for going on three years now. A nice enough guy, Joy figured she'd probably wind up marrying Ed when he asked. She honestly believed there was no one better out there. Her principal was married anyway.

Three years already and *when* was he going to ask? Joy found it ironic that if she had made up her mind to "settle" she'd have to wait for the man to whom she'd resigned herself to propose already. *Settle* was an unfair word, too harsh. Ed was a good man, though lacking that edge others had.

Three months into her first academic year at Hillcrest, Joy fit right in with the rest of the staff, some of which had beenwith the program for years. The job was challenging because of students such as Joey, the job frustrating but rewarding in its own ways. Kids like Joey, with so much to offer, they could sit attentive in class, absorb information, use it to pass exams, even state exams at the end of the year, but these same students were unmotivated, never turning in assignments, never cracking a book open at home, not once attempting to capitalize on the god given gifts in their possession.

Still, Joy knew that without Hillcrest, many of them had no hopes of graduating. They'd fall through the cracks. No child left behind, right?

Fourth period was a free one. Joy considered going upstairs to the staff office. There were a couple of parents she needed to call. Alex was continuing to take his meds when he woke in the morning, meaning he spent most of his first three periods off the wall, driving his teachers nuts. Kid needed to take the medication *before* he went to sleep. She had had this conversation with Alex's mom more than once before.

Shanice, on the other hand, persisted in wearing clothing way too revealing—belly shirts and spaghetti straps—causing a distraction in Joy's seventh period math skills lab. Joy thought back to when she'd been in high school, not that long ago really, when you wore a belly shirt if you *didn't* have a belly. Today these girls wore whatever they wanted, whatever they looked like.

I can call later. Joy decided she'd walk across the street, buy herself lunch at the deli. She hadn't anything to eat since a protein shake before she left the apartment. Thin, in shape, Joy worked hard to keep herself that way, so that she could wear belly shirts when she was out with Ed. A turkey breast sandwich wouldn't be so bad.

Boar's Head low sodium. And American cheese. Yellow.

Joy locked her door, walked down the hall, admonishing a few stragglers to get to their next class before they were so late they received cuts from their teachers.

Out on the street a beautiful early November day. There'd been a brief cold spell at the end of October—Ed persisting in keeping the window open when he slept over, claiming he "breathed better", Joy always prevailing, the window always eventually closing—the cold followed by a return of warmer weather. Close to sixty degrees when it should have been much cooler. A late summer's last hurrah, an Indian summer.

The sky was beautiful, blue, limpid for the most part, some puffy cumulous clouds over in the distance.

Joy walked down the street towards Gary's deli. Hillcrest's location in downtown Bedford Hills put it in the middle of the shopping district. Quaint little stores, dog groomers, Judaica, a consignment shop, a Cold Stone Creamery. Off campus privileges, a draw of the program, once earned granted students the ability to spend their lunch hour eating in one of the delis or pizzerias, checking out the latest arrivals at the video game store, or browsing the CDs at Borders. Hopefully they weren't off smoking weed somewhere.

Weed. Joy smirked. Buddha, ganja, moocah, funk, chillums, hay, she heard new ones everyday between the kids and the rap music Ed liked to listen to. The low level dealer she dated her freshman year in college called it Aunt Mary or Baby Bhang. No one called it weed anymore.

Gary's deli was adequate but Walter's two blocks down better. The extra two blocks was not something Joy felt she wanted to commit to. Gary's was competent enough to put together a turkey and American sandwich. On whole wheat. With lettuce, tomatoes, maybe a little mayo. But not too much. Better the light Hellman's. She had spin class at the gym tonight.

"Joy!"

Susan McGreevy, a teacher's aid at Hillcrest for the last six years, was well liked by the students. Middle forties, married with three boys. Susan was always up on the latest gossip, from Hollywood celebrity to Hillcrest staff member.

"Hi, Susan."

The other woman looked spooked.

"What's wrong?"

"I don't know—I was in the deli and I heard something on the radio, rioting in the city or something."

"What?" Joy said, not comprehending.

"It's bizarre. They interrupted the music, said the National Guard was called in to put down some kind of gang violence or something. It was spreading up Fifth Avenue, from downtown."

"I haven't heard anything," Joy said, realizing it was a dumb thing to say. Of course she'd not heard anything. She had been in the classroom teaching all morning, going over factoring with her students.

"If you find anything else out, let me know." Joy could tell Susan was antsy, wanted to get going,

Saying she would, Susan made her way back towards Hillcrest, Joy resuming her walk, thinking. *Rioting in New York City? Moving up Fifth Avenue? Gangs? What the hell is going on?*

She stopped, breathing in the November air. Not as cool and crisp as it should be yet, the way Ed liked it. That would come.

Something about Susan's story bothered her.

Ed worked on Fifth Avenue. Up between forty-fourth and forty-fifth. His building was well protected with its own security. Ed himself was on the sixtieth floor, away from any street protest turned violent, away from anything that was going on.

Still…

The turkey sandwich not as tempting as had been a few moments before, even with the thought of mayo.

Joy turned, heading back towards Hillcrest, picking up her pace. Not running, but moving ahead with determination in her stride.

Her cell phone was locked in her desk.

Inside the building, Joy was relieved to find the halls empty. The kids were all in their classes.

She let herself into her room, letting the door close behind her, not locking it.

Sitting down in the executive chair at her desk, unlocking the drawer where she kept her valuables during the day. Joy liked most of the kids at Hillcrest, but she didn't want to put them in a position where they were tempted to rifle through her purse.

The ten seconds it took her phone to power up when she thumbed it on felt more like ten minutes.

Joy checked the digital display, pressing the keys, Ed's office number stored in her phone's memory. No messages.

The tiny screen: Connecting…

The phone beginning to ring.

"Hello?"

"Ed, listen, it's Joy, what's going on?"

"Joy, Jesus, you're not going to believe this shit. Things are fucking crazy out there, on the street. I've never seen anything like it. Turn on the news. Joy, they're fucking eating people—"

"Ed? Ed?"

Disconnected.

Redial. A quick succession of beeps, a ring, then a recorded voice, all circuits busy.

Exhaling, she redialed again.

All circuits busy.

Snapping her phone shut, she walked across her classroom and out into the hall, not bothering to close the door. Directly to the staff office on the second floor, redialing twice more, getting the same message, Joy found her principal making some copies on the Xerox machine.

"Joy, what's up?" He read the concern in her face.

"Can we talk in your office?" She gestured.

Her principal cast a quick look around the staff room. Hillcrest's secretary was on the phone, on hold, ordering supplies. The English teacher was surfing the net.

"Sure, come on."

The principal's office adjoined the staff room.

He shut the door behind them, the secretary holding the phone out and looking at it quizzically, "Huh?"

On the edge of the couch, leaning forward with her hands clasped together on her knees Joy motioned to the television set on the shelf. A TV/VCR combo, anyone who needed it for class was free to sign it out.

"Does that thing get any local channels?"

From out in the staff office they could hear the English teacher say to the secretary, "Holy Christ. Check this out."

"Yeah, it does," said Mr. Harris, already moving.

"Turn it on, please."

He did so.

"**Listen, Harris,**" **Buddy** said, taking his friend over to the side, away from the others, out of earshot.

Overcast spring morning, an intermittent moan from the undead beyond the wall reaching their ears, the stink of them wafting in, ever present.

"What's up?" Harris asked the big man.

"I want you to keep an eye on Diaz," Buddy said, casting an eye towards the others. A dozen men and women gathering around the manhole in the middle of the block, a rummaging party preparing to head off in search of supplies for Eden.

Diaz was a young buck, born and raised in uptown Manhattan, something he made sure everyone knew. A Dominican flag flew outside his house in Eden. The apocalypse gripping their world hadn't jarred the piss and vinegar out of him, at least not until this point. If anything, it had just raised his intensity, an intensity always there, sometimes hidden, sometimes exacerbated by all the PCP he toked.

Buddy continued, "He's going through a lot right now. Not sure what he's capable of."

The wind had been blown out of the braggart's sails the night before, when his girlfriend Shannon was infected. She was in Diaz's house now, her last hours fading fast, tended by some of the others. Julie couldn't stand Diaz but set aside her revulsion and went to bring what comfort to Shannon she could. Amazing, everyone said away from Diaz, that Shannon could hold out so long.

Once you were bitten, it was only a matter of time.

The outcome was inevitable.

"You think he'll come unhinged?" Harris asked Buddy.

Bobby Evers went over a list of supplies with Sal Bianaculli. Harris heard the word "Ibuprofen."

"Come unhinged?" Buddy raised an eyebrow. "Fucker's already unhinged if you ask me."

Harris thinking he knew, asked anyway. "How you mean?"

This was a pattern they'd established. Harris turning to Buddy as something of a father figure. Sometimes a game between them, sometimes earnest on his part.

"Usually young brah all up and at 'em, but notice how quiet he's become. Withdrawn, even."

Harris nodded. Diaz was definitely keeping under the radar. When Shannon was wounded Diaz went nuts, screaming his head off, Spanish and English, the Spanish too fast for Harris to get. Harris, Buddy, Davon, four or five of them were forced to subdue Diaz, trying not to hurt him, let Evers, Tina, and Bianaculli's wife Camille help stop Shannon's bleeding, get her back into Diaz's house. After they'd wrestled him down, Buddy asked him, "You alright?" Diaz's eyes were spacey, hyper-alert; his body limp was under them. This said he was. When he didn't say anything, they let him up and he went to be with Shannon.

Thompson adjusting an empty knapsack on Panas' back. The idea was to go out empty, return knapsacks full.

"Plastic wrap," Sal Bianaculli read from the list.

"Yeah," Harris said to Buddy, "I know what you mean."

Buddy chin-nodded him, turned to the group. "All right then, we good?"

Assorted nods, verbal assents, a grunt.

Buddy lifted his saddle bags from the cement, slinging them across his wide shoulders. His shotgun—the big semi-automatic with the cylinder clip that held 12 rounds—hung over his back. Buddy nodded towards Thompson, the younger man prying open the manhole cover with a crow bar.

Thing must have weighed a couple hundred pounds or more. Harris remembered when he'd lived in Queens, before he and Raquel moved out to the suburbs. One night there had been a huge explosion down the block, everyone out of bed, thinking terrorism. Harris had worried an airplane had gone down somewhere near their house. That'd happened before.

Turned out to be an explosion of gas in the sewer system, which had sent a manhole cover skyward. The thing returned to earth through the roof and windshield of someone's car.

Harris never liked the look of the manhole, a gaping man-made maw in the earth. Made him feel uneasy, like something in a horror movie. Didn't like going down into the sewer system, but to this point the miles of tunnels somehow remained empty of the undead.

A spiraling undulation passed the wall. They never shut up, even when feeding.

"Okay, lets' go," Buddy said, climbing down into the manhole, grasping the ladder below. Harris bent forward, passing him a Maglight.

Buddy was waist deep in the street, setting the flashlight on the asphalt, unholstering his nine millimeter, the silencer not threaded on. Checking to make sure a round chambered, Buddy returned the piece to its holster on his waist, and took his flashlight back up.

"Hey," Harris said, beckoning. Buddy looked up at him from that place.

"*You* da man," Harris said with thumbs up.

"No," Buddy said, grinning, correcting as was their habit. "*You* da man."

It never ceased to amaze Harris. After all the carnage, all the slaughter, after the drama with Graham and the Pole and Dom with his wife, the nights on the run, the innumerable times their backs were to a wall, certain this their last, after all that, Buddy's indefatigable smile was a mile-wide and his laugh so life-affirming and optimistic, inexplicably ineffable.

"Peace." The big black man laughed, starting his descent into the city's underground. Sal Bianaculli, his list and their hand-made map charting various tunnels and outlets explored over the months, following. Panas, Larry Chen and Biden went after. All the men carried shotguns or assault rifles, one or two pistols apiece. Larry Chen drew the shortest straw and lugged the flame thrower.

The earth swallowed them up.

Harris stood there, staring and thinking, until he became aware of Thompson looking at him.

"That's it then," Thompson said.

Harris bent down, helping the other slide the cover back into place. The rest of the day they'd take turns sitting beside it, waiting to hear the foragers return.

Harris saw Julie leave Diaz's house, come walking towards them, noted Thompson watching her too.

A lot of men looked at Julie, it was easy to do. Harris briefly considered what was wrong with him, why he didn't seem able to appreciate her the way he thought he should. The way another could.

"Want a smoke?" Thompson had a pack of stale Parliaments.

"No, thanks." Harris never liked smoking.

"Guys," Julie greeted them. Harris was aware Julie knew Thompson had the hots for her, conscious also that although she found Thompson less annoying than Diaz, because Thompson, unlike Diaz, never got high and let everyone in Eden know what a magnificent lover he thought himself, that he'd show all their women what a true man was about. Though Thompson was nowhere near that obnoxious, Julie wasn't interested in him or any man other than her own.

If Thompson had such thoughts he kept them to himself, which was just fine by Harris.

Should he or Diaz or anyone else ever act on them, Harris could deal with that when the time came.

"How's Shannon doing?" Thompson inquired, flicking his Zippo, firing up a Parliament.

Julie shrugged her shoulders and frowned, her look said it all and none of it was good.

They knew what was going to have to be done soon.

Thompson drew the smoke deep into his lungs.

Harris sighed, thinking of Shannon, of Diaz, knowing it couldn't be anything but ugly when the time came. Not knowing this the last time he'd ever see his friend Buddy.

HOOFING IT TO THE corner, Adlard held up a hand, halting everyone else. Hunkering down in place on the street, squatting behind cars strewn pell mell, Harris next to Bear between an SUV and a Lexus, the other trying to be as inconspicuous as a three hundred-plus pound man mountain could be, Harris signaled the others behind.

Daylight, all of them were exposed in the street, far from the relative safety of Eden's walls.

Adlard motioned, Buddy crouch-ran forward, passing Harris and Bear, Bear gripped the ancient mace, which someone now dead had procured from a museum somewhere, the chainsaw slung over his back. There was some fat on Bear but most of it muscle and bone and girth, one eye dead in his head, always staring off somewhere else, looking like a rock troll, some monstrosity from a fantasy novel. Harris always wanting to ask Bear about the eye, never did.

Buddy was abreast of Adlard, pressed to the wall.

"What we got?"

"Round the corner, on the avenue," Adlard keeping it low, his AK-47 pulled in tight against his torso. "A few hundred of them. At the minimum."

Buddy nodded, leaned forward and chanced a glance around the building, pulled back.

"Damn."

They spoke quietly to one another, Adlard bobbing his head, agreeing to whatever was being said. Buddy hoofed it back to Harris and Bear's position, waving the others, Davon, John Turner, Orlando. They all gathered close.

Six of them were in the street, between the cars, among the piles of bones in empty clothes scattered about the road, blood stains long ago washed away by the elements. The street in front and behind was much the same, vehicles everywhere from the panic, cars connected like dominoes, some crunched together, doors ajar, occupants long gone, abandoning the general congestion, having made their gamble on foot. Each of the six was aware of his vulnerability, wary of the desolate stillness of the block, leery an undead should stumble into sight.

"Here's the deal," Buddy said, speaking quietly, straightforward. "We got an avenue at the end of this block and it's packed." Every man knew with what.

"How far are we from the warehouse?" asked Bear, drumming the flanged end of the mace up and down in his massive palm.

"Two blocks," John Turner said, consulting the map.

"We sure there's even going to be anything in it?" Orlando hadn't wanted in on the rummage, so why, he kept asking himself, was he even here?

"There better be," said Harris, scanning the three-family row houses on either side of the street, windows vacant, staring down upon them, skull's empty sockets, curtains drawn in some.

Bear asked Buddy, "What're you thinking?"

Adlard was out of sight up ahead, somewhere between the cars.

"I'm thinking we cross this intersection," Buddy said, laying it out, "one by one. Car to car. Cover each other. We keep quiet, we keep our heads down. We can do this."

"What if they spot us?" Orlando said, worrying.

"They spot us. We run."

"No, they spot us, I run like hell," Davon spoke up. "I'll lead them off."

"And what about us?" John Turner wanted to know.

"I don't know, you guys hide or some shit."

Orlando shook his head. "Hide where?"

"In the cars, in a house," said Davon, thinking better of it, thinking of the skeletal remains locked in the cars around them, of the people who'd died doing just that, hiding, trying to wait out the predators beyond. "Shit if I know. Run or something."

Bear scoffed good-naturedly. Put him under a thousand pounds in a powerlifting competition, he'd squat it into the hole and bring it back out again, the bar bending over his shoulders the whole way, but ask him to hustle, well, there just certain things some men were not meant to do.

"You want to go back?" Buddy asked them all.

The temptation to say "Shit-yeah" strong, Orlando held his tongue waiting for someone else to say it so he wouldn't have to.

"Let's do this," said Harris, a nine millimeter in each hand. People in Eden depended on them. "And let's do it fast."

"All right then," grinned Buddy.

They darted, one by one, from stalled car to truck to SUV, Orlando the next to last before Adlard, only getting a move on when Adlard from the corner hissed at him to do such. Orlando was duck-walking, trying to retrace as much of the route he'd watched Turner take, staying as close to the ground as possible. He went out into the intersection, the traffic lights hanging dead above him, not chancing a look up the avenue, not needing to see the hordes there.

He heard them just fine.

Turner made it to the other side, touched the wall, and let his breath out, conscious for the first time he'd been holding it. Buddy, Harris, Bear, and Davon all lined up, backs to bricks. Bear was sweating profusely. Buddy whispered to Davon, telling the former high school football star to go on ahead and scout their way.

Harris followed Orlando's progress as best he could, the other man appearing and disappearing among the cars. Adlard was in plane view of Harris, tucked away around the corner where the undead could not see him.

A bunch of pigeons nestled on the power lines overhead.

Orlando misjudged the path, deviating slightly, a little too high and too slow to boot, out in the open between a BMW and a motorcycle momentarily, and he had a perfect view of the mob down the street, he of them and them of him.

"Sheeee-it," Buddy drawing the word out, raising his silenced nine millimeter.

The ruckus from the zombies was unmistakable, the ones capable were screaming, bawling; the faster ones already dashing madly to the intersection, the stumbling mass behind them roiling, moving as one, a tide rolling in.

Fuck! mouthed Adlard from across the intersection, looking from Orlando to the other men, bringing the AK to his shoulder, wondering what the hell he should do.

Orlando hugged his knees behind the motorcycle, pissing himself, risking a look over the seat of the Harley.

Buddy waved Adlard off, pointing back the way they'd come, Orlando stood up in the open now, and started to scream hysterically.

"Fuck!" Yelling out loud now, Adlard stepped round the corner, the pigeons scattering above as the AK-47 started bucking on semi-auto into his deltoid, firing at the advancing mass, spitting shell casings out into the street. "Orlando, move your fucking ass fucking now!"

Harris readied the nine millimeters, moving to step out onto the avenue, when Buddy stopped him. "Run, we gotta run!" Louder to Bear and Turner, "We out!"

The other two did not need to be told twice, and hoofed it in Davon's direction.

Across the avenue, Adlard dumped a mag, zombies in the fore running over those brought down, scrabbling their way towards the intersection, Orlando extended his pistol and fired out the clip, not hitting a single one.

"Run, bitch—run!" Adlard himself fired more rounds from the assault rifle, turning and hauling ass back in the direction they'd come. Buddy pushed Harris— "Go!"—Harris didn't move fast enough, Buddy shoved him ahead, propelling him with his free hand. Orlando tried to reload his pistol on the run and fumbled a fresh clip; it bounced to the asphalt out of sight under a car. Orlando shrieked, legs moving faster than they'd ever moved before, burning him his own zig-zag path down the avenue between the lifeless vehicles.

Half way up the block on the fly, Harris risked a look over his shoulder. "Oh shit!" A dozen or more of the things had turned on the street after them, the majority pursuing Orlando, his yelps and cries diminishing with distance, the last anyone from Eden ever heard from him.

"Up ahead," Buddy said, pointing. Davon signaled from an alley between two buildings.

"Harris, Buddy," Bear said in the alley, rivulets of sweat streaming down his face, looking like he was prepping for a coronary, summoning them further along the path, Davon and Turner at the opposite end.

Passing a dumpster, Bear stopped, hands on knees, the breath gone from him. "I can't."

"Alamo time." Buddy didn't think about it, tracking the nine towards the mouth of the alley, shrugging the shotgun off his back and into his free hand, tensing it on the sling.

"Wait," Bear gasped squatting down, finding a grip under the dumpster, a rapid succession of grunts and jerks and he'd cater-cornered the metal bin, cutting off the alley.

"Nice." Harris patted the giant on his sweaty back.

The next hour was spent navigating back alleys and roofs, avoiding the mass of zombies on the avenue streaming past, all heading in one direction.

The street outside the MJ's Wholesale Club was deserted, most of the zombies in the area hot on the trail of Orlando or Adlard. It was unsettling to the men how one street could be empty of them, another thronged.

The parking lot behind the discount warehouse was equally barren, save an un-hitched trailer from an eighteen-wheeler.

Inside the building's cavernous depths Davon and Turner wheeled the gate shut and fastened the chain from the inside. Dust motes swirled in the beams of their flashlights and the high powered torches they fanned out, their cursory glances through the looming aisles meant to ascertain they'd not stumbled upon a warren of them.

John Turner said, "Doesn't look like anyone's been here since we were last time."

"Hmmm." Buddy was concerned. Eden was not the only enclave that periodi-cally raided this store. He didn't envision any of the refugees in Jericho across town making it this way, but the place they called the Farm had to be less than a mile from this spot. No one from Eden had ever met the survivors from the Farm, but they knew of its existence from those at Jericho.

As the younger Turner had said, it didn't look like anything had been touched since their last visit.

"Let's get working on those lists." No time to mull it over, "Somebody check the pharmacy section, see if they're any inhalers left for Bobby."

Bear filled two gunny sacks, leaving them next to the gate with his chainsaw. Against his better judgment he walked over to what had been an employee office. He'd been there before, knew what he would find, the lure still inexplicably strong.

A suite of rooms. The first the largest, tables and chairs for staff, a refrigerator long dormant, a row of cubbies for personal belongings. Two doors leading off into smaller offices, one with a copy machine and water cooler.

There were three dead zombies outside one of the doors, decomposed, crum-bling into flakes on the tile floor. That door broken open. Inside, a skeleton in a chair hunched sat over a desk. On the desk was a flashlight, couple of framed pictures, a family with two kids. An organizer with pens and a ruler sticking straight up; a faded white monthly desk calendar took up much of the surface area.

One other item on the desk lay a personal journal, closed.

Bear shined his lantern about, the same as last time. Over their visits to this place he'd pieced together a tale, what he thought had happened in the room. The skeleton, judging from the clothes in the chair a man—a manager? Employee? Hapless schmuck wandered in from the street?—whoever he had been, locking himself in the office, the three zombies outside.

Whoever he'd been, he'd written entries in the journal: some long, others two or three sentences. A few were moving, personal. Others detached, written in the third person, the first person interjected randomly. Bear imaged the man in the chair, the door locked, listening to the things outside, the things that kept him from the water in the cooler the next door over, the things waiting for him. Bear pictured the man writing in the journal by flashlight, filling pages as he slowly dehydrated and starved to death, the flashlight dimming and dying, leaving the man alone in darkness with the noises outside.

Bear imagined someone else, someone from the Farm, maybe some other anonymous group of wanderers, first gaining entry to the warehouse, finding the three zombies outside the door, the man inside long dead. The zombies felled, the office door forced, anything worth taking gone. If the man had any weapons with him, they were part of the booty, but Bear couldn't imagine the man inside with a weapon and not using it, opting instead to wait for death in the dark. Either the original plunderers hadn't read the journal or they'd decided to leave it on purpose, as Bear abandoned it each time.

He'd read from the book before, sometimes only getting a few sentences before he'd had to close it and leave. The words written there were nouns, adjectives and verbs, yet too much for him. Bear looked at the journal, wondering if he should, knowing he would. Placing his lantern on the desk, the calendar beneath it brittle, he opened the diary at random, crossed himself, and picked up at the first full paragraph, reading an entry he hadn't before.

We had to call them something, so we came up with a variety of names. Undead, walkers, zombies, ghouls. Other more colorful, less polite terms. Whatever one chose to call them, there was no doubt to what one referred.

They own the world. There is no telling where the first undead came from, what made them sally forth and seek human prey, though in the first few weeks of contagion there was no shortage of theories. As world governments and military forces scrambled to at first annihilate and then contain the spreading threat, scientific establishments, rooted in empiricism and rational thought, sought to cope with the very irrational—but nonetheless real—idea that the dead had come back to life, kept coming back to life, attacking the living.

Within a couple months of the first outbreaks, the human population had pitched into a frenzy. Towns, counties, provinces, then whole countries crumbled. Large urban areas, home to great populations, were the first to fall.

Zombie numbers expand exponentially. For every one felled two take its place.

The major communications media broke down within the first week, followed in short order by the infrastructures of most countries. On the streets and plains it became chaotic, sheer pandemonium, with humans doing their best—our best—to arm ourselves and find refuge. Safety wasn't necessarily found in numbers. Isolation is the key. Being able to lock yourself away someplace safe from them. But no refuge is completely impenetrable, either from the undead without or from demands within. Human beings need food and water, supplies, some word of what the hell is going on outside everyone's individual little private sanctuaries, and eventually they set foot outside their areas of protection to be pounced upon by the waiting undead.

They, the undead, are nothing if not patient. If they chase you into a room and the door is solid enough to keep them out, they will wait, standing around outside the vicinity of the door, just as those outside now wait for me. Others would join them in the following hours, in the ensuing days and weeks, knowing something edible is locked away behind that door, something worth the wait. But I suppose when you're already dead, you've got a lot of time to kill. Eventually hunger or thirst would drive survivors out of their hiding places, in weakened states, and they'd be no match for what awaited them. I will not leave this place.

Those who managed to survive for some length of time did so because they found out a few things quickly. The undead "rules" so to speak. First and foremost, there are only a few ways to bring them down. The easiest way involves destroying the brain, just like in the horror movies. Head shots, bludgeoning the skull, even a well-placed blow to the temple, one powerful enough, all can fell an undead. Burning works too, although one has to be careful to really fry them, to burn them until they collapse and stop twitching and then, just to be sure, to burn them even more or shoot them in the head.

Blowing them up works, but not well, because explosions cause massive damage but not all of it to the brain. This strategy worked well enough for the armed forces early on, when their helicopters and bombers would rain missiles and bombs on cities and large concentrations of the undead. Poison gas and nuclear weapons didn't do shit to them. Horrendous toll on the civilian population though, but what could one do?

The brain has to be destroyed. That's all there is to it. An undead can literally lose its head—have it severed—and the thing's mouth will still attempt to bite at human beings. Zombies with their legs blown off by explosives or weapons fire will crawl after living prey. The disemboweled stagger forward tripping over their own intestines. None of their major internal organs seem to be necessary.

They are driven by hunger and human beings are their favorite meals. But they also eat cats, dogs, any other animals they can get their hands on. Unlike other mammals, people often rise as undead themselves after being bitten. It all depends on the severity of the feasting. If a slew of the undead take a human down and eat him, devouring most of his innards, separating limbs from trunk, rending flesh and muscle from bone, for some reasons these dead humans remain dead. They will not get back up. They will not start walking around.

But if an undead takes a few bites out of you, or even one nibble, you are doomed to walk the earth as one of them. It is from that point a matter of time, and the length of time seems related to the severity of the bite and its proximity to the brain. Humans with their throats torn out, writhing on the street while their arteries pump out the last of their precious life blood will often get back up within a minute of dying. I have seen this all too often with my own eyes. If the zombies are gathered around to start feasting on the newly dead they immediately stop when the dead one stirs, signaling his ascension to their ranks.

On the other hand there are human beings who sustain relatively small bites, mere scratches to their ankles or feet, and the wounds will often appear to start healing over the next few hours. But they too turn, within a night or two at most. At least the dogs and cats, the rats and goats, the horses, whatever else the undead get their hands on and their teeth into, at least these things don't return.

There are different types of the undead that we survivors armed ourselves against. The majority of the undead are shamblers. These creatures stagger through the streets and country, moving relatively slowly. In open areas you can see them coming from a distance and easily avoid them. In the dark or in enclosed spaces they are especially dangerous. Such are at my door now.

The bookers are so-called because they really move, they could book after you. These undead (were they spry human beings?) launch themselves into a sprint in pursuit of fresh flesh. Some are fast, others extremely fast, and most human survivors do their best to avoid these creatures. Not only are they quick, bookers, unlike the survivors they chase, don't tire. They are relentless. The silent bookers are especially dangerous, as they are on you before you're even aware of their presence.

Howlers can be either shamblers or bookers. These undead scream, literally howling, their range covering everything from shrieks of frustration to roars of anger. They're never able to keep quiet, so you can hear them well in advance of their appearance on a scene.

Only one of the things outside this room now makes noise and it won't stop.

Most of the undead appear to lack anything but rudimentary intelligence. They don't work together. If a group corners a human being they attack all at once as individuals, each jockeying for position and attempting to secure the choicest meat for itself. At times they appear aware of the presence of other zombies, but mostly they ignore one another, shuffling past each other with the bookers racing between slower moving shamblers.

The most dangerous of the undead are the brains. They are cunning. They will stalk prey, awaiting the best opportunity to pounce. They also work as individuals, but their stalking and waiting behavior is like a form of hunting. Brains could be shamblers or bookers, but there aren't many howlers amongst their numbers, probably because stealth and blood curdling cries don't go well together, those that combine both easily noted and brained.

Each time the undead eat, it is as if they are eating for the first time. Their hunger cannot be satisfied, but they can go weeks or months without eating until a human being or a rat shows itself. They don't appear capable of starving to death, and they aren't deriving energy from their feedings. Their feedings hedonistic frenzies, pure bacchanal gluttonies. Three bookers—they eat as fast as they run—could denude a human being to the bone within five minutes of its being brought down. Shamblers eat more slowly, seemingly taking their time, perhaps even savoring the experience more than their booker cousins. I will stay in here rather than suffer that fate.

The elements don't seem to bother the undead. Rain, snow, extreme heat. There they are, moving around the countries, invading cities and farmhouses, waiting out human strongholds until supplies and patience disappeared and those safe inside are forced to venture beyond their confines. Standing around in rain and snow storms, the weather burns and rots their undead skin. Some of them no more than walking skeletons with shreds of flesh and the clothing they died in hanging from exposed tissue and bone, yet they also seek food.

Some survivors refer to the coming of the undead as "the plague." The more religious amongst us dub it "the apocalypse" or "end times." No savior has appeared. The origins of the outbreak are unknown. The nature of the contagion, spread by bites, is unclear. But there is one stark reality left we survivors: being human after the outbreak isn't easy, and the tenure usually isn't long.

"Bear, we're ready to get out of here," Turner called from outside the office.

"Just a sec." Bear gently closed the journal, considering, as always, taking it with him, but deciding, as usual, not to.

He retrieved his lantern, cast its beam towards the door, looked back towards the desk and chair at the clothed bones in the sightless dark.

"YOU SHAVED." JULIE'S look of surprise transitioned to a smile. She'd never seen him clean shaven before.

"Yeah." Harris rubbed his smooth chin between thumb and forefinger. "It was time for a change."

His dirty blonde hair, streaks of grey showing through, was still shoulder-length, shaggy like some aging British rock icon.

Julie, Bobby Evers, Bobby's third wife Gwen, and half a dozen other men and women worked throughout the house Harris and Julie shared, carting off trunks and limbs, scrubbing walls and carpets, trying their best to get things back to the way they'd been before the pre-dawn assault.

"Damn, look at you," said Keara. "A new man."

"They never could get one over on you, Harris." Mickey saluted and Harris sighed, forced a smile. He got along well with Mickey because Harris liked movies and Mickey, well Mickey *loved* movies. But this was tough, keeping it together in front of all these people.

He'd stitched the bite wound on his left upper arm as best he could, wrapping it with gauze, securing the gauze in place with surgical tape. Changed to a fresh set of clothes: loose carpenter jeans, a flannel over a ribbed tank t-shirt. Different boots.

"We got lucky," Harris replied, still not sure what to say. Telling them he'd been bitten was not an option. He knew what they'd do. He knew what *he'd* do if he was in their situation. Julie might hesitate and he loved her for it. She loved him, love lending itself to hope, even when hope was absent.

Bobby Evers, decent man that he was, Harris knew what Bobby would do. And he knew Bobby would do it with regret, probably an apology. Not the way Buddy'd do it, but still, Bobby would do it anyway. Which would be doubly awful, for both of them, seeing it coming. When the time came, he'd figure something out, maybe tell Bobby then. Let Bobby handle it.

Or maybe he'd deal with it all himself. In the meantime, he had the remainder of the day at most to figure things out, put things right.

"Here's what I don't get," Keara stopped scrubbing at the polyurethane-coated floors. "How they got into Eden. Harris, you and Bobby said the security door was open, right?"

"Aye," Bobby Evers piped up from across the room, him and Gwen loading a cadaver onto a make shift stretcher to lug outside and cremate. "That would be open as in unlocked."

"Well, what sick fuck would purposefully open that door?" Paul asked. His partner Larry Chen had disappeared with Buddy and the others down the man hole months back, they had heard nothing from them since. "I mean, they put us all in danger, whoever did it."

Harris didn't say anything about the door to their domicile being forced open. He didn't speculate aloud why someone had chosen *that* particular security door in the gate, with half a dozen possible entrances and exits in the walls around Eden, *that* door to leave open, as they undoubtedly knew doing such would place the undead as close to Harris and Julie as could be. Someone had attempted to murder him and Julie, and Harris knew this. But he kept it quiet, watching and listening to Paul very carefully, hearing his words, reading his eyes, watching his hands, looking for any sign of …

Of what? Nervousness? Harris was almost a hundred percent sure he knew the one responsible. Still didn't hurt to pay attention, be alert for as long as he could, figure out if this was the work of one man alone or of many. Harris needed to know who he had to kill before his own demise.

"No way it could have been a mistake?" asked Mickey. "You know, someone checking the locks last night, accidentally unlocked the gate?"

"Even if it was a mistake," Gwen responded, as she and Bobby lugged the body outside, "this needs to be treated like it was intentional. Like Paul said, it put us all in danger."

Mickey shook his head at the absurdity of it all and went back to his task of plastering the buckshot and bullet pocked wall.

"There he is," said Julie, Mr. Vittles meowing, watching them work, his tail swishing slowly.

"This stain on the floor is tricky," said Paul. "But I think I can get it out."

"Hey boy," Harris called to the feline, crouching down and beckoning him over. The cat sidled up to Harris and started to rub up against his thigh but thought better of it, cast him a look, and disappeared under the dining room table.

Harris went to Julie, wrapping his right arm around her, pulling her close to him, thinking of the poison, the virus or whatever it was coursing its way through his blood, consuming him. He kissed her on her kerchiefed head, excused himself and went up to the roof.

The sun wended its way to the meridian, and Harris alone surveyed that what left of the neighborhood. Eden a walled one square block area, part of a place formerly called Queens, one of the five boroughs of the City of New York. Manhattan itself was uninhabitable, Staten Island inaccessible, Brooklyn was much like Queens, and no one who'd ventured up into the Bronx or further ever returned to tell what they'd found.

Harris couldn't blame them.

Beyond the walls a congress of the undead in their mass like some perverse charade, a mortiferous simulacra of an everyday that was nothing and no more, consigned to memory. Their stink. Their wails. Their future.

The wall surrounding Eden constructed shortly after the beginning of the outbreak, dozens of people working night and day, dozens more patrolling the perimeter, keeping the zombies out. So the story went. The story they told themselves. No one inside the walls today had been around then, no one here witness to their erection.

Harris thinking how insane that must have been, building this wall with the undead gathering, hundreds of the things, thousands, innumerable.

Beneath him was a normal looking block, cement sidewalks, cars neatly parallel parked, little squares of green dotting the sidewalks in front of each house, stoops, an American flag or two still flying on someone's porch, Diaz's Dominican standard announcing his residence. The homes were, for the most part, attached on two sides. Alleyways were a premium on this block before the outbreak, Harris suspected, as there were only two on each side of the street.

The only things that looked out of place on the block were the public baths: corrugated metal jerry rigged affairs, roofed to protect from the sun and possible peeping toms. These and the overhangs covering the generators. The generators supplying their energy needs, giving them light, air conditioning in the summer, refrigeration, lending Eden some semblance of normality.

Harris had grown up on a street very much like this one as a boy, albeit in Brooklyn. With his wife he'd moved to the suburbs, she accepting a Wall Street lawyer position. The move cut down Harris's commute, and he didn't need to worry about Raquel as she could take the Metro North into the city.

If he closed his eyes, if he imagined, he could almost hear the block as it once had been. Children crying out, playing stick ball, tag, and chalked hop scotch on the sidewalk. A Mr. Frostee ice cream truck blared its tune, kids screaming to mom and dad for money to buy bomb pops, Nutty Buddies, soft serve. A chopper barreled down the block, car alarms set off by the barely muffled V-Twin engine.

When one looked at the walls and beyond, one realized just how different things had become. Normal had done a complete one-eighty.

The walls, twelve feet high, two feet thick, were built up around a steel mesh for added durability. Security doors were placed strategically, each locked, bolted from the inside. There was a much larger opening in the northern wall, large enough to let a truck through. The original architects of Eden had built a sliding steel door there, with bulletproof windows.

After a vote by the community, Panas painted over the glass, blackening it out. It was appreciated by the residents, who were more than a little unnerved by the zombies on the other side.

The northern and southern ends of the block were the most vulnerable to breach. There, cargo containers were placed flush against the wall, reinforcing it. Atop the cargo containers were stations where one could look over the wall to the other side, and keep tabs on the things beyond.

The walls continued around the back of the houses. Whoever had originally designed them had done such that the backyards of each house were still intact. Fences separating the yards from residential days had been torn down, and it was there, along two strips of green on the west and east behind the homes, that crops were grown. Corn, tomatoes, squash, green beans, melons, and some wheat. Wheat was a tough one to grow, given the climate. As it was there was never enough food, and sometimes it seemed that everyone was slowly starving to death.

The tops of the walls were ringed with thick loops of concertina wire, which was stringed with aluminum cans. If, somehow, an undead managed to scale a wall, the idea was that it would tangle up in the wire, its struggle to free itself alerting those inside.

They'd never made it over the walls, but sometimes the undead did get inside.

Harris looked to the east, out beyond the mass of the undead, past where the breech had occurred that morning. The cacophony of battle had attracted a plentitude of zombies. He looked pas the burnt-out homes, the empty cars. The walls of Jericho were visible even at this great a distance. Harris didn't need binoculars to see what had befallen Eden's sister stronghold.

The undead got into Jericho. Harris and Buddy and a few others went to investigate. What they'd found when they'd stealthed their way inside something none of them likely to forget. Jericho was an outpost of the dead now.

He looked at his watch: noon. This time tomorrow he wouldn't be remembering anything ever again. The thought sobering.

"No matter how many times I see the bloody devils," Bobby Evers said, on the roof behind him. "It never ceases to amaze me…"

The undead ringed the walls, thousands of them along the southern wall where the gate had been left open earlier. Some were milling about, others standing in place, shifting from one leg to the other. A booker darted past, disappearing down an alley.

"Look at that one," Evers said, with his thirty-thirty hunting rifle to his shoulder, sighting along the barrel. He said "pow" as he exhaled.

"The one behind the school bus?" Harris asked. It was important to appear normal these last hours, a task certain to increase in difficulty as time passed.

"Yeah." An undead peered from the back of a yellow bus at the two men on the roof. It could see them clearly, watched them intently. "I hate brains."

Harris knew Bobby Evers had a reason: the smart ones had been responsible for the death of the man's second wife.

"Ever wonder, Harris, what they're contemplating? Like, what is that sneaky son of a bitch behind that bus thinking as it looks at us?"

"You want to know what they're thinking?" For a moment, Harris felt like the man who had gotten into bed the night before. "Think of the best meal your mom would make when you were a little potato over in Ireland."

"Okay." Bobby laughed, still staring the thing down over the barrel of his rifle. "What is it?"

"Pepper steak."

"Pepper steak?" Harris thought it would be something else. Bobby Evers, naturalized American citizen with the Irish brogue.

"Eh, what'd you think I'd say? Corn beef and cabbage or something?"

"Actually, yeah."

"Cop on, Harris."

They laughed together.

"Anyway, remember when your mom would spend the afternoon cooking that pepper steak, and you'd smell it? Then she'd call for dinner and you'd all go and sit around the table, and just seeing the pepper steak there in front of you, knowing how good it was going to taste and that you'd be digging in in a few minutes, remember how good that felt?"

Harris said all these things like he knew they were how Bobby had experienced them, but in fact Bobby had been a stranger to him outside of Eden, whose past could have been anything and nothing Harris could imagine.

"Yeah." The barrel of the thirty-thirty pointed muzzle-down at the rooftop.

"Well," said Harris. "That's how that thing feels looking at you and me."

The other scoffed. "That's fooked up. Go way outta that, Harris."

Bobby was quiet a moment.

"Thanks for ruining a memory," he laughed.

"Harris, listen," he said, serious again. "This morning. You and I both know that was no accident."

Harris nodding slowly. "Yee-app."

"Question is, *who* would have opened that door? And why *that* door?"

If Bobby or anyone knew what Harris was thinking of doing, they'd try and stop him, or at the least tell him to take some time to think it over. Time was the one thing Harris did not have, yet he couldn't let Bobby know that. He'd rehearsed answers to questions like this in his head.

"Probably that door because we only have the watch on the north wall."

True enough. When Harris and Buddy first arrived in Eden, all four walls had been guarded at all times. Eden had been a different animal then, an armed camp under Graham the dictator.

When it became apparent that the undead were incapable of scaling the walls, when Graham and his thugs were out of the way, with attitudes somewhat more lax, the western watch was pulled first, then that on the east, finally the south. The north, with its huge sliding door gate, was the only side of the compound to have a full time watch with rotating shifts. Those looking to Eden as a refuge from the horror outside usually tried to get in that way.

No one had tried to get into Eden for a long time.

A Quonset hut sat atop the cargo container at the north wall. Whoever was on watch sat inside the hut with a view of the block and the southern wall, remaining tucked away, out of the direct line of sight of the zombies on the streets. Otherwise, dozens, then dozens of dozens, ad infinitum, would gather, spying the human being atop the wall.

At night, when people were trying to rest, the screams and howls of the undead were nightmare-inducing at best, sleep-depriving at worst.

"I already thought of that," admitted Bobby Evers. "And you know Turner was on this morning."

Fred Turner had never been the same since his son John died. The man's A-game had left him, and if it wasn't for the safety of the armed garrison Fred would be meat on the street, just so much more food for the undead.

Harris felt for Fred Turner. Turner, who'd tuned out. Diaz had been out of it, too, since Shannon. Where Diaz pretty much kept to himself, smoking his PCP-laced marijuana, spending his time blitzed out of his mind, Turner at least *tried* to fit it. But Fred wasn't like everyone else anymore, and that was something everyone knew.

Last night wouldn't have been the first time Turner fell asleep on watch. It used to anger Harris to no end, yet he never said anything. The reforms in the wake of Graham's ouster encouraging public opinion, group decision making, and the group had decided that Turner was to be left on rotation, like everyone else. With the undead unable to climb walls, Turner's position was more a sinecure than anything anyone took seriously.

Except now Harris was dying from a lapse in security.

"You know how I feel about Fred and his whole situation," Harris said, chosing his words carefully. "The man's been through a lot."

All in Eden had been through a lot, only Fred's nightmare was communal, the dead taking his son shared by all.

"Okay, here's the thing of it then," said Bobby Evers. "I can't think of anyone here would want to see the camp destroyed. Can you?"

No, Harris could not. However, he could think of one man who probably thought life much easier with Harris out of the way. He had the man's lighter in the pocket of his carpenter jeans.

"I'm stumped," said Harris. Out of the corner of his eye he was aware of Bobby studying him, looking for something not being said.

"But you know what Bobby?" Harris said, turning, facing his friend squarely, a smile on his face, thinking *God damn you Bobby, you try and stop me and I will pitch you off this goddamn roof, tell the others it was an accident,*. Instead, he said, "I want to thank you. You and the others came running real fast this morning. I don't know what would have happened otherwise. Actually, I mean, I do."

Bobby Evers holding Harris' gaze, his words belying how he felt inside. "The noise you made holding down the fort brought us cavalry, Harris, F-Troop," both laughing, Bobby steering the conversation somewhere he thought Harris more comfortable. "This is Eden, Harris. We stick together, or it's all over."

"I hear that," Harris agreed.

"What's that line from *The Wild Bunch*?"

Harris laughed. "Ask Mickey."

Bobby sighted along the barrel of the thirty-thirty, wanting to ask Harris why he'd left the door to his house unlocked last night. Bobby had spent enough time at Harris and Julie's to know that Harris still locked the door at night, *every* night. But how else could the zombies have gotten into his house?

The brain was under the bus now, staring at them from the shadows beside a flattened wheel. Safe as Eden could be within its four walls, it wasn't like Harris to *forget* to lock the door at night. Bobby decided he'd ask Harris more about it later.

"One day soon, lad," Bobby promised the brain. In the meantime, he'd keep an eye on his friend. Maybe it was nothing. "One day soon."

Maybe.

"If it was that easy," sighed Harris, thanking Bobby silently.

"YOU SURE THIS is what you want to do?" Buddy asked Siobhan McAllister.

Her hair up in a bun under her best Sunday bonnet, the septuagenarian replied, "I think it's for the best," Her voice was young, strong, not cold towards Buddy since what he'd done to Graham, since Markowski failed to return from their sewer trip. Though not cold, not the way she'd been. Didn't deign to voice judgment on the situation, her silence was judgment enough.

Siobhan reminded Buddy of his grandmother: the slow, steady gait, the way her eyes would lock on his, not hostile yet implacable, the soft, firm, no-nonsense manner.

They came with stories of what was happening "out there", but when they left they were never heard from again. Maybe they found a better place.

She'd grandkids before all this, Buddy was sure of it.

McAllister was seated in the back of a Hyundai Sante Fe next to Vanessa and Mel, her cane on her lap. Paul and Bert circled the vehicle, giving it a final once-over, making sure everything looked good. Everybody else in Eden was standing around, watching them as they loaded the Sante Fe, offering hands and helpful tips.

"Ms. McAllister," Buddy said, genuinely concerned, leaning in through the window, looking Siobhan directly in her eyes. "I know you're not happy with what I've done here. You haven't said anything and I know you won't. But you don't have to."

"This isn't about anything you did or how I feel about it, Buddy," she said.

"It's dangerous out there ma'am, I know you know that. I worry about you."

"Bless your heart son," she said, laying an arthritic, liver-spotted hand on his. "But remember, I wasn't born in Eden, and it was a dangerous place out there before I got here, but I did alright. The Lord'll look out for me."

"And I don't doubt it, but if you stay here, I can look out for you. Stick around, you'll see, things will be different here."

"Things are already different," said Vanessa next to the old woman, not meant to contradict Buddy, but not so much to dissuade McAllister either. Just an observation. Discussions and deliberations—things not allowed in Eden under Graham and his stooges—were now the order of the day. The world had gone to hell outside their four walls, but inside there was progress, all now having a voice where once one voiced all.

"Believe me," Siobhan McAllister said, letting go of Buddy's hand where it rested on the window, and patting it. "This isn't about anything you did. Yes, I wasn't happy you doin' what you did to that man, but I ain't pig-headed enough not to admit things are better here without that bad man and his evil ways."

Buddy pressed on, sensing this was a battle he could not win. "So why leave?"

"It's been a long time coming, son."

Buddy looked down, shook his head, laughing a bit. His grey hair, the lines in his face. No one had called him "son" in a long time.

He didn't want to let Siobhan McAllister go. The others, Vanessa, Bert, Mel, had beenplanning to leave Eden for weeks, talking about armored caravans out west, maybe in Pennsylvania by now, about hooking up with one of those troupes, about getting north into Canada, the winters there enough maybe to freeze the zombies, grant a seasonal reprieve.

Bert could leave Eden for all Buddy cared. The man had been contributing jack shit since Graham forcibly abdicated. Bert sat around at their community meetings, if he showed up at all, doing only what he was told to do when it came to the crops. The whole time it was obvious the man would rather be elsewhere. The wind had left his sails since Markowski and Buddy had gone down into the sewers, with only Buddy coming back.

Siobhan McAllister was a whole other story. No way the woman was capable of making it out there, in the world beyond Eden's walls. She refused to even carry a gun, claiming if she got into a situation where she needed to use it, her good Lord would look out for her, do "what's right" by her. Buddy had his doubts, having seen too many people eaten alive hollering the entire time for divine intervention.

Maybe it was a miracle of sorts that Siobhan had made it to Eden to begin with. Not a lot of old or young folk around Eden, the most vulnerable getting picked off first, early on.

"There's nothing I can say, make you change your mind?" He knew the answer.

"Bless you, Buddy. I do believe in your heart you are trying to be a good man. I need you to understand, this is what is meant to be."

Whatever, he thought, but Buddy was not going to argue with her.

"Okay, you're ready," Paul announced, Bert climbing into the driver's seat. Panas and Al Gold began fitting metal plates into place over the windows, welding them to the vehicle body.

Seeing the concern on Buddy's face and appreciating the sentiment, Siobhan took Buddy's hand from the window frame, squeezing it, her grip a vise.

Buddy squeezed back.

"You watch out for yourself, Buddy," the woman who reminded him of his grandmother said. "You watch out for all these people here, too."

Buddy nodded, said, "I will," and walked away. Harris and Brenner got to work on the passenger side of the SUV, acetylene torches hissing.

On the southern wall, Bobby Evers stood with his thirty-thirty, and some others began sniping on the undead, the cracks of their weapons reverberating throughout Eden, the gunfire drawing the zombies.

The SUV was sealed, the windows welded with plate metal, meant to keep anything from breaking its way in. A large plate with pre-welded eye slits replaced the windshield. They had enough food to last them five days to a week, water, extra gasoline.

Buddy thought that so long as Bert kept the vehicle upright, could navigate between everything cluttering the streets, and they car didn't catch a flat, they'd be okay.

John Turner was on the north wall giving a thumbs up from the hut.

"You're clear," Harris told Bert, patting the side of the SUV.

The northern gate rolled open, in the street beyond was a lone zombie, sitting in its wheelchair. It had been a paraplegic, half its face, most of its chest and neck gnawed off, enough having been left for it to come back. It couldn't operate the wheelchair any longer, and had been sitting there in the street for a couple weeks.

Buddy had no clue how the thing got there in the first place.

The Hyundai eased out of Eden, through the gate, around the wheelchair and the zombie. The undead thing moaned, turning its head the few degrees it could, trying to follow.

"They're a crazy bunch of motherfuckers." Diaz exhaled a long stream of marijuana and something else, people gave him dirty looks.

The gate rolled back, secured, Evers still yelling at the zombies from the southern wall, like a cowboy slapping his horse's rump, "Yeeeaaaah!" He whooped it up between rifle shots.

Staring at the southern gate, Buddy thought of Siobhan McAllister, the vehicle already out of ear shot.

"There they go," said Buddy. "Doomed souls."

"Their souls aren't doomed." Bear spoke with a quiet self-assurance.

"You alright?" asked Harris.

"Yeah, I'm cool. What's the Irishman up to?"

"Shoot," smirked Harris. "He thinks he's John Wayne or someone."

"SHANNON," DIAZ WHIMPERED, all cried out.

"She's gone." Julie glanced around nervously.

Bitten the night before, most of Shannon's throat had been torn out. Getting to her quickly, fending off the undead, they'd staunched the wounds, bound them, and carried her back to Diaz's house.

Diaz sat on the floor next to her bed all night, holding one of her clammy hands, while she drifted in and out of consciousness, unable to speak. Lisa administered the syrettes of morphine the way she'd done as a nurse practitioner, the syrettes from the National Guard armory. No way to know what Shannon was aware of in her finals hours.

Diaz cried silently, the tears burning down his cheeks, as he sat there with no gun.

There were always other people in the room with the couple. Julie, Beth Evers, Al Gold, and Davon there when Shannon passed, the deathwatch fulfilled.

Julie looked at Al Gold, who nodded, pulled the flask from his back pocket, and swallowed a mouthful of whatever it contained.

Big, strapping Davon, his high school football career ending with the rest of the world, stepped up, a 40 mm Glock by his side.

"Diaz," said Davon. "Diaz you hear me?"

Diaz stared at the wall.

"Diaz, look man. You gotta go with Beth and Julie. Get out of here man."

"Just shoot her kid," said Al. "Shoot her now."

Diaz looked up from the wall, eyes unfocused then moving to his girlfriend. All Shannon had been through, she looked peaceful, at rest. Diaz knew they were going to take his Shannon and do horrible, terrible things to her, shoot her in the head and then burn her beautiful body until there was nothing left.

"Diaz, come on…"

Diaz stood. Julie backed away from the bed, uneasy in Shannon's presence now that she was dead. Soon. It would be soon. Shannon'd been tough. The bite had been bad, she'd almost bled out on the spot. Julie was surprised the woman made it through the night.

Beth Evers placed a gentle hand on Diaz's arm, began to guide him towards the door, Diaz going with her a few steps, appearing to comply.

Lighting fast, he tore free of Beth's grasp, lunging at Davon—Davon standing over the bed, his back to Diaz and Beth, above Shannon, bringing the Glock up—and Diaz bashed the black kid in the back of his thick neck.

The blow caught Davon by surprise. He stumbled, went down across the bed, the Glock falling from his hand and thudding on the floor.

Diaz scooped up the pistol, waving it wildly at the others.

"Stay the fuck away from her!" he screamed. "Leave her alone."

"Diaz!" Al took a step forward, one hand hovering over the holstered .45 on his right hip, his other hand still holding his flask. "Let's talk—"

"Fuck you, Al, you fucking drunk fucking fuck! Fuck all of you! That's my Shannon you *putas*, leave her alone."

Diaz backed himself against a wall, fear in his eyes, spittle flaked around the sides of his mouth. The pistol in his hand was unsteady, wavering.

"This is insane." Julie looked from Al to Diaz to Beth, to the bed where an unconscious Davon was sprawled across Shannon's sheeted legs. "Just insane."

She started walking for the door.

"Where the fuck are you going?" Diaz demanded, wiping at his nose with the back of the hand gripping the Glock.

"I'm getting out of here. This is nuts," Julie said calmly, exiting the room. They could all hear her break into a run in the hallway, down the stairs.

"Now what?" Al Gold looked at Beth Evers.

Davon groaned, got up on his hands. His head groggy, everything out of focus.

At that moment Shannon came back, so sudden the others could not react. Davon had no idea what hit him. The undead sat up in bed, grabbed his shaved head in its hands, twisted his face towards her and ripped away a hunk of his cheek and nose.

Davon bellowed, rose to a kneeling position on the mattress, pushed the zombie off him, the former Shannon, a booker, sprang off the bed, across the room at Al Gold, his flask dropped, fumbling with the flap of his holster, trying to get the .45 out.

Beth Evers screamed, a cry of pure terror. Diaz backed against the wall, the Glock aimed nowhere, eyes zoned out.

Davon lost his balance perched on the bed, fell backwards and cracked his skull on the dresser with a dry thump.

Beth looked towards the door, the way out, instead she rushed to Al, tried to pull the undead off him. She got an arm around the thing's neck, tried to put it in a full nelson. It stood, Al writhing on the floor, one eyeball on his cheek, hanging from its optic nerve, the other missing completely, his face ground up, his flask gurgling out onto the floor.

Beth Evers hung on for dear life, the undead wheeling around the room, her on its back, the thing's fingers trying to pry her arm from its neck, into its jaws.

Al cried out, sightless, kicking at the air, trying to regain his footing, and slipped in a puddle of alcohol and blood.

The undead slammed its back, Beth attached, against the wall. The wind was knocked out of her, but Beth held tight, knowing she couldn't let go. A second collision with the wall weakened her grip, the third dislodged her entirely. Slumping to the floor, breathless, the back of her head split, pulsing.

Davon was bleeding out all over the floor, a puddle of blood gathering around his skull.

Beth looked up, blinking, a vision from hell, the undead pouncing, all teeth and nails.

She started shrieking.

On a lawn chair in the middle of the street Harris kept an eye on the manhole cover. He wouldn't say it to anybody, but he was worried. Buddy and the others should have been back a long time ago.

The 12 gauge rested across his lap.

"Harris!" Julie ran out of Diaz's place, screaming for him.

"Diaz," Harris spat. Buddy had been right.

He ran, reaching Julie, saw she was not hurt—

"Shannon's dead—Diaz pulled a gun on everyone—Davon—"

—broke back into his run, aware of Bobby Evers and others following.

Through the open front door, up the stairs to the second floor, down the hall to the bedroom where Shannon had been taken earlier.

Pausing outside the doorway, Harris listened to the sounds from within and did not want to enter. He tightened his hold on the pump, leveling the barrel at his hip.

"Beth!"

Bobby barreling up the stairs wheezing, Harris stepped into the doorway before Evers could.

"Oh no…"

Al Gold was lying on the floor, blind, an eye out of its socket. Al had managed to draw his .45, waving it in front of him as he lay there shaking, quivering, whimpering in agony, his free hand, blood covered, tentative, gingerly touching the ravaged mess, his face.

Davon was dead, lying in a pool of red on the floor, ankles still resting on the bed. Harris could see part of the kid's face had been bitten off. Smelled like someone had evacuated their bowels.

Beth Evers was still alive, swatting at the undead Shannon, ever-weakening cuffs from her right hand—her left arm mangled, chewed through to the white. The zombie ignored the blows. It had Beth's stomach open, intestines unroped, lassoed on the floor about them, blood smeared on its face as it gorged itself.

The room, the stink, blood, booze, feces, the dead.

"Oh, Beth…" Bobby Evers's lament jarred Harris.

Harris aimed the shotgun at Shannon, whistled. The booker looked up, reared back on its knees with something from inside Beth's body clenched in its hands and cracked open its blood caked maw. Most of its head disintegrated as Harris fired, a splatter of blood and bone and brain splashing the wall behind.

Diaz was hoarse, crying out from the other side of the bed.

Harris stepped fully into the bedroom, Bobby Evers went past him to his wife.

The shotgun pumped, on Diaz, the man down on the other side of the bed, sobbing. Harris kept one eye on him as he moved over to Al Gold. Al all fucked up, Harris said, "Al, it's me, it's Harris," a little too quietly so then louder.

"It's okay now, Al."

Al's free hand clutched at Harris's shirt sleeve, then his arm, getting a firm grip, his mouth moving trying to say something, speechless.

"Don't Al, it's okay." Harris clenched the man's shoulder, turning to stare back at Bobby and Beth, placing the shotgun on the floor next to him, drawing one of the twin nine millimeters.

Seated next to Beth on the floor, Bobby stroked his wife's hair tenderly. She cried, the color draining from her face. Bobby's .38, the one he kept on his ankle, was in his right hand.

Harris tried not to look directly into Al's ravaged face. Al clung to Harris's arm like a drowning man, trying to talk, to say something.

Harris aimed the nine millimeter at Al's forehead.

"Al, it's okay, now? You hear me? It's okay now."

Al swallowed, quieted for a moment, his grip on Harris's arm never loosening.

"It's okay, Al. You were a good man, you hear me? You *are* a good man."

His ears still ringing from the shotgun blast the nine millimeter was not as loud as it normally sounded.

Another crack behind Harris.

Bobby Evers gently laid his second wife's head down, rose, having done what needed doing.

"Bobby."

He looked at Harris, and nodded.

Harris nodded back.

He sighed. A different situation with Bobby's first wife. Harris had had to take care of that.

Drawing its knees to its chest, the thing that had been Davon rolled over, began to get into a position where it could push itself up.

Harris aimed at the big guy's head, Bobby beating him to it, striding over and putting one in the left side of the undead's skull. Bobby stood over the fallen zombie, firing a second and a third shot in the back of its head.

"Diaz."

Diaz was comatose in the space between the wall and the bed. He'd dropped the pistol, and was curled in the fetal position.

Harris looked him over, deciding the man had not sustained a bite.

"You got any objections…?" Harris asked Bobby, indicating Diaz with his gun.

Bobby shook his head, nothing to say.

Harris straight armed the nine millimeter in Diaz's direction. Undead or not…

"Harris."

Julie stood in the doorway with the AR-15. Mickey was behind her with an assault shotgun. Mickey was the one who had spoken.

Julie was pale from the sight in the room, her eyes finding Harris', a question there.

"Mickey," he said, lowering the nine millimeter, "Do me a favor and get Lisa in here to look at Diaz."

Julie waited until Harris holstered the handgun under his left arm.

HE WOKE TEN minutes before the alarm, and it was still dark outside.

Harris didn't get up. He popped the ear plugs out, rested them under his pillow. Could hear the birds outside. They were always loudest in the hour before the sun rose.

He rolled over, wrapped an arm and leg around Raquel, who was sleeping quietly.

Harris kept his mouth closed, and could taste his breath. He always slept with his mouth shut, which was good. Nothing could fly into it. He'd seen too many *Three Stooges* as a kid, the one with the feather aloft from Curly's breath. But a closed mouth meant sour breath when he woke.

As a kid he'd wake to piss and *have to* brush his teeth at the same time. The taste used to bother him *that much*. That continued up until the first year or so of his marriage, at which point he stopped brushing his teeth every time he woke. These days he brushed once in the morning and once before he went to bed, kept his mouth shut next to Raquel.

Theirs was a quiet block, a cul de sac, but he needed the ear plugs to sleep. A dependency from a time long ago. Without them, he found himself lying in bed, listening to the creaks of the house, the occasional car going somewhere, the dog roused by a raccoon or skunk outside. It wasn't so bad in the summer, with the low steady hum from the central air conditioner vent lulling him to sleep.

With two minutes left before the alarm clock would ring, he pressed his nose to Raquel's head, breathing deep. The scent of her shampoo and conditioner, her natural smell under that. He liked her smell, even that slight musty smell she got after a long day when her deodorant wasn't up to the task. Not full blown body odor, the type that made people on the subway wrinkle their nose and turn away, just that vaguely discernable emanation, it embarrassing her should he mention it. It secretly turned him on.

As he got out of bed, pulling the sheet and light blanket back up over Raquel, Harris wondered if that made him a pervert. She would sleep for another fifteen minutes before he woke her, up as was their custom.

He thumbed the selector on the clock radio one notch turning off the alarm. Had to be careful, two notches and the radio station would pop on.

He pulled on a white t-shirt to go with his boxer shorts, stepping into his slippers. His robe hung up on the door, he slipped it on, leaving it hanging open in the front. The bedroom door opened without noise, and Daffy looked up at him with expectant eyes and wagging tail, her whole rear starting to shake, the door closing silently behind him.

"Good morning, Daffy-doggy."

The one major concession he'd made for Raquel: keep the dog out of their bedroom when they slept. Part of the reasoning had been they were going to have a kid, and maybe keeping the dog away from the sleeping baby would be good for everyone involved, but they hadn't been able to have a kid, and somehow Daffy was still relegated to the hall.

"How's daddy's little girl?" She followed him.

In the bathroom he urinated, shook it out, farted loudly, a trumpet blast but no smell. Good to know his gastro-intestinal track still worked. He yawned, his breath rank. Harris flushed, put the seat down, a common courtesy when living with the opposite sex.

Heading downstairs, he could smell the hazelnut. Every night before they went to bed, Raquel set up the coffee machine. Fifteen minutes before Harris stirred the automatic timer kicked the brew off, a full carafe waiting by the time he got to the kitchen.

Harris went to the refrigerator, poured himself a glass of orange juice from a 96 oz. plastic jug. Fresh, not from concentrate. Raquel liked pulp. He preferred none. Sometimes they compromised, as with this container. *Some pulp.*

He looked at the calendar hung on the fridge with a magnet as he drank his juice, farting twice more. Daffy cocked an eyebrow.

"Damn squirrels," he said to her though she didn't care.

Another week and a half, he'd have two days off. Thanksgiving. Five weeks after that, a full two weeks for the holidays.

"Come on girl," Harris said, beckoning Daffy. She wagged her tail, slipped out through the sliding glass doors in the dining room, and ran into the backyard. Harris watched her do her business from the house, drank his juice, yawned again, and tried to squeeze out another fart: empty. He noted the squirrels chasing each other in the tree, thought he should get up on the roof this weekend sometime, clean out the gutters, check the tiles. Three years ago, they'd had to replace the original roof and it had cost over twelve thousand bucks. The joys of home ownership.

Daffy finished what she was doing, came back to Harris. He let her inside the house, closed the sliding glass doors.

In the kitchen, he fished out a dog cookie, made her give him a paw. "Good girl, good girl," he said, letting her have the treat. Harris rinsed the glass out, put it in the dish washer.

He thought about breakfast as he went to the front door, opened it, looked outside. The blue plastic of his New York Times home delivery greeting him on the lawn. The glow from the sun started to spill over the horizon.

Harris cinched the robe shut, walked outside to retrieve his paper. The grass was wet, but he couldn't feel it for his slippers. The neighbors were not out yet. Still, it wouldn't do for a man in his early forties to go outside and get the newspaper in his boxers. People would talk. That's what people did.

He could always make eggs, it would only take a few minutes. Mix two or three in a bowl with some milk, a little pepper, pour the concoction in a frying pan with some melted butter coating the bottom. Mrs. Harris' oldest boy was no Emeril but he wouldn't starve to death. There was a box of Cheerios on the kitchen counter beside the fridge, and a second box of some sugary breakfast cereal. Raquel occasionally liked the sweeter stuff; he shunned it the way he shunned bologna for breakfast. Harris was convinced some things just not meant for consumption before noon.

He slipped the paper out of its plastic container and laid down the international news section, the metro section, and the sports, casting a cursory glance at the headlines as he did so, figuring out what articles interested him enough to read when he was ready. Another suicide bombing in the Middle East, four U.S. soldiers killed. The Fed raising interest rates another quarter of a point, the third time this year. Albany struggling to find a few billion in funding for the state's school systems. Looked like there was going to be a hockey season this year.

He unscrewed the top of the insulated carafe, poured three quarters of a cup of coffee for himself, added a good dose of milk, lightening it up. He stuck to decaf these days at home, as all they had at work was regular, he with this image of his gut rotting out from too much caffeine. The hazel nut smelled great, tasted delicious, but he'd heard they sprayed the beans to get them that way, and that couldn't be good for him.

Daffy had settled herself beside the kitchen table, front paws stretched out before her, head resting between them on the cool tiles.

Harris looked at the clock on the wall. He straightened his arms, hearing his elbows crack, and headed back up the stairs. Time to wake Raquel.

"ANY OF YOU fuckers run, I'll kill you myself!" roared Lieutenant Bonham, the look on his face telling them he meant it.

PFC Udit steadied his M-16 at the plate glass entrance to the office tower. The entrances were all locked but the zombies were pressing up against the glass, banging on it. The sheer weight of their numbers—it had to be hundreds of them out there—might shatter it eventually.

Around PFC Udit, the rag tag group of National Guardsmen, Marines, Army soldiers and police officers that'd grouped together in the lobby of the building leveled their weapons.

"Hanging in there, Udit?" PFC Kimberly Sams asked. Sams was a big, tough German-Puerto Rican broad. She'd dragged Udit in from off the street, their platoon overrun down on Columbus Circle. Sams had the squad's M-240 B Machine Gun set up on an overturned leather couch. A uniformed cop she'd grabbed stood next to her to feed the ammunition.

"I'm good, Kimmy," he said, mustering his courage.

A broad-shouldered black cop was up in the lieutenant's face.

"What the fuck are you talking about man? You don't be threatening me and my people!"

Bonham's face going from red to crimson. Udit thought he might kill the other where he stood.

Around the elevators the crowd had thinned, but there were still dozens of civilians waiting to hitch a ride up into the building, out of the lobby, away from the hordes of zombies filling the streets. Three firefighters were overseeing the loading of the elevators, making things go smoothly.

"Get out of my face, nigger!" Bonham screamed at the black cop pausing between each word. Udit looked down, shaking his head. *Oh boy...*

"Nigger? Who you calling nigger?" Another black cop stood up.

"You're out of line—" A white officer started to put Bonham in his place, but the lieutenant flipped and brought his M-16 up and fired a three round burst into the first cop's chest.

Udit ducked as things got crazy again.

The cop's two buddies fired their service revolvers at Bonham and the lieutenant pirouetted, screaming about "niggers" as blood geysered out of him. Bonham triggered a second then a third three-round burst from the M-16 before he dropped to the marble floor.

Seeing their LT lit up, Hale and Kucharyk fired on the cops. The white cop was lifted off his feet and slammed back down, deceased. The second black cop ducked and rolled, got up firing, the bullets from his Glock missing their targets. One errant round pierced through Sergeant Gloria Grant's lower back, below her body armor.

The cop who'd taken the chest full of lead from Bonham thanked his god: he was saved by his vest. He was down but still in the game, firing his pistol, blowing holes in Hale's center of mass.

Grant grunted and fell forward, firing her M-4 as she went, a full auto rip punching through a hapless emergency service worker and the glass windows of the lobby. The firing stopped just as suddenly as it had started, all eyes watching the spider webs rippling across the glass, then sheets of it cascading down, shattering on the floor. The zombies poured in, more glass breaking around them.

Civilians by the elevators started screaming and didn't stop.

"Fuck!" Kimberly Sams let them have it with the M-240B. The squad machine gun started rattling off six hundred rounds a minute, the 7.62 mm belts flying through it, shell casings and links spitting out, littering the marble floor.

Everyone opened fire. The noise was deafening. PFC Udit lost his nerve and fired out his first clip in a matter of seconds, full auto. Not a good move, as none of his shots brought anything down.

The first zombies that went into the building absorbed the withering salvo, limbs severed, dropping off, blood exploding across their torsos. The few humans who kept their cool brought many down. A pile of undead built up, but more invaded the building, climbing over their fallen.

PFC Udit swapped magazines and moved his weapon's selector to single shot.

Sams screaming at the zombies as she mowed them down, Udit couldn't make out a word she was saying.

He was so close he didn't have to aim, just point and shoot, and PFC Udit did so, starting to hyperventilate. Legless zombies dragged themselves across the floor towards the line of defenders, leaving streaks of blood on the waxed floor behind them.

Sgt. Gloria Grant was pulling her own paralyzed body across the floor when a group of zombies fell on her and started chewing up her legs. She couldn't feel anything but cried anyway, yelling through the tears for them to "Get off!"

Around PFC Udit, people were up and running. And not just the cops and National Guardsmen.

"Fall back!" a Marine screamed, firing a pistol out as he retreated towards the elevators.

"Udit, let's go!" Kimberly had the machine gun by its handle, lugging its thirty pounds around with a belt of ammo slung over her shoulder, the muzzle glowing red.

PFC Udit followed her and they merged with the crowd trying to push their way into the elevators. Only six elevator banks.

Sporadic gunfire continued as the zombies bore down on those inside the lobby. One of the black cops from the shootout dived over the counter behind the front desk, half a dozen undead right behind him. Several gunshots and then the man was up, trying to get back over the counter, three arms pulled him cursing back down out of sight.

"Move!" A National Guardsman pushed some women and men in office attire out of the way to squeeze himself onto an elevator. There were too many people and the doors couldn't close.

Someone tossed a grenade and it detonated knocking down several of the undead and sending clouds of plaster dust roiling through the elevator bank.

"Get out, get the fuck out!" the guardsmen threw a hysterical secretary out by her hair. The doors closed.

Ding!

At the end of the elevator banks another car opened. Sams and PFC Udit moved to it, humans screaming and dying around them as the zombies tore into their flesh.

Someone was on a full-auto tear, and their friendly fire mowed down civilians, cops, Guardsmen.

The secretary was dragged out of the elevator car by her hair, on her knees, crying, hugging herself.

The elevator was pretty much full by the time Udit and Sams got to it.

"Shit," muttered Udit.

He turned, watching in horror as the zombies overran the elevator banks. One elevator's doors were closing when a zombie forced its way in, the automatic sensors opening the door. Someone inside shot it in the head but others pushed in behind it. People were screaming in that elevator, and someone fired what sounded like an M-16 wide-open.

The kneeling secretary was enveloped and buried under a huddle of the undead.

"Move!" a Marine screamed desperately, a big brawny guy crying out high-pitched, and when nobody got out of his way fast enough he sprayed his M-16 into them, bodies collapsing around another open elevator. The Marine jumped over the dead and dying, into the elevator, kicking the bodies out so the doors could close.

"Fuck you!" someone else yelled at the Marine, tossing a grenade in as the doors closed.

"Go, Udit!" Sams pushed PFC Udit into the elevator.

"Kimmy!" he cried out but it was too late, the doors sliding shut.

There was a muffled thud as the hand grenade in the elevator with the Marine exploded.

"Fuck," Udit cursed.

The people in his elevator, some crying and breathing heavily, one babbling desperately.

That was the second time that day Sams had saved his life. Udit wondered if he'd ever have the chance to thank her.

THE DAY IT all began Harris did his best to keep his cool, for his own sake as well as that of his staff and students. Joy Noddings told him to turn on the television. The science teacher, Gus Cupolo, stumbled across an MSN web page news bulletin on the outbreak.

The first thing Harris did was make a call to his superintendent at Central Office. The superintendent was not in, and her secretary didn't know when she'd be back. The secretary was puzzled that Harris asked her about any instructions left for the district, so he told the woman to turn on a television or radio.

He called the main campus of the high school next. Got through to an assistant principal, a woman named Burns. Harris liked Burns. She always shot from the hip.

"We're going Code Green," the A.P. explained, suggesting that Hillcrest should do likewise.

Code Green was basically a lockdown, the entrances to the school sealed so no one could get in. The color code system had been implemented a few years back following a spate of high school shootings, national tragedies.

In the Hillcrest staff room, Joy Noddings punched numbers into her cell phone. Cupolo alternated between the web site, reading to the secretary and Susan—"attacking people, eating them"—to casting quick glances out at his car in the parking lot.

Best thing to do, thought Harris, *is be honest with the students and faculty.* He stepped into the hall, knocked on the door of the nearest classroom. Ms. Hernandez's Art class. He asked her if he could borrow two students for a moment. She sent him a junior, Yasmin, and Benjamin, a sophomore.

"Listen, I need you guys to do me a favor, okay?" He looked them both in the eye. "I need you to go from class to class, tell everybody we're going to have a community meeting downstairs in the lunch room. Right now. Yasmin, you get the classrooms downstairs, all right. Ben, up here. Thank you both."

They agreed, Benjamin asking, "Mr. Harris, this got something to do with the calls and texts students been getting in class?"

Harris nodding, cell phones and text messages, these kids probably knew more than he did. "That's *exactly* what this has to do with."

They wheeled the big 35-inch color television into the lunch room. Three dozen students and staff members sat around in chairs, on the edge of tables, craning their necks to get a better view of FOX.

Harris stood, hands on his hips. Channel 5 was reporting live from the West Side Highway somewhere in the mid-thirties, a National Guard unit engaged in a firefight. The cameraman delivered some amazing footage. The audio from the reporter not clear, but the gunfire and shouts were crystal.

Some individually, others in groups, people staggered into view, emerging onto the West Side Highway from side streets. Before them ran other people, screaming, wounded, bleeding. The National Guard were doing their best to separate assailants from victims, gunning them down, the pandemonium proceeding up the highway.

The *brrrrrrrrpt* of a light machine gun nonstop, tracer rounds zipping down the street, meeting the humans running their way. Many of the humans were going down, others were crushed by the slugs, blood jetting from their wounds, yet staggering on, running even.

The mass closer, the reporter saying something about how he "didn't see anything like this shit in Iraq," then apologizing to the audience for his choice of words, stumbling over his own, chalking the imprecation up to the situation, the Guard firing indiscriminately, full auto, their position being overrun.

The cameraman zoomed in on a stringy black man keeping his head down, trying to outdistance three others chasing after him.

The man yelled, grasped his knee and went down, friendly-fire. He twisted around on the asphalt, gripping his ravaged leg, blood pulsing from between his fingers, and was then pounced upon by those who gave chase.

Harris and the others stood transfixed by a close up as the attackers began tearing into the fallen man, while he screamed, punching at them. One of the aggressors chomped furiously around the bloody knee, and Harris shut the television right after the lower leg came off.

A complaint, *why-are-they-shutting-off-the-television.*

"Jesus Christ," the secretary said.

"Why'd you shut if off, Harris?" demanded the Phys. Ed. Teacher.

"Enough of that," said Harris. "The kids don't need to see that."

The students and staff murmuring, the noise rising. They were upset, some scared. Others thought it cool.

"Did you see that one with one arm chasing that lady? That was hella dope!"

"Listen up!" Harris shouted once, injecting as much testosterone into it as he could, his loudest, deepest, *I-command-thee-to-listen-to-me* voice, the one usually reserved for the few times a year he had to break up a student fight.

"Do I have your attention?"

The murmurs quieted down.

"Yo, listen!" someone hissed.

"*All* of your attention?"

He had it.

"Okay." He was winging it, not knowing what to say. "Something real bad is going on in the city. We're not sure what, and from what we can tell, the people on the television don't know either. A lot of us have family and friends down in the city, and we're going to be worrying about them. I understand that. It's natural."

He worked his way to the center of the room, pitching his voice, turning his head, at one point or another facing everyone in the place, making eye contact with all.

"The main campus is on Code Green. That means no one gets in and no one gets out.

"No one," he said this again, the gym teacher looking away.

"Best thing to do is sit here until 2:00," dismissal time, when the busses came to take the students who didn't drive home, "wait it out. We don't know if, whatever this is, is confined to the city, or if it's up here too. I don't want any of you getting hurt, not one of you, and that means we stay where we are until we hear otherwise."

Harris said it again, "That means *all* of us."

"Can we turn the television back on?" a student asked.

"No. We don't show you R-rated movies, I'm not showing you that crap. Somebody get a radio out of one of the classrooms, hook that up. Bruce, you still have that boombox in your room?"

The Phys. Ed. Teacher said he did, and left to get it.

"Okay. Staff, I want the kids here or next door in Joy's classroom. I want people accounted for. I don't want people wandering around. The main thing is to try and stay calm. We aren't helping anyone out if we go crazy here, right?"

A few "Yeahs" and "A'ights," even an old-school "Word". Some silent nods. A couple of the girls were crying. The kids here long enough knew Harris would never steer them wrong.

"Mr. Harris," said Shanequa, a scared ninth grader with afro puffs, "are those things gonna get us?"

"I'm not going to let those things get you, Shanequa, any of you."

No one who heard his promise doubted it.

The gym teacher came back with his radio, said he was going to Ms. Noddings' room to plug it in. Several of the students and staff followed him.

"Susan," Harris stopped her. "I'm going upstairs, make a few phone calls, Central Office, the police. See what I can find out. You okay?"

Susan shrugged, the look on her face saying she didn't know what to do or feel.

Harris reached out, placed a reassuring hand on her shoulder, left it there for a moment.

"Everything is going to be okay, all right?"

"All right," said Susan.

In case anyone was watching he walked calmly down the hall and up the stairs.

In his office he closed the door, then thought better of it and opened it again. Harris tried to call his wife.

BREATHE IN, BREATHE out, in, out. The man concentrated on his breathing, the inhalation and exhalation of air, conscious of the rise and fall of his chest, his eyes closed to his surroundings. He was aware of an itch on his arm, but ignored it, striving to center himself.

The counting of breaths was a technique he'd practiced for years. He'd had the time on his hands to do so. A breath, another, again. Assigning each a number, focusing on the numeral in his mind, envisioning it in empty space, concentration on the number allowing him to void all else around him, the itch not so much forgotten as no longer mattering.

The numbers, the visuals cast on the screen of his mind, dissipated, his awareness now of breathing alone. Somewhere his corporeality continued, the inflation of his chest, blood coursing through his veins, electrical impulses through his brain and sensory-motor system, processes external to him, his sense of self transcended.

He was one with the emptiness, one with everything, a clang of keys on metal brought him back to his world, out of meditation, the hack over his cot, looking down on him, suited out in riot gear. One hand pulled in close to the guard's body, injured, the other steadying a mini-14 on him.

The man made no moves, not the slightest indication that he had a stake in what transpired next.

"You're free," said the corrections officer. "As much as it pains me, as much as I wonder and worry if what I'm doing here is the right thing, the *just* thing, I'm letting you go.

"But before you leave, I'm going to tell you something, and you're going to listen."

The man sat up, hands on knees.

"You think I'm kidding don't you? That this is all some sick joke, right? You think I'm going to blow your brains out all over this place, spit on your body? Part of me wants to do nothing *but* that. But this is no joke, and I'm not kidding."

The turn-key glanced, over his shoulder, into the hall of D-Block, wincing, looking down at his hand.

"Now you listen to me. I hate you. I fucking detest your very being. Everything you are, everything you represent, you're an abomination to me. I've spent the last twelve years of my goddamn life trying my best to make the last twelve of yours as miserable as I fucking can.

"Hell. That's all I ever wished for you. *Hell* for your soul in death, but also here on earth while you lived out whatever was coming to you. I did what I could to make hell real for you here, for all of you death row scumbags matter of fact, but especially *you*.

"'Specially you. When I look at you, I don't see a man, I see a beast. Ain't no man capable of what you done, nothing human. I see all those little girls, their arms cut off, struggling up out of those ditches, screaming and crying their way down the side of the road, all bloody between their legs.

"I see their mommies and daddies weeping, wondering why God would let that happen to their children. I see little ones, robbed of their innocence, their futures. I see families robbed of the promise, the covenant, the idea that if they do right by the world and God, that world and God would do right by them.

"I ask myself, *who* are you? Who are you *really*? What kind of man…what kind of *thing* could do this, could visit this upon others? It's not so much the mechanics that concern me. I been here in this place long enough, I seen enough what one human being can do another. It's the motivation, the thought process. You're something I don't understand, something I can't understand. Best thing could have happened is they killed you when they took you, but they didn't.

"I'm a religious man, but I don't know. I'd kill you right now. That's why I came down here to begin with. But death is too good for you. If you die and there's a hell I have no doubt there's a special place reserved for you. If you die and there ain't nuthin', well, I don't believe that, but on the off chance there ain't then death for you ain't nuthin' but a reprieve, and I'll be goddamned you're gonna get that.

"That's why I did what I did in here over the years, kept you alive. There were those wanted you dead, you know. Dead for what you did outside, dead for what you did others in here. Inmates, guards. I *kept* them from you. Death isn't enough for this one, that's all I kept thinking. You die, no matter how painful, no matter how much suffering anyone or anything could inflict upon you in your final hours, it's still all over for you, the way it's all over for some of them kids, mercifully. The other ones…

"The ones that lived… I don't even want to think about them.

"I came down here to kill you. You'll see what's going on outside, the world's gone to hell. If I killed you, no one would notice. Even if they did, fuck, nobody'd give two shits now. So I come down, and in my heart of hearts I'd made up my mind to end you, but then this motherfucker—a man I know, a good guard, a man I've known longer than I've despised you, he attacked me, and I had to kill him, shoot him with this gun."

He raised the barrel of the mini-14 to the ceiling, his eyes running up and down the stock, contemplating the instrument in his hand.

"He bit me, that fucker. Don't know why. That's when I changed my mind, thought how death too sweet a deal for you. Maybe I don't know what I'm doing…I'm not feelin' so hot right about now. But, you know what? Fuck you. You *live.*

"But before you thank me, you go on, you see what this world holds for you. You've no idea what I'm letting you out into. You might not make it long out there, but I think you will, and I hope you do. That'll be your punishment, and I pray it's punishment enough."

The man on the cot stood, stretching, rotating his head on his neck.

He took nothing with him, stepping into the hallway, leaving everything in the cell as it was. All the cells along the block were rolled back, open, empty, and somewhere there was a ruckus, muted clangs of metal on metal, the screams of men.

"Everything's gone to hell, buddy. I think the world is ending." The corrections officer walked off down the block, calling behind him, "And don't you walk my way."

The man in the cell sat there for some time considering this turn of events.

Buddy, he thought, *that'll do*. With no destination in mind he strolled off in the opposite direction, towards the bedlam.

"OKAY, FAVORITE JUNK food," invited Fred Turner.

Fred, his son, John, Bobby and Beth Evers, Buddy, Harris, and a bunch of others sat around some patio tables set up in Eden in the middle of the street. Well past midnight, most asleep, Mickey on watch along the southern wall, Sal Bianaculli on the northern, this group up late, under the stars and luau lamps, ignoring the occasional moan and yelp coming over the wall, drinking and talking.

"Favorite junk food," mulled Beth. "You know those little chocolate donuts, the kind Hostess used to make?"

"Yeah," someone else.

"Well, those. But only if they're frozen. I don't like them when they're room temperature."

"That's how I feel about my Devil Dogs," Davon nodding in agreement.

"Chocolate cream pie," said Bobby Evers. "But what I'd give for some of the Black Stuff."

"You talk about other women that way in front of your wife?" John Turner asked, pushing his glasses up on his nose.

"You're twistin' hay there, boyo. I'm speaking of me Guinness."

"This is America, Bobby," said John. "Speak American."

"And not the instant pudding type either," Bobby continued, "the one with the pudding you gotta make with milk and stir."

"Jeez, you guys were made for each other," said Buddy. "All these qualifications and what not."

The game continued around the loose circle.

"Crumb cake," said Isabel, following it with another shot of tequila.

"Tiramisu," was Fred Turner's answer. He was glad Mickey was on watch, otherwise they'd probably be talking movies, because between Harmon and Harris they could talk on them all night. Turner'd grown up when the radio was still America's number one form of entertainment. Talk about the Shadow, he was in his element. Spielberg or Cameron, he could keep up; Kurisawa or Truffaut, he couldn't.

Buddy raised his eyebrows, proffered, "Lemon meringue pie."

"What about you Harris?" Isabel asked the other directly.

Isabel a good looking woman, early 40s, buxom. Buddy used to kid him those were the two good things about Isabel, the twins, and Harris thought she had been flirting with him on occasion.

"I have one," said Harris, "But like my Irish friend and his lovely bride here it comes with a qualification."

"Uh-unh, here we go." Buddy rolled his eyes in his head, mock annoyance.

"Like my brother from another mother Buddy it's chocolate—"

Bobby Evers interrupted in a good naturedly way, "Jay-sis, Harris, always gotta bring race into it, eh?"

"You noticed that too right?" Buddy just as quick.

Harris ignored their ribbing. "There used to be this chocolate shop, and they sold everything, anything you could want in chocolate. You know, chocolate bunnies at Easter, chocolate covered nuts, chocolate this and that. What I really liked there, they sold this loose chocolate, think they called it 'chocolate chunks' or something. Could buy it by the pound, they'd scoop up these nuggets of milk chocolate for you, put them in a bag. Good stuff."

"Sounds like it," said Isabel, and Harris noticed she wasn't wearing a bra. She never seemed to be wearing a bra. "Where was this store?"

Harris said the name of the place. "Not too far from where I grew up."

"And where was that?" asked Isabel.

"Not too far from here." Again, almost to himself. "Not too far from here."

MICKEY HAD A huge collection of DVDs. He'd had a couple thousand before the outbreak, and often lamented the loss of his collection. In his months in Eden he'd steadily amassed thousands more. When rummage expeditions for canned goods and supplies Harmon always kept an eye out for another flick to add to his library.

One time Harris had been in Mickey's home. The walls of the man's living room stacked with DVDs. Mickey had them arranged according to genre, from French new wave, to Hollywood blockbuster, to Hong Kong shoot 'em ups. Mickey's living room had beenconverted into a media room, a plasma screen television with a surround sound home theater system. The television was from Palmer and Ryan's house. Mickey had asked and they'd let him have the television, even helped him carry it over and set it up in his place.

Mickey facilitated a weekly Eden movie view-and-discussion group. He'd studied film in school for two semesters, but most of what he knew was self-taught.

When spring came to Eden, Mickey enlisted the aid of several of the men and women and they all set up an outdoor theater. Folding chairs, recliners, and couches were all arranged to face a white screen on a stand. Phil Caputo, an electrician in real life, hooked a lap top to a projector, and a whole bevy of speakers to the lap top. They watched movies on the big screen in nice weather, carting the lap top, projector and other electronic devices indoors when the weather inclement, covering the seating arrangements with tarps. Everything up on two-by-fours, out of the run off from the rain showers.

If a sofa or rocking chair got ruined it'd be easy enough to burn it, toss it over the wall. Replacing it not a problem. There were whole houses on the block left to raid, empty of inhabitants. Guys like Harris and Buddy preferred to have their own places. There were shacked up couples, some married like Bobby and Beth, Sal and Camille. Those who didn't want to live alone had housemates like Palmer and Ryan, the unlikely pair of Davon and Al Gold.

Tonight a western was showing. Harris had seen it several times before.

A dozen or so men and women lounged about. The volume was turned way up, almost drowning out the sound of the undead beyond the walls.

"You could at least have the decency to draw your guns," the sheriff told his old friends Butch Cassidy and the Sundance Kid. Newman and Redford. A classic. The duo on the run, relentless foes on their trail.

"Come on Sundance, start trussin' my feet."

This part of the movie always making Harris sad. He'd seen the movie the first time as a little boy, *Million Dollar Movie* late one night. Butch and Sundance going out in a hail of Bolivian lead. The ending was effective in large part because you didn't see the two men check out. They just come running out of the building they're holed up in, wounded and bloody, toting two six shooters each. The frame freezes, the first hail of rifle fire, a screamed command, a second volley. Harris always felt sad; you just knew they were shot to hell.

But that part wasn not until later in the film. Right now the sheriff was laying it out for them prophetic, though they knew it not.

"There's something out there that scares ya, huh?"

Redford was peeking through the drawn curtain out into the night.

"But it's too late. You know you should have let yourselves get killed a long time ago when you still had the chance."

Harris got up, walking away from the others.

"It's over, don't you get that?" He could still hear the sheriff scolding Butch and the Kid. "Your times is over and you're gonna die bloody. And all you can do is choose where."

When the sound of the movie was inaudible, he sat down on somebody's stoop, looked at his feet. He thought he was doing a good job, holding it all together, everything considered. He'd avoided taking to drink, to other drugs. Al Gold polluted half the time. Harris wondered if Al had been that way before all this, or if circumstances had changed the man.

Who was he kidding? The situation had affected him, was affecting him every day he woke up and every night he went to sleep. How else did he explain the way he'd reacted to that psychic that time? Harris liked to think he was not a violent man. Hadn't his years teaching and being a principal shown him he had a vast reserve of patience? Yet the last several months, he'd been doing what? Hacking people up with a machete, shooting them in the head. Okay, maybe they weren't exactly *people* anymore. Or were they?

Harris' existence, and everyone else's, devolved to nothing other than a question of survival. Questioning it was a luxury possible only in the relative safety of Eden.

His wallet was in his back pocket, an old habit. He pulled it out, noting how much thinner it was. He'd never been one to carry cash in his pocket. He'd used a rubber band as a young man, later a money clip. He'd already chucked his credit cards, his library card. Old habits did die hard, though. He'd cut up the credit cards before he tossed them, still held onto the social security card.

He still had the pictures, but there weren't many. He looked through them, starting with the last one, working his way to the front of the wallet. A group shot of his parents, his brother, their wives, his brother's kids. He'd taken the picture, so he wasn't in it. Tonight he was here, and they were all gone.

A picture of Daffy girl, sitting in the grass of their back yard on a hot day, tongue lolling out of her mouth.

His wedding picture. He'd never been a big one on ceremony, and neither had Raquel. They'd done the whole church thing and reception for the sake of their families. That and the idea they didn't want to grow old one day, regret not having done it.

A headshot of Raquel, the first picture of her he ever possessed. She'd always been beautiful to him, the black and white photography lended her an ethereal quality.

Her face just wouldn't leave him alone. Harris wondered when this haunting would stop. He hummed a few lines of the Status Quo's *Pictures of Matchstick Men* to himself.

"What are you looking at?"

The tall girl, Julie. She'd come over and was standing at the foot of the steps holding an open can of beer. In her other hand the plastic webbing with two more unopened.

"Ghosts," he replied, more to himself than to her.

"Mind if I sit down?"

"Go ahead." Harris made eye contact to be friendly, hadn't lost all of his social skills.

"Thanks."

Harris wondered why she'd wandered over. He'd talked to her once or twice since the day she arrived in camp. No denying was Julie an attractive woman, beautiful even.

Harris hadn't thought about another woman in years, not seriously. He'd left the dating game behind him with Raquel, the both of them pledging each to the other, never expecting it to be easy. But at the end of every single day, when he went home to her and she to him, Harris knew he'd made the right decision.

Thinking about Raquel bothered him. This world had robbed him of her.

"Did that hurt?"

Harris asked about Julie's arm. She wore a t-shirt, cut off sleeves, her right arm covered from shoulder to elbow with tattoos, some intricate-tribal-art-black-ink-thing.

"Oh man, did it," she laughed. "Especially on the underside of my arm, inside of the triceps, right here."

She held her arm out, pointed to the area she meant. Her arms long, tight, flawless.

"You have any? Ink, I mean?"

Harris blushed, "No."

She didn't say anything, so he continued. "My generation was the one where everyone started doing that, getting tattoos, piercing themselves. I always meant to get around to it—"

"What, a piercing?"

"No," he laughed a little. "A tattoo. But I'm glad I didn't."

"Why, you don't like tattoos?"

"No. I don't like what I had in mind then, now. I mean I would have been one of those regretted getting it."

"Why, what did you have in mind?"

"You ever seen that Bad Boy logo? You know, the one with the jar headed kid with the short hair flexing one arm?"

Julie laughed, "My brother had a decal of that on his truck."

"Yeah, well, when I was eighteen, *that's* what I would have gotten on my body if my parents wouldn't have thrown me out of the house."

"The Bad Boy Logo, hmmm," she mused. "Maybe it's a good idea you didn't get a tattoo."

"Yeah, I think so," Harris smiled.

They sat quietly for a minute, comfortably.

"You mind if I ask you a question?" asked Harris.

"Ask it first."

"How old are you?"

"How old do I look?"

"Well, I, uh…"

"I get it, you're worried if you answer too old or too young I'll be offended. Don't you know you shouldn't ask a woman her age to begin with Mr. Harris?"

"Social niceties were never my forte."

"Oh, I don't believe that."

"I'd be willing to bet I'm a bit older than you."

"So, was your question about me, or about you?"

"I'd have to think about that one."

She told him her age, asked him how old he was.

"Yeah," she said, "you're really older than me, old enough to be my older brother maybe."

"And have a Bad Boy decal on my truck?"

They both laughed, Julie sipping her beer.

"You want some?" she offered the can.

"No, thanks." Harris gestured. "I never did like the taste."

"Wish I could say the same," sighed Julie. "If you had known me in college you'd have thought my major was hops and barley or something."

"Hey, to each his own. Speaking of which, you have any others? Tattoos that is."

"Yeah, I do."

"Okay, do tell."

Julie pulled a leg of her jeans up over her calf, a little purple and red and green butterfly with circular motion arrows on her ankle, Harris thinking he could probably wrap his thumb and forefinger around that ankle.

"Nice. Nature girl?"

"No, my friends and I all went together, got the same tattoo on our ankles when we turned sixteen. Had to lie to the tattoo artist about our ages. I don't think he cared though. He didn't check our i.d.'s."

Harris admired the little butterfly.

"Here hold my beer will you?"

Harris took it, Julie turning around, lifted her t-shirt, showing him her back, a multi colored rendering, a girl's head and shoulders. Her bra strap hiding the girl's eyes, Harris still recognized it.

"Cosette," he said, pleased.

"Yeah, how'd you know?"

"Everyone knows Victor Hugo," said Harris, then thought, *no, surely enough, not everyone does.*

"*Les Mis* is my favorite musical," Julie pulled her shirt back down, turning to face him again.

"Yeah, ours too—mine and Raquel's, my wife's I mean," Harris wondering why he'd added that part about Raquel—"my wife's I mean" —and why, the thought vexing him just as equally, just why *shouldn't* he have?

Julie only missing one beat.

"I thought you were married, that ring on your finger and all."

Harris held up his hand, looking at his wedding band.

"I haven't seen you with a woman around camp," she said.

"No, my wife… my wife was in Manhattan," Harris told her. "I don't know what happened to her. I mean, I think I know, I mean…What about you? Were you with anyone before… well, you know what I mean."

"I had a boyfriend, if that's what you mean. But things weren't working out for us."

Harris found himself looking at her, really looking at her. She had a beauty mark above her lip. It looked like it'd been placed there on purpose. He liked it.

"I guess it was only a matter of time, before things ended officially. Then this," She gestured with both hands.

"I still find myself, it's just, damn, it's crazy isn't it?"

Julie finished her beer, "Yes, it is."

"It's one of those things, words can't do it justice."

"I agree."

"Let me ask you…"

"Go ahead."

"Why aren't you watching the movie?"

"I've seen it before."

"Big western fan?"

"My mom, she had this thing for Robert Redford. Always said if Robert had come along before my dad…"

Harris laughed, "My mom had this thing for the guy who played Tom Tom in *March of the Wooden Soldiers.*"

"That one I *didn't* see," she said.

"Laurel and Hardy?"

"I've heard of them. Let me guess, your generation right?"

"What do you mean?"

"Before, when we were talking about tattoos, you said something about your 'generation,' like you're some old man."

"I only feel that way sometimes."

"Let me ask you, Harris, this might sound strange, all this time I've been here, you haven't… how should I put this. You haven't talked to me. How come?"

"Oh, was I supposed to?"

"No, it's not that, I just—look, I'm sorry, Harris. Let me ask you another question."

"Go ahead," he smiled.

"You and Buddy, are you two, *you know?*"

"What, gay?"

"Yeah."

"You're serious?"

"Yeah."

He laughed. "That's a good one. He'll love that. Oh man will he love that."

"Well, I mean, it's not like there's anything wrong if you two were…"

He laughed harder.

"It's just you're always together, you know? I mean, I usually have a good eye for that kind of thing, but I couldn't really tell."

"Is that what your gay-dar was telling you, that me and Buddy were an item?"

"No, I wasn't sure, I didn't think so…"

"Julie, Julie, Julie," said Harris. "No, I'm not gay. And I don't think the big man is either. He's just my boy, you know what I mean? I wouldn't be sitting here talking to you if it wasn't for Buddy."

Was the look on her face relief he wondered.

"I'm sorry if I offended you—"

"No, you didn't. Don't worry."

"It's just that, you and him are also, oh, how can I say this without sounding conceited?"

"Just say it."

"Buddy. You. Neither one of you guys have tried to hit on me, on *any* of the women here."

"That's a bad thing?"

"No, that's a *great* thing! You don't know what its like for a woman around here. All these guys have this mind set, like, it's time for everyone to pair off and hook up or something, you know?"

Harris considered it. "Yeah. The only single woman I can think of here, aside from yourself that is, would be Isabel."

Julie rolled her eyes. "And with her, oh, well, you know *how* she is. And some of these guys, well, I think they think *all* women should be like that around here."

"Why, did someone get pushy with you?"

"Well, Diaz is a jerk."

"Diaz was born a jerk. Don't worry about him. Shannon will kick his ass if he tries anything with you. Come to think of it, though, I have noticed how Thompson seems to like you."

"He's a nice guy, Harris, but he follows me around."

"That's not good, huh?"

"No, that's not good."

"Well, tough luck for Thompson, then. But now that I know how you feel, I'll make an effort to show you some attention in the future."

"That's not what I meant."

"You don't mind if I stalk you sometimes, do you? Leer a little now and then?"

"You're a funny guy, Harris. You shouldn't sit here brooding by yourself."

"I wasn't brooding. I was contemplating. There's a difference you know."

"Do tell."

"You gotta see for yourself. So, give me one of those beers. Sit here and contemplate with me."

She looked at him directly and he winked at her. It felt natural.

"Okay," said Julie. "All right."

She handed him a beer, he popped it open, she doing likewise.

"To Cosette," said Harris as they tapped cans.

"Damn. This stuff still tastes like crap."

HARRIS THOUGHT ABOUT the fact that last night had been it for him, his last night of sleep. *Ever.* It was a staggering realization, and part of him felt detached as though it was not his fate that he was cognizant of but that of a stranger.

The bite so small, only a few teeth impressions on his upper arm. But the skin had broken. He could never figure how rotting corpses had such strong teeth.

All the way he'd come. Evading death on the streets, alone at first then with Buddy. He'd managed to avoid catching any contagious diseases, the things all that death and decay brought in their wake.

And here he was, hoping maybe he'd make it through the day. He thought of Diaz's girl. Shannon suffered a horrendous wound, but she'd lasted a night, into the next day. Thing was, what kind of an existence was it? Things started to happen once you were infected. Harris looked forward least to the bloody shits he knew were on their way.

He changed the bandage, put his shirt back on.

Part of him really wanted to tell Julie, but he couldn't. He just couldn't.

He didn't think *she'd* shoot him. Julie was still shaken up herself waking with a house full of undead attacking them. Throwing something like this at her, right now...

The others, *they* would shoot him if they knew, if they had the nerve. Harris knew Bobby Evers suspected something was amiss, that the other man knew something wasn't quite right.

He wondered if the time came would he let them kill him, could he let them. If he marched out onto the street and exposed the wound and told them what happened would he let them draw down and blast him away on him? Would he pull the nines and take as many of them with him as he could with no good reason?

Felt a bit nauseous already but nothing debilitating. A general sense of not feeling well. Not feeling the way he should, the way he used to.

Maybe this wasn't anything out of the ordinary. Harris'd suffered from some kind of slight depression most of his adult life, or at least convinced himself he had. He could never put a finger on it. Noticed it on Sundays mostly, a certain sense of dread with the ending of the weekend. Harris liked work, especially teaching, and administration, so it wasn't like he was ruing going back to the job, whatever the job was.

He'd found keeping busy helped. If he occupied his hours, didn't give himself much down time, he wouldn't get caught up in the blues. Raquel always said she admired that about him, his ability to manage time, to always have four or five things going on at once, and as soon as he completed one thing he'd move seamlessly into a new task.

Thompson, Harris thought, fingering the lighter in his pocket.

Leave it to human beings, he thought, *everything goes to hell and you'd think we'd pull together.* Some did, and he thought of Dom, he thought of the old man in the boat, of William Richardson, of the good ones. Where were they all now? Here in Eden, where for all he knew, for all anyone knew, what was left of humanity had gathered, here some wanted to put one over on the rest.

Harris had a pretty good idea regarding Thompson's motivation. But Thompson had let zombies into Harris's house while Thompson knew Julie was there, and that didn't make much sense. Then again, the more Harris thought about it, maybe it did make sense, maybe it made a lot of sense.

He considered running his idea past Evers. Bobby was a pretty level-headed guy, considering. Evers would listen to Harris, and of course Harris would leave out parts, the parts about his being bit, about planning to murder Thompson. *Maybe later.*

Harris left the shower area of Eden. Water had stopped running in the houses a long time ago, so the people constructed a public bath area. Toilets with cess pools, hot running water for the showers collected when it rained. Everyone had job assignments and everyone rotated amongst jobs, unless it was a task demanding certain skills only specific people possessed like Phil Caputo the electrician, and then those people were expected and encouraged to teach what they knew to others lest they die and with them their knowledge.

Harris had been on bathroom duty last week, cleaning the toilets, gassing and torching the cess pools, scrubbing the showers. Bathroom duty was a necessity, but one he wouldn't miss.

"Harris." A few people gave him small waves as he walked down the street, smiles, from Ryan a thumbs up.

Harris nodded back, forced a grin, let them know he was okay. He wore the twin nines, one under each arm. Everybody was armed in Eden, and nobody gave it a second thought. He imagined the old west might have been this way, minus the zombies.

Thompson was up the block, sweeping his property. Harris was careful *not* to avoid eye contact, though he didn't go out of his way to make it, and once it had been established Harris didn't allow it to linger, worried less his eyes gave something away, sent Thompson the message, *I know it was you, and I'm going to kill you.*

"Harris!" Julie hugged her man.

Harris hugged her back, hard, because he still could.

She'd taken a shower, cleaned up after carting the last of the bodies the other end of the block to add to the smoke and stink of the pyres.

"Harris, have a listen to this," said Palmer. "Idea a few of us had."

Harris sat himself at a folding table in the street. Funny, the scene reminded him of block parties they'd had in his neighborhood when he was a kid, all the neighbors sitting around, talking, having a good time. Difference being, this block was surrounded by an army of flesh-eaters, zombies clawing at the walls around them.

"Remember that couple came through here about two weeks ago?" Brenner asked.

Everyone remembered them. They'd driven in with an armored personnel carrier. Nice couple. Young. Heavily armed.

Brenner continued, "They mentioned there's whole cities and towns, further north, south of here too, hold outs."

"They mentioned they'd *heard* there were towns and cities where it was safe," Kate Truman corrected.

"True that," admitted Brenner. "But they'd *heard* about them from someone who'd been there."

"So what do you want to do, Kile?" Harris asked him.

"Look, we got the vehicles, we got the guns," Brenner addressed the larger group. "I say we get out of here."

"Eden's safe though," said Truman, crossing her arms in her folding chair.

"Yeah, Eden's safe," agreed Brenner. "But Eden's... Eden's a cage. Look at us. We're like pets, those fucking things are toying with us."

"Those fucking things don't think," said Phil. "At least, not like we do. They're not toying with us. They're waiting around for us to get antsy, come out. *That's* what they're waiting for, if they're waiting for anything."

"It's a good idea, Brenner," said Harris, "but I ain't buying it right this second."

"Harris, come on man," Brenner trying to persuade him. "You and me, Julie," he nodded at her beside Harris, "We can make it out of here. Others have before us."

Harris thought about those come and gone. Graham and Markowski had a way of chasing away folks, but there were fewer zombies outside the walls back then. Time went by, the streets teemed with more and more of the undead, Eden went from Graham's rule to everyone's, those who came for respite, those already here more amenable to staying, to stick it out between the four walls.

People left. Harris thought about old Siobhan McAllister, how her departure had bothered Buddy so, Buddy never saying anything about it. Whatever happened to all those people who came and went, to all those people on the outside he'd met when he and Buddy were jogging through the streets just trying to live another day, to Raquel, to Daffy? Harris longed for closure, willing even to accept the certainty of something he didn't want to hear.

"Just promise me you'll think about it, Harris," said Brenner, "All of you."

"Yeah, we'll think about it," said Phil. "From *here*, safe."

Harris coughed suddenly, bringing his hand up to his mouth. He couldn't control it, the coughing spell lasting long enough for people to notice it, which made him uncomfortable.

"Whoa, that's some cough you got there, Harris," Palmer said. "You coming down with something? Come by the dispensary, we'll hook you up with some antibiotics."

Harris thanked Palmer, excusing himself. Life continued as usual in Eden in certain weird ways. People got colds, the flu. Bobby Evers battled his asthma flare ups.

Julie made to follow Harris but he turned, stopping her.

"What is it?" she looked concerned.

"Nothing. It's all good. I want to get something out of the house. Meet me up the block by the grill. I'll be there in a few minutes. You've got to be starving. We haven't eaten."

"Okay," the look in her eyes said she didn't want to leave him and he loved her for it.

Harris turned, started towards their house, thinking about how he'd turned his back on Julie in other ways in the time he'd known her. Julie loved him, and a part of him really loved her, but there was always Raquel in the back of his mind and he thought Julie knew this.

Harris wondered if he was capable of giving himself *fully*, emotionally, to Julie. So much of what he'd felt had been blunted by all the death. Maybe this was the best he could do, given the times in which they lived, the man he now was.

He just didn't want to shortchange Julie, as she loved him deeply and unconditionally.

Harris thought these things as he unlocked the door to their house. About three months after she'd come to Eden, Julie had moved out of her own place, moved in with him.

Inside he closed the door, leaned against it. He opened his left hand, the hand that came away from his mouth wet, the same hand he'd kept down by his side, clenched tightly, hoping no one would notice. Harris stared into the palm of that hand, at the blood freckled from the cough.

He didn't have much time.

BUDDY AND HARRIS kind of stood back, following the National Guardsmen's lead as they secured the supermarket. These weren't full time troops, but they were trained, even if only one weekend a month and two weeks every summer. It was best to follow their direction, not step on their toes, go along for the ride for as long as it seemed feasible. That plus the fact the guardsmen outgunned them with some pretty heavy weaponry, compared to Harris's six-shooter, Buddy's sawed-off and the pistols and whatever other stuff the big man had in those saddle bags.

The supermarket had been closed. They'd forced their way in, blasting the locks off one of the riot gates, pulling it down behind them, the Guardsman named Shapiro going to work with an acetylene torch. *Standard Guard gear?* Harris had wondered, *or something useful picked up along the way?* The others fanned out, canvassing the aisles of the supermarket.

No zombies inside the store. All the exits seemed secure. Sergeant Edmond posted his men in what looked to be the strategic spots. The windows were protected by pull down riot gates, like the one covering the entrance, the gates meshed at eye level. Looking through the links Buddy watched the undead outside on the street.

The zombies were looking back in at them, several with their faces pressed to the grating, pulling and pushing at it futilely, moaning.

"Don't do it," Edmond cautioned Annunziata. The man was sighting down the barrel of his M-16 at one of the undead staring in at them. "Conserve ammo."

"You seen what the fuckers did to Bevilacqua and Gordon, Sarge," growled the other. "Look at Koster. They bit the shit out of Koster. You know what that means? He's got a five year old at home, Sarge."

"Annunziata, you listen to me." Edmond took his hand and forced the barrel of the other man's rifle down. "You stand the fuck down. We'll have our payback, but until I say fuckin' so you fuckin' cool your heels. Got it?"

Cowed, Annunziata said "Yeah."

Hundreds of zombies were gathered outside, joined every minute by dozens more of their kind.

"Roof access through the back," shouted Gill.

"Let's check it out," the sergeant invited Buddy and Harris, motioning one of the other men to stay with Annunziata.

"Have you ever seen this many of them gathered together in one place?" Harris asked Buddy and the sergeant on the roof.

"Manhattan was worse than this," said the sergeant. He shook his head, "Manhattan was bad."

"You were in the city?"

"We got out before the jets, and we barely got out at that," explained Edmond, "hopped the Seven train in Times Square, pulled into the station in Grand Central and there were I don't know how many hundreds, maybe more of these things all on us at once."

"We lit their shit up," noted another guardsman on the roof.

"Barely made it out of there ourselves," Edmond continued. "Hoofed it through the train tunnel. Had to carry Koster."

"He would have died on that train," said the other guardsman. "Sarge dragged him off himself."

"And maybe I should have left him," mulled the sergeant. "As it is, it doesn't look good. Any of you guys ever see someone get chomped on by one of these motherfuckers and then get better?"

"No, I haven't," said Harris, Buddy just shaking his head silently.

"Well then, ain't we in the…"

"Shit, huh?" offered Buddy.

"Shit's right," Edmond agreed.

"I understand Annunziata though," he said as if someone had asked him. "It sure is tempting to just open up on those freaks."

"You guys low on ammo?" Buddy inquired.

"Nah, we're okay, I guess," the Sergeant didn't sound too sure himself. "We picked up a lot along the way. Lot of dead soldiers out there. Thing is, *how many* of these motherfuckers are there?"

"Looks like they're going to hang downstairs, see if we don't come out to play," responded Buddy.

"Shit no," Edmond cursed. "Homie don't play that. Me and my boys are going to stay right here. Keep Hernan on that radio, get our asses extracted first-things fucking first."

The roof itself was huge, and as they walked it they saw they were surrounded on all sides by undead. Most of the zombies were congregating where they'd come in earlier at the front entrance.

"Sarge." Brophy came up to them, still lugging the general purpose machine gun, Burdett beside him, festooned with links of ammunition. "Where you want me and Burr to set this bitch up?"

The Sergeant went off to consult with his men, leaving Buddy and Harris.

"What you thinking?" Buddy asked.

"This is nice and all," said Harris. "But I am *not* into this."

"I'm with you on that man," the big man replied, thinking of their options. Manhattan was out. They'd both seen what had happened there and heard what Edmond had said.

"You seen that alley in the back?" asked Buddy.

"Yeah," Harris smiled. The rear of the supermarket fronted a large alleyway running between buildings. It was big enough for 18-wheeled delivery trucks to pull in and drop off their freight. There weren't too many zombies down there when they'd looked.

"Man might be able to mosey on off in that direction," said Buddy, "If he had a mind."

"Yeah, I bet he could," Harris said. "If he had a big enough distraction to cover him."

"Now we're thinkin' the same," Buddy grinned. "You da' man."

"No. It was your idea. *You* da man."

When they told Edmond what they were planning he looked at them like they were crazy.

"You're fucking with me right?" He could see by the looks on their faces that they weren't. "Oh Lord, they are not fucking with me."

Harris and Buddy, for their parts, watched Edmond very carefully. He'd been extremely cool with them up to this point, but facts were Edmond had more men on his side with bigger guns. If he tried to force them to stay it would get violent fast.

The sergeant remained true to form, playing it straight with them, no matter how harebrained and hell-bent of destruction he personally found their scheme.

"Okay, I guess if you're crazy enough, we can make a racket out front, rile them up down there," Edmond smiled the more he thought about it. "Give my boys a chance to let off some steam."

"But I got to let you guys know. I think as soon as you get off this roof you've got about two minutes left of breathing between the two of you."

Harris and Buddy returned downstairs for some impromptu shopping, taking items they thought they might need, Harris stowing things away in his knapsack, Buddy in his saddle bags.

"What the fuck?" smirked a guardsman, his face in a bag of chocolate chip cookies. "You guys looting?"

"Hey Chris," another guardsman called to the first. "You remember them assholes running out of Best Buy with the flat screen TVs, getting pounced on by zombies, still trying to carry off those television sets?"

"I do, and I hope every one of those Puerto Rican motherfuckers got eaten."

"You got a problem with Borrequas, Gill?"

"No. I got a problem with Hispanics in general. Puerto Ricans are the niggers of the Latino race."

"You never met a Hispanic you liked, Gill?"

"I don't know Hernon, I like your sister just fine."

"Ohhh—"

"Milk," Buddy said in the dairy aisle. "Drink up. Once this shit spoils it might be awhile before we ever have any again."

Milk's good, Harris thought, chugging from a half gallon of two percent.

"Damn if I ain't lactose intolerant though," said Buddy. "One time they had me locked up overnight, in holding with this white boy. He loved him his milk, so I let him have mine, he gave me his orange juice."

It was the first time Buddy had mentioned anything to Harris about having been away, yet it didn't surprise him. Harris could tell Buddy was a hard man, a tough man. Buddy had proved himself a good sort, although he was quiet about his past. Out on the street a perverse form of survival of the fittest was quickly shaping up, and Buddy was one tough son of a bitch. Harris only wondered how he himself had come this far. He wondered when it would end for him and how, hoping it would be quick and as painless as possible.

Back on the roof they were ready to go. The drop from the roof to the alley below was too far to make without risk of being injured. Harris spied a dumpster they could hang-drop onto, and from there leap to the ground. He and Buddy stood away from the edge of the roof, not letting the zombies below see them.

"When we go, I go first," Buddy told Harris, withdrawing the silenced nine millimeter pistol from the saddle bags.

"You guys about ready?" Edmond asked.

"We good," said Buddy. "Thanks Sergeant."

"Yeah, sergeant," agreed Harris. "Thanks."

"Then luck to you men," Edmond said. "We'll be thinking about you when the helicopter comes to take us out of here."

Edmond shook both of their hands, left them where they were, went to the front of the roof where his men lined up.

Annunziata stood there with a mad-dog look on his face. Most of the others were nonchalant, aloof almost, like it was perfectly normal, even natural to be stuck on a roof, looking down on thousands of cannibalistic reanimated corpses.

A couple of them had carried Koster up to the roof, laying him on the side. The color was drained from the man's face and he was wrapped tight in a government issue blanket, shivering.

"Give them hell, Sarge," Koster shouted weakly and there was the sound of fluid in his lungs.

"Okay, guys, when Brophy starts, let's rip." Edmond pulled a grenade from his web belt, his assault rifle taut on its sling. He'd seen what the grenades could do. They'd knock those things down, and a few of them wouldn't get back up, shrapnel to the head. But most would.

Still, the idea was to provide a diversion for the two crazy bastards about to step off the roof.

Edmond looked back at Buddy and Harris. The two were crouched across from him, at the edge of the roof, keeping low.

"Okay, Brophy," Edmond told his machine gunner. "Light those motherfuckers up."

"I ain't no sniper and this isn't a precision instrument," Brophy warned lackadaisically.

"I don't care," his Sergeant hocked a loog. "Just make some noise. Burdett, feed the pig."

The M-60 came alive, laying down hundreds of rounds a minute, the other men joining the fray, unloading on the zombies below. Edmond pulled the pin on his grenade, threw it as far as he could, letting off a "fire in the hole" no one heard as he did so, shouldering his Mike One Six and firing on semi-auto, one round at a time, aiming for heads.

The grenade blew and a dozen undead were swept off their feet, with at least two or three of them not getting back up. Brophy strafed them across their chests and heads, their bodies jerking backwards as the M-60 did its deadly work, the shell casings spitting out one side of the machine gun, Burdett feeding a link-belt into the other.

Edmond emptied a thirty round magazine and as he changed mags he cast a look over his shoulder but Buddy and Harris were gone.

He turned back to the carnage on the street below. He and his men fired and reloaded, hundreds of the things collapsing in the street, and soon little piles of them were forming, yet still they came, fresh ones pouring in off the side streets, heedless of the hot lead flying down from the roof. *Stupid almost*, Edmond thought, *like lemmings following one another over a cliff.* The incessant chatter from the weapons fire punctuated by grenade blasts.

"Whoo-hah!" Annunziata screamed when there was a lull in the shooting. "Look at 'em, Sarge. They keep coming."

"How many you think are down for the count?" Shapiro wondered.

"Not enough," Gill spat. "Kill more."

"*Goddamn* that felt good! 'Nother round, Sarge?" Annunziata almost begged.

"Okay, one more salvo," granted Edmond. "Then we lay low until the choppers come."

"SHOULD I MAKE reservations for the Greek place tonight?" Raquel asked, applying her make up with the mirror affixed to the visor above the passenger seat.

Harris thought about it as he waited for traffic to let up, wanting to make a left turn. "You know what? I don't really feel Greek tonight."

Raquel reached over, squeezed his thigh with one hand, her other applying mascara. "You're right. You *don't* feel Greek."

"Hah-hah." Harris made the turn, accelerated, heading towards the train station. "Here's an idea. Why don't you make reservations for Antica."

They'd been going there for years, the Italian restaurant a favorite of theirs since they'd lived in the little studio apartment in Queens.

"I'll meet you in the city this afternoon."

Raquel seemed pleased, "Can you do that?"

"Shoot," Harris said, mocking an authoritative tone. "I'm the principal. I can do whatever I want." He laughed. "Yeah, it's Friday, today shouldn't be a hard day. I can meet you at the office at, let's say what, six?"

"You're going to take the train in?" Raquel asked.

The train ride from their station to Grand Central was only fifty five minutes, but then it was a pain in the ass to get from the city to Queens and the restaurant by public transportation. It would involve a subway ride followed by a bus ride, and then they'd have to do it all over again after dinner with a carafe of the house red in them.

"No, I'll drive in, pick you up at work," Harris said. He could drive safely, soberly enough if he split half a carafe with Raquel. A full carafe would have been another story.

"No need to do that, just meet me in Woodside at six. How's that?"

"That'll work."

Depending on what time he got out of work on Friday afternoons, the ride into Queens could be a pain in the ass. The kicker was he'd be going *against* traffic and it'd still be a hassle. Everything seemed to slow down around the Whitestone Bridge. The Throgs Neck wasn't much better. There was always construction on the damn things, those and the Long Island Expressway.

Harris didn't miss his Queens-Westchester commute, hadn't since they'd moved north out of the city.

The thought that Raquel would meet him in Queens, that he wouldn't have to cross the 59th Street Bridge, or worse the Mid-Town tunnel into Manhattan after that, was music to his ears.

Woodside had always been their favorite subway stop. It held a lot of memories. Harris used to drive into Queens after work and park there, walk past the Irish bakeries and bars, the Korean corner store, the newsstand owned by Middle-Easterners. He'd hop on the 7 train, head to grad school back when he was working on his administrative degree. They'd lived in the area, so Raquel had been able to take a local bus to the train and into work at her firm.

"What about Daffy?" Raquel asked.

"I'll stop by the house before I head in, let her out. We still have that thing at your mom's on Sunday?"

"Yes, the shower." Raquel was reminded. Her second brother, the black sheep of her family, was getting married for the *third* time. The first two marriages had ended in a divorce and a separation, with two kids in there, because Chad was a piece of work. A piece of shit, actually, although Harris never said that to his wife. He let her say it when she wanted to. He just listened.

Harris thought maybe he'd drive in on Sunday again, take Raquel in and stop by his brother's for a few hours, see his niece and nephew. Wait around, pick Raquel up and take her back home. He told her so.

"Sounds good," Raquel said, pleased. They'd been married ten years now and it had gone fast. They still enjoyed their time together, which was a lot more than what could be said of many of their friends, who seemed like they couldn't wait to get away from a spouse for a boy's or girl's night out. "Thanks for the ride, honey."

Harris slowed the Lexus to a stop at the curb outside the Metro North Station.

Raquel gathered up her attaché and the gym bag she kept her dress shoes in. She had her running sneakers on. She'd change at the office.

"Love you honey." She leaned over, kissed him on the cheek. "See you to-night."

"Let me get some more of that," Harris said, and she leaned in again for a deeper, more animated kiss.

"You're an animal." She quickly checked her lipstick in the mirror, the flipped the visor back up.

"I'm a sexy beast baby." Harris did his best *Austin Powers* as she got out. "Love you babe."

"Six o'clock in Woodside then?"

"I'll be there."

She blew him a kiss, and closed the door. Harris tried to ignore the stirring in his slacks. After all these years, first dating and then marriage, she still had what it took to get him going. Sure they didn't do it like they had the first few years they were dating and married, but who did? Harris knew other men his age who relied on testosterone therapy, Viagra, or a mistress. Not him.

He watched Raquel disappear into the entrance of the station, put the coupe in drive, and pulled onto the main street headed towards route 35 and his way to work.

Friday. He drummed the wheel with one hand, twisted the volume on the radio up. They'd had it set to 1010 WINS, "the world" in twenty-two minutes, but the volume was down on the ride so they could enjoy small talk. He was hoping to catch something about the weather and traffic—were they still doing construction on the Whitestone?—but got something about "doctors and authorities are still unsure about the nature of the contagion infecting some city residents but assure that this is nothing to be alarmed about" and that didn't interest him, what with all the hype and unwarranted scares surrounding the Avian flue, West Nile, Pam Anderson's hepatitis, whatever it was this month. He flicked over to satellite radio, the Stern show.

Howard was interviewing some porn star, talking about double anal, asking her if she'd been molested as a kid.

It was another concession he made to Raquel. He could listen to the shock jock all day. She had her limits, wasn't too crazy about Stern. Maybe it was the lesbians, the phony phone calls, or the always grating Eric the Midget. Harris listened when he drove to work, but by the time he got to work and got out of the car, he was all business.

WILLIAM RICHARDSON PRIDED himself on being a family man, and he was doing his best to keep that family together.

They'd all made it back inside the house. The kids had been in school, Maggy at work, and he was on the road when news of the outbreak first came in over the radio two days prior.

Today they were hiding in their house, doors and windows boarded up from the inside. Empty gallon milk jugs were filled with water, as were the bathtubs. He knew the water would eventually stop working and it wasn't like they were going to be heading out to the dairy barn to pick up some more anytime soon.

Nothing new on the radio. When the news station had interviewed the evangelical preacher and the old man started spouting off about liberals, gays and feminists and their responsibility for this, Bill had changed the station, looking for one playing music, but the stations had all switched to talk, and despite all the talk no one had any answers.

Maggy was downstairs in the kitchen with Billy and Sarah, listening to it, trying to occupy the kids with a board game.

William sat in the upstairs hallway, looking out the only window not boarded up yet. Several planks of wood, a hammer and nails rested under the window, just in case.

So far no one had bothered their house. No one had tried to gain entry.

William had heard them out front in the street. Cars early on, some screeching around the corner, the roar of a heavier military vehicle, then people on foot, many of them calling out as they went, finally silence punctuated by an occasional otherworldly caterwauling, something human but not quite.

Last night there had been a muffled crash, like an accident, somewhere nearby, but he couldn't see anything from this vantage point.

He'd listened to the radio when he could. He had some idea of what was going on out there. He knew about those *things*, the zombies, what they would do to his family if they got into his house.

Will knew because he'd rescued his daughter Janis from one of them only a few hours ago. She was resting in her bedroom now. The door was only a few feet away from William's chair where he sat looking out the window into his backyard.

He had the cop's nine millimeter Glock. Will knew how to use it, although he wasn't comfortable with it. The pistol was on the lacquered floor of the hallway next to him.

When things had gotten *really* crazy the night before, when William had gone out, to the dairy farm as a matter of fact which though open was unattended, when he had left his house to get milk and bread he got a hold of the pistol.

His car had been abandoned several blocks from the house, the road ahead consumed in fire from an accident involving a brown UPS delivery truck, an SUV and a motorcycle. A police cruiser had pulled up as Will watched from half a block away, and two officers had come out, weapons drawn.

One cop circled around the flaming mess behind the smoke and fire out of Will's and the second officer's sight.

Will got out of his car, called out and waved, walking towards the first cop.

"Who are you?" the cop yelled. He didn't look strong and confident the way Will thought a cop should, the way they looked when they pulled you over on the road with all their lights flashing.

"I'm William Richardson. I live nearby."

"What are you doing out of your house? Jesus man, don't you know about the curfew? I could have shot you."

Gunfire erupted from where the second officer had disappeared and then three people—all quite dead—came running around the flames towards Will and the police officer. William ran back to his car and locked the doors, ducking down below the dash.

Pop-pop-pop-pop he heard the Glock sound off, and then something jumped onto the rear of his car, over the roof and across the hood. More pops, about a dozen of them followed by silence.

When Will dared to peek over the windshield it looked safe enough so he got out of his car.

The cop was feebly trying to reload his piece. The three undead were sprawled in the street, a fourth only a few feet from the front bumper of Will's Oldsmobile.

Will approached the officer and saw that the man was hurt. Deathly pale. The cop's uniform shirt was soaked with blood, lots of it.

"Officer, you okay?"

The cop jacked back the receiver of his side arm, looked up at Will and tried to say something but only blood bubbled up in his mouth and welled up and out down the front of his uniform.

The police officer collapsed on his knees and caught himself with one out-stretched hand, refusing to go flat on his face in the street, with the crackle of the flaming vehicles and the disembodied moans drawing closer.

Will walked over to him. The fire still raged in the street behind them and there was no sign of the second cop.

After all he'd seen and heard on the radio and TV, Will did not hesitate. He pried the Glock from the officer's fingers. The man was still alive but he had been wounded somewhere and was unable to talk. There was a pleading look in his eyes and when Will had forced open his grip and taken the pistol the man tried to grab onto Will's shirt, a silent imploring for help, but his blood-slicked hand slipped right off Will's sleeve, and this time he did collapse on the street in a bloody heap. But he was not yet dead.

He lay there panting, looking forlorn and defeated.

"I'm sorry, officer. I'm really sorry."

Will stood up and there were four or five of them coming down the block, slowly but relentlessly lurching in their direction.

The cop clawed at Will's sneaker, gargling something incoherently.

"I really am sorry," Will said, then ran off between two homes, leaving the wounded cop out on the street, leaving his groceries in the car.

He made his way home through backyards, clambering over fences, cutting himself on one of them, avoiding the streets because of the things in them.

Today he sat in his window looking out onto the backyard. He had a pretty good view of the whole of his property, the wooden fence surrounding it and the back of the house behind his. He could also see in between that house and the houses on either side of it, to the street beyond. All morning he'd watched, and once he had seen one of the things stagger into view on the street beyond, unaware it was being watched.

He'd recognized the thing too. Jim Harrison. Lived three houses down. Used to, at least.

Jim listed into view and shuffled off.

Not much had been going on since.

There was smoke in the distance, and Will worried whether his house would catch fire if his neighbors' houses did, like those wildfires out in California.

The squirrels that routinely raided his bird feeder clung to their tree. He hadn't gone out to replenish the bird feed and didn't plan on it.

A man ran into Will's yard.

"*Jesus.*"

The guy looked to be in one piece. He wasn't a zombie. But he looked cornered, and he had a big revolver in his hand which he kept aimed in the direction from where he'd come. The man had a knap sack, similar to Janis'.

Will considered his options. Hopefully the guy would go away. He'd run into the backyard, which made Will pretty sure he was being pursued. If this man was being chased, then those things couldn't be too far behind, and the last thing Will wanted was for them to come hanging around his house while Maggy and Billy and Sarah played Cranium and Janis tried to rest.

Yeah, hopefully the guy would disappear as suddenly as he'd appeared.

He didn't.

The man was bent over, holding his knees and that big revolver, catching his breath. He walked over to the fence separating Will's property from that of the house behind his, and then peered over it on tippy toes, appearing to weigh his options.

That's when he turned and looked right up at Will in the window.

"Jesus," Will said a second time, ducking down below the sill, one hand going for the Glock, not knowing why. He wasn't going to shoot the guy unless he had to.

The man outside was smart enough not to yell out, which would have given away his position to anything out on the street.

Will waited a couple of minutes, getting a hold of himself, hoping the guy would do the smart thing and scoot, thinking that's what *he'd do* if he was in someone's back yard and that person was purposefully ignoring him. Maybe the man hadn't even seen him. When he sat up in the chair the man outside was gone.

He breathed a sigh of relief.

Sure, the guy hadn't even seen him.

Will looked over at the door to Janis' bedroom. Keep his family safe. That's what it all boiled down to.

Tap-tap-tap.

He almost wet himself. The man from his backyard was standing outside his window, having climbed up onto the first floor roof. How the hell had he gotten up here and what did he want?

"Damn," Will muttered, then, loud, "What? What do you want?"

The man kept quiet, gestured to Will to open the window. Will noted that the revolver was tucked in the waistband of the man's pants. He didn't look like he meant any harm.

What choice did he have? His play with the police officer still bothered him, leaving the guy like that on the street yesterday. It didn't take much imagination to figure what had happened to that cop. Will opened the window.

"Thanks for letting me in, I *hate* heights," Harris said. "They're all over the place out there."

"How'd you get up here?" Will Richardson asked incredulously.

"You left a ladder in the backyard," Harris said.

Will pictured it, the twelve foot aluminum one he used to change the bulbs of the light in the driveway. Even though they lived in a safe neighborhood in Queens, Will didn't like Maggy coming home to a dark driveway.

"I pulled it up behind me," Harris explained. "So none of those things could get up here. I don't know if they can climb."

"They're following you?"

"They were. I think I lost them."

Will noticed Harris's shirt was black with sweat.

"Man," said Harris. "Some of those things can *move* too."

"Any news?"

"Nothing, I was hoping you could tell me something."

Will shook his head. "Same old crap on the radio. TVs been out for awhile now. 'Stay in your house, National Guard'll handle it', that kind of thing."

"Yeah, the National Guard and the army are shooting anything that moves. Looks like you got this place pretty well secured. I noticed that on my run down the block."

"Yeah, well." Will thought of his family and their safety. "You can't stay here."

"I wasn't planning to," Harris said, no hesitation, no anger. "If you'd be kind enough to just let me catch my breath for a few minutes, I'll be out of your hair."

"It's just that..." Will had a tough time being tough, especially in a situation like this. "You know, food, water, provisions—we got enough for us for a few days but that's—"

Harris cut him off, gently, genially, "That's fine. No need to explain yourself."

Will saw something in the other's eyes and understood he was right not to fear this man.

"What's your name anyway?" Harris asked. Will told him and Harris reciprocated.

"Well, Will, let me rest up just a bit if you don't mind, and I'm gone."

"Where you in a rush to get?" Will couldn't understand why anyone would want to be outside with those things.

"Manhattan."

"The city?"

"Yeah."

"Why?"

Harris was quiet for a moment, then he said, "My wife's there."

Will mulled this over. He thought how lucky he was to be with Maggy and the kids in the safety of their own home, when so many others had been dislocated and separated, like this man here.

"Listen, Harris," Will decided. "Stay awhile. At least *eat* with us. The gas and water are still working. Amazing right? Hell, catch a shower. You can have a change of my clothes."

Harris nodded, thanking Will, overcome by the man's generosity. Harris knew in stressful situations people could be real jerks or stick together, and he was lucky that this man was the way he was.

"Let's close this window up and then come on downstairs. Meet Maggy and the kids."

Harris stepped aside while Will secured the storm window.

"Daddy?" a woozy voice came from the bedroom next door.

"I'll be right there, honey," Will spoke loud enough for Janis to hear.

"Daughter?" Harris asked.

"Yeah, my girl, Janis. She's resting. One of those goddamn things bit her leg earlier today."

Then down the stairs, "Mag, come here a second, sweetie. We got company."

"THEY SURE AREN'T like in the movies, are they?" Larry Chen asked. Keara shrugged her shoulders alongside the others looking over the wall at the undead drawn together on the street. From a moan to a howl, the crescendo of a cold dead lament peaked then ebbed.

It reminded Larry of the collective noise the crowd at a Mets game made, the sound when there was no direct action on the field, when anticipation of the next line drive or strike out hovered in the air like something real, something tangible.

Whenever someone inside Eden climbed up onto one of the cargo trailers fronting the walls, they were in plain view of the zombies. The walking dead would gather, reaching up, motioning, trying to draw one of them down, to no avail. They were packed down there ten deep, with dozens and dozens of others stumbling along the street to join the mass. A few were running, dipping in and out of buildings, around corners out of site, down the alleyways and side streets between the abandoned shops and homes.

"I don't know, they ran in that *Dawn of the Dead* remake," John Turner pointed out.

"Yeah, but not all these guys run," Buddy said.

"Thank Christ for small favors," Diaz said, and spat down onto the upturned faces of the zombies below.

"Why'd you go and do that for?"

"Fuck off, Buddy, all right. Don't tell me it bothers you that I spit on them. Don't try and give me any of this respect for the dead shit, okay?"

Buddy gave the other man a look.

Diaz continued, "Why don't you go down there and try talking to *them* about respect for the dead and all. How 'bout respect for the living? About how it's rude to spit on a bunch of motherfuckers trying to eat you?"

Buddy considered pushing Diaz off his perch into the crowd below.

"You're a flaming asshole, Diaz."

Diaz spat something back in Espanol but Buddy chose to ignore it.

"Boys," said Keara, "Could you both shut the fuck up? We're having a conversation here."

"I wonder how that works," Larry Chen put it to the group. "I mean, the ones that run, *why* do they run? What's special about *them* that they can run like that? The ones that can't run, why can't they?"

"Rigor mortis?" volunteered the younger Turner, pushing his glasses back up on his nose with an index finger.

"Granted the slow ones move kinda stiff," said Al Gold, "But they can move too."

"It's futile," announced Buddy.

"How's that?"

"It's like wondering why dead people are coming back to life in the first place. Wondering why they're attacking the living. You'll knock yourself out searching for an answer."

"Any of you guys ever seen *Zombie?* The movie, that is." Mickey had seen movies no one else had ever seen, movies maybe no one would ever see again. "Directed by that Italian guy, what's his name?"

"Fuck them, fuck their mothers, and fuck movies about them," shot Diaz. He stared down at the massed undead with contempt.

"Hey, that's no way to talk about Eye-talians," tried John Turner but no one laughed.

Diaz enjoyed dusting off the Walther WA 2000 he kept over the mantle of the faux fireplace in his living room, sniping at the zombies from time to time. The Walther was a beast of a weapon. It vaporized heads and once he cut an undead clean in two with it, watched the upper half of the thing roll itself over and crawl away.

Lately the Walther wasn't shooting straight and Diaz didn't know how to fix that. Sometimes now when he took aim and fired he wound up hitting something he never meant to. Twice people in Eden had warned him not to snipe on the zombies, those pendajos worried about attracting more of the things.

It was different with Graham and the big Pole. They'd let Diaz pop as many of the fuckers out there as he wanted, even invited him into Markowski's basement from time to time to get some up close hand to hand knife action with one of the things tethered to a pole. *That* had been some crazy shit.

"I think it was directed by Argento," Mickey rambled on. "You know his daughter Asa starred in Romero's *Land of the Dead* right? Romero's nod to the old man."

What Diaz really wanted was to get a flame thrower up there, torch a two or three hundred of the things. He'd seen it done before, watched the things burning up, still staggering around until there was nothing left to walk with and they'd crumple to the ground, smolder, and put off a smell worse than they did now, though not by much.

Diaz had plans. When humans once again regained control of this world, he'd open something like a game reserve, charge wealthy, bored tourists to pick up a rifle and bust a few caps at these things. He'd heard once that you could fire a rocket launcher at a water buffalo in Cambodia or some other God-awful place. That kind of thing.

Mickey asked if anyone had ever seen *Return of the Living Dead* and had better luck with that one.

"Is that the one where they're looking for brains?" asked Keara.

"Yeah, they eat brains."

"I remember that one," John Turner laughed, mimicking the zombies in the movie when they'd gotten on the radio in the police cruiser. "*Send more cops.*"

Diaz shook his head. "Mamaciyalla." He climbed down the ladder to go in search of Shannon.

Buddy watched him go. He thought he might have to kill that man some day. Thought not too long ago he would have done just that. He thought about that.

The work for the day had been done, a couple hours of daylight left still before they'd crank the generators up to power the lights. There was a badminton game going on in the street.

Isabel wore short shorts and a halter top. She'd probably looked good twenty years back, Buddy though, but now her ass was too big and for Buddy, being a man who could appreciate a big ass on a woman, that was truly saying something.

Hanging out of those ripped shorts like that, the thing almost scared him. He could imagine her butt all wrinkly, cottage cheese-like from too much cellulite, and way too dry from time spent in the sun trying to perfect her tan. Buddy'd known a guy inside, an old Italian who was supposed to be somebody, who used to spend his hour of rec out in the yard lying there shirtless with this big aluminum thing, sunning himself. It'd made it all the more easier for the Guatemalans when they moved on the guy, shanked him right there on the yard, and no one'd seen a thing.

Most of the men in the camp seemed to like Isabel. Many had slept with her. Buddy hadn't and he was pretty sure his boy Harris hadn't either. 'Bel wasn't the type of woman Buddy would want to hook up with, and it had nothing to do with her sex life. Hell, her sex life probably would have turned him on back in the day when he was a younger man.

Buddy knew people like Diaz dealt with their stress by climbing up on the wall, unleashing a hail of lead into the things below. Others, like Isabel turned to sex to help clear their minds of the anxiety and bullshit that came with this so-called existence. Buddy preferred to close himself away and focus on one spot, or count his breaths, to go inside and beyond himself. He'd learned that during his time with the state.

"Okay, favorite horror movie," said Larry Chen. "I go first. *Friday the 13th.* The first one, when it was Jason's moms killing everybody."

"That's a good one," said Keara. "I remember we were afraid to get in the bathtub after that one, what with that little creep popping out of the lake at the end."

"Yo, what was up with Jason?" asked John Turner. "Not the grown-up Jason behind the hockey mask. I mean the kid in the lake. His face was all messed up."

"Maybe he rotted down there all those years in the water," offered Keara.

"No, no, no," explained Mickey. "He had Down's Syndrome. He was born deformed. Remember, Jason was conceived out of wedlock. That's a whole theme with those early-eighties slasher movies, premarital sex leads to all sorts of bad shit."

"Yeah, it's always the teens who are having sex that get killed in those movies," noted Keara.

"Right," said John Turner, "like when Johnny Depp got killed at Camp Crystal Lake, that spear head stuck up under the bed, right through his neck? That was awful!"

"No, that wasn't Johnny Depp," corrected Mickey. "That was Kevin Bacon. Before *Footloose*. Johnny Depp died in the original *Nightmare on Elm Street*."

"How about *C.H.U.D.?*," John Turner asked, and Buddy chuckled, "*C.H.U.D.?*"

"*Cannibalistic Humanoid Underground Dwellers*." Mickey knew the movie and the acronym. "Lots of cheap slasher films came out in the eighties, following *Friday the 13th* and *Halloween*."

"That's what I was going to say," said Paul. "*Halloween*. But since you mentioned it I'll go with *The Thing*."

At least now they were talking about movies Buddy had heard of or seen.

Mickey asked, "You mean the original or the remake by John Carpenter?"

"We were just talking Carpenter and *Halloween* here, right?" said Paul. "So I'm talking about the remake with Kurt Russell."

Mickey thought it was one of Russell's finest roles, albeit one that never won him much acclaim. That last seen of MacCreedy and the other guy sitting there waiting it out and freezing to death just awesome. People didn't tend to take horror movie seriously, not at least until *Silence of the Lambs* took home an Oscar.

"What about you, big man?" Larry Chen asked Buddy.

"Well, if we were sticking to a John Carpenter motif, I'd have to go with *The Fog*."

"Ooooh, nice," Mickey agreed.

"What's *The Fog*?" asked John Turner.

"What's *The Fog*?" Buddy shocked. "Man knows *C.H.U.D.*-somethin' but don't know *The Fog*."

"I saw the remake," offered Keara.

"*Don't* go there," warned Mickey, then to John, "*The Fog*'s a ghost story."

Buddy nearly protested, never thinking of *The Fog* as a ghost story. Ghost stories were lame ass movies that never scared him when he was a child watching channel 11. Or kid-friendly stuff like *Casper*. But he thought about it and Mickey was right. *The Fog* was a ghost story. Blake and those guys on the boat with the burning coal eyes, looking for their gold, they *were* ghosts.

"But it's a *kick ass* ghost story. Anyway, since I'm old fashioned, you know I'm going to have to go with one of them late '50s-early '60s joints. Maybe *The Blob* or *Day of the Triffids*."

"*Day of the Triffids*," Mickey laughed. "I used to watch that movie on Sundays when I was a kid. They'd always run it."

"I've seen *The Blob*," Keara said. "But again I think it was the remake."

"Yeah, they did remake it," explained Buddy. "In the 1980s. But I'm talking about the original, with my man Bullitt, Steve McQueen."

"There was a sequel to that too, to the original," Mickey pointed out.

"Yo, wasn't the blob supposed to be an allegory for the cold war and all?" asked John Turner. "I think I took a class on that in college."

"Yeah, well," Mickey took over. "A lot of those 1950s movies were influenced by the Cold War. That ever-present threatening menace. We couldn't really stop it but maybe we can contain it. The blob gets frozen at the end too, remember? They can't destroy it."

"Blob was red too," the younger Turner held up a finger.

"Blob was red in the sequel, *Beware the Blob*. Blob was red when they colorized the original," said Buddy. "But the original Blob was black and white."

"Blob was supposed to be red, even in the original," proclaimed John Turner. "You know, communism, reds?"

"Oh I love that movie!" said Keara. "Warren Beatty is so sexy."

"Warren Beatty's dead," announced Larry Chen, gesturing with his chin. "Think these fuckers out here—think they can be destroyed, all of 'em I mean?"

They were all looking at Buddy, like he'd have an answer for them.

"What, you think because I'm old I got all the knowledge or somethin'? Hell, I don't know. It's a waiting game, that's what it is."

"True, true," said Larry, looking all serious.

JULIE DID HER best to stay in one place in the backseat as Bob swerved the Thunderbird, weaving between the undead and the abandoned automobiles, trying to avoid those he could, clipping the ones he couldn't. The windshield was spider-webbed, smeared with gore in two places from zombies catapulted over the hood and smashed against it. Bob doing his best to avoid a full-on collision with them, as it could do more damage to the car.

"Right! Go right!" Lex yelled back into the car, leaning out the front driver's side window as he did so, firing an AK-47 at the undead. The zombies stood off to the sides, staring at the spectacle, were slower to react, so Lex didn't bother with them.

The AK-47 locked open, fired out. Mika took it, seated between Lex and Bob up front, handing over the smaller nine millimeter Spectre submachine gun.

Gus, Phyllis and Snyder yelled, banging inside the trunk, hysterical in the en-closed space, the sounds of chaos thundering from outside. They'd drawn straws to see who could sit inside the car and who would have to ride it out in the trunk. Those three had drawn the shortest.

Julie was glad she didn't have to ride in the trunk. If she was going to die this morning, she wanted to see it coming. She gripped the .45 in her left hand, her palm sweaty. The gun was too big for her, but she knew how to use it.

The Thunderbird swerved and Julie pitched first into Mitchum on her left and then into little Kelsey on her right. "Sorry!"

Mitchum was turned around, looking out the back window.

"I don't see the Lincoln!" he yelled.

There had been almost thirty of them, holed up in a warehouse less than two miles from this spot. For two weeks they'd watched the compound across town through binoculars as their own stores ran low. The night before it was decided their only chance was making it to the walls of the compound and hoping the people inside would let them in. Less than ten minutes before they'd piled into four cars.

"I don't see the fuckin' Lincoln," Mitchum barked again.

"I heard you, I heard you." Bob pressed harder on the gas.

"We ain't going back—" shouted Lex.

"We can't go back!" Mike sounded like she was crying.

"—we ain't fucking going back!"

Julie wondered what Floyd had been thinking. He'd driven the Lincoln Navigator right *through* the garage door. The door gave but the Lincoln had been damaged, one tire running on a rim, steam coming up from the engine block. The Lincoln had fallen last in line as the four vehicle convoy raced through the streets.

The Hummer, which Julie had hoped to ride in because it looked safest, had missed a turn a few blocks back and was nowhere to be seen.

"I'm out!" Lex barked and Mika passed back the AK, fully loaded, a live round chambered.

"Hold on!" screamed Bob, wrenching the steering wheel hard to the right. They fishtailed around a corner, the rear driver's side of the car smashing into a zombie, flinging it into the air. The thing landed on its head and didn't get up.

Julie looked at the twelve-year-old next to her. She wanted to say something, anything, to Kelsey, to reassure her, but what was there to say?

They were on a long straight avenue, a clear view ahead and behind. The mass of the undead were forming behind, only a dozen or so ahead of them, slowly responding to the sounds of the onrushing cars and the gunfire.

"Fucking Floyd!" yelled Mitchum, causing Julie to turn around and look.

The Lincoln, both front wheels flat, rolled to a halt behind their Thunderbird and the following station wagon. The windows on the Lincoln down, gun muzzles flashed, cracks from semi-automatics, rips on full auto.

Bob, spying all this in the rearview, slowed the Thunderbird down. Lex ignored what was happening behind them and continued to fire ahead, his aim more accurate now with the Pontiac slowing up, undead dropping with head shots up the street.

Someone in the trunk screamed something that sounded like "What's happening?"

The station wagon had stopped as well, was in reverse, picking up speed as it headed back down the street.

The steam coming out from under the hood of the Lincoln obscured her view, but Julie clearly saw two of the doors on the Lincoln open and people clamber out, firing as they did so. No sooner had they exited the Lincoln then the first of the sprinting undead were on them.

Lex fired with the Spectre, a spray of blood jetting up from the back of an undead's skull. He picked off the two or three bookers loping their way, burning through the submachine gun's fifty round box magazine.

Julie watched as three zombies took down one woman outside the Lincoln. Another man fired a shotgun repeatedly, blowing other bookers down. Muzzle flashes still sparked from one side of the Navigator, and Julie thought, *What the hell are they doing, they've got to get out of there!*

But it was too late for the people in the Lincoln Navigator. The shamblers were on them and for as many of them that collapsed head-shot in the street, innumerable others swarmed the car, climbing up onto the hood and roof, the man with the shotgun dropping it, firing out a pistol as he was tackled down into the street, behind the SUV, out of their site.

If he was screaming Julie could not hear him.

"Mika!" yelled Lex, the Spectre out, Mika twisted around in the front seat trying to watch what was happening down the avenue behind them. She jerked back around and handed Lex the freshly loaded AK she had been holding, taking the empty Spectre.

The driver of the station wagon, sensing the futility of attempting to reach the broken-down SUV, stopped again, shifted to drive and peeled out, barreling back down the street in their direction. Three undead shamblers barred the car's path and the station wagon never slowed, plowing over and through them, sparks flaring between the undercarriage and the street. Something under the station wagon damaged, the car veering one way then the other, not losing speed, not picking any up either.

"Bob, let's go!" Mitchum yelled.

Julie stayed twisted in the back seat, one arm around Kelsey now, the little kid crying. Julie watched as someone in the Lincoln slammed the doors shut, probably trying to lock themselves in. The undead were all over the SUV, punching at the windows, trying to pry the doors open.

Julie knew there was no hope for anyone inside that vehicle.

Turned and facing the opposite direction as she was, Julie did not see the booker that came sprinting out from behind a dumpster on the sidewalk, reaching their Thunderbird as Bob really began to feed it gas. The thing latched onto Lex from behind as he fired the 47 at the undead up the block.

Lex made a noise somewhere between a scream of pain and a roar of anger as the booker wrapped both decaying arms around his upper torso and sunk its teeth deep into his back.

Julie didn't hesitate. With her right hand she shoved Kelsey's head into her lap and with her left she straight-armed the big .45 across her body and started pulling the trigger. The pistol bucked in her hand, and she should have maintained her calm, but she was panicking, and Lex was being savagely mauled, the undead hanging from his back, its feet dragging in the street, skin scraping off onto the asphalt. Lex attempted with one hand to dislodge the creature, the other holding onto the window frame so as not to be dragged from the Pontiac.

Most of Julie's shots missed, even at this close range, but two of the .45s buried themselves in the undead's back and it let go of Lex, rolling away into the street as the Thunderbird accelerated past.

Mika pulled a wounded, bloody Lex back into the car, chunks of his pink raw back ripped out. His eyes squinted with pain and he punched the dashboard in front of him in rage and frustration.

"Fuck! Fuck! Fuck! Fuck! Fuck!"

Bob accelerated down the street, reaching thirty five miles an hour, the undead less massed here, the turn coming up.

"Oh Christ," Mitchum breathed, and Julie looked again.

Behind them the station wagon's axle was broken or something, she could see it bent under the car, sparks flying. As the Thunderbird turned the corner, they watched the Station wagon try the same thing, lose control and ram into a parked van.

Someone in the front seat of the station wagon came through the windshield head first, smashing against the van, sprawling on the street.

Julie couldn't understand a word of what the people in the trunk were screaming.

At the end of this street awaited the wall of the compound. A half dozen undead stood about the wall and turned to look as they veered down on them. Zombies came shuffling out of the building on either side as the car roared by. Atop the wall, one or two figures with guns watched as the Thunderbird raced down the block.

"It hurts! It fucking hurts!" Lex screamed, clenching his fist. Mika was hugging him, crying. Lex's back bowed as the pain seized him.

Mitchum yelled up at the driver, "Bob, slow down, slow this thing the fuck down!"

Bob had both hands on the steering wheel, and they were white from his gripping it so hard. He was bent over low in the seat, manipulating the wheel, avoiding the undead reaching out for them.

"Bob, slow down!" Mitchum barked.

The people on top of the wall were firing now, sniping at the undead.

Julie looked up and saw the wall and knew Bob would never be able to stop in time. Bob waited until the last second and then slammed on the brakes, the Thunderbird sliding out from under him, turning sideways and skidding the final twenty feet until it slammed into the wall of the compound, flush on its driver's side, air bags deploying.

Black.

Movement next to her… Mitchum?

Black.

Lights going off in her head. Stars. Julie saw stars.

Julie shook her head and cleared it of all save the enveloping dark. *Not now!* She felt something in her hand, the .45, Kelsey with her head in her lap. Her vision came back to her, and with it came screams, a pounding from the trunk as Snyder, Phyllis, and Gus shouted, wanting to be let out, terrified in the confines demanding to know *what the fuck was going on.*

The gunfire was closer, more people firing from atop the wall. Julie looked out the open door on Mitchum's side, saw the parade of dead things coming down the block towards them. Mitchum kneeled in the street, firing the Stoner M63 Light Machine Gun, seeing its flash, shell casings from the box-contained 150-round belt arching slow motion into the air, its report muted, her head swimming.

Mitchum hollered something at the advancing ranks of the undead.

Julie closed her eyes, held them that way for a second, opened them and could see clearly. Suddenly the racket from the machine gun nearly deafening.

"Come on you cocksuckers! Come on then!"

Bob, blood streaming out of his nose, was screaming to Mika that they had to get out of the fucking car. Lex slumped in the front seat, his head smashed back by an air bag. Mika was having a time of it reaching around Lex, trying to pry the passenger side door open.

Mitchum fired.

"You want some, bitch! Eat this! You too, motherfucker!"

Kelsey did not move. Julie looked down at her. She looked peaceful, her head twisted at an awkward angle. Julie would have cried, but she wanted to live.

The people in the trunk were going crazy in there and the gunfire on the wall picked up. Atop the wall men and women were yelling things too but Julie couldn't understand them.

"You like that? You like that? Fuck you, then!"

She only understood Bob but something wasn't right in her head because while his voice was crystal clear it was like the volume on everyone and everything else had been muted.

The rear window. The windshield and rear window had both come out in the crash. Or, maybe Mitchum had blown it out when Julie was out of it.

She glanced down one more time at Kelsey, pulled herself out of the back of the Thunderbird, cutting her palms on the glass, rolled onto the trunk, over the chunks of glass there. She could feel the vibrations of the people pounding inside.

"Come and get some, assholes!" Mitchum standing none too steadily, wobbling a few steps towards the hundreds of zombies advancing down the block, two dozen bookers ahead of the pack. Julie watched three go down. Six others shuddered as bullets pounded through them, but they kept coming.

Julie became aware that the people on the wall were calling out to her.

"Up!" a voice commanded and Julie, kneeling on the trunk, spotted a rope ladder hanging down from the wall to the roof of the Pontiac. Funny, she hadn't noticed it a moment ago.

"Mitchum!" she cried, clambering onto the roof, almost losing her footing and toppling off to the street, grasping at the rope ladder and pulling herself up hand over hand, the .45 gone, arms reaching down for her, pulling her up onto the wall. Hhalf a dozen people fired at the onrush.

Julie lay atop the wall where the arms placed her, turning her head in time to see an alleyway off to the side of Mitchum come alive as zombies poured through between the houses.

"Who invited you, bitches?" Mitchum started walking backwards, firing the Stoner M63, chunks of flesh exploding from zombie bodies, and yet they came on, reaching the car. Mitchum eyed the ladder which he could reach if he made it to the roof of the car, but he never even made the trunk, the undead pulling him down, dragging him down. Mitchum didn't scream or cry or beg. He unsheathed the big knife on his belt and began plunging it into their heads as they grouped on him and smothered him on the street.

"There's someone in the car! There's someone in the car!" a person atop the wall gasped, and Julie knew Lex had changed then, chewed up as bad as he'd been. Mika was screaming, and then Bob as well. Those on the wall aimed their fire down into the vehicle, above the front seats, the bullets pounding through the roof and into the car, peppering whoever or whatever was inside with hundreds of rounds.

At that moment, somehow, the trunk popped open, and Gus, Phyllis and Snyder popped out, only to be swarmed by the undead, Snyder firing his shotgun once before he was overwhelmed, dragged down braying. It was so bad down there Julie couldn't even see what was going on, but she heard Phyllis cursing for a moment. A zombie made off with Snider's arm, the shotgun still clutched in its hand.

"Julie!"

In amazed horror, Julie watched as Kelsey, apparently not dead, rolled out of the back window frame onto the trunk, the trunk closing under her weight.

"Kelsey!" Julie yelled, reaching out to her from where she lay, and the twelve-year-old started to haul herself up onto the roof of the car, as greedy hands from the horde of undead latched onto her ankles and feet and pulled her off the car and into the street.

For a moment she was born aloft, a crowd surfer at an undead concert.

Julie would never forget the look of terror she saw in Kelsey's eyes as the young girl was pulled down onto the street to be eaten alive.

"Grenade!" someone yelled and everyone on the wall hunkered down, the explosive tossed into the sea of ghouls in the exact spot where Kelsey disappeared. Some man pulled Julie away from the edge of the wall and shielded her face as the grenade exploded, the blast muffled by the press of bodies below.

Another man on the wall opened up with a flame thrower, incinerating the undead, driving them back away from the wall and the car.

"Let's get you off this wall." A woman took Julie by the arm, but Julie said "Wait," and looked back over the lip into the street below.

Kelsey, scorched by the flame, disemboweled by the undead, one arm chewed or blown off by the grenade beneath the elbow, lay on the street, her flesh bubbling. As Julie watched, the little girl sat up, looked around, stood, the last of her innards spilling out of its ruptured stomach, and staggered down the street.

"Oh my god," was all Julie could say. They were dead. All of them.

HE ALWAYS KNEW he was going to die, but to know with certainty the approximate time and situation, that was somewhat overwhelming to Harris. Up until his mid-twenties he'd suffered from the all too human delusion that mortality was something that affected *other* people.

Then he'd gotten the hernia which he'd eventually repaired with surgery. The procedure was elective, his intestine wasn't strangulated or anything, and he was back in his parents' home recuperating later the same day, but just the thought that his guts had broken through his abdominal wall made him realize that he too was going to die one day. He was, after all, like everyone else.

On the day he'd been bitten, Harris spent the early afternoon around people. He liked people. Always had. He'd never been one to seek attention, but he played well with others, and his people skills had helped him a lot in life, from being a competent administrator to meeting and marrying his wife.

He spent what remained of his time with the people he liked in Eden. He worked with Bobby Evers in the garden, turning the soil for the coming planting. Evers was back to his usual jocular self between hits from his inhaler.

Harris avoided those he disliked. Thompson kept his distance, but he always had since the night Harris put him straight about Julie, about respect.

Harris avoided Diaz. Diaz had never done anything to him, but he didn't like the man. The Dominican just wasn't his type and ever since Harris put Shannon down, he'd gotten a vibe off Diaz, something he didn't care to pursue.

Isabel was another one he steered clear of. She was harmless, her infant on her hip and her flirty talk. But again, not the kind of people he wanted to spend his last hours with.

He figured he would spend his time around other people for as long as possible. He was starting to cough more, and carried around a bandana so no one would see the blood and sputum. He still felt relatively well, though bouts of cramping came and went, seizing his stomach. Fortunately, they weren't too frequent as of yet and he could feel them coming and get away from the others before it gripped him.

"Can I ask you something, mate?" Bobby Evers rested a hairy forearm on a shovel, wiping his forehead against it.

"Go ahead."

"Through all this, you ever done… you ever done something that you regret? Something that really bothers you eh?"

Harris stayed silent for a moment thinking that as long as he could put up a good front he knew he'd be safe around everyone else for a little bit longer. He had no intention of letting himself become one of those undead and harm any of them, but he was going to kill Thompson.

"Yeah, we all have. Why, Bobby, what's bothering you?"

"Shite, I'm that obvious am I? Well, I wouldn't mind tellin' you."

"And I wouldn't mind listenin'."

"When Graham and his blackguards—goddamn them all I say—when they were here, this one time a group of people, I don't remember, six, maybe seven of them, showed up on the other side of the wall.

"Fred Turner let them in but we could see something wasn't right with them from the get-go. There was one man with the group and he was kind of jumpy, had him a shotgun he did, and he kept himself close to this woman and child in the group, the both of them two all bundled up, and this is a spring day, mind you.

"Graham and Markowski, that mentaller, they come over talking about put down your guns, and they got theirs leveled mind you. But that man with the shotgun, he refused, saying they just needed a place to rest for a few days, that they'd be movin' on soon enough.

"Well that wasn't good enough for that header Markowski. He snatches one of the group, an old lady and puts his gun to her head, and now we've got ourselves a regular Mexican standoff."

Harris listened to Evers, thought how he could walk up to Thompson right this minute and execute him, take him out quick fast like Buddy'd done Graham, but Harris was envisioning something special for the man who'd dropped his lighter, who'd dropped his lighter and in so doing revealed his intentions.

Thompson would die, but he wouldn't die fast. The slower, the better.

"There's a bunch of shouting and cursing going on from both ends and the little kids crying fit to break your heart and finally Markowski just straightens that pistol of his and blows a big hole through that man with the shotgun. Just like that. End of conversation. Then he lays a big wet one right on the old lady's cheek, the wanker. I'd a thought she'd faint."

Harris needed Thompson to know he was dying. He had never been a cruel man. If anything, he would avoid or walk away from a fight, that incident with the self-proclaimed psychic notwithstanding. He'd never taken pleasure in the hardships of another. *Schedenfreude* was a word Harris knew, but not a word in his vocabulary.

This was different, though. Harris wanted Thompson to really *experience* his death, to be aware of his every last minute, every second of each. That involved getting Thompson alone, being able to implement whatever his plan was going to be. Time was running out, and Harris really didn't have a plan yet.

"Anyway, Graham orders them all to strip, and they do, and guess what? Three of them have been bitten, including that woman and that little boy the man was so keen on protecting."

Harris thought about just walking up to Thompson, throwing him a beating in the street. He had no doubt he could still do it if he acted right away. The time was quickly approaching when he'd be too weak and his coherency too compromised.

That, he thought, is what it all boiled down to, no matter what he had fooled himself otherwise all these years. Man sizes other men up, figures if he can take them. Whether it was a dance club, a conference room, or an octagon, that's the way it is. People might like to kid themselves about human beings, their higher natures, but Harris had read his Freud in college, and he thought there was a lot of truth in what the Austrian had written, about man's instinct for aggression, about man being a wolf to man. Civilization had let them tell themselves something different.

Since the undead had come back to life to wreak havoc on the living, Harris had seen and learned a thing or two about his fellow human beings. Some of it was sheer beauty, but much of it stuff he would have cared to ignore or deny.

So, yeah, Harris knew he could physically take out Thompson, even though the other man was younger. That real primitive mindset, in another time it had been superseded by other considerations, but it was coming out again and he did not fight it..

"Graham doesn't even hesitate. He has Paul and a couple others line the three up against the wall and Markowski mows them down. Just like that. Nobody says anything, I don't say anything. And that's what bothers me."

Walk up to Thompson, Harris thought, slug him in the face, squash his nose against his cheek. Break his jaw with an uppercut. Drag the man across Eden, up onto one of the trailers. In front of all the people—they'd try to stop him of course, so he'd need to get them to hear him out—get Thompson to cop to it, to admit, *yes, I let them in, I broke the door to your house. If I can't have her neither can you, Harris!*

Hip toss the loser over the wall while he still had it in him, let Thompson fend for himself amongst all those goddamn freaks out there.

Harris stopped himself. Bad plan. The people would move in quick to break up the fight and by the time everything had been sorted out Harris would be showing symptoms and Thompson would have the satisfaction of watching *him* check out first and that was a satisfaction Harris silently vowed to himself he would never deliver the man.

Even if that idea worked, Thompson's death scenario wasn't nearly as long and drawn out and vicious as what Harris wished for him.

Bump that, Buddy would have said.

He looked at Bobby Evers who was staring at him expectantly, waiting for him to say something, and Harris realized he hadn't heard one word Bobby had said.

"Sometimes things just happen," Harris picked up the ball effortlessly. "And we don't know if they were meant to be that way or not, they just play that way. The plays aren't written in stone, Bobby, not before we have to deal with them."

"So you're saying there's no use me beating myself silly over it, then, is that it?"

"That's it."

"Hmmm," Bobby thought it over.

Harris squatted down to pull some weeds from around a tomato post when the thought came to him. The post was a pole sunk into the ground, a much smaller version of the metal poles embedded in the concrete of his basement floor, the house Markowski used to live in.

He thought about it some, and then Harris knew how Thompson was going to die.

BUDDY WAS AWAY inside himself, so he didn't hear Adlard come down the dark street, zombies taking steps towards him and then shuffling off away from the man, Adlard's every step deliberate as if each required an effort.

He leaned up against the burned-out hull of a car, and while he caught his breath he gazed at Buddy atop the wall and smiled to himself, shivering. His body quivered briefly under the crescent moon. It took everything he had and more to climb onto the hood of the vehicle and seat himself against what was left of a cracked windshield, which mercifully held.

Adlard was sitting there like that, watching him, when Buddy opened his eyes on the wall.

"Buddy."

"Adlard."

The greetings were spoken as if not out of the ordinary.

"Why are you out there, Adlard?"

"The zombies aren't going to bother me, Buddy."

Buddy saw that the undead nearest Adlard did indeed seem disinterested in the man atop the car.

"And why's that?"

"I'm diseased, Buddy. Infected."

"Bitten?"

"A bite wouldn't stop them."

"What then?"

"I'll tell you...how're the others?"

"Not enough to eat, but besides that as well as can be expected."

Adlard stared off into the night for a moment.

"Adlard?"

"I'm still here, Buddy."

"Where have you been?"

"I been all over."

"What have you seen?"

"It's bad, Buddy. It's really bad."

"This is all over then, isn't it?" Buddy gestured down the street, to the stalled cars and undead.

"Yeah."

"You meet any other people out there?"

"Some." Adlard was gripped by a series of tremors and couldn't speak for a minute or two. Buddy watched the man from the relative safety of the wall. When he was able to, Adlard resumed.

"Most of them don't have half a chance, Buddy. This is a dead world."

"You know about Jericho then?"

"Yeah, I know about Jericho. And I found the Farm, Buddy."

"So it exists."

"It did."

"Not anymore? Zombies?"

"No, this." Adlard motioned with his hand, encompassing himself. "Disease. The zombies never got inside. I found everybody there dead."

"What kind of disease is it?"

"I don't know. But I've seen what it can do."

Buddy nodded. Even the undead were steering clear of the man on the street.

"Buddy, listen, I'm glad I found you. I heard rumors, talk. There's places, farther north, where the winters freeze *everything*. There's people, societies, life. *Good* life. Or so it's said."

"So it's said," Buddy echoed the other.

"Everybody has to get out of Eden, Buddy. You're all going to die there. The plague'll come and you'll all get like this."

"I don't think most people here want to move on, Adlard. They feel reasonably safe."

"They're safe from these things without, but there's worse things spawned in this world, Buddy. Just take a look at me."

Buddy couldn't make Adlard out in the dark and told the other man so.

"You got a light? Shine it on me."

Adlard raised his head high as Buddy centered him in the lantern. There were black splotches on Adler's face, like welts made of tar.

"Look at this, Buddy." Adlard reached up, gripped one of the welts on his cheek between an index finger and thumb and pulled, taking a chunk of skin off his face.

"Oh, Jesus."

"Yeah, it's real bad, Buddy. I'm losing fingers and toes."

Adlard held up his other hand and in the lantern light Buddy could see the man was missing two digits and a thumb.

"What can I do for you, Adlard?" Buddy asked.

"Nothing you can," the other said calmly. "I wouldn't come in if you invited me. And I won't get closer. I'm contagious, Buddy."

Buddy breathed out and turned his head, looked inside Eden. The street was empty and the houses were dark. He was alone out here on the wall talking with

Adlard. When he turned back to the other, Adlard had slid off the hood of the car and was standing, albeit barely.

"Well, I should be moving on."

"Where you off to?"

"Oh, here and there. Maybe catch me a little nap soon. I'm tired, Buddy, I'm tired."

"Adlard—"

"You listen to me, Buddy, you've got to get those people out of there. Eden won't hold. Head north."

"They say there's people and all, huh?"

"They do. But a man needs a purpose, doesn't he?"

"Adlard, you want a gun, food, anything?"

"Nah, these things out here don't bother me any more. You take care of yourself, Buddy."

"Yeah, you too, Adlard."

Buddy watched the other man walk away until he was swallowed up in the night.

PANAS COULDN'T TAKE any more of the man's bullshit, so he got up and walked away. Harris sat where he was, taking it all in, his anger mounting.

"I see a man, a young man, *no,* an old man," said Philip, looking beyond the people seated in front of him, as if he could see something they couldn't.

"An old white man? Anybody have a grandfather, an uncle, maybe a friend? His name starts with a J, yeah a—*no,* a T. *Terrance* maybe? Troy?"

"Thomas!" said Siobhan McAllister, "My grandson's name was Thomas."

Philip smiled at her.

This asshole might actually believe what he's doing, thought Harris, *but he's full of it.*

"Ms. McAllister, was your grandson white? Because this spirit I see is definitely Caucasian."

"Well, he was *light skinned,*" admitted McAllister. "Our family used to call him Red Bone."

"You sure the name isn't Toni?" asked Camille Bianaculli. "Sal had a niece named Toni."

"Toni?" Philip called aloud, looking into empty space. "Toni? Yes, that's it, her name is Toni!"

There were a few gasps, Camille Bianaculli clutched her husband, looking like she was going to cry. Sal did his best to look aloof, but it was clear by his face he *wanted* to believe. Markowski looked like he thought Philip had two heads, spit tobacco juice into a plastic cup. Larry Chen elbowed Mickey and the two of them tried to suppress their laughter. Philip ignored them.

Harris and Buddy had pulled into Eden two weeks prior, and Harris thought maybe it was best to keep his mouth shut, although this guy here was pissing him off to no end. A couple of the people in camp had recognized Philip from some late '90s cable-access late-night television show where he was touted as having psychic powers, that he could contact the dead, channel whatever it was they were thinking and feeling.

This kind of thing had never really bothered Harris in years past, largely because he was able to tune it out, ignore it, change the channel. Circumstances being what they were here and now, though, this son of a bitch was getting to him. Harris didn't feel the blood rising in his face, but Markowski saw it, and he nudged Bert, nodding towards Harris.

"Yes, Toni," Philip all smiles. "He says he's glad to be watching over his Aunt Camille and Uncle Fran."

"Sal," corrected Sal, the correction not shaking his faith one iota.

"God, Sal," gasped Camille. "We've got our own little guardian angel looking out for us! How is she, Philip? What happened to her?"

Philip bowed his head, kept his eyes up, quiet for a moment, like someone was whispering something in his ear.

"Toni says she misses the both of you. She says not to worry about her, that where she is now, there's no pain, that it's really very peaceful and wonderful. She says she's got someone with her you might want to talk to, a little girl, little boy maybe?"

"Giovanni!" cried Camille. "Sal, it's our Giovanni!"

"Yeah," Philip was nodding. "It is Giovanni. He says he misses his mom and dad. He says to tell you not to worry, that when his end came it came peacefully. None of those things hurt him too bad."

Sal looked at Philip out of one eye. "Giovanni died when he was a year and half, childhood leukemia."

"Is that so? Hmmm. Who's this? Rachel? Someone know a woman named Rachel, Rhianna, Rebecca or something?"

Later Buddy would wonder why he was surprised Harris had it in him, what set the man off like that. Something came over Harris' face, something primeval and bad, and he launched himself out of his chair and started towards Philip, sputtering, "Shut up, shut your goddamn fucking mouth!"

Julie startled, took a step back.

"Stay clear little lady," said Markowski, spitting into his cup. "This should be good."

"Look," Philip held his hands up, palms out, "Take it easy pal—"

Harris pushed Philip, the man stumbling backwards several steps, regaining his balance in time to take a crushing right hand to the side of his head. He dropped to the street.

Markowski was smiling, nodding his head, holding his spit cup.

"Harris!" Buddy was up next to Harris, gripping his arm.

"You see that?" Bert half-whispered to Markowski.

"Yeah," the big Pole smiled. "But why didn't he. *He's* the psychic."

Harris couldn't take his eyes off Philip. He was seething and trying to say something, overcome with emotion, tears streaming down his face, tears of rage. Philip did the worst possible thing he could do at that moment. He got up.

Buddy wasn't expecting Harris to break free of his grasp, but his friend did, shrugging off his hand and laying into the psychic again.

Harris delivered a hard right directly to Philip's nose, then an uppercut with his left to the man's torso. Buddy wrapped his arms around Harris' trunk, pinning his arms to at his side, hauling him back.

"Day-yem!" Bert shouted approvingly.

Markowski snickered, spit in his cup.

Philip stayed down this time, bleeding from the face, retching. A few of the people gasped and gawked at Harris.

"Harris, Harris!" Buddy turned Harris and let him loose in the other direction. "What the hell got into you?"

Harris looked past Buddy, looking like he'd love to jump on top of Philip, beat the man some more. He breathed hard, shook his head as if to clear it and stalked off the opposite way.

Markowski raised his spit cup up in a mock toast, laughed, and pitched the contents onto Philip where he lay.

"Oh, sorry about that."

Bert laughed.

Buddy ignored them, following Harris. He didn't say a word to his boy, just shadowed after him as Harris walked to the house they'd claimed.

Harris walked right through the front door, Buddy behind.

Harris was inside, on the couch in the living room, crossing and uncrossing his legs.

Buddy settled down in a recliner across from him, didn't say a thing.

Harris bent forward with his head in his hands, laughed nervously. He sat up, "Jesus, that was uncalled for, huh?"

"You cool now?"

"I'm good, Buddy. What was I thinking?"

"I don't know, Harris. Why don't *you* tell *me* what you were thinking."

"It's just, it's just that those people out there. They've been through a lot man. We all have. And this guy shows up, and he's going to pull the wool over their eyes?"

"You gotta remember he's telling them what *they* want to hear. You saw Camille and Sal eating that shit right up."

"Yeah, but they don't *need* to hear that."

"Who are you, Graham? Markowski? Who are you to decide that?"

"But man, it's so, so, I don't know, condescending? So *wrong*, man. On many levels. I mean, these people, all of us. We've lost people, Buddy. We've lost people in bad ways."

"You don't have to lecture me on loss, Harris."

"I'm not trying to, I know. I just don't, I—Christ, what was I thinking?"

"Harris, look, man. I don't buy the guy's program either, but you've gotta ignore him, okay? Just avoid him as much as you can."

Harris sat for quite some time.

"Did I hurt him?"

Buddy smiled. "Nothing that can't heal. Looks like you busted his nose pretty good. I figure you would have done worse if I wasn't there to stop you."

"Man, I hope I didn't hurt him," Harris said, genuinely apologetic.

"Sit here awhile, Harris, chill out. Then I'll go find out what kind of damage we've done."

"We, huh?"

"We're in this together, right?"

"Completely."

"Well, I need you to keep as cool and clear a head as you can, Harris. Time is coming and it's coming quick when we're going to have to make a move on Graham and his crew or they're going to move on us."

"You think it's going to come to that?"

"I've seen it before. It'll happen."

"People are going to die, aren't they?"

"People always die, Harris. It's part of what we do. Question is, which people and how many."

"Well, it's not going to be us."

"That's what I'm thinking."

HE GOT HOME a little after five in the afternoon. Harris stayed at Hillcrest until all the buses had come and gone. One driver freaked out and didn't show up for his run, so another had to be brought in, which delayed everything for a half hour or so. Harris dismissed his staff as soon as the majority of the students left, knowing they'd want to get home to their families. He waited with the last kids until the final bus arrived.

The science teacher, Gus Cupolo, had boogied soon after they'd all met in the lunch room. A part of Harris was really angry at the man for sneaking out like that, but part of him understood Gus all too well. He'd talk to the science teacher later.

Neither his cell phone nor any land line in the building worked. All circuits were busy. He needed to hear from his wife, to know she was okay, that the National Guard had things under control where she worked downtown, that she was safe in her building. Hers was a major law firm, after all, and it had its own security. Maybe she was already on her way home to him.

When the last school bus pulled away, Harris locked the front door behind him and walked briskly to his Lexus in the parking lot. He'd never cared much about cars as a young man, something which set him apart from his other friends, but as he got older and settled into a comfortable upper middle class lifestyle, he started to pay attention to people's rides. The Lexus was still considered a luxury ride, and Raquel and he had agreed to buy it when it became apparent that they couldn't have their own child.

No need to save for college, so why not splurge and buy each other nice sedans?

In the last couple of months they'd been talking about adopting. They had friends who'd adopted from Russia, a cute little girl. Harris didn't care where the baby came from. He knew a lot of white couples adopted from European countries because color was important to them, and they couldn't get a white baby here in America.

Color wasn't important to Harris. Working in public education had taught him that there was good and bad in all races. He saw it with the kids, and even other adults. If a child went home to a family that valued education and kept their kids off the streets, that child usually turned out a lot different than a kid who returned to a home where one or both parents were absent, either from walking out or because they had to work two or three jobs to make ends meet, or a home where schooling wasn't considered important, where resentment against the "system" for perceived ills festered.

As Harris drove to their house, he thought back to how his mom and dad had never let him and his brother hang out on the corner when they were younger. The way his parents spoke of it, the corner was some mythical evil place teeming with drug use and wayward youth. Truth turned out to be it was just a bunch of kids with no adult supervision and way too much free time on their hands, and a good many of them did wind up getting themselves into hot water for it.

Harris' dad used to troop him and his brother down to the park, play some ball, keep them active.

He'd have to call James when he got to a phone that worked.

There was surprisingly little traffic on the roads home, and Harris made the commute quickly, staying five to ten miles above the speed limit the whole way, trying not to freak out about events over which he had no control. He didn't see any police cruisers on his whole ride.

He parked the coupe in the driveway and let himself into their home. Daffy greeted him at the door, licking his hand.

"Good girl, good girl." Harris petted the dog on her head and she followed him through the first floor where he unlocked the sliding glass door and let her out into the backyard to do her business.

While the dog squatted on the grass, Harris tried his house phone. Not even a dial tone.

"Damn, " he breathed. *Calm. Gotta stay calm.* Freaking out wasn't going to get anything accomplished. His wife hadn't made partner in a prestigious Manhattan law firm on her looks alone. Raquel was bright, sharp, much more conservative and, he sometimes thought, on the ball in many more ways than he. Harris could trust Raquel to put herself in a position where she'd be safe.

But he worried about her. Raquel also had a side of her that liked to help people, and he could picture her stopping on the street to assist somebody who was hurt, the rioters closing in—

Whatever. Harris forced himself to stop thinking about it. Raquel was either safe somewhere, probably as worried to death about him as he was about her, or she was on her way home, or… anyway, there was nothing he could do in the meantime.

Daffy's pawing at the sliding door made him blink.

"Come on in girl." Harris let the big blonde Collie into their kitchen. He squatted down and patted her neck and back. "Somebody needs to be brushed." She licked his hands.

He turned on their home computer, checked his email accounts. He had three, one for work, one for home and an old Hotmail account he'd had since forever. He checked each. Nothing but *Bigger-Harder-Longer* and *Stop-Hair-Thinning* spam advertisements. Not a thing from Raquel. As a lark, he clicked on an email she had sent him a week before and replied to it, letting her know he was home waiting to hear from her, just wanting to know she was okay or that she was on her way to him and Daffy.

He wanted to get back in the car and drive down into the city. He decided to wait around the house for awhile. What if Raquel came home when he was out, and then she would be stuck here alone wondering about him?

He left the computer booted up.

He fixed himself a plate of leftover roast pork and mashed potatoes from the night before and sat in front of the television. Daffy sat obediently at his feet, eyeing the plate.

Some of the local television stations were off the air. One was playing reruns of *Battlestar Galactica*. The cable news stations were live, and it appeared that whatever had happened in Manhattan had spread. CNN was broadcasting from Russia where tanks were rolling across Red Square and rifle fire punctuated the anchor's words.

Harris was staring incredulously at Fox TV's coverage as a line of soldiers in South Africa fired on a wall of human beings coming down the street when the station cut live to a press conference with the Vice President.

Harris ignored the plate of food on his lap.

He didn't particularly like this guy, but Harris listened to the man's every word. The Vice President usually delivered his talks extemporaneously, unscripted, but today he stood at the podium with the flag behind him and a sheath of papers in his hands. The announcer introduced the Vice President, who put on his glasses and began to read.

"Ladies and gentlemen, fellow citizens, men, women and children of this great Republic. The events of the past day, unfolding as I speak, have caused some people to—" *yadda yadda yadda*, Harris waited to hear something substantive, something that would tell him the fate of Raquel, "—the armed forces of these United States are acting now to contain this outbreak of rioting, and we believe that order will be restored within 12 hours at the latest—"

Daffy whined and looked at Harris with pleading eyes.

"—furthermore, I urge all citizens to stay in their houses, with doors and windows locked. For those of you for whom returning home at the present moment is not feasible, be advised that temporary relief stations, where you will receive food, shelter and first aid, have been erected in nearly all—"

At the bottom of the screen, a scroll listed the neighborhoods and the nearest relief stations.

"—above all, do not attempt to counter this threat on your own. The men and women of our armed forces are the best trained in the world, and you have my assurances that this threat will be curbed within the next few hours."

That was the end of his speech, and the Vice President looked like he was ready to leave, but there was a rustle from the reporters and a "Mr. Vice President, Mr. Vice President!"

"The Vice President won't be answering any questions," one of his aides said off camera.

"No, no, Jim, it's okay, I've got this one. I'll answer a few questions," the Vice President looked at his watch, like answering questions was the last thing he wanted to do, an imposition, "and then I've got to go."

Harris wondered where the man was in a hurry to get off to. *Smug bastard.*

"Yes, Peter," the Vice President pointed.

"Uh, Paul, sir," a reporter off screen spoke. "Mr. Vice President, is it true sir that some of the rioters are *eating* people on the streets?"

The Vice President shook his head derisively and waved a hand, dismissing the idea. "Listen, in trying times like these, there are stories concocted—concocted, hear my word? Fabricated. People embellish what they think they see, they hear one thing from one person and it becomes another thing when they pass it along to another person, but no, cannibalism? No, I don't think cannibalism—"

"Mr. Vice President," another reporter interrupted, causing a vein to stand out on the V.P.'s forehead, "We have footage of a group of rioters eating their victims."

"Look," the Vice President sounded peeved now. "In any situation of great stress, you've got individuals who pursue extreme measures. But cannibalism? I wouldn't be surprised if a few fanatics are resorting to it, God only knows for what reason. Probably to strike fear in the hearts of the people. And that's exactly what we can't let them do, we have to retain our resolve and stand firm in this attack on our freedom."

"Who's that Mr. Vice President?"

"Who?" The Vice President looked at the woman like she was retarded.

"Yes, *who* can't we let strike fear into our hearts? Who is attacking our freedom?"

"I'm not at liberty to divulge that information at this time," the Vice President glanced at his watch. "But make no mistake, the enemies of America, the enemies of freedom, are not to be underestimated."

"You're not at liberty Mr. Vice President or you have no clue?" another reporter off camera.

The Vice President turned crimson, wrapped his hand over a microphone, released.

"Who are you with? What organization?"

"Z Magazine."

"Huh, 'Z Magazine.,'" The V.P. nodded to one of his aides who wrote something on a legal pad.

"Mr. President," one reporter mistakenly called, and there was a chuckle from the press pit. Even the VP smiled.

"Go ahead, Fran," said the Vice President of the United States.

"Will today's events have an effect on next week's elections in the Middle East?"

"Good question, Fran," and he launched into a three minute answer, towards the end of which the Vice President started to look a little queasy. Once or twice he placed a hand on his chest. When he looked like he was going to vomit his handlers hustled him off the podium and out of the camera's view.

His press secretary too the podium. The man looked like a shark.

"The Vice President has taken ill and—"

"Has the Vice President been bitten, Randy?"

"Is it his heart?"

"You've got mail!"

Harris hopped off the couch and crossed the room to his computer. He checked the subject heading from the sender: *Hi I Victoria From Russia You Meet Me?* Harris deleted the email, went back to his couch.

"Who exactly do you think the Vice President could be implying when he said enemies of America might be responsible for today's events, Harry?" Two network talking heads were engaged in an after-address analysis. "The Venezuelans? Al Qaeda? The Iranians?"

Daffy was licking her lips now, looking from Harris to the plate of food he'd taken three bites from and back to her owner.

"—one thing we haven't considered in all this, Sam, is nanotechnology and its potential for abuse—"

THEY MOVED QUICKLY and silently through the sewer system, no map necessary. They'd visited their destination enough to know every turn and straightaway needed to get where they were going.

An hour before, the heavy gunfire emanating from Jericho had given way to thick white smoke on the horizon. Even with binoculars, the best view from Eden had revealed nothing but thick plumes rising from several burning houses in the other camp.

Harris was behind Buddy at the front of the pack, his twin nines holstered each under an arm, a Mossberg ATPS 500 12-gauge with mounted bayonet in both hands, a flashlight duct-taped to the barrel.

Buddy had the Striker shotgun with the rotary-drum magazine, tensing it on its sling, a Mag Light in his free hand illuminating the path before them.

The three men behind were similarly well-armed. Evers had left his hunting rifle behind, opting for an H&K MP-5, more suitable for the close-quarter fighting they might be walking into. Aside from the MP-5, Evers had three pistols holstered on his person and an M-79 single shot grenade launcher strapped to his back.

There was only one reason Jericho might be burning. If what they suspected were the case, no amount of firepower was likely to prove adequate for what they'd find.

Harris reached the ladder and paused.

There were two functional sewer entrances into Jericho. One led directly onto the main street. They avoided that one. Whatever had befallen the camp, they didn't want to come up in the middle of it.

The manhole cover looming above them would deposit them in an alleyway behind a row of houses. The homes and store fronts of Jericho were set up exactly like those of their own Eden, with community driveways in the same spots. The only major difference was a series of fire escapes built onto the rear of the houses in Jericho. They could access the fire escapes a short distance from the manhole cover.

Harris stared warily upwards and Buddy followed his gaze.

There was a big slab of light where there shouldn't have been, the manhole partially uncovered.

A crescent of weak sunlight from the overcast sky filtered down on them, causing Thompson to squint.

"You smell that?" he scrunched his nose.

Harris had rallied this posse, deciding to bring Thompson along. They'd had their little "to do" a few days ago, but Harris was resigned to a few facts since. One of them was that he might be living with Thompson at Eden for a long while yet. Asking Thompson to come along was meant to be a first step in letting the younger man back into his good graces and a public means of allowing Thompson to save face.

Buddy hadn't questioned Harris's choice. He understood Harris' thinking.

"Yeah, that's not good," said Fred Turner, shifting on his feet. Turner hadn't been the same since his boy had died.

"Give me a second," Buddy said, handing his shotgun to Thompson. "I'll have a look."

Buddy drew his nine millimeter from its spot on his hip and threaded the silencer. He'd left the saddle bags back in Eden just in case they had to move fast in Jericho. He hadn't counted on the manhole cover being like this.

None of them had.

Harris watched Buddy ascend the ladder, climbing with his feet and one hand, the silenced nine aimed at the gap between the manhole cover and the street, in case anything tried to come down while he worked his way up.

Fred Turner was shining his flashlight on the tunnel where it continued on ahead of them. Harris thought he knew what the man was thinking, if the man was thinking normally. If that manhole cover was unsealed even slightly there was no telling *what* was down here with them now.

Harris banished an image of being chased in the dark tunnels from his mind.

Bobby Evers must have been thinking the same because he was keeping an eye and a light on the tunnel they had just come from, with all its sinister pitch black connections stretching off unseen in the distance.

Buddy came back down the ladder.

"Can't see much," he said. "Didn't see anybody or anything, but I didn't get much of a view either."

"What do you want to do?" Harris asked the older man. Buddy's thinking had kept both their asses alive up until this point.

"What I *want* to do," said Buddy, "Is close that manhole cover and go back to Eden."

"Class idea, that," agreed Evers.

"What we're *going* to do, Harris, is you, me, Thompson, we go up there, we check it out. Fred, you and Bobby stay here, close that up behind us when we're out. Keep an ear cocked because we might be coming back fast."

"You sure you want to do this?" asked Bobby Evers. "Is it even necessary?"

They had all listened to the volley of guns in Jericho dwindle, then disappear. They'd seen the plumes of smoke billow from black to white. What was done was winding down up there, and the best thing was to probably to pull that manhole cover back into place, get the hell back to Eden, forget about Jericho forever.

"Closure," said Buddy. "Right?"

"How about payback?" Thompson asked.

"No. Matter of fact, we leave the big guns down here with Bobby and Fred. Pistols only. This is pure sneak and peak, get the fuck out. Can you handle that?"

Thompson looked reluctant to discard his nine millimeter Colt sub machine gun. "Yeah, I can deal with that."

"Bobby, you keep an ear out on that radio, right?"

Buddy, Harris and Thompson stacked their assault rifles and shotguns against the curved wall of the sewer and started up the ladder one at a time, Buddy at their head.

"Be wide!" Evers whispered, telling them to be careful.

At the top of the ladder, Buddy reached up, braced himself with his feet, grunting as he pushed with one hand and slid the man hole cover back over his head, wincing at the noise it made. He moved it just enough to allow him to slide out with the silenced nine millimeter, scanning the alleyway directly in front of him, not seeing any zombies, but hearing the noises from beyond the buildings, the acrid smoke hitting his nostrils.

He got up out of the hole in the ground, turned to cover the blind spot behind him and understood how the manhole cover had come ajar.

The remains of a young man—everything below the sternum gone, bits of flesh and clothes hanging off his spinal cord—lay with its arms askance. Buddy didn't recognize anything that was left of the face.

There were three zombies kneeling around what was left, finishing it off, seemingly engrossed in their task. One looked up at Buddy as he shot the other two in their heads, the silenced nine laying them down.

"Fuck you." Buddy shot it through the upper lip, the exiting round lifting off most of the top of its skull.

He covered Thompson and then Harris as they climbed out, Thompson scrunching up his face at the sight of the half eaten man.

"I know that guy," Thompson whispered.

Buddy and Harris looked at him.

"John or Joe or something, maybe Jim. Something with a *J*."

Their view of the alley ahead and behind them was obstructed by fences. Where Eden had wide open areas behind its houses, Jericho's lots were fenced in. Each fence had an opening that let out into the next area. A home four or five houses up was ablaze, and Buddy figured they were probably all burning, but he got up onto the fire escape anyway, ignoring the scraping shriek made when Evers pulled the man hole cover back into place.

All three froze as a final, ragged salvo of gunfire sounded from somewhere out front, followed by silence.

Buddy looked at Harris.

He went up the fire escape to the first landing, squat-walking past the windows in case anything inside cared to look out, up the stairs to the next landing, repeat. The higher they got the more smoke Buddy could see and the more difficult breathing became. Smoke was billowing from a house three down.

They made the roof. Buddy peered over before climbing up. Wisps of smoke obscured his view, but it looked like the roofs between their position and the blaze were empty and intact. No zombies.

Buddy wasted no time, duck-walking to the other side of the roof, getting down onto his hands and knees, then elbows and knees, crawling up to the lip. He peeked down over the gutter onto the street below, into the heart of Jericho. Harris hunkered down on his left and Thompson on his right.

"Oh God," said Thompson.

Jericho had been overrun. It looked as if the undead had breached the electrified fence at the southern end. Smoke and flames from the buildings and the streets obstructed their view of the other end of the block.

Beneath them an undead bacchanal was in full swing. There were bodies and zombies everywhere. Many of the zombies were unmoving, head-shot or skulls caved in, bludgeoned. There were also dozens of the people who had lived here, people who'd broken bread on various occasions with Buddy and Harris, with Thompson and everyone else in Eden.

Zombies grouped around bodies like wild animals, tearing at the flesh and viscera, gnawing through limbs and carrying them off to eat alone. Blood was smeared all about the street where people had been felled, dismembered and disemboweled, fought over and dragged off. There were two or three close to skeletons, bones glistening white through all the red.

As Thompson watched, a zombie reared its head back out of a mid-section where it'd been buried like an ostrich, its entire skull slick with blood, something sausage-like between its masticating teeth. Thompson turned to the side and vomited all over the roof.

"You hear that?" Harris asked Buddy.

The other man wished he didn't. Somewhere down there, beyond the smoke, people were still alive. As they listened someone screamed, another called out, a few scattered gunshots. The smoke masked their view. All they could see were the already dead bodies below, the undead feasting on them.

They stared at it in shock and disgust for some while, absorbing it all.

Buddy keyed the walkie talkie. "Bobby, we're on the roof."

"What have you got?" the Irishman came back.

"It's not good. We'll talk."

Harris watched a zombie chewing the toes off a severed, charred foot.

"Payback time, right?" Thompson asked.

Buddy didn't hesitate, "No."

"What do you mean *no*?" Thompson asked Buddy. "You see what they've done down there. Fuck them. Fuck them all."

Slowly, calmly Buddy replied, "It's too late for everybody down there. But it isn't for us. It isn't for Eden. We just go."

"What do you mean 'we just go'?"

"If we go and open up a can of worms just to get some satisfaction for something we can't change, we'd only be putting more lives in danger."

"Bullshit." Thompson said it more to himself than to either of them.

"Where are you on this?" Buddy asked Harris.

"I know what you're saying, Buddy. And I know you're right too. But I'm with the kid this time."

"Shit," Buddy breathed.

"Buddy, listen to me man," said Thompson. "You know up the block they keep that big 18 wheeler of gasoline, right? You've seen it before, right? If I can get over there, maybe across the roofs and down a fire escape—"

"No, forget it," Buddy interrupted him, but Thompson continued unabated, fighting to keep his voice down.

"—if I can get over to it, I can unseal the valves, flood the fucking street. Then we either torch it or one of those fires already burning down there will destroy them all. Look at them, Buddy. There must be thousands of them down there."

"Thompson, Harris, now you both listen to me. What's done down there is fucked up. No doubt. But it's *done*. We aren't doing anybody any good risking our lives. All for what? A little payback against fuckers that don't even know what payback is? Fuckers won't even know what's happening to them as its happening?"

Thompson stared Buddy dead in the eye and Harris saw the edge of the younger man's mouth quiver.

Someone below cried out, something that sounded like "Oh God no!"

Thompson looked away from Buddy, and with his face averted asked, "That sound 'done' down there to you."

"This ain't open to debate," said Buddy.

"Guys." Harris rolled away from the edge of the roof towards its center, bringing the twin nines up.

From the smoke billowing across the roof a few houses down emerged first two then three then half-a-dozen more zombies.

"Fuck!" Thompson brought his Colt Detective Special up and started firing the .38.

"Ah hell," Buddy aimed slowly and deliberately, the nine millimeter coughing and a zombies falling back into the smoke.

Harris stood and fired the nine millimeters two fisted, "Let's go!"

Thompson fumbled a speedloader and dropped it on the roof. Buddy pushed him towards the fire escape.

Harris covered the other two men as they started down the fire escape, firing out the nines, knowing he'd taken at least six of the things out for good. He dropped the magazines, not bothering to gather them up, reloading and holstering them both, the Colt M1911 up and out, booming, blasting through the nearest zombie. The undead had cut the space between them and were only two roofs away.

Harris had one hand on the ladder and was starting to lower himself when there was a shriek, and a booker came tearing out of the smoke, bearing down on him. He straightened the .45 and fired once, a hole the size of a fist blowing out of the zombie's back. He fired again, catching the dead thing in the shoulder and twisting it in mid-stride. His third shot took off the side of its head, the thing stumbling off course, pitching over the roof to the yards below.

Harris ignored the shamblers heading his way and started down the ladder.

What they could see of the alley below was still empty. Buddy got on the radio as they descended to the last landing. "Open up, Bobby, we're comin' down!"

The manhole cover immediately slid back a foot and a half.

Buddy squatted, his nine tracking for a target, Thompson slipping down below. He nodded, indicating Harris next. Harris disappeared and Buddy passed him his nine, reaching up and over as he balanced himself on the ladder under the ground, pried the manhole cover forward and slid it into place.

Harris and Thompson had looks on their faces conveying to Bobby Evers everything he needed to know, and to not even ask.

"What you seen up there?" Of course Fred Turner asked.

Buddy didn't say a word. He'd watched with Turner as Turner's boy had perished. He was glad that he hadn't had to actually see anyone else go the same way out there in Jericho, that the smoke and flame had hidden most of it. Slinging his shotgun, Buddy stalked off the way they had come, flashlight bobbing.

Harris felt like he had to say something to Turner, so he told him it wasn't good. Bobby Evers nodded, laid a hand on Fred Turner's shoulder.

Buddy stalked off ahead and the others quickened their pace to catch up.

Buddy had seen some bad shit in his life, and a good deal of it he'd been responsible for. He'd seen some straight up horrible shit since all of this had gone down. But today took the cake. The scale, the mass. Just a waste, what a terrible, terrible waste.

He figured he'd remember what he'd seen in Jericho all his days.

BY THE TIME Harris reached exit 12 on the Hutch, traffic on the southbound lane was at a standstill. People were out of their cars, standing around in groups, calling over to one another.

Harris put the Lexus in park. There were already cars pulling up behind him, stopping, boxing him in, the queue lengthening.

Only two or three cars passed in the north-bound lane, and Harris wondered if they had gotten out of Queens or were just coming from some spot further south, maybe Yonkers or the Bronx.

All the radio stations had gone over to news. Reporters and officials were telling people to stay in their homes, not to panic. The Vice President had suffered another minor heart attack but it wasn't believed to be life-threatening. Only on satellite radio did some of the channels continue to play music.

Harris tapped on the steering wheel and grew agitated. This was *bullshit*. Raquel was waiting for him. Maybe in Manhattan, maybe in Woodside, somewhere in the city.

He killed the engine, got out of the car, stretched. He had changed at home to jeans and his running sneakers, and had thought enough before leaving the house to pack an extra change of comfortable clothing in the duffel bag.

He'd put Daffy out in the yard with food and fresh water, realizing it might be some time before he saw her again, hoping it wouldn't be, hoping it wouldn't rain, and figuring she could wait it out under the deck if it did.

"They say the bridges are shut down," a man standing beside the car next to his announced. "Is this nuts or what?"

"Yeah, it sure is," Harris muttered, trying to control his temper. He'd be damned if he was going to be stuck here on the highway, not moving an inch, while who knew what was going on further south, his wife somewhere out there.

Raquel would hold on, find a place to lay low until he came to her.

He checked his watch. He had missed their six o'clock in Woodside.

Harris shook his head, thought *never the time*, the slang his kids at school would use, reached back into his car and pulled the duffel forward. He reached in but didn't take out the .357 Colt Python he'd brought along, loose rounds for the revolver strewn about the bag, also a full box of shells. Instead he took out his sweat pants, stepped out of his shoes right there on the side of the parkway, unzipped his jeans, pulled them off, placed them on the front seat.

"Mommy, what is that man doing?" a little kid outside the car behind his own asked her mother. Harris in his white boxer briefs, pulling the grey sweat pants on, untying his running sneakers so he could put them back on and lacing them up, double knots each.

He rummaged through his jeans, pulled out his wallet and money clip, dropped both in the duffel bag. He folded the jeans and laid them in the bag. Zipped it up.

He considered taking the car keys, but decided against it. He put the keys in the ignition so the automatic locks wouldn't kick in, closed the door, cinched the duffel bag tight across his back, ignored the little kid and her mother, and started jogging off down the Hutchinson River Parkway at a steady pace, southbound.

"Hey mister!" the woman called out to him but he ignored her. He stuck to the median, the asphalt under his feet, his knees feeling good, passing row after row of unmoving cars, people staring at him curiously as he passed.

One fat guy leaning on a town car stuffing a donut in his mouth muttered "jerk" as he went by.

"YOU BELIEVE THAT?" Harris asked Buddy.

They were sitting in lawn chairs on the street, playing *Uno*. Isabel, pregnant and starting to show, was sunning herself down the block, wearing a thong and a string bikini top. Palmer and Diaz were sitting in chairs next to her, and Diaz was openly staring at her ass.

"Hey, it takes two to tango," said Buddy.

"Yeah, but I hear sometimes she takes on teams with more than one player," Harris joked, but it wasn't really a joke because Isabel was quite open about her sexuality in camp.

Uno was a kid's game but Harris enjoyed it. He had never learned it until he became a teacher. The kids needed something to keep them busy those last fifteen minutes of study hall before the end of the day, when they were itching to go and maybe get in trouble elsewhere in the school. A poker resurgence had swept the nation but he didn't feel right playing Texas Hold 'Em with high school students.

"I wouldn't let it bother you, Harris. She's just living her life the way she wants. God only knows we might not have much time left to us, so I can't blame her for trying to enjoy herself."

Buddy laid down a blue six.

"So you don't judge, huh?" Harris asked.

"We all judge," said Buddy. "Even when we say we don't."

"Yeah, I guess you're right," Harris admitted, putting down a red, green and yellow stack of sixes atop Buddy's blue. Isabel had come on to him a couple of times but he hadn't gone there. It wasn't because she "slept around" or anything. Harris was beyond that way of thinking. There were other reasons.

"What about you?" asked Buddy, nailing him with a draw two. "How's your love life these days?"

Harris snickered, plopping down a draw two of his own. "What love life? Draw four my friend."

Buddy gave him a knowing look, drew the four cards. "I see how that girl Julie is around you."

"You're crazy, old man."

"I might be crazy, that's true, but you're blind. That woman lights up when you come around. Why don't you talk to her?"

"I *do* talk to her."

"No, I mean *talk* to her. And don't try and tell me you don't know what I mean. You're a man, Harris. What have you got to lose?"

"Right, Buddy. I don't see it, but if you say it's so… Draw four by the way. *Again.*"

"You don't want to see it," said Buddy. "Look man, it ain't wrong. Think about it. Draw eight."

Buddy had plopped his own draw four down on Harris's.

"Anyway," Harris said dismissively, looking down at Buddy's draw four card on top of his. "Thompson seems to have a crush on her. He's closer to her age as it is."

"Yeah, I seen that too," Buddy agreed. "And I also seen how she doesn't pay him no mind. She's not interested in him, man."

Harris set a draw two on top of the pile. "Ever occur to you that she's playing hard to get?"

"You should know, way you're treating the pretty lady," Buddy threw down a second draw four. "What's the story?"

"Damn," Harris mumbled, "Hang on, Sloopy." He started to draw fourteen cards from the remainder of the deck.

"That's another twenty you're going to owe me," said Buddy. "Not that I'm counting."

"You haven't won yet."

"Yeah, but you have half the deck there in your hands."

"Okay, wise guy. Watch this."

Harris put down a green skip card, followed by two more skips, a blue reverse, red reverse and green reverse, and on top of it all a wild card, saying, "Draw four. Color is red."

"Man. You used to play the kids cut throat like this?"

"Are you kidding me? Those kids would have beaten the pants off the both of us."

"Funny though," Harris observed. "How money doesn't mean anything any-more."

"That's all it ever was, just paper. Only reason it meant anything is because everyone believed it meant something. Hey, get a load of this."

Down the block Diaz and Palmer were lathering sun tan lotion on Isabel's back and legs.

"Arturo!" Shannon, Diaz's girlfriend, stomped over to the spot.

"What is it baby?" smiled Diaz his hands hovering over Isabel's thighs slick with oil.

"I need to see you, in the house." Shannon was fuming and casting evil looks from Diaz to Isabel and back. "*Now.*"

Isabel didn't avoid eye contact but she paid the other woman no mind. Palmer continued to apply lotion to Isabel's angel wings.

"Okay, I'll be up in a minute," said Diaz.

"No, Arturo, *now!*" There was no room for negotiation in Shannon's voice. "Let's go! And you—" Shannon glared at Isabel, the latter propping herself up on her elbows, craning her neck around to see what Shannon wanted, "You should be ashamed of yourself!"

"Ashamed of myself for what?" Isabel looked like she was going to laugh.

"Why you fucking whore—"

Shannon took a step towards Isabel but Diaz grabbed his girlfriend and started to manhandle her back towards their house.

"What?" Isabel said, "Are you going to attack me? Kick my pregnant ass? Is that what you're going to do?"

"Stay away from him, slut!" Shannon yelled and Isabel laughed at her as Diaz carried her away.

She said something to Palmer that neither Harris nor Buddy could hear. People on the street and in their windows who had watched the little drama went back to whatever it was they had been doing.

Palmer alone oiling her up with a shit eating grin on his face.

"He's in now," noted Harris.

"Think he's been *in* once or twice before." Buddy threw down a green two. "Uno."

Harris still had a bunch of cards in his hands. He thought about it, put down another green card.

Buddy smiled, lay down his last card. It was a wild card.

"One more game?"

"Not a whole lot else to do, right?" said Harris.

"I deal this time. Let me see them cards."

OFFICER TRICIA MORGAN hunkered down in the closet, half-blind and scared out of her wits.

She'd been here like this for the past four hours.

Tricia'd lost her primary weapon in the melee outside, and all she had now was the .38 back-up piece she kept on her ankle, the gun in her hands.

Her knees were drawn up to her chin in the back of the closet where it was dark. She couldn't see anything without her contacts, anyway.

She'd lost them in a wrestling match with a Hasidic zombie out on the street. She'd been helping corral people up Sixth Avenue. It hadn't been orderly or calm at all. Anybody who could was running. People were getting knocked to the ground and trampled.

Morgan didn't know if it was because she was a woman or because she was only two inches over five feet tall, but people didn't listen to her as she first implored, then screamed at them to slow down. She realized they were just frightened out of their minds by what they'd been fleeing. As she was this moment.

She heard gunfire before she saw any zombies. When they came they came fast, though most of them seemed to be pretty slow. In her three years on the force she never had to draw her pistol on duty but she didn't hesitate when the first zombie showed up. The thing was easy to spot, the stream of people screaming and making room around it, breaking away from it. The zombie had blood all over its mouth from whatever it'd been eating. Tricia aimed carefully but missed, accidentally shooting a man behind it in the arm.

The guy hadn't stopped, just pulled his wounded limb close in to his side and disappeared up the street.

Though Tricia was shaking her second shot caught the zombie square in the chest and the thing jerked back a step, then righted itself and kept coming. She put three more rounds from her Glock 40mm into it but the thing wouldn't go down. Finally, when it was six feet away from Morgan, when she was considering turning and running herself, she nailed it between the eyes and the beast went down for good.

That's how she learned headshots were all that counted.

Within the next fifteen minutes she had killed seven more and swapped magazines twice. Ammunition was going to be a problem.

The crowd started to change. There were uniformed soldiers hustling up Sixth Avenue. Morgan tried to get her commanding officer on the radio but the line was in use, frantic conversations between people she didn't know, yelling back and forth and talking over each other.

Several times she considered leaving, juts running, finding a way back to the station or even to her family on Staten Island. But something, a sense of duty, she wasn't sure what, made Morgan stand her ground.

She figured she'd be in enough trouble when all this was over and the guy she'd shot in the arm sued the department and the city.

What finally made her mind up for her was when the Bradley tank came barreling up Sixth, zombies clinging to its exterior, two battling with a soldier in the hatch. The tank didn't slow down or attempt to go around the crush of people and Morgan felt sickened watching people go down under it, human beings popping like ripe fruit beneath its treads.

She heaved where she stood, vomiting up the dirty water dog she'd scarfed down from a sidewalk vendor. Morgan wiped her mouth and started up Sixth.

The Hasid attacked from behind when she had gotten about eight blocks up. At first she didn't know what was happening, someone grabbed her from behind and pulled her down. They rolled and she managed to turn herself around, but not before one dark suited arm rubbed up against her face and dislodged her contacts.

Morgan grabbed the creature by its payos and pulled its mouth away from her face. She fired one shot into its head and it went limp.

She sat there on Sixth Avenue for a minute, blinking, feeling with her fingers. One contact had come completely out. Another was half way in but as she continued blinking it too came free.

She'd been wearing glasses since she was a kid. Her eye sight was bad. Not legally blind bad but not too far off. Glasses or contacts corrected that. She'd lied on the police medical and then when she got into the academy she'd never had a problem with her contacts. There had always been the fear that she'd lose her contacts in an altercation with a perp, and she usually had a pair of glasses with her in a sunglasses case on her utility belt, but she hadn't seen much action on the job and grown lax. Got to the point where she wasn't bringing her glasses with her everyday. Today was one of those days.

Without her contacts everything was a blur. She could make out people going past her up the street. She could see the buildings on either side but couldn't discern any details. She couldn't even see the license plate of the car parked less than ten feet from her.

Morgan knew she had to remain calm. She had seen too many people this afternoon screaming their heads off, tearing ass for who knew where, seemingly out of their minds. She stood up and brushed herself off. She had dropped the Glock and now couldn't find it. Maybe someone running past had snatched it up? If she got down on her hands and knees to search for it she might be trampled.

She pulled her back-up piece off her ankle, glad she carried one.

Morgan tried to get someone on the radio but no one responded.

And so she found herself hours later hiding in the back of a closet in an office on the thirty ninth floor of a building off Sixth Avenue.

It had been a hell of a process just getting into the building and onto an elevator. No one was willing to stop and help her. It seemed like everyone was trying to get *out* of the building, and she was the only one taking the elevator up.

She was in some kind of doctor's office or something. She'd passed through a waiting room and a hallway with examination rooms on either side. She'd tried the phones but they weren't working. Maybe she'd done something wrong. Zero didn't bring an operator.

What she had on her hands now was a waiting game. At one point she had to sneak out of the closet, find the bathroom. Fortunately the doctor's office had their own. After she'd peed and washed her hands, she'd heard noises out in the hall and stepped into the receptionist's area so she could hear better.

What she'd heard wasn't good. A man's voice screaming, someone running. At one point it sounded like a fight right outside the office door.

Tricia Morgan went back to her closet then, shutting the lights in the doctor's office. Only the light in the hall remained on.

Sitting in the dark she considered her options. She could try and find any other people on this floor. Being with *someone*, anyone, would be preferable to being alone. But she was scared of venturing out into the halls after what she'd heard earlier.

She could sit where she was and wait. Things had been pretty hairy out on the street, but would that last? The city had to have some kind of plan. If not the city, Albany. Still, the way the soldiers were running away, the way that tank had come down the street crushing people…

One thing she was determined about. She *wouldn't* be eaten. *No way, no how.* She'd seen the people running past her, many gripping arms, shoulders, other areas of their bodies torn open. That Hasid had been trying to bite her face off when she'd shot him.

She hadn't wanted to believe the early reports, that whatever these things were, they *ate* people. But it was true.

She had the revolver. It only had six shots.

She hoped they wouldn't find her in this place. Yet she feared they would.

There was nowhere she could go. No place to hide. If she heard them come into the office, she would stay where she was, listen. If they made it into the doctor's room and there was only one of them, maybe two, she could shoot it out. If there were more than that…she would put the gun to her own head. If they opened the closet door, she'd—

Tricia would do what she felt she had to do when she felt she had to do it. The police officer sat back in the dark closet, watched the shadows, and waited.

THEY STAYED TO the roofs as much as they could, coming down only to cross streets where necessary, keeping out of sight. The few undead they encountered on the roofs they dispatched silently. Buddy passed Harris his silenced nine, opting for his knife. Taking his targets from behind when he could and driving the blade up where the skull met the back of the neck, twisting it around before withdrawing.

Other times Buddy walked right up to the slower moving zombies, grabbed them by their chins and the tops of their head and wrenched their skulls to one side, necks breaking audibly. That a bold move to say the least, one Harris sure as hell wasn't going to try. Breaking their necks didn't kill the zombies, but it left them paralyzed, incapable of pursuit. They lay in place, immobilized, opening and closing their mouths as Harris and Buddy passed them.

Leapfrogging from building to building, avoiding discovery, they squatted atop an apartment building directly up the block from their destination.

"There it is," said Buddy, scanning with his binoculars.

"How's it look?"

It was a whole street walled in on four sides. The walls were dense and high and there were people atop them moving about and more people down on the walled-off street. Regular people. *Live* people.

"They got themselves a whole little community going on down there. I see something, looks like generators. Looks like they have themselves showers and latrines too, maybe."

"That wall all around?"

"From what I can see, yeah," Buddy panned with the binoculars and found himself looking directly into the face of another man, this one man tall and cradling a bullpup assault rifle, staring back at Buddy with curiosity and something else in his eyes. Something Buddy recognized and did not like.

"Made contact," Buddy chanced it, stood up against his better judgment, waving, and Harris reluctantly joined him, looking behind them and then down to the street. The zombies below hadn't noticed the two men on the roof.

"Hello, big boy."

The man on the wall was joined by others, and some of these began to wave back to them. The tall man made no moves, calling out over his shoulder to someone instead. The undead, drawn by the presence of those on the wall, started to mill about beneath it.

Buddy pointed to himself and Harris, then at the walled camp.

There was some discussion on the wall, everyone there armed. The tall man talking with a shorter fat man, a third man apparently arguing with the both of them. The tall man turned aggressively on the third, lashing out at him verbally, their distance too great for Harris or Buddy to hear any of their words.

Buddy watched it all through his binoculars, Harris making out most of what transpired, though he was unable to make out the expressions on the individual faces.

The third man cast a glance towards Harris and Buddy, shook his head in resignation, and got down off the wall, disappearing from view on the other side.

"That doesn't look good," muttered Buddy.

The taller one, apparently done consulting with the fat man, turned to look directly at them once more. He shook his head, held up a hand, thumb down. Then he waved them away, once, showed his teeth, and turned his back on them.

"You gotta be kidding me," Harris murmured.

"You saw that, huh?" Buddy didn't sound perturbed, almost amused. Harris getting to know that in situations such as these, when Buddy would laugh or seem entertained, the other man was actually starting to seethe inside.

"What do they want us to do," Harris said with disgust, "just lounge around out here with these things? Wait 'til it gets dark, see how long we last?"

"Well, looks for sure like they don't want us joining them. But you know what, Harris?"

"What's that?"

"Like I give a *fuck* what *they* want."

"So what's our plan?"

Buddy started laying it out for him and Harris listened. Although dangerous, Harris knew it was better than sitting around on the roof waiting for the zombies to find them.

Ten minutes later they'd crept down the stair well of the apartment building. Along the way they'd taken out ten zombies, silenced shots, up-close knife work. Harris and Buddy were learning that the undead, one on one, could be dealt with, so long as they didn't surprise you in a tight spot. Especially the slow ones, which seemed to be the majority of them. The faster ones were a different story.

The lobby of the apartment looked out onto the street. The wall was a good hundred yards at the other end. Between the apartment building they were in were parked cars, a bus stuck in the middle of the street, and a couple hundred zombies.

Buddy sheathed his knife on his ankle, checked the silenced nine millimeter, made sure it had one in the chamber and placed another round in the magazine. The sawed-off shotgun jutted out of his saddle bags, and the H&K G3 was strapped to his back, two twenty round magazines taped together. He cradled the Milcor MGL, the South African multiple grenade launcher squat and brutish looking.

Harris checked the loads on the twin nine millimeters he wore under his arms. The Colt .357 which had served him so well was holstered on his right hip, a .45 on his left. He wore a machete strapped to his back next to an M-16 carbine fitted with an M-203 A1 grenade launcher. Like Buddy's G-3, he'd taped the magazines of his M-4 together. Harris unslung the M-16/M-203 combo.

"You ready?"

Harris nodded, "Let's do it."

"Hey, Harris, if we don't—"

"I said let's do it, Buddy, before I lose my nerve."

"Nah, nah, man," grinned Buddy, "I wanted to tell you not to worry about it. I don't think they were being unfriendly to us 'cause of you bein' white and all."

Harris laughed, "You're cracked man."

There were two undead at the bottom of the stairs letting out from the apartment building and Buddy let Harris put one in each's head with the M-16, the double cracks alerting everything else about. The zombies looked their way, mouths cracking open, hisses and screams, the fast ones breaking into long loping strides.

Buddy braced the grenade launcher on his hip—Harris fired the M-16 on semi-automatic from his shoulder, sighting down the barrel and letting off single rounds into the heads of the runners as they came—and squeezed the trigger, the launcher bucking slightly in his grip, firing again, swiveling at the hip and tracking up and down the block, launching 40 mm grenades at clusters of undead and the vehicles they stood around.

The grenades detonated, drowning out the sound of Harris's 16, cars parked along the curbs rocked, lifting off the ground as the fragmentation rounds detonated, secondary explosions as their own gas tanks went up. Shrapnel from the grenades and the cars ripped through the undead, decapitating some, driving shards of metal into the heads and brains of others, tearing limbs off more, knocking any too close to the blasts from their feet, flinging them through the air like rag dolls.

Harris fired out the magazine at the runners, dropped the mag, flipped it over, slammed the taped mag home. He wrapped his hand around the magazine and sighted along the barrel at another booker, triggering the M-203, the 40mm grenade catching the zombie in its stomach, vaporizing the top half of its body.

"Nice shot," said Buddy, all six rounds from the Milcor expelled. He abandoned it, motioning for Harris to follow as he brought his H&K G-3 to play, firing single shots up the street, undead closing from behind them pirouetting and collapsing.

They broke into a run, past the flaming metal of cars, past the undead standing there gawking, around those knocked flat from the explosions, some beginning to get up. They stayed clear of the creatures staggering towards them, looking out for bookers, seeing none, heading for the wall at the end of the block.

A single man on the wall, Buddy recognized him as the third guy who'd been chastised by the tall one, was laying down covering fire, the cracks of his hunting rifle sharp.

As he ran, Harris tried to watch his step, avoiding any undead that were getting back up onto their hands and knees, kicking one that blocked the path in its face, sending the thing over backwards out of the way. He'd never been out on the street with this many at once, and the situation was hairy. Small fires were burning and they ran through a mist of smoke.

The people on the wall were watching them intently, seeing if they were going to make it, the lone gunman doing what he could.

A zombie popped out from behind a truck stopped half-on-the-street, half-on-the-curb as they passed, going for Buddy, Harris slamming it back with three shots from the M-16, not bothering to finish it, just letting it lie in the street where it fell struggling to right itself, the two human beings already past it racing up the block.

Twenty yards from the wall they veered suddenly towards the left, aiming for the storefronts and stoops of the houses. Ahead of them on the street in front of the wall their path was blocked by a crowd of the undead. They didn't need to look to know that the zombies were massing behind them as well, new ones drawn by the racket, emerging from side streets and doorways.

"We do this quick!" Buddy yelled, and Harris brought the reloaded M-203 A1 grenade launcher mounted under the barrel of his M-16 into play, firing another 40mm grenade through the doors of the single story building before them. It had been a home once, but nothing human lived there anymore.

The grenade took the doors off their hinges along with most of the molding.

The smoke wasn't even clear and Buddy was inside the building. Harris could hear him firing the G-3.

Harris turned when he reached the smoking ruins of the entrance, coughing from the smoke. The undead were coming for them down the block, an impenetrable wall of them.

"Dammit," he turned and ran into the building, into a veritable zombie nest.

"Harris, heads up!" Buddy yelled, ramming his blade into the face of an undead. Corpses lay sprawled in the hallway. Doors on either side of the hall opened or were opening, undead staggering out, going for the man.

"Buddy, down!" Harris roared, and Buddy launched himself forward, tackling a runner, the two of them bouncing off the hallway floor.

Harris flicked the selector on the M-16 to full auto and sprayed the remainder of the magazine down the hall, geysers of blood and gore erupting from the heads and shoulders of the undead, plaster exploding off walls in clouds.

With one hand wrapped around its throat to keep its teeth from his face, Buddy drove the index and middle fingers of his free hand into the eye sockets of the thing beneath him, sinking them up to the first knuckle, the beast beneath him fighting, squirming. He drove his fingers the rest of the way, twisted them about, the zombie going limp.

He was up, yanking his blade out of the head of a felled undead, ramming it through the throat of another that was already on him, pinning the thing to the wall behind it, finding his saddle bags, yanking the sawed-off out, straight arming it and letting both barrels off at the same time, three forms knocked down by the buckshot.

Harris used the stock of the M-16 to beat in the head of a zombie, a stain streaked on the floor of the hall. Letting the M-16 fall to his side, the sling keeping it on his body, Harris drew the .45 with his left hand and the .357 Magnum with his right, firing as undead emerged from a doorway.

Buddy and Harris moved, working their way down the corridor. The doors here opened outwards, into the hall, Buddy slamming them shut as he went. Harris, bringing up the rear, flinging the doors open as they passed, aiming to make it more difficult for the zombies following, even if only momentarily. There were undead stirring in the rooms beyond those doors, they could hear them, but there were now dozens more starting to pour in from the front, crowding on the street, drawn by Harris and Buddy's mad dash and the din of battle.

At the end of the hall a window which Buddy blew out with his nine millimeter. He launched himself through whatever remained of the glass without looking, landing on the grass four feet below, his saddle bags still on his shoulders. Harris followed suit, vaulting off the skull of a felled zombie, shrugging off reaching hands.

They found themselves in a small space between the wall of the compound they'd spied from the roof top and the house they'd just jumped out of. The other two directions were blocked by wooden fences. This house had once had a yard, and the people who had constructed the walled compound had built their wall through it, leaving the fences of the yard standing until where it reached their wall.

The wall a good ten or twelve feet high, too tall for even Buddy to leap up and grab onto.

One of the people on the wall saying, "I cannot believe they made it this far!"

"You goddamn right we did, now get us up there!" Buddy yelled back at them, thumbing new shells into the sawed-off.

Harris put a magnum round between the eyes of the first zombie that appeared in the window.

"No deal," the tall man yelled down, "I told you before not to come here."

"Come on Markowski," another person on the wall plead. "We can't just leave them down there."

A booker leaped through the window and Buddy grabbed its wrist as it landed. He yanking forward, its momentum slamming it into the wall. Buddy fired the sawed-off, the blast taking off the thing's head and the hand it'd extended in front of its face, blood and matter dousing the people upon the wall, someone screaming.

Another zombie dropped from the window into the yard and Harris gunned it down with two blasts from the .357.

A third was gripping the window frame and had its legs on the sill, Buddy giving it the other barrel, punching it back into the house out of sight, the zombies inside ululating.

The wooden fence separating the two men from the street rattled and shook violently under protest from the undead grouped against it. Harris knew if they didn't get into the compound they were not going to make it.

"*Fuck them.* You heard what Graham said," the tall guy named Markowski spat.

Harris aimed the .45 and .357 at the darkness of the window, into the hall beyond. He waited until he saw shadows inside then fired both pistols.

Buddy snapped the breach shut on his sawed-off and sent the contents of both barrels through the window, a spray of blood splashing out. Harris holstered the empty .45 and .357, cross drew the nine millimeters, filling both his hands.

Buddy reached into his saddle bags and took out a big lump of grey-looking clay. Harris had never seen him with it before.

"What the fuck is that?" someone on the wall dumfounded.

Buddy slapped it on the wall of the compound where it stuck.

"That's plastic explosive," he yelled up, taking a grenade from the saddle bag, tossing it to Harris, pulling out a second.

Harris pulled the pin on his and put it through the window frame without having to be asked. Everyone on the wall ducked as the grenade inside the house exploded, plaster dust billowing out. A caterwauling from inside the house as the zombies clambered over their dead numbers towards the open window.

The people on the wall stood up, brushing themselves off.

"Oh no he didn't—"

Buddy had plugged the second grenade into the plastic explosive pressed to their wall. He had one finger around the pin of the grenade, his nine millimeter in his other hand.

"Hey, big guy!" he called to the tall man. "You see this? You let us up, or we let them all in."

Buddy's finger didn't leave the pin of the grenade, even as he swiveled to fire three shots into the head of an undead that popped up in the window.

Gasps and stirrings on the wall now, and the tall guy named Markowski had a Bullpup assault rifle on Buddy.

The zombies did not relent. Two or three heads would appear in the window at a time, and Harris would let them have it with the nines. The wooden fence was threatening to collapse under the weight of the undead hoarding against it.

"Evers, what the fuck are you doing?" Markowski roared.

A rope ladder dropped down to them. Buddy nodded to Harris and the later holstered his nines, scrambling up. Men and women at the top reached down to him and helped him.

"You're not the full shilling, Markowski!" Evers yelled back. "Ya mad man."

"Help my friend out!" Harris yelled, mounting the wall, drawing the nines again and firing them out at the window of the house where undead spilled through into the yard.

People on the wall opened fire on the zombies below, a withering hail of lead from an assortment of assault rifles, shotguns and a hunting rifle.

Buddy popped the grenade out of the plastic explosive but left the explosive itself in place on the wall.

He was reaching for the ladder when a zombie laid both its hands on his shoulders. Buddy whirled and rammed the barrels of the shotgun through its mouth, shattering the thing's jaws and teeth. He fired a barrel and the explosion ripped out the back of the creature's neck, decapitating the zombie directly behind it.

The zombie dropped to its knees, Buddy's shotgun still impaling it through the mouth.

Buddy clambered atop the wall out of breath.

"Fuck!" he wheezed, staring at the men and women around him. They stood on what looked like an empty cargo container pressed against the wall, something usually mounted on an eighteen wheeler.

Most looked as surprised to see him and Harris as he and Harris were to see them. Only the one named Markowski still looked disgruntled, but at least he had the barrel of the FEMAS in his hands cast down.

"Fair play out there!" said Evers, the curly headed man with a hunting rifle and an Irish brogue, the third man Buddy had seen arguing with the first two through the field glasses. He reached out to take first Harris's and then Buddy's hand. "Welcome to Eden."

"Yeah," said Buddy. "Thanks."

THEY LOADED ANOTHER batch of their wounded onto the chopper.

Marcos kept low, remembering his days in the Gulf aboard the aircraft carrier when that poor schmuck had gotten the top of his head taken off by the rotor blades on the flight deck. Someone had taken pictures of it afterwards, put the pictures up on one of those web sites, one of the ones with all the porn and death vids. Marcos never understood who would want to mix the two.

They were seventy stories up, which was a bad thing for Marcos because he hated heights. He kept well away from the lip of the roof, working with the firefighters, EMTs and other rescue personnel to transport the wounded onto the helicopters setting down and lifting off, ferrying as many people from the building as they could.

The street below no longer an option, hadn't been since last night. Soldiers and armed citizens held the stairwells, picking off the zombies as they lumbered up towards the roof.

Marcos wondered how long it'd take them to make it up seventy stories. He lent an EMT a hand, the woman had a man on a stretcher, the man's face all eaten off, dying from his wounds. They carried the stretcher across the tarmac, keeping their heads low, passed it up to the men aboard the helicopter.

There was a spare tire around his middle these days but Marcos found the discipline from his old Navy days came back fast. He'd feel safer if he had some kind of weapon, preferably a gun. He set his mind to the task at hand and tried not to think about his family at home. He had to trust they were still safe, as they were when he spoke to them last days ago, when he came down here looking to volunteer to help because he thought his country needed him.

A man on the helicopter signaled the craft was full and Marcos and the EMT hustled away from it.

Marcos turned from the downdraft and looked over the roof. Even with all the evacuation flights shuttling in overnight, there must have still been a good hundred and fifty, two hundred people left on the roof.

As the chopper lifted off Marcos could hear the words of the EMT next to him, "Poor bastards."

She was pointing across the street to a roof top slightly below their own. Dozens of people were stranded there, waving their arms, gesticulating wildly. Marcos could see them but he couldn't hear them. Helicopters couldn't land for them because the building nestled between taller ones with no clearance for rotors or their draft. Imagine, Marcos pondered it, making it off the street alive, climbing sixty-something flights of stairs—he assumed the power out in that building like the one he stood on, so elevators out of the question—and finding yourself struck on the roof, no place to go, no one to come and take you away. Those people were all trapped.

"Oh God no!"

Marcos looked up. The helicopter they had just loaded tilted crazily in the sky. Something was going on inside it, the pilot losing control.

"Oh shit—" the EMT beside him cried, but Marcos was already running for the door to the stairwell, the helicopter coming back down towards them, skewed at an angle that defied its physics.

He knew he wasn't going to make the stairs so he rolled behind the air condition ducts and kissed his ass goodbye.

Screams lost in the deafening vibrations of the rotor wash, a wrenching collision and three loud explosions following in rapid succession. Marcos felt the heat lying where he was and watched bodies catapult through the air past him, one motioning with his arms and legs like he was swimming in the air. The bodies pitched over him and off the roof down to the street seventy stories beneath.

He heard a ringing in his ears like the kind he'd get when he tensed his jaw, but this was involuntary. There was a muffled clanging that diminished in volume and then a muted crash somewhere far below.

When the heat had subsided he dared to stand.

Nearly everyone was gone. Bodies and parts of bodies littered the place. It looked like the helicopter had smacked into the roof, exploded, and bounced down to the street. The rear rotor had come off and sliced through dozens. Some of them were still alive, dragging legless torsos away from the burning fires, or lying, flailing their arms and screaming, but Marcos couldn't hear them for the ringing in his head.

He watched a woman cut in two pull her upper half from her lower, feet, legs and thighs still standing, draped in strands of burnt up skirt. She got about two feet before she didn't move again.

A man stood in place, hopping around, his clothes burned off from the knees up, his skin bubbling and coming off in dollops. Like a man stepping onto the scalding sand of a beach and hotfooting it back and forth from one foot to another in place.

Marcos felt something warm down the front of his pants and felt there, finding he had pissed himself.

A man or woman on fire—Marcos couldn't tell which—ran past, arms beating at the flames engulfing its body. Marcos wondered if the person were screaming and he just couldn't hear them. Man or woman. it went right over the side of the roof.

Maybe twelve or fifteen people were getting up, some wounded, others miraculously unscathed.

He looked up into the sky. Off in the distance he saw a few helicopters, but they were heading away from the building and there were no others coming back.

He sat down behind the air conditioning ducts where he wouldn't have to see the severed arms and legs and burned flesh, where he wouldn't have to watch the survivors writhing on the rooftop.

He wondered what had become of the female EMT he'd stood next to moments earlier.

Through the ringing in his ears he discerned a low roar, increasing in intensity. He stood once more and looked in all directions. The jets were coming in low.

Across the way zombies had breached the roof and the people were fighting them.

He turned his back on the carnage and the incoming jets. Marcos stared into his lap and thought of his family. Looking over the edge of the building scared the hell out of him. He was petrified of heights. He sat with his back against the air conditioning ducts and prayed like he had never prayed before.

HARRIS WATCHED THE young guy, Thompson, put fire to his cigarette with a Zippo lighter.

"Thanks for bringing Harris over, Thompson," said Graham, his chins jiggling. "Why don't you wait in the next room."

It wasn't a question, and Thompson left.

"So, Harris, what did you guys think of Jericho?" The fat man sat on the other end of the table, his little sausage fingers tented in front of him, wrinkly elbows resting on the table. Graham' house was a mess, a pig sty. It fit the man. Harris thought that wasn't true: it was unfair to pigs.

Graham and his lackey were looking at Harris, waiting for an answer.

"The people were nice enough," he recounted. "A bit hippy-ish, if you ask me."

"Bunch of sixties rejects," spat Markowski. "Don't eat the brown acid and all that shit."

"They're in there pretty tight though," continued Harris. "Only concern I have about them is that electrified fence. If that thing fails they're out of luck."

"If that thing fails, they're *fucked*," said Markowski in his usual brusque manner.

Graham had sent Harris and Buddy with Markowski and a few other men from Eden to visit the neighboring encampment. The walk through the sewer system had been a little freaky and claustrophobic at first for Harris, and he wondered how the zombies were unwise to the system of tunnels and passageways running beneath the streets and houses of the city, but they had made it and the people of Jericho had welcomed them with open arms.

"Hippy-ish," said Graham, "I like that."

Harris had noticed that about the heavy man: the guy would repeat something you'd said two or three sentences ago. Harris figured Graham was doing it because he wanted to appear profound. That or the guy had slow processing speed.

He and Buddy had been in Eden a few days now, and things were coming to a head fast. Graham ran this place with his thugs, chief of whom was Markowski, the tall Pole with the crappy attitude. The people in Eden did what they were told because Graham kept them safe from the undead and they feared Markowski.

Harris had been getting the vibe that Graham was trying to win him over to his side, which he found funny because he detested the dictator and his ways. If the shoe had been on the other foot, if Harris had been in Graham's position, he'd have tried to win Buddy over to his side, because Harris considered Buddy a much more dangerous adversary than himself, and that would make him a more valuable ally.

But Graham steered clear of Buddy as much as possible, and Harris suspected race may have been involved. It definitely was an issue with Markowski, who peppered his speech freely with references to "jigs" and "niggers." The Pole might be six and a half feet tall, but he was cruising for a bruising or worse with Buddy.

"Hippy bullshit," Markowski literally spat on the floor, which didn't seem to bother Graham one bit. "They're pussies, all of them. Let them have their Neil Young and flower power."

"You'll have to excuse Kowski here, Harris. He's a Skynyrd fan himself."

Markowski was right about one thing. The roughly five dozen people who lived in Jericho didn't seem very tough. Not that anyone here in Eden was. People listened to Graham because they were afraid. Graham reminded Harris of the schoolyard bully who was a mess himself. But there was a cruel streak to Markowski, something fundamentally wrong with that one. A mentaller, as Evers referred to him.

Harris wondered how everyone who had come to Eden or Jericho had survived as long as they had. They had to be tough, right? He and Buddy got where they were fighting hard, ready to die hard if necessary, but they always tried to deal fairly with anyone they met on the outside, never burning anyone. Harris imagined Graham getting by on cunning and deceit, weaseling his way here, and Markowski on brute force, shooting and slashing his way inside Eden.

One thing he couldn't imagine was either Graham or Markowski in Jericho. Over there the people smoked a lot of pot, danced, and did seem somewhat frivolous. But they'd had their crap together enough to put up an electrified fence and get the tanker of gasoline in to fuel their generators.

"There's a reason I'm asking you about Jericho, Harris." Graham leaned forward on the table, as if he were taking Harris into his confidence.

"See, I made an overture, an offer, to Jericho three weeks back. Asked them if they wanted to join us here at Eden, you know, somehow consolidate what we all got into some kind of confederation, a co-op for the benefit of everyone involved."

For the benefit of you and Markowski and anyone who does your dirty work, thought Harris, although he was careful his face did not give away any of how he thought.

Graham held up a finger, like the next thing he was going to say was the loftiest sentiment known to their species. "And they refused."

"*Pussies*," Markowski plugged one nostril with a thumb and blew a stream of snot across the room. A strand of it dangled from his nose and he wiped the back of his hand across it dismissively.

"They want to be off on their own, Harris, but you saw how things are there. They're smoking pot and carrying on like it's the goddamn fucking age of Aquarius. In the meantime they've got thousands of zombies massed outside their quaint little experiment in communal living. They ain't going to make it without our help."

"So what are we talking about here?" Harris asked carefully.

"It's like with a child Harris. You have any children?"

"No."

"I do," said Graham. "I mean I *did*. Your child wants to run across the street you aren't going to let him do so, right? He'll run right into traffic thinking nothing of it, get his little skull peeled open for him by a Mack Truck. That's how those people in Jericho are, Harris."

"Fuckin' infants," emphasized Markowski.

"They're going to tune in, turn out, drop in and Woodstock their way into the mouths of those things."

"Turn on, tune in, drop out," said Markowski but Graham ignored him.

"I don't think I'm following you," Harris admitted, although he knew all too well where the heavy man was going with this.

"We're going to have to go in there and run things *for them*, Harris," said an exasperated Markowski, and Harris couldn't tell who the big Pole was short with.

"Take *care* of them," amended Graham. "If you will."

"What are you talking about here, Graham? They already told you they're happy the way they are."

Graham looked perturbed and Markowski shot his boss a look that said, *he just don't get it*. Graham looked down hard at his hands. When his eyes came back up they had softened.

"I know what they told me, Harris. But I also know what needs to be done."

Harris figured Markowski for the true threat in the room, and if he had to he'd need to take the Pole out first, which was easier said than done. There was a roomful of other men next door and Harris found himself wishing Buddy were with him.

"That sound too harsh to you?" Markowski asked Harris, the challenge in his voice unmistakable, inviting.

Harris thought about what he was going to say before he said it, choosing his words, "Spell it out for me then. What are we thinking here?"

The word "we" seemed to put Graham at ease, the fat man casting a reassuring glance at Markowski. The tall man didn't lose his scowl. Harris wondered how many rounds from the .357 Markowski could take and keep coming.

"I'm thinking we send in a small team, maybe six or seven at first." Graham laid out his plan with all the gravity as though he were discussing MacArthur's landing at Inchon. "I'd want you on that team. Kowski told me how you handled yourself in the drug store. Going back in there for Evers."

"Mick faggot."

"I wouldn't have, but that's just me. Then there's that whole incident with the psychic. You know what that shit shows me?"

Harris waited.

"It shows me, one, this guy Harris here can handle himself. He's got balls. Big hairy fuckin' man balls. Two, it shows me you don't take any bullshit. And three, let's face facts, Harris, you're a tough man but you're not a hard man, not like Kowski here. And see, I'm not expecting anybody in Jericho to give us a hard time, but if they do I'd feel better knowing I got guys like you alongside Kowski to handle it. You got a way with people Kowski lacks, and he's got a way with people you lack.

"Your friend there too," Graham meant Buddy, and Markowski snorted, mumbled something about "spear chuckers" but Graham ignored him, "you guys go in there, explain to those peaceniks how things are going to be, set up some kind of government or some shit."

"You think they're just going to agree to this?"

"Let me tell you something about people, Harris. You walk into a room, you pop the biggest, toughest guy in there in his goddamn mouth, leave him cradling his nuts crying on the floor, everyone else is going to pony up to whatever it is you've got to say."

"Whatever you're selling," added Markowski.

Graham spoke like he knew what he was talking about from experience, but Harris couldn't imagine the overweight man being able to pull that off. Still, the guy had Markowski tame enough, however that had happened.

"So if any of them want to kum-by-ah or any of that shit," Markowski said, and drove one balled fist into the other open palm for emphasis.

"And we're doing it for their own good, Harris. They might not see it that way at first, but they will."

"Of course we aren't going to benefit at all from this, are we?" Harris asked, trying to sound like he hoped they would, like *wink-wink come on fellas*.

"But of course we will," Graham picked up on his tone, broke into a leer. "I mean, to the victors go the spoils, right? This ain't a democracy here in Eden, but it works pretty goddamn well. And to those who come up with the plans and protect the others go the lion's share. Nothing too indulgent mind you, but we're gonna get our fair share."

"Should I tell him about my idea, Graham?" Markowski all eager. "About the community of women?"

"Nah, save it for later. I'm gonna have need for guys like you, Harris," Graham laid it on thick, trying to seal the deal. "Guys who can think on their feet. Guys people respect and will follow. Me and Kowski here, believe it or not, we can show you a thing or two."

"Yeah, like how to make better friends," Markowski growled. "The only time I want to see black and white together is on a fucking cookie."

"Calm down, Kowski," said Graham. "You know, Harris, even your pal, Buddy, man's got a lot of promise if he'd just learn to lighten up."

"I'll talk to him," reassured Harris. "He'll come around. I think he's still angry that you—" Harris nodded to Markowski "—didn't want to let us into Eden in the first place."

"That old shit?" Markowski dismissing it like it was something happened twenty years ago and didn't mean anything.

Graham showed his palms, "Harris, you and Buddy have to understand, you know how many people we've let in here and they've turned out to be dangerous?"

"Motherfuckers come in here bitten."

"That's true. They come in here bit and they don't want to show us and then things gets violent, or they come in here with their own ideas about how things should be in Eden…"

"And then shit gets violent," gloated Markowski.

"Same thing with those fruitcakes over in Jericho. Would you believe they kept a few of their own, a few of their own undead? The religious among them tried to minister to them, heal them."

"They tried all sorts of bizarre shit," said Markowski.

"Aromatherapy even."

"Crazy, right?"

"Dangerous," Harris admitted.

"You know what we do with the undead here, Harris?" Markowski asked, a sneer plastering itself across his face.

"For some reason I don't think that's to Harris' taste, but you can show him in a minute. Now, Harris, we got an understanding, between you and me that is?"

Harris mulled it over, more for the sake of show than anything else. "Yeah, we do."

Graham smiled, and Harris couldn't believe how someone so stupid could get into such a position, lording it over everyone else.

"Good. I'm glad to hear that, Harris. I'll keep you informed, and when the time comes, and it's coming up soon, I'm going to ask you and your pal there to go with Kowski and some others over to Jericho."

"I'm up for that." Graham ate it right up, smiling at Markowski.

"Kowski, why don't you show Harris how we keep the boys entertained around here?"

"Come on Harris, rock out with your cock out. I'll take you to the play room."

Markowski's chuckle was devoid of mirth as he motioned for Harris to follow him.

Harris stood, nodding at Graham, glad the other man didn't want to shake hands.

In the next room, Thompson was flicking his Zippo open and closed while Bert stood around looking bored.

Markowski led Harris through the house, into the kitchen to a basement stairwell and downstairs.

Half way down the steps Harris stopped, reaching for his twin nines. Markowski stopped as well, turned to Harris bemused, smiling, "Relax." Harris heard *pussy* in there unspoken, implied.

The tall man ducked and continued down the staircase, flicking a light switch as he did, laughing to himself.

Harris didn't like what was down in the basement one bit.

Metal poles had been driven into the middle of the floor and cemented into place. A chain attached to one pole tethered a zombie. She was topless and rotting, flesh hanging from her shoulders and back. She'd been a red head in real life and tufts of her hair were gone, revealing the skin of her scalp.

When she saw Harris and Markowski she pulled at her chain, coming as far in their direction as she could, hungry, trying to get at them, stretching out her finger tips. Her rotting tits swayed like decaying pendulums.

"Frisky one this one. Hot, ain't she?"

Markowski reached out and gave the zombie a mock high five, then back-handed it in the side of the face, the thing moaning.

Harris felt disgust.

"You're probably wondering why in the hell we keep undead tied up in the basement," Markowski said.

Harris didn't say anything. He didn't like being this close to the undead, even one tied at bay.

"Well, Harris, let's face facts, a man has needs. And while we're facing those facts let's face this one: zombie pussy is still pussy, right? Another fact for ya, Harris, one not widely known. Zombie pussy is goddamn tight pussy. Tighter than a man's ass. You have any idea how tight that is Harris? You ever have you one? Zombie pussy I mean."

Markowski started laughing, "I'm fucking with you, Harris. We don't fuck 'em. Although, there was this one kid here who did just that, and you know what happened to him? He got sick and died, but not before his dick fell off."

The Pole got all serious, "And that's no joke. No, Harris, we use them for target practice."

Markowski drew his pistol, pointed it right at the undead's head. The thing reached for him, fingers clawing at the barrel, mouth lopping open.

"*Pssh! Pssh!*" Markowski mimicked the sound of a gun firing, moved the barrel around a little, leading the undead that reached for it.

"Yeah," he said, "she probably was a hot piece of ass in real life, don't you think? And she's a real redhead too, this one."

Harris didn't respond and Markowski didn't seem to expect him to. The tall man holstered his pistol.

"Sometimes I like to get down here close with one of them, use a knife or a hatchet. You ever use a blade on one of these things, Harris? It takes balls, man, 'cause you gotta get in close. And up close, that's where these fuckers can do the most damage.

"Natural inclination is going to be to drive that bitch right up into their chest or kidneys, maybe gut them, but these fuckers, they couldn't care less about that. Cut their heart out and show it them, they still come and get you. No, man, you stick them in the head, scramble whatever brains they got left."

Markowski finished with a look like he was immensely satisfied with himself.

"That's what we use 'em for."

"**WHAT ARE WE** going to do about Dom?" Buddy asked Harris one night on the roof. It was a question Harris had been meaning to ask Buddy, and he was perplexed when the other man asked him first because he'd hoped Buddy would have an answer.

They were a few feet apart in their respective sleeping bags on the roof of Dom's fortified house.

"That's what I've been thinking about," confessed Harris.

Harris and Buddy had been holed up with Dom for nearly a week. Eating Dom's food, sleeping under the stars on his roof, spying on the undead as they filed by on the street below.

"Do you think he'd want to come with us?" Harris asked.

The both of them looked across the roof to where Dom sat in a folding chair, next to the Viking Grill on which he cooked their meals, listening to oldies music on the battery-powered boom box he'd dragged up from somewhere in his house. Dom didn't go down into his house much since the incident with his wife.

"Well, I kind of have to ask you this question, Harris. Where are *we* going exactly?"

Dom liked the old novelty songs from the '50s and '60s, songs Harris remembered hearing when he was a kid driving around with his dad.

Gary Paxton was singing about the toughest caveman we all know, a cat by the name of Alley-Oop.

"I had an answer to that one once," said Harris, thinking of Manhattan. "But not anymore."

Dom was a big man who smoked like a chimney. Even now he was dragging on a Marlboro. Neither Harris nor Buddy could realistically imagine him hustling along with them on streets teeming more and more each day with zombies.

"Anywhere's as good as somewhere," added Harris. "I've got no place in mind. But I don't think I can just hang out here for ever."

"Yeah, I know. And all we're doing is eating this man's food."

"We'll talk to him in the morning."

"Sounds good," Buddy turned over on his back in the sleeping bag and looked up into the night sky. So peaceful above, continuing as it always had been and always would be, oblivious to and uncaring of to the hurly burly underneath.

Harris woke with the sun as Dom emerged from the port-a-potty. He'd been meaning to ask the heavy man how he'd managed to get the grill and the portable toilet up on the roof in the first place but it always slipped his mind when he had the opportunity.

The radio was low but Harris could hear the singer asking if one's chewing gum lost its flavor on the bedpost after a night.

"Morning," Dom said, firing up the grill and a smoke at the same time. The roof itself was butt-free because Dom would grind them out and toss them down into the street when he finished.

"Hey, Dom," Harris yawned, stood and stretched, prodded Buddy in the side with his foot, waking the other man.

"Who sings this song?"

"Lonnie Donegan," said Dom. "You know it?"

"My father used to listen to these songs when I was a kid. CBS FM, you know?"

"I knew it well," said Dom. "The Do-Wop shop, Cousin Brucie. Couldn't believe they did that to New York, took away our only oldies station."

"They brought it back."

"Yeah, they brought it back. But they brought it back without the fifties music. Just the sixties, seventies and eighties. Eighties *oldies*? What does it say about a man Harris when the music he grew up on isn't even considered oldies anymore? Has time really passed him by?"

"Minds much greater than our own have no doubt pondered this question and its ramifications, Dom."

They ate breakfast together, the last of the eggs Dom had stocked up in his fridge in the house with bacon and coffee. The milk was all gone but Dom had creamer and Harris sprinkled it liberally in his coffee.

"Damn this is a good cup of coffee, Dom," said Buddy. "Strong."

"How I've always drank it."

"What song is this?" Harris asked.

Dom smiled, "The Jolly Green Giant."

"Like in the vegetable commercials?"

"Remember those, huh?" Dom exhaled a stream of cigarette smoke. "Thought this band might have been before your time."

"Well, I never heard this one. Or if I did I just don't remember it."

"You ever heard the song 'Louie, Louie'?" asked Dom.

"Of course," said Harris. That song was an anthem at keg parties back when he went to college.

Dom winked, "Same band. The Kingsmen."

"Yeah," said Buddy. "But the Kingsmen *borrowed* this song from the Olympics."

"Now you're taking *me* back," admitted Dom.

Buddy continued, "'Big Boy Pete' was the name of the Olympics' song. And that wasn't the first time they inspired a song either. They did 'Western Movies.' You know, 'My baby loves the western movies.'"

"Yes they did that indeed," acknowledged Dom.

As they finished their meal Harris looked at Buddy and Buddy at Harris and Dom finally said, "You guys got something you want to say?"

"Yeah Dom, there's something me and Harris been meaning to talk to you about."

"You're thinking of leaving, right?"

"Yeah," said Harris.

"You want to come with us?"

"We want you to come with us Dom."

Dom laughed, "No, but thanks. In case you haven't noticed, I'm not exactly in any shape to be hotfooting it down these streets. And that's what we'd be doing. You've both seen how many of those things are down there, right? Every day they add to the collection."

Harris and Buddy nodded both. Things were getting depressing on the street. Over the last week the undead had grown thicker and it was rare now when the road below was scant of them. Some of the things screamed and cried out, which would have kept Harris awake if not for the ear plugs Dom gave him. Sometimes their wailing kept him up despite the plugs. And then there was the smell. Always the smell.

Buddy slept through the stink and the noise yet Harris suspected he could sleep through anything once he lay his head down.

"Where you guys planning on going anyway?"

"We don't know." Buddy told him the truth. "We're just going to do what we were doing when we met you."

"Run around looking for something better than what you got?" Dom put out the cigarette on the asphalt of the roof, filliped it over the ledge and lit up another.

"That's about it." Harris smiled, aware it was a stupid idea, knowing they'd probably die soon, hunted down by the zombies, boxed into a situation from which they couldn't escape. Thing was, sitting up on this roof, as pleasant as it was with the affable man's company, his food and music, Harris and Buddy were starting to feel boxed in already.

"Papa-oom-mow-mow, papa-oom-mow-mow," the Trashmen sang.

"What about you?" Buddy asked Dom.

Dom smoked. "Shit. I got enough food for another week or so still. Think I'm just going to sit up here and do my best to smoke myself into cancer. Keep an eye on the street, watch what happens."

"You sure that's what you want?"

"Yeah, Buddy. This is my house. I paid for this. Paid off the mortgage, put a lot of work into it. My castle you could say."

Dom laughed. "I couldn't figure another place I'd want to be, all things being equal of course.

"Don't go looking all serious, Harris," Dom exhaled a long plume of smoke. "Every man has to die. At least I know where I'll be. It's you two I'd worry about if I were you. Some of those bastards down there move quick."

"Yeah, I know."

"What we're saying though, Dom," Buddy tried, "Is if you wanted to come with us, it'd be cool man. You wouldn't slow us down. We'd stand with you."

"Yeah, we owe you, Dom. You been looking out for us, feeding us, letting us eat up all your food—"

Dom waved a hand, cutting him off, "Don't mention that, it's something I would have done for anybody, something anybody would have done for anybody."

"That's not true, Dom," said Buddy. "And you know it. Fact is, me and Harris have seen a fair share of the good in people brought out by this, but we've seen a lot more of the bad."

"It's the situation. You gotta remember you guys helped me out too." Dom moved his head, gesturing to the trap door that led down into his house, his meaning clear. "But I ain't going to stop you both from doing what you think you have to do. I'm going to ride this one out up here."

Buddy gave Harris a look that said, *we tried.*

"We appreciate all you've done for us," Harris told Dom. "And if we make it out of this, if there is some way to make it out of this, we'll come back for you."

"Don't worry about me," Dom waved his hand again. "You guys find a safe place somewhere, stay there. Send me a post card. Maybe a couple cartons of Marlboros."

Buddy smiled, but it was a smile bereft of joy, one of resignation. He looked to Harris and wondered how far they would get. If they left today would they live to see its close? Everything up for grabs, indeterminable, unwritten.

"UGH. HERE WE go again with the theology talk," said Brenner somewhat derisively, though these discussions never failed to elicit some small amount of mirth for him.

Al Gold stood up. "I'll leave the pondering of the imponderables to the goyim. Goodnight, gentlemen."

Gold left the fire for the shadows, the fifty-five gallon drum radiating warmth as the wood and fuel inside sent flames licking up.

"All I'm saying," Davon continued from where Brenner had interrupted him, "is something like *this* happens, makes you think there's got to be a god or something, don't there?"

"And why exactly would that be?" asked Panas, Eden's resident atheist.

"Because when some supernatural evil foul shit like this goes down," the football player reasoned it out, "it makes you realize there's got to be something more powerful than humanity at work in the universe."

"You know, Davon," Panas smoked a cigar and as he spoke he exhaled and watched the plume dissipate. "Before the scientific revolution people assumed any natural disaster was the work of God. You do know there was a noticeable decline in miracles with the spread of science, don't you?"

"Natural disaster?" Buddy asked. "Is that what this is, a natural disaster?"

"Just a turn of phrase, Buddy. Who knows what caused any of this."

"I'm not sure how I feel about the hand of any god in all this shit here," said Buddy. "But I'm trying to keep an open mind."

Beyond the northern wall a screamer let loose like a wild hyena, cackling and pounding on the sliding door.

"Nothin' natural about that shit, Holmes," said Brenner.

"See," said Davon, "thing is, God is like, *testing* us, man. Separate the wheat from the chaff, right?"

"Is that what all those billions of people that died are—chaff?" the contempt in Sal Bianaculli's voice obvious.

"Nah man, that's not what I'm sayin'."

"I don't know what it is about you people—"

"Sal," Camille put a hand on her husband's arm.

"'Scuse me?" Davon narrowed an eye.

"You people?" repeated Brenner. "No he just didn't."

"Yeah, you people."

"You mean us *niggers*?" asked Davon.

"No that's not what I mean and don't go making it fuckin' sound that way."

"Then what exactly do you mean then?"

"I mean 'you people' like me and my people, the Italians."

"Your people?"

"I mean 'you people' the same way your leaders could talk about 'their' people and that was okay and no one would bat a fuckin' eye. Don't try and insinuate that racism bullshit with me."

"If it sounds like a duck and quacks like a duck and—"

"Don't give me that bullshit. You have any idea how my people were treated when they came to this country?"

"Were Sacco and Venzetti brought here in chains?" Davon shot back.

"Fuckin' hear me out, all right? You guys get to talkin' about God, like belonging to the Mount Zion Church or whatever it's called entitles you to spell it out for everyone else."

"And you, Sal?" asked Brenner. "You take your marching orders from the pope?"

"Sometimes. But I got peoples out there, *my people*. And I know all of youse got yours out there past these walls, somewhere. And I re-fuckin'-fuse to believe my people are chaff. Some of them are good as gold."

"Come on man," Brenner implored Fred Turner. "You a preacher and whatnot."

"Not anymore," the elder Turner shrugged his shoulders. He'd lost his faith shortly after his wife had turned and tried to devour him. The only thing he had left of this earth was his boy.

"Listen," said Buddy. "I never could get into all this talk about God, man. I mean, there's so much fucked up about the world, even before this—" he gestured past the walls"—I mean, a tornado wipes out a trailer park and one person's left alive, right, one person, and the holy rollers jump on it like that's a miracle right there, a miracle that that one man or woman lived."

"And why it ain't a miracle?" demanded Brenner.

"No. Why *is* it? What about all those other fuckers got deposited all over the Wal-Mart parking lot? No one pipes up and says, 'Oh, there goes God again, He was responsible for that.'"

Davon asked, "So you're wondering if God is all knowing how can he be all mighty right?"

"I would if I gave a damn."

"How can a God that knows all be all good?" mused Panas, drawing on his cigar.

"And the opponents of religion," said Davon, "they say that if God knows all and still allows all this bad shit to happen, then God must be one sadistic motherfucker."

"Well, why isn't She?" asked Panas.

"You're fuckin' wit' me, right?"

"Just a little. Whereas the religious say that their God is *testing* them. You said it yourself a minute ago."

"I don't know." Buddy thought it out loud. "I always used to tell myself, if I ever saw something, like a ghost or something, that *that* right there would prove it to me, that'd reaffirm my faith. But this shit, I don't know. I got no clue. I ain't believing much of anything any more."

"My whole point," conceded Panas. "There has to be some rational explanation for this. An answer science can give us. We don't have to throw ourselves on the mercy of some mountain god or anything."

"Yeah, well we're not going to try and capture one of those things and start tinkering with it," said Brenner. "See if it got a soul in there somewhere."

"You can argue about this all night, guys," said Fred Turner. "Religious faith requires just that, faith. We aren't going to reconcile reason and belief. Theologians and scholars been trying that for thousands of years."

"For real," said Davon.

"And we aren't going to choose one over the other. For those who believe— that's what they need. For those who don't, I guess as long as they're okay with that, that's good enough for them then."

"That's what I've been saying all along," said Panas.

"So what you think happens when you die, Panas?" Brenner asked. "That's just it, man?"

"Yeah, that's just it. Like before you were born. What you think? Pearly gates and cherubs and the little baby Jesus and all?"

"On the for realla my nigga'," affirmed the other.

"What are you, an infant, Brenner?"

"Panas, that's not really helping things," said Buddy.

"What I never got was the whole purgatory thing," confided Sal Bianaculli. "Maybe that's what this is?"

"This right here is hell," said Davon.

"Tell me something I don't know," said Sal. "Tell me somethin'."

BEAR CAME BY his handle because of his look. At 6'2" and 320 pounds, the guys he rode with in the Pagans used to call him Bam Bam, partly after the wrestler, partly after his propensity to make like Barney and Betty Rubbles' adopted son on people he took a dislike to. Those were the days when wrestling was still cool, when hercs like Davey Boy Smith, the Ultimate Warrior, and Jake the Snake Roberts *owned* things. And he did resemble Bigelow. He shaved his head back then, at first because he thought it looked cool and it kept motherfuckers from grabbing onto his hair during brawls and tough man contests, but then his hairline started to recede and he would never consider being one of those suckers who did the comb over so, he kept it clean. But, like a bear, the rest of his body was covered with a thick, curly down.

Unlike Bam Bam, Bear had no tattoos on his skull, although there were others on his arms and calves. He'd earned the tear drop tattoo beneath his eye and the spider webs on his elbows the old fashioned way: he'd killed for them. The '90s came and everyone started getting ink on their bodies, trying to make some kind of fashion statement. One night hard looks from idiots who should have known better led Bear to beat the daylights out of five college boys in a bar. The one guy had his elbow spider-webbed. Bear had the frat boy outside on the street, grinding the unconscious kid's elbow back and forth on the cement between swigs of Jack. He had done a pretty good job of scraping most of the kids' tattoo and skin off when the cops surrounded him and let him have it with the tasers.

Those were the old days, and Bear feared for his soul because of them. After he nearly died fighting four men in the parking lot of another bar—one let him have it half a dozen times in the torso with a butterfly knife—he'd a couple months to lay around in a hospital bed and think about his life. Sure, his bros from the Pagans came by, even kept vigil early on from around the bed when it looked like he wasn't going to pull through.

But Bear made it and when he was finally able to get around the hospital in a walker he started to visit the chapel. At first he would sit there by himself and think. The third or fourth time he ran into the Chaplin and they started to have conversations. As he convalesced, Bear found himself looking forward more to his talks with the Chaplin than to his visits from his biker brothers. He decided that the life he'd been leading wasn't the one for him any longer, that down that road lay only despair and damnation.

He checked himself out of the hospital without letting any of his buds know. Bear sold his Harley and moved to a new city where he found work as a home health aid. The woman who hired him took one look at him and measured up his immense size as a boon. Bear was easily able to lift and carry his wards from their beds to their bathtubs or their toilets, whatever the job might entail. Years before he would have laughed at the thought of carrying frail old men and women around, of digging between their asses with rubber gloves to keep their shit from getting impacted, but that was before he'd been left for dead like a stuck pig in a parking lot and accepted Jesus Christ as his personal savior.

Years earlier he would have laughed and dismissed the holy rollers and high priests he saw on the television. He would have dismissed the hundreds of cars crammed into the mega church parking lots that he passed every Sunday on his chopper. If there was a God, Bear had believed back then, then that man was a pussy for letting everything get out of hand. Now Bear understood otherwise.

No more drinking, no more fighting, Bear found new ways to relieve his aggressive impulses. Powerlifting. He'd always admired the look of bodybuilders but thought them too prissy, too into their bodies. Besides, dieting wasn't much his thing. Bear joined a gym and started to hit the weights, learning from those around him that the form he had learned in the big house wasn't necessarily the way to lift. He'd always been naturally muscular but also heavy, and when he began lifting he gained more muscle fast. People who met him thought Bear a linebacker or, like Bam Bam, a pro wrestler.

He watched a group of powerlifters in his gym doing their thing and he was immediately hooked. Bear asked if he could train with them and they took him under their wing. He learned correct technique and before he knew it his squat, bench press and deadlift skyrocketed. Bear began to accompany the gym's power-lifting crew to meets and competed in the superheavyweight class. His first competition in upstate New York in Tribes Hill he squatted nearly 800 pounds raw, *without* a squat suit, and people's jaws just dropped.

At home or on the job as he watched over a snoring patient, Bear considered how he'd stumbled onto something at which he might be conceivably great at the same time as his spiritual awakening was blooming. Coincidence? He thought not. God intended him as a witness to his salvation, of this Bear was convinced.

The lifts continued to go up and soon everyone in the powerlifting world knew Bear by the name his parents had given him. He was squatting over 1,000 pounds in competition, benching in the mid-eights with a bench shirt, and was poised to possibly be the strongest man on Earth. Every chance he got, every interview, every appearance, he plugged his God and how he believed everything he did stemmed from His goodness.

The outbreak began and Bear survived, having to revert to his old ways somewhat. The killing scared him this time around because it still came so easily, but it allowed him to make it through those first few weeks, allowed him to keep others alive. Early on he wondered if killing these things trying to eat him and everyone else was wrong. But Bear figured if God didn't want him to be able to do it, he wouldn't be able to do it. His facility with violence allowed him to save who knows how many people. God *wanted* him to do that, just like God had wanted him to squat half a ton for the greater glory.

For some reason God led him to Eden. When Bear arrived he couldn't believe it, that this place was called Eden. Bear wasn't a fundamentalist. He didn't buy the Bible hook, line and sinker. But he thought that this too, was more than a coincidence, another of the serendipities in his life that spoke to something greater than the flesh and the blood. Of course there were assholes like Graham and Markowski, but Bear hoped he would be able to serve as an example to these men, to show them the correct way. And if the Lord ever revealed to him the need for it, Bear could easily utilize his baser skills to remove the two men from the planet.

So Bear wasn't afraid as he raised the man hole cover and peered out onto the street. But he wasn't stupid either. As much as they needed certain supplies, if the street they had chosen was filled with the undead, they wouldn't embark here. His God would let him know when it was his time. He didn't need to take added risks.

There were several zombies on the street but none had noticed him. Bear looked down the ladder at Markowski. Harris, and the others.

"We're good here."

"Then move your big ass," snarled Markowski, "and remember to keep it quiet."

Bear had to believe that there was hope even for the soul of a man like Markowski.

He shifted the cover out of the way and squeezed himself through onto the street. The steel pipe he carried clattered a little on the street as he rolled over and got up, and some of the undead turned to look. They started over, one of them running.

The booker reached him first. Half of its upper body was clothed and the other half exposed. The exposed half was denuded of skin and its rib cage and spine were clearly visible. Its condition didn't seem to slow it down.

"Here," Bear said, attracting the booker as it closed in on the manhole where Bobby Evers struggled out onto the street and Markowski only now gained his feet.

Bear wore thick leather gloves, similar to the ones he used to ride with, though the fingers on these were intact. The zombies couldn't bite through these gloves.

The Booker ran into the former biker and abruptly stopped like it had hit a brick wall, Bear's massive gloved hands wrapped around its throat. Keeping it at arms length, ignoring the swiping hands and gnashing teeth, Bear looked with pity upon the thing and brought his steel pipe down on its skull. A single blow brained it.

The other zombies, shamblers, were almost upon them. Markowski, Bobby and Stephanie Evers, Al Gold, Davon, Harris, and Buddy were all up on the street. They carried an assortment of clubs, machetes, knives, and other blunt instruments in addition to the holstered pistols, shotguns and assault rifles slung over their backs with and the empty knap sacks and duffel bags they'd brought along.

Buddy handed Bear his chain saw by its sling and Bear slung it across his broad back. He would never have been able to squeeze out onto the street with it such.

"What now?" Harris asked Markowski. It was Harris's first time outside of Eden since he and Buddy had arrived, and he didn't feel safe out on the street as eight or ten zombies bore down on them.

"Watch and learn," Markowski muttered, shifting his baseball bat and stepping forward to meet the first of the undead.

"Close it up," Buddy spoke down to Panas, "And keep an ear out on that radio."

Markowski swung and connected with the first zombie's head, knocking it down. It struggled to sit up.

"Fore." Markowski swung the aluminum bat like a golf club, catching the thing on the chin. It lay in the street and didn't move.

"There." Al Gold pointed to the store. "Pharmacy."

Harris felt the machete in his hand and watched as Markowski and Bear dispatched the zombies. Bear went about it with determination, treated it as something that needing doing. Markowski seemed to be enjoying it, relishing each swing.

"Hey, Buddy." Markowski pointed into the sky like Babe Ruth, got into his stance, and swung. The head on the half-rotten zombie he'd chosen popped off its body and rolled down the street.

Markowski laughed, "Aw shit, you seen that? Home run! Barry Bonds ain't got shit on me."

Davon clipped the locks of the riot gates over the entrance to the pharmacy store. The locks lay broken and useless on the sidewalk, and he rolled the gate up.

"Open the door, Buddy."

Buddy leveled the Striker shotgun and fired once. The lock mechanism and most of the door's glass disappeared. Davon pushed it open and entered the store.

"Here they come to play," said Markowski. "Look at them, Harris."

The shotgun blast had drawn the undead, dozens of them coming from seemingly everywhere.

"Harris, let's go," Bear took his arm. "Get what we came for."

They filed into the drug store, everyone except Markowski.

"You coming?" Buddy called out the door.

"Don't go getting any ideas, locking me out here with these things," Markowski said, and clubbed a zombie over the head repeatedly. "Not that I wouldn't enjoy it."

"Then let's go."

"Let me get a few more licks in."

"I'm closing this gate, Markowski."

The big Pole glared at Buddy but turned and entered the store, muttering under his breath. Buddy pulled the riot gate down behind them.

"How do we secure this?"

"I got it," said Al Gold, preparing an acetylene torch. Gold went about welding the gate closed.

Stephanie Evers took a look around. No electricity meant the alarm hadn't gone off but there were no lights either. The store was huge and eerie, even disquieting.

She had been in other stores like this before and had a general idea as to their lay out.

"Okay," said Markowski. "Get your shopping lists out."

Without another word he stalked off down an aisle by himself.

"Best thing is to pair up, stick together," Bobby Evers told Harris and Buddy.

"Come on, Harris," motioned Bear, and the other man followed him.

Buddy walked off in the opposite direction with Davon.

"Al," Bobby said. "You keep an eye on things up here."

"No problem." Al popped himself up onto the counter between two cash registers. He leaned back and looked behind the counter, made sure nothing lurked there. And not a thing did. When Bobby and Stephanie disappeared down another aisle he reached into his coat and pulled out his flask.

God damn that whiskey tasted good.

Stephanie followed Bobby past an aisle of greeting cards, gift wrap and bows.

Harris and Bear moved their flashlights back and forth as they walked.

"Look at that," said Bear.

At the end of the aisle they were in, where another intersected, boxes of female hygiene products were scattered across the floor. Some of the boxes were open. Tampons and pads lay all over. Many of the pads were soaked with blood, as if someone had tried to staunch a wound with them.

Bear whistled. "Let's keep our eyes open."

His flashlight lit her up at the end of the aisle. Markowski saw it standing alone next to a display of batteries. Batteries were on his list anyway so he walked towards the zombie, making as little noise as he could.

In life she must have been hot. She had her back turned to Markowski so he got a good view of the low cut jeans, the whale tail thong peeping out. Her skin was ashy and grey now but he could still make out the tramp stamp tattoo, some kind of bullshit sun rise, the rays radiating across her waist and up her lower back.

"Hey, sexy."

She turned and moaned at him.

"Oh baby, you've seen better days."

Her halter top torn open revealed the remains of a mutilated breast. Someone had done a number on her face as well, one eye missing and most of her teeth knocked out. Looked like she'd had her head stepped on a few times.

Markowski didn't wait for the zombie to stagger towards him. He moved in, grabbed her by a shoulder and spun her around, reached down, grasped the thong at her lower back and tore it up and out, ripping it free.

"Goddamn, I always wanted to do that," he laughed.

As the zombie turned to face him again he thrust the baseball bat like a pool stick, cracking it hard in the forehead. She went down and started to shake on the floor.

"Believe me darling," Markowski unzipped his pants and pulled out his cock. "I ain't taking any pleasure in this."

He relieved himself on the seizing zombie.

Al Gold worked at keeping his buzz going. He didn't buy all that shit people said about alcoholism being a disease. No one chose cancer, but he chose to drink. He'd stop drinking when and if he was ever goddamn ready, or when the alcohol ran out. No one was making it anymore. Like Insulin. Al wondered how many people had died because they couldn't get that or other medications they needed.

He got the shakes in the morning until he took that first slug of whiskey, but he had long since stopped caring that the others would notice. The black kid, Davon, he didn't say nothing about Al's drinking, and Al didn't say nothing about Davon's pot smoking and porn watching.

Al popped himself up off the counter and panned his flashlight up and down the bank of registers. The candy bars and chewing gum all looked intact. He thought how everyone could go for some chocolate once in awhile and decided to fill his knapsack with candy. The others would be stocking up on the vitals.

Hope they like Hersheys. Al dumped boxes of plain chocolate bars, chocolate with almonds, and peanut butter cups into his bag. Some of the stuff had a shelf life of two or three years, so he figured it was all still good to eat.

He spotted the box of peanut chews under the licorice and knew he was in luck. He'd enjoyed peanut chews since he was a kid. As he dumped the contents of the box into his bag with the others, Al spied a spiral notebook closed on the counter.

"What's that about?" he asked aloud.

Davon was jittery. "You hear something?"

"It's all that weed you be smoking," said Buddy. "Making you paranoid."

"Being paranoid has kept me alive up to this point."

"Can't argue with that. Just keep an eye open and let's fill up on these cans."

Buddy and Davon had found the grocery aisle of the pharmacy. There were several shelves of canned items and packaged foods. They steered clear of the wrapped breads and boxes of moldy cookies and cakes and instead tossed cans of vegetables, soups, and meats into their bags.

"Spam," said Buddy. "I never thought I'd be eating this stuff."

"What's wrong with Spam?"

Stephanie Evers looked back at her husband as she knelt, rummaging through her pack, trying to make room for more toilet paper. Bobby was an aisle down, loading up on over-the-counter pain medications, his flashlight aimed in the opposite direction so nothing could sneak up on him. Stephanie thought how it would be easier if they could just take a truck or van, fill it up with all the stuff they needed and drive it back into Eden. That had been done once or twice, until the streets began to swell with all those zombies and the last van expedition that'd gone out hadn't come back.

She wondered what had happened to those people. They were probably dead. No way they could survive for long without shelter on the streets. Stephanie could imagine there being hundreds of zombies pressed against the riot gate they'd come in through. Getting into stores was the easy part. Getting out required a distraction.

What was that?

Stephanie jerked her head to the left and stared towards the end of the aisle, bringing her flashlight up at the same time. As the beam lit it up she thought she saw an arm pass, swinging like someone walking might do.

She trained the beam there and listened. Nothing. The only sounds came from her husband working down the aisle.

Still…

Stephanie wrapped her hand around her pistol. It was a .380 and she had had plenty of practice with it. She stood with the pistol and the flashlight and looked back at Bobby, but he wasn't paying attention.

"Bobby," she whispered to him, but he didn't hear her, and she didn't want to call out loud in case there really was something there.

Stephanie started forward, slowly, carefully, the pistol extended ahead of her, ready to shoot anything that popped around the corner.

"Bingo," said Bear. Harris had climbed over the pharmacy counter and opened the door to allow the larger man in. Around them loomed shelf after shelf of prescription items.

"You got that list?" Harris asked.

Bear produced it from under his leather vest, unfolded it and shined his light on it.

"Harris, you keep an eye open, I'll find this stuff."

Harris walked the aisles behind the pharmacy counter, bathing each with the flashlight. There was no one to be seen. Nothing to be heard aside from the rattle of a bottle of pills as Bear picked it up and examined it.

Al Gold opened the marble notebook and examined it. Someone had written *Journal of My Life* and their name on the first page. There was a month and a date, both coming after the outbreak. He leafed through it. There were only twelve or fifteen pages written in, but the person who'd kept it wrote small and neat in cursive.

This should be interesting, he thought.

He looked around and then opened to the first entry.

December 2.

I'm going to keep this journal or diary or whatever the hell it is for as long as I can. Whether I make it or not, those things don't eat books, so maybe some day people will find this and use it to make some sense of just what the hell has happened to us.

I really don't know where to begin. There are twenty-five of us hiding out here. The news said to stay put, but there hasn't been any news in a few days. We pulled the gates and locked them from the outside—they don't seem to be able to break the locks, thank goodness for us—and have been holed up in here since.

Al yawned. *Boring.* He took another swig from his flask and turned to the last page of writing to see how this story ended.

Harris shined the light on the closed metal door. There was a deadbolt on his side of it.

He'd agreed to accompany Markowski and Bear on this foraging mission only when Buddy had said he'd go. The more he got to know the men, the more he thought he'd misjudged Bear. The man had badass written all over him, but he wasn't made of the same stuff as Markowski. Or, if he had been, he wasn't anymore.

Bear didn't laugh at Markowski's crude jokes the way others did. The others, like Bianaculli or Bert or even that young guy Thompson, they laughed at Markowski's garbage because they were afraid of him. Bear didn't laugh, and Harris thought it was because Bear didn't find Markowski humorous.

Markowski seemed to have a hard on for Buddy. Little comments and looks, busting his chops, jig-this and jig-that. Buddy did a good job ignoring it for the most part, but he and Harris had talked. Harris wondered where Bear would stand when things went down. Who's side? He'd hate to have the big tattooed biker type to contend with.

Harris pressed his ear to the door and listened.

Where did it lead? Outside? Maybe a basement?

He shifted the Colt Python to his left hand and took the flashlight in his right. It looked like the door opened towards him on the left and he'd want to shine that light down the stairs or wherever it was he was going to be opening it up onto.

He used the thumb and forefinger of his right hand to twist the deadlock and tried the door again.

Stephanie reached the end of the aisle and moved the light as far to the left and as far to the right as she could. Dust particles fluttered in the mote of light.

She stepped out of the aisle. There was a film processing counter in front of her, stretching down to the pharmacy. She thought she could see some light in that direction.

No zombies. Just to be sure, she walked around the end of the aisle she had just stepped from, giving herself a wide birth, and shined the light up the adjoining aisle, this one running parallel to that she'd just exited. Empty.

Now I'm seeing things, she thought and went back to her knapsack, setting the .380 down on the floor, picking up a four pack of ultra-soft Charmin, thinking of the old Mr. Whipple commercial, hearing her husband coming up behind her—

"You know, Bobby—"

She turned but the thing upon her was not her husband.

February 7

I don't know what is going to happen now. First they got through the door down in the basement and then one of them bit Cheryl. Mark got bit too, but no one is going to fuck with him. He's got a gun, the only gun in this goddamn place. He already shot the store manager, dumb-ass stupid enough to go near him when he said not to. Tried to get the gun away from him. This place is insane.

We did what we could for Cheryl but when it looked like she was dead we opened the door and tossed her down into the basement with all the others. Thing is, she wasn't dead. We had to listen to her scream and cry as those things in the basement got her. With that door to the outside open there's no telling how many of them are down there. Christ, we should have just done what Burns said, wait for her to come back, bash her fucking brains in.

Somewhere in the dark, Stephanie screamed.

"Oh shit," muttered Al Gold, tossing the notebook down and hauling ass up an aisle, yelling for Markowski as he ran, for Bear and for Buddy, for anybody and everybody.

The door slammed into Harris, flying open under the weight from the other side. He lost the pistol and fell backwards, dumped on his rear. He managed to hold onto the flashlight and directed it upwards—

Zombies avalanched through the doorway, a tangle of arms and legs, massed at the top of a stairwell, with more behind them. Harris braced his feet against the metal door and pushed, fighting the weight pressing against it.

"Bear!" he yelled, losing the battle, the door inching open.

Stephanie Evers brought her arms up to protect her face as the zombie jumped on her, howling like a banshee.

Bobby Evers ran towards his wife, the light from his flash jolting up and down. Fear coursed through him. Steph's light rolled about on the aisle floor and all he could make out was a struggle, an undead thing on top of her.

"No!" Bobby screamed, reaching the two of them, not thinking, leveling the .30-.30 hunting rifle he carried and firing it.

The zombie reared up and turned, its mouth bloody. Bobby shot again, the bullet punching out the back of the beast's head in a shower that streaked the cartons of plastic wrapped toilet paper.

"Stephanie," Bobby dropped his rifle and knelt with his wife. She was wheezing and there was a hole in her throat from which blood bubbled and squirted. She was trying to say something to him, and as he watched and held her the color in her face waned and her life seeped out between his fingers.

"No, baby, don't die on me," begged Bobby, trying to staunch the blood with his fingers, "Don't die! Don't die!

"I'm sorry baby, I'm sorry."

The wound in her neck had been caused by his first round.

"Oh-Christ-Oh-Jesus-Oh-Mary-Mother-of-God-I'm-sorry-I'm-sorry-I'm-sorry…"

Bobby failed to notice the bites on his wife's hands.

Harris lost his battle with the door at the same moment Bear materialized behind him. The door flew open, spilling zombies out onto the floor, others staggering through the opening, a decomposing booker leaping into the air, intent on landing on Harris.

Bear grabbed the thing by its throat in mid air and slammed it into a wall of shelves, hundreds of pill bottles scattering over the tiled floor. His hand still around its neck, Bear whipped it against the next wall of shelves like a child's doll. He squeezed his hand, the muscles in his forearm tensing, and Harris watched in disbelief as the man tore the thing's head from its neck.

Harris scrambled, found his Python, and fired from his back, aiming around Bear's legs—the man mountain standing there blocking the aisle, swinging his pipe in the enclosed area and busting heads—at the faces of the zombies thrashing on the floor, at the domes of the ones appearing at the top of the stairs.

"Let's go Harris," Bear threw the cylinder with all his might, the pipe catching a zombie across the chest like a clothesline, knocking it from its feet.

Bear reached down and dragged Harris up with one hand, freeing his mini-Uzi at the same time. The mini-Uzi looked like a toy pistol in Bear's big paw, and he fired it in crisp controlled bursts, ripping holes in the necks and faces of the nearest undead as he backed away from the door, pulling Harris with him.

Bear let him down and Harris holstered the Python, cross-drawing his twin nines and following the big man.

"Get my bag," Bear shouted, opening the door to the pharmacy section.

Harris scrambled behind the pharmacy counter, finding Bear's bag, aware that the undead were pouring out of the basement as if someone had loosed a faucet of them. He pulled the zipper closed and launched himself head first over the counter, knocking down a display with pamphlets on health insurance plans.

Bear pulled the door to the pharmacy closed behind him. It had a glass window waist-high and the zombies started to rattle against it as he reloaded the mini-Uzi with a fresh stick.

Harris considered himself lucky that he didn't break his neck as he splayed on the floor and scrambled to get up. Zombies started to try to pull the same move he'd just made, albeit much slower and even less gracefully. As they clambered over the counter from the other side, Harris fired his nine millimeters. The limp zombies were pushed out of the way, dragged down by the ones behind as groans filled the air.

"Oh shit," Markowski said, reaching Harris and Bear. "You guys throw a party and don't invite me?"

"Markowski! Bear!" Al Gold reached them, out of breath.

"One minute, Al," Markowski picked his targets with his FAMAS bullpup assault rifle and blasted them as Harris reloaded his pistols.

"No, Markowski, there's too many of them," Gold nearly stumbled over his words as he tried to get them out.

Buddy and Davon reached the group and dropped their sacks, bringing their weapons up and firing.

For a moment it looked like the humans would be successful in repelling the undead. The rips of Bear's mini-Uzi, the pops of pistols and cracks of assault rifles fired on semi-auto seemed like they might drive the beasts back.

But the supply of zombies wasn't dwindling. If anything, there were more, moving about in the shadows of the pharmacy. The glass portion of the door broke and a dozen arms reached through.

"Let's go!" yelled Buddy, snatching up his saddle bags, slinging them over his shoulder and jetting down an aisle-way.

The others shouldered their packs and followed, reloading on the run.

Markowski pulled the pin on a thermite grenade and handed it to one of the reaching arms. The zombie took it, its arm disappearing inside the door frame.

"Oh shit!" Markowski half laughed as he turned and ran. The explosion knocked him off his feet and half way down the aisle. He brushed himself off, found the FAMAS assault rifle and flashlight and shined the halogen lamp back the way he'd come.

The blast had taken the door off the frame and zombies poured through onto the main floor. They burning and bellowing as they came.

"Oh, we're in some shit now!" yelled Davon. "Stick near me, roommate!"

Al Gold looked over his shoulder and decided that's *exactly* what he would do: stick to the younger, bigger guy like glue.

"Markowski!" Buddy drew their attention to a side door.

"Where's that lead?"

"Let's find out!"

Buddy blew the lock off the door with one barrel and Bear followed up with a kick when they reached it. Bright sunlight poured in. The six of them shielded their eyes from the sudden change in light and burst out into a deserted alleyway. Davon pushed the door closed behind them and leaned against it.

The passage ran between the drug store and another building. At one end a brick wall, at the other a green fence. There was a space of about six inches under the fence and they could see that the fence bordered the boulevard fronting the burning store.

"That way," said Markowski.

"Wait," said Harris. "Where's Bobby and Stephanie?"

They looked at one another and then at the door.

"Ah shit," Al Gold shook his head.

"They're dead," Markowski spat like that was that.

"Not yet they're not," Davon almost whispered.

"This is some bullshit," Buddy summed up their situation.

"Come on, we don't have time for this shit," protested Markowski.

Bear didn't say anything. He reloaded his mini-Uzi, unslung the chainsaw and cranked it up.

"What the fuck are you doing?" Markowski's words were half drowned out in the roar.

Bear placed one giant hand on Davon's shoulder and moved him out of the way. The door swung open and the huge man disappeared inside the building. Al Gold shrugged and slammed it shut again, leaning against it.

"Buddy, you've got the walkie talkie," said Harris, slamming a fresh clip into one of his guns. "Don't let him leave without us!"

Before Buddy could object, Harris pulled Al out of the way and followed after Bear.

"Well fuck me."

"Shut up, Markowski," growled Buddy.

"Wah tah dah then, Pootie Tang."

"Uh, guys." Al Gold pointed down the alley. The green fence was mounted on hinges and swung back as zombies stumbled their way.

"Come on bitches." Markowski shouldered the FEMAS. "I've got something for all of you! I'm Tony Montana, baby!"

Gunfire. A lot of it. But Bobby Evers ignored it.

Stephanie gurgled one last time and went limp.

"Oh Jesus, no," cried Bobby, pressing his wife's head to his chest.

He sat there holding her, sobbing. He'd shot her. Shot his own wife. Hadn't aimed good and blown a hole in her neck. Stephanie had died because her husband, the man who'd sworn to love and cherish and protect her for always, had shot her.

There was no more gunfire inside but he could hear... something. He smelled smoke.

Bobby wiped the tears out of his eyes and followed the beam of light cast by Stephanie's flashlight. At the end of the aisle there were legs moving his way. He didn't recognize any of them.

Stephanie moved in his arms and he pushed her away involuntarily.

She sat up and hissed at him.

Bobby started to move, slipping in the blood that had puddled on the floor, fighting to keep his body from freezing on him.

Stephanie stood and lurched his way. The aisle behind her was a wall of zombies.

He took up his .30-.30 and leaned against a shelf in a crouching position.

"God help me," he cried and aimed at his wife's head, but he couldn't pull the trigger.

He only hoped his own end would be quick.

"Stephanie!"

Bobby screamed as his wife's body shook, gouts of blood spouting from her shoulders and chest, jolting her back. He turned around and Harris come walking down the aisle firing both of his nine millimeters over Bobby where he sat.

Bobby turned back around in time to see Stephanie's corpse catch one in the upper lip, and then he was firing his hunting rifle at the undead that stepped on and over her body where it lay.

"Let's go, Bobby!"

Harris motioned behind them. Evers followed the other man and they ran in the dark. A glow emanated from one end of the building where fires spread. Around them the sounds of things moving, knocking into shelves, searching.

Harris found his flashlight where he had it jammed it in his jeans and flicked it on. They were cornered. At either end of their aisle the zombies gathered. *Damn*, thought Harris, *they move fast for things that move slow.*

"This is it, Bobby," he thought of saying as he reloaded his nine millimeters one last time, jacking fresh rounds into the chambers. He didn't say it. Bobby had just seen his wife die and he would be dead soon enough.

Harris and Bobby waited, letting the undead get closer. They hissed and spat and moaned as they came. The first group was nearly on them when lightning exploded, a stream of lead ripping down into the zombies, skulls popping, bodies dropping.

"Bear!" Harris yelled, adding his nines to the mix. Bobby swallowed whatever was in his throat and followed suit, sending rounds through the undead.

"Praise Him!"

The mini-Uzi fired out, Bear cloaked in shadows where he crouched atop the shelves, the sound of an engine firing up, almost catching, then again, this time catching, and Bear launched himself from the ceiling, chain saw swinging.

He landed amidst the swarm, his sheer size bowling many down. Bear regained his feet and howled back at them like some insane beast of a man, brandishing the chainsaw, cutting through legs, torsos and heads. Blood gushered and jetted and he felt it splash across his face and chest and arms and he was lost in the fury.

Harris fired out the nine millimeters and reloaded.

The zombies around them were down but dozens more advanced.

The chainsaw revved mightily once again and then idled.

Harris shone his light on Bear. The man looked like something born of a slaughterhouse, covered from head to toe with gore, blood and pieces of flesh dripping from the chain saw in his hands. Zombies and parts of zombies lay around him, some limbs still kicking.

Bear sawed through the shelves on one side of the aisle, plastic and wood chips flying, clearing a path into the next.

"Harris. Bobby. Go."

"You too Bear," said Harris

"Not today."

Harris looked at the other. Blood dripped from his brow and glistened on his shaven dome. He was awash with gore. Harris couldn't tell how much of it, if any, was Bear's. The look in the man's eyes was something from another planet, something beyond intense, maybe insane.

"I know my path," Bear said as if to himself. He turned, cranked up the chainsaw and waded into the next group of zombies.

"Now, Bobby!" Harris pushed Evers through the sawed-off shelves into the next aisle. He squeezed himself through and didn't look back.

They hustled up the aisle and reached the intersection where another crossed.

"This way!" Harris coughed, smoke and noise all around them, the shuffling sounds of moving feet in the darkness, the crackle of greedy flames, the chain saw's drone muffled. Then Bear roaring at the undead in tongues, his words indecipherable.

A square of light opened up before them with Al Gold and Davon peering through at them.

Harris pushed Bobby ahead into the alley, into the light, the chain saw buzzing well behind them, silenced as he pushed the door closed.

"Where's Buddy?" Harris asked.

"In the street with Markowski," said Al Gold, fumbling with his acetylene torch.

"Not now," Harris said, "let's just go!"

"Where's Stephanie and Bear?" Al asked on the run.

Harris shook his head.

In the street in front of the store Buddy and Markowski stood back to back in a circle of zombies. Markowski swung his aluminum bat, cracking skulls, cursing at the undead. Buddy steadied one hand with the other, squeezing off rounds from the nine millimeter. Markowski was roaring lines from *Scarface* at the undead, "You want to go to war? We'll take you to war!"

"Down!" Harris swung his M-16 into play.

"Hey assholes!" Davon called at the zombies.

Buddy looked at Markowski with his bloody bat, thought otherwise, and hit the deck.

Harris opened fire with the sixteen, Davon and Al Gold joining him in a fusillade that peppered the street.

When their weapons were empty Markowski stood in a circle of unmoving zombies with the blood-streaked baseball bat in his hands. The Pole looked down at himself and then at Buddy who shrugged as he reloaded the Striker shotgun, and finally at the three men on the street, smoke rising from the barrels of their weapons.

"You pussies, you could have shot me."

"He said get down," noted Davon.

The street on either end was filling with zombies.

"There!" Al Gold pointed out a manhole cover a few buildings down.

Everyone ran towards it except Markowski. He stood there muttering to himself, reloading the FEMAS, the baseball bat resting against his leg.

The sound of rending metal and sparks and the front gate cleaved in two, roiling plumes of black smoke rolling out onto the boulevard, something big and bloody in a leather vest with a chainsaw bursting from the pharmacy.

"Nice of you to fucking join us again," Markowski spat between rounds from the FEMAS.

"Bear!" Harris yelled to the man from down the block where they were clambering down into the sewers.

"You bit?" demanded Markowski.

"No," said Bear.

"How do I know?"

"You bite anyone? You'll have to take my word for it," Bear walked off up the block towards the others, zombies reeling out of the pharmacy and smoke, the one in the lead shorn of both arms, several alight.

"Goddamn frog piece of shit." The FEMAS was empty, and Markowski threw it down. He took his own sweet time walking up the block, stopping along the way to brain zombies with the bat.

"Let's go, Markowski!" yelled Buddy, the street filling with zombies.

"Yeah, yeah. I'm coming!"

GRAHAM SENT THEM into the sewer as an advance squad meant to infiltrate Jericho, lull its inhabitants into complaisance through an overwhelming show of force and, if need be, overcome any resistance and enforce compliance. "Time for the empire to expand," he had only half joked.

Unbeknownst to Graham, there had been a change in plans.

Buddy fell to the back of the line as they slogged their way through the subterranean channels, Harris up ahead, second from the front. The men moved quietly, the route second hand from their previous travels.

As always the underground was dissonantly still, the only sounds their discordant own, the only light their flashlights and the beams of weak sunlight coming through the perforations in the random manhole cover overhead. It had rained the day before and water dripped down onto them from drainage pipes. Some tunnels were already flooded, inaccessible. No maintenance, no upkeep, no passage.

Harris looked back in the gloom and it looked to him like Buddy chin-nodded. He hoped he'd seen right.

"Hold up." Harris leveled the M-16 with the M-203 mounted under the barrel at Bianaculli ahead of him, the assault rifle taut on its sling, the .357 filling his right hand, covering the men behind him, an awkward position he hoped no one tested him in.

"What the fuck is this?" asked an incredulous Bert.

"This is that time when shit don't go according to plan." Buddy jostled Paul and Markowski forward, the muzzle of the Striker shotgun threatening.

"Okay, all together now," Buddy continued coolly. "Put your firearms down, nice and slow."

Markowski, caught off guard, looked pissed, the barrel of his AKS-74 lowered. Buddy watched him. The stock of the AKSU folded, it'd take Markowski only a moment to bring the weapon up into firing position. A moment was all Buddy needed to blow the man in two.

"Go for it, Markowski," said Buddy. "You know you want to."

Bianaculli placed his assault rifle on the wet ground, but Bert and Ralph searched the dark for Markowski's. The big Pole growled and did not acknowledge them.

"Lay 'em down," Harris ordered, the .357 holstered, both hands on the M-16/M-203.

Harris and Buddy covered the remaining three men as they placed their assault rifles and shotguns on the cement floor. Their pistols were still holstered and their knives were sheathed.

"What the hell, Harris?" Ralph asked.

"Like the man said, Ralph, change of plans. Sal, get back there with the others."

"I ain't with these guys, Harris. You know what I mean."

"We look like we give a good goddamn fuck?" said Buddy. "Get back in line."

Markowski snickered, "You can take the nigger outta the jungle, but…"

Buddy slammed him in the face with the barrel of the Striker and Markowski staggered back, but didn't go down. He regained his footing, brushed a hand across his nose, looked at the blood there. His tongue darted out, tasted it. He said, "Mmmm," laughed again, stepping back to his original position.

"First blood drawn, Buddy," said Markowski. "Won't be the last."

"Can we just shoot this son of a bitch right here right now?" asked Harris.

Markowski glared at him.

"Wait," was all Buddy said to Harris. Then to Bert, Sal and Ralph, "Now look. Graham's been running Eden like he's some goddamn liege lord. That shit's about to end. What ya'll four need to do is think on this. You want to leave with Graham when he leaves, or you want to change your ways, try and fit in with the new Eden?"

"Shit, man," said Bianaculli. "You don't got to convince me."

"Pussy," spat Markowski. "I'm going to kill you right after I kill the nigger."

"It's about staying alive, man," pleaded Bianaculli.

"Up here, Sal, do them for me." Buddy extended a handful of plastic handcuffs.

"Oh, you got to be kidding," said Ralph. "What the fuck are you two planning?"

"We're gonna go back to Eden," said Buddy, the barrel of the Striker and his eyes never leaving Markowski. "Have a little talk with Graham."

"Do it Sal," Harris gestured with the sixteen.

Mumbling apologies, Bianaculli fastened the hands of Bert then Ralph behind their backs.

"Use two pairs each," said Harris.

"Two?" Bert asked. "Goddamn, Harris."

Buddy and Harris kept their flashlights and their firearms aimed at the men as Bianaculli bound them.

"Get behind that asshole when you handcuff him," Buddy told Sal, referring to Markowski. "He tries to use you as a human shield, I will kill you both."

"You read my mind with those voodoo-jig powers or something?" Markowski growled.

Sal stepped around Markowski and took the big Pole's wrists, securing them behind his lower back.

"That's right, Sal," said Markowski. "Leave a little slack, just like that."

"I ain't leaving any slack, Buddy," Sal sounded worried that Buddy would believe the other.

Markowski mimicked him, a high pitched whine, the contempt clear in his voice.

"Now you," Harris said to Bianaculli when the latter had finished.

"You're kidding, right Harris?" pleaded Bianaculli. "Look, I said I'm not down with these guys's program."

"That's all good," said Buddy. "But you still need to shut your mouth the fuck up and listen to the man."

Bianaculli turned around with his hands behind his back, Harris using two pairs of the heavy duty plastic cuffs to immobilize his arms.

Harris and Buddy moved quickly from that point, stripping the men of their side arms and knives, their grenades, anything that could be used as a weapon.

"So that's it then?" spat Markowski. "You're gonna leave us down here while you go and talk it out with Graham?"

"Talk it out," Buddy mulled it over.

"I'd suggest you guys just sit here and wait, we'll be back," said Harris, stuffing two pistols in the waistband of his jeans, slinging Ralph's AK-47 over his shoulder.

"Directly," added Buddy.

"Sit here with no weapons?" Panic crept into Ralph's voice.

"Oh come on man," Markowski said to Buddy. "We both know how this is gonna end."

"Tell us how's it going to end then?" Harris buried the muzzle of his sixteen in Markowski's jaw.

The Pole turned his eyes to look at Harris, then focused them on Buddy, moving his head to get the muzzle out of the side of his cheek so he could talk.

"Me and your buddy here, the nigger, we're gonna go toe to toe. One of us isn't going to walk away."

"Bullshit," said Harris. "If you don't shut up I'm going to end it for you right here."

"Don't kid yourself, Harris." Markowski's eyes never left Buddy. "You don't have it in you."

"Harris." He looked over and Buddy was stripping off all his weapons, the Striker, the pistol, grenades, lying them all atop his saddle bags away from the water pooled down the center of the sewer pipe.

"What are you doing Buddy?" demanded Harris.

"Me and Markowski going to go do just like he said."

"Buddy, come on."

Markowski grinned, anticipation in his eye.

"Buddy, you're crazy."

Buddy bent down and retrieved his blade, then went over to Markowski's pile of stuff and found the Pole's knife.

"When we're finished," Buddy told Markowski. "I'm going to cut your head off with your own knife. And then I am going to bring it back here and give it to these men."

The Pole laughed derisively.

"When *we're* finished," Markowski cackled, "I'm gonna pop your eye out and skull fuck ya. Fuck, I'm gonna cut *your* head off and stump fuck ya. How's that sound?"

"Get up," Buddy told him.

"When I'm finished, I'm gonna hang you from a fuckin' tree in Eden. Goddamn Mississippi wind chime."

"Buddy—"

"Harris, wait here. I'm not back in ten minutes, means I won't be. He comes back here, kill him. Kill him dead."

"*When* I win," said Markowski, "I will not be coming back here. Fuck all of you, and fuck Eden too. Buncha pussies."

"Move." Buddy prodded Markowski with the flat of his blade, angling the halogen bulb ahead of them.

Harris and his three captives listened as the steps of the other two men receded, the light disappearing around a bend. Soon they heard nothing.

"Harris, come on man," said Sal. "Untie me, man."

"Sit tight, Sal."

"I'm not *with* them man, you know that. I went along pretty much just so they wouldn't mess with me and Camille."

"Markowski always had his doubts about you, Bianaculli," said Bert. "Said we had to watch that Italian nigger. That's what he called you."

"Shut up, Bert."

"No, you shut up, Sal. Markowski told me day came we made you disappear, I could have Camille."

"Fuck you, you piece of—"

"Idiots!" hissed Harris, "You keep carrying on, the zombies are going to hear you and they *will* find a way down here. And I will not stick around to keep them off your sorry asses."

The thought seemed to sober both men up and they were silent.

"Who do you think will win?" Ralph asked nervously sometime later.

"Markowski's a goddamn animal," opined Bert.

"Yeah, but Buddy's no joke either," proffered Sal.

"But Markowski is a fuckin' maniac," Ralph shook his head.

"Has it been ten minutes yet?"

"Shut—up," warned Harris, a pause between the two words. "Listen."

Someone was coming towards them. They could hear him before they saw him, and then they saw his light reflecting off the corner up ahead.

"Damn," said Sal. "Untie me, Harris! If it's Markowski he's going to kill me as soon as he kills you!"

Harris had the M-16 raised to his shoulder, sighting down the barrel.

The man rounded the bend and spoke as he came, "Muck a lucka high..."

"Mucka hiney ho," Harris finished and raised the light and shined it on his friend.

He let out his breath and lowered the sixteen and breathed hard.

Buddy came to them and tossed something that landed in the dark by Bert's sneakered feet.

"What the hell is—"

Harris shined his light on Markowski's severed head. The eyes lolled in their sockets.

"Christ, Buddy," sputtered Sal. "You keep your word."

Ralph retched off to the side.

Harris didn't know what to say, so he said, "You da man."

"You da man," Buddy shot back with a short laugh. Like he hadn't just finished sawing someone's head off.

"What's next?" Harris asked Buddy as the other man retrieved his gear.

"Let's secure these guys to some of these pipes, take their stuff, go and get Graham."

"You guys can't leave us here!" Bert immediately protested.

"Shut up idiot!" Sal told him. "Be glad they're not killing us. We make too much noise, we're *fucked*. You will come back for us, right Buddy?"

Buddy looked at him, nodded.

Beneath Eden Buddy grunted, clearing the man hole cover aside.

It was midday and most of the people who called Eden home were on the street. Several eyebrows raised at the site of the two men, people wondering what was going on.

Bobby Evers looked at Harris, Harris nodding, Evers nodding back.

Graham made his way towards them, a look of disbelief on his face, and Buddy spoke his name.

"What's this all about, Buddy? Where's the rest of them then?"

Harris scanned the gathering crowd, watched what was transpiring before him. The M-16 in both his hands, the barrel slightly below hip level, ready to come into the mix. He wasn't one hundred percent sure how this was going to go down, and there were a few amongst the crowd he wanted to keep an eye on.

"I said what's this all—" Graham reached Buddy and lighting fast Buddy drove his booted foot into the man's crotch, hard. Graham's face turned beet red as he doubled over and vomited on the street. Buddy took the man by the ears and brought his head down onto his knee. Graham rolled over onto the street, his shirt riding up, his stomach jiggling.

"Afternoon, Bear," Harris said to the big biker.

"Afternoon, Harris," responded the bald man. "If it's all the same to the two of you, I'll just head over there, mind my own business."

"That's fine by me," Harris said, relieved.

Pistol-whipping Graham with his snub nosed .38, Buddy dragged the bloody man up to his knees and pressed the muzzle of the revolver to the rotund man's split head. "Things are gonna be different around here from now on," he said to the people gathered around. "No more fat man here telling ya'll how to live."

Graham expelled blood and a few teeth, rasped, "Don't listen to him. Who's going to protect you?"

"Harris, where's Sal?" asked Camille.

"He's fine, Camille."

"We're all going to protect our own selves now," said Buddy. "We're all going to make decisions together. Not no one man by himself for everyone else. Together, that means all-uh us."

"Democracy," someone in the crowd offered.

"That's goddamn right," affirmed Buddy.

"They're fucking crazy," Graham spluttered, a line of blood dripping from his mouth to the asphalt. "They can't protect you."

"Always the bully," said Harris. "That's how you been working Eden, Graham? Make these people think they need *your* ass to protect them? Why don't you tell them how you were sending us over to Jericho to take over the place, to kill whoever stood in your way?"

"What the fuck would you two know," whined Graham. "You just got here. Fuck Jericho and fuck the two of you."

"I know tyranny when I fucking see it," said Buddy.

"Where's my husband, Harris?" Camille had a pistol leveled at him and Harris damned himself for not paying close enough attention.

"Camille, be a good girl and put the gun down," Bobby Evers was sighting down the barrel of his .30-.30 hunting rifle.

"Blow his goddamn brains out," Graham spat to Camille. Buddy had a hand in the fat man's hair and he twisted mercilessly, pressing the .38 deep into the man's temple. "That hurt? Does that hurt? *Good.*"

"Where's my husband?" Camille demanded. "Where's Sal?"

"He's okay," Harris kept the sixteen lowered, thinking there was no way he'd be able to twist and knock Camille down before she plugged him at least a couple of times. "He's down there with the others. We had to tie them up, but they're okay."

"He had a conversion experience," added Buddy, twisting Graham's hair again, forcing the fat man to grunt and spit out another tooth.

"Graham was going to have Sal killed eventually, Cam. Give you to his men."

"Bullshit!" Camille shouted.

"No, it's not," said Harris. "Bobby, you do me a favor, take Camille down to Sal. Ask him yourself, Cam."

"If he's dead Harris…"

"He's not, Cam."

"You telling me the truth, Harris?" she asked, trying to hold back sobs. "My Sal's alright?"

"Camille, I wouldn't lie to you," said Harris.

"I believe him," Al Gold said from amongst the spectators.

Various murmurs of agreement followed.

"Jew fuck," Graham rasped and Buddy rubbed his face in the vomit on the stone.

"Okay…" Camille sounded unsure, but she slowly squatted and placed the pistol on the ground. "Go with me, Bobby?"

"Aye lass," Evers lowered the thirty-thirty.

"Okay, now what do we do with Graham?" someone in the crowd asked.

"Cap that bitch," said Davon.

"Let's put him outside with those things," offered another.

"You motherfuckers," whispered Graham. "All of you. I'll get you for this, all of you. Each and every single one of you. All of you."

"If we let him go," Harris explained to the crowd. "He might come back later with more like him. He might try to overthrow Eden, just like he wanted Jericho."

"That is if his fat ass can outrun them zombies," said Brenner.

"Well, shit, I don't want him living here with us," said Isabel.

"Me neither," agreed Panas.

"Fuckers. All of you."

"Shut up." Buddy smacked Graham on the head with the .38, not hard enough to knock him out, just enough to instill more pain, open up his scalp in another area.

"I'm a say it again, kill this son-of-a-bitch!" shouted Davon.

"If we kill him, we're no better'n he is," pointed out Larry Chen.

"Amen," chimed 74-year old Siobhan McAllister.

"Nah, the kid's right," said Diaz. "This maricn get out of here, he gonna come back, fuck us all again."

The crowd louder now, debating what to do with the dictator. Graham looked angry and ready to kill someone if he could wrestle free from Buddy, but he never looked scared. Hurt, but not afraid.

"Yo, listen up." Harris watched as Buddy spoke. "Way I see it, we got three choices of what we can do here."

"Listen to yourselves." There was contempt in Graham's voice. "You can't even reach a decision by yourselves. Talking and arguing. Have your democracy, cocksuckers."

"Democracy ain't nice and quiet, Graham," said Panas.

"One," Buddy ignored the side comments and spoke as loud as he could, his voice booming in the afternoon. "We can let him go, put him over the wall, let him fare his way with them outside."

A few nods in favor of this.

Davon said, "He'd come back."

"Bet your asses I'll be back," hissed Graham.

Buddy pistol whipped him again, blood spattering the asphalt. "Two," he continued calmly, almost detached, "we can kill him. End it right here."

A few more murmurs greeted this suggestion but there were also some skeptical voices raised.

"Or three," added Harris. "We could continue this discussion. Don't have to decide right now. Tie him up."

"Let's vote," said Panas.

"Yeah, let's vote right now," nodded Fred Turner.

"Okay," Buddy looked at the man he held at arms length by the hair. "Show of hands, right. All those in favor of letting Graham go?"

Some hands went up immediately, among them Siobhan McAllister's. One or two more ascended in the next few seconds. Fred Turner the last one to raise his hand, casting a look over at his son John.

"Two, we end this shit right here." Buddy spelt it out for them. "We kill this man now."

A majority of the hands went up. John Turner raised his.

"You seen that, right Graham," Buddy said matter-of-factly.

"Hey wait a second," someone said, "We got a couple people here voted twice."

"Fucking cocksuckers," fumed Graham. "Every last one of you."

"Three!" Harris yelled out quickly, "We lock him up, talk about it some more."

Harris raised his hand as some others did, including people who had already raised theirs.

"Look, again dammit!" the same person cried. "You get to vote once, one choice, get it?"

"Still choice two, Graham," Buddy let go of the man's head, splayed his palm at arms length to guard against the blow back, placed the barrel of the .38 two inches from Graham's bloody head and fired. Graham collapsed, a chunk of the back of his skull gleaming white amongst his hair.

"Holy shit," whispered Al Gold.

People looking at Buddy, astonished, afraid.

"What about the third fucking option?" said Davon, "You know, the 'Let's-talk-about-this-some-more-some'? I seen a lot of goddamn hands up for that one."

Buddy wiped the blood that had splattered across his palm on Graham's shirt.

"Listen to you, man," said Brenner, "talking one minute about let's ice this motherfucker, now getting all third option up in here."

"Yeah," said Panas, "You raised your hand for the death penalty man."

"Yeah, I did," said Davon. "But shit, I raised for the third part too."

"One man, one vote," said someone.

Siobhan McAllister looked at Buddy. She said nothing but her silence said it all. Buddy met and held her eye.

It had to be done, Harris figured. A guy like Graham wasn't just going to disappear. What Buddy had just done wouldn't go down well with some of these people, and in other circumstances he himself would have been one of them, but... people respected action, and this was a time to act.

"Okay, listen up," he called out, "Now I know some of you aren't going to be cool with what you just saw, and that's okay. If you want out, no one will think the less of you for it. You're free to leave anytime you want. The only thing you're not free to do is lord it over everyone else and try and rule Eden the way Graham did."

"What about Camille and Bobby?" someone asked. "They didn't get to vote."

"We got things to do around here, people," Bear sidled up.

"Like what?" asked Henderson.

"For one thing," said Harris, "We've got to send some people to Jericho, let them know things are different here now, that relations are going to be a lot friendlier."

"We stand together out here," said Buddy. "Or we don't stand at all." He looked towards the wall keeping the zombies out.

"What we gonna do with Graham's body?" asked Larry Chen.

"Any body want to volunteer to lug him out back and burn him?" asked Buddy.

"Flop his fat ass over the wall and let them feast on it," said Davon.

There were one or two smiles but most people looked uneasy.

"You want to feed them now?" Panas asked, half-joking.

"No, this is how we gonna do," Buddy looked at Siobhan MacAllister but she wasn't looking at him. "Two or three of ya'll, carry him around back. We're gonna burn him like we do the rest.

"It's what's right."

"HOW WE GOING to get across?" asked Harris, he and Buddy looking beyond the East River at the subdued Manhattan skyline. Whole buildings and blocks remained dim.

"Well, we're not going to swim," Buddy said, looking around. "That's for sure."

The moon passed in and out behind ominous rain clouds.

The streets in Queens had been mostly quiet. Occasionally they'd passed another car, a desperate-looking family inside, searching for a place to go, a way out. They'd avoided those wobbling and lurching along, the ones motioning towards their own car, starting for it.

Manhattan, Staten Island, even Brooklyn and Queens were all islands or parts of islands. The boroughs were connected with bridges, but the bridges had been closed and the soldiers guarding them fired first and asked questions later.

Only the Bronx was connected directly to the rest of the land mass forming New York State, but Harris knew he'd been lucky to get out of the Bronx and into Queens days earlier. He doubted his luck would hold in a reverse attempt, so he wondered what he would do if and when he found Raquel, where they would go, where they could go. He hadn't heard anything about the expressways or parkways leading east farther out onto Long Island being shut down, so there was that possibility. Who knew.

Raquel. Harris looked across the river into Manhattan. He and Buddy were in someone's backyard and couldn't see much of the city from this distance in the night. Just the skyscrapers, the lights of vehicles moving back and forth across there the size of ants from their vantage point.

The gunfire and explosions were muffled but audible. The caverns of Manhattan acted as an echo chamber, the steady clip of a machine gun firing full out reverberated back to them, faint yet discernable. An occasional *whump!* as some ordinance detonated. For all that, neither man could see any explosions. Everything, buildings, skyscrapers, the Empire State building, the Chrysler building, all still stood where they should be and always had been.

"How bad you want to get across there?" asked Buddy.

"I'm going," replied Harris. "One way or another. Does that answer your question?"

"You see that?"

Harris followed Buddy's pointing finger out onto the water. At first he saw nothing, but then he discerned it. There was a boat not too far from shore. It appeared anchored and not moving.

"Let's go," Buddy said, hitching his saddle bags back onto his shoulders, gripping the sawed-off shotgun around the barrel with one hand as he made his way through the backyard to the property line, following the fence looking for an opening.

Fifteen minutes later they were down where the land dropped off into the river. They'd made their way through the empty spaces between barren, desolate factories. They had not run across anyone. Still, Harris felt jumpy, like it was only a matter of time. He reached down and touched the cold steel of the Colt .357 for reassurance.

The boat was closer, clearer. It reminded Harris of the fishing boat his grandfather had when he was a kid. Not a huge affair, big enough to seat two or three people inside the cabin.

"You see anybody on board?" Harris asked. It was still dark and he couldn't see anyone deckside on the boat.

Buddy scanned it with the binoculars, said he did not either.

The binoculars had come from the saddle bags and Harris wondered if there wasn't anything the big man didn't have in those bags. Kind of like Mary Poppins pulling what she needed from her carpet bag when she'd arrived at the Banks's.

"I don't know, Harris. I still don't see anything. Have a look."

Buddy passed Harris the binoculars and Harris focused in on the boat. It bobbed gently in the river.

"You know how to operate a boat, Buddy?"

"No, man, you?" Buddy took the binoculars back and panned the island of Manhattan.

"No."

"How hard can it be, right?" Buddy put the binoculars down and rubbed his eyes.

Buddy looked around. It was creepy here on the wharf fronting an industrial area. "Question is, how do we get out to that boat?"

"Those saddle bags don't float?" quipped Harris.

"Man, I ain't in a rush to ruin my leather."

"I'm only kidding. We don't want to swim in the river anyway. Currents. I'm not changing my mind, Buddy."

"I'm not asking you to."

"Then make it fast."

"What do you expect we're going to find over there, man? I mean, besides your wife, if we're lucky."

"Nothing but a load of trouble. Death. Lots of that. Probably our own."

"But that's not going to slow us down one lick," said Buddy and Harris wasn't sure if it was a question or a comment, and if a comment how it was meant, and he was exhausted and on the verge of collapse and couldn't really care at the moment.

"Look there," he said and pointed into a darkness that was just beginning to hint at breaking, the sky to the east purpling.

Buddy stared off down at the water to their right.

"What's—" then he saw it also, a dinghy tethered further down. "Oh, you got a good eye, Harris. You da man."

They came around the front of the small fishing boat, lest anyone exited the small cabin aft and spied them. The dinghy was a small yellow rubber life raft, durable enough to get them across to the other boat, but not something either man would want to try and float out to the ocean in.

Buddy looked uneasy, and Harris wondered if the other was sea sick.

"You alright?"

"My grandmother took me to see *Jaws* when I was thirteen or fourteen years old," explained Buddy. "I was afraid to swim in a pool afterwards. It's irrational, I know, but I can't help it."

They paddled with their hands as there had been no oars or anything else suitable.

Buddy shook his head. "Sharks man. I hate sharks."

"There aren't any sharks in the East River."

"Bullshit," said Buddy, "Sharks everywhere. And this boat ain't much of anything to keep one out."

The echoes of automatic weapons fire were clearer and cleaner out on the river.

"That's going on over there," Harris nodded towards Manhattan, "and you're worried about Bruce the mechanical shark?"

"Now why'd you go and name him, Harris?" asked Buddy, a serious look on his face. Harris couldn't tell if he was for real or pulling his leg. He decided to say nothing, to just continue paddling with his palms towards the other boat. He was running on adrenalin again and he was lit up.

"Damn," Buddy laughed nervously.

"Back on shore we got dead people coming back to life. You're not worried about them. But *Jaws* bothers you?"

"Damn it, Harris," said Buddy. "I know what to do against a zombie, but a twenty-four foot shark?"

"That's what they are then, zombies?"

"What else to call them?"

"I wouldn't worry about any aquatic life, Buddy, we're good here. I saw this interview with Rob Zombie on VH1, some show about the scariest movie moments. Zombie said he saw *Jaws* as a little boy, then went to Denny's to eat. He's in the bathroom peeing and he's scared the whole time the shark was going to get him there in that bathroom."

"Okay, Harris, so you all tough and what not. Ain't afraid of nothing right?"

"I didn't say that, man. Heights do it for me. I can't stand them."

"See then, we both got somethin'."

"But honestly, these zombies have me freaked."

"Let's be quiet," Buddy said a minute later. "Try not to make too much noise the closer we get. Anybody aboard, we don't want to spook them into gunning the engine and leaving us."

Or worse, Harris thought, noting how Buddy propped the sawed-off within easy reach.

Another fifteen minutes of paddling and they were alongside the boat.

Harris wondered if they should yell out something, as this was private property. If there was someone alive inside and he was armed, they might think they were being pirated, but Buddy had already left the dinghy, swinging his saddle bags over the side of the fishing boat to the deck, where they thumped. The big buccaneer stepped foot on the ship, the sawed-off leveled in one big hand, directed at the cabin door.

Harris followed, fastening the rope from the dinghy to a stern cleat. He followed the other man's lead and produced his own revolver.

Buddy held up a hand and signaled Harris to take the left side of the door. Harris pressed himself there, the .357 trained on the door, as Buddy reached out with his left hand, the shotgun held steady with his right, turning the knob. It gave way and opened.

Curtains drawn over windows blocked the new light creeping over the horizon with the coming of day, but a single unprotected bulb hung from the ceiling. Harris could see the place was small andthat it was a mess amidst the shadows.

Thunder rumbled overhead.

Buddy nodded at Harris and stepped into the cabin.

A drunken roar met them. "What the hell?"

"Easy, pops," said Buddy, loud and clear.

Harris followed. The cabin itself was cramped, small, with a hammock hanging along the starboard side. An old man with a week's worth of white stubble on his face was floundering in the hammock, trying unsuccessfully to extricate himself from it. A bottle of whiskey lay on the floor beside his berth, empty and on its side.

"Take it easy old man," said Buddy. "Here let me help you up."

"Help me?" the old man sputtered, flummoxed. "You board my ship and *you* want to help *me*? The nerve of sons of bitches these days."

The man and the room reeked of drink, and when the boat's captain finally managed to get out of his hammock—he was wearing a flannel shirt, unbuttoned around a sleeveless white t-shirt and a pair of boxer shorts—he had difficulty keeping his feet.

"Goddamn ocean swells," he cursed.

"Mister-mister-mister," tried Harris. "We aren't going to hurt you. We need your help."

"My help?" said the old man. "Well, let me help get both of you the hell off of my boat, God dammit!"

He was obstreperous but he wasn't swinging yet.

"Sir, listen to my friend," smooth talked Buddy. "We just came aboard to inquire if your boat is for charter, that's all."

The old man cocked one eye at Buddy.

"We were calling from outside but no one answered," offered Harris.

"No one answered because no one wanted to be bothered," spat the old man, but then his look softened up. "You fellas want to know if my boats for charter?"

Buddy smiled, showing his pearly whites, "Yeah."

"Has either of you dimwits noticed what in the hell is going on around this city?" There was a look of drunken disbelief bordering disgust on the old man's face. "And you nimrods ask me if you can charter my boat."

"Yeah, we know what's going on out there," Harris tried to remain calm. He needed to get across the river.

"Young man," the old man said, and it had been awhile since Harris had thought of himself as a young man. "I may be drunk, but I'm not stupid. Okay?"

"We know that pops," Buddy said. "We just really got to get across that river."

"Do you men know what is going on over there? Listen!" Inside the cabin the thumps and tat-tat-tats sounded like fireworks.

"Yeah, we know," said Buddy.

"Why'n the hell would you want to get across to *that*?" The old man looked at them like they were the drunk ones.

Harris didn't say anything.

"My man here," Buddy laid it out. "His wife is down in that mess."

Buddy thought the old man was going to go and say something stupid to Harris, something like, "Young man, I got some news for you. Your wife ain't alive over there," or something truthful about a lot of people being over in that mess. He wondered how Harris would handle it if the old man did. Harris seemed cool, but Buddy knew something about having his buttons pushed, knew what it could do to a man, the conditions being right.

The old man looked Harris up and down, apprising him, stopping at his eyes, looking thoughtful.

"Says your wife is across that river?" the codger said clearly, the drunk out of his voice.

"Yes mister."

"Well, then…oh what the hell." The old man threw his hands up. He'd made his decision. "Let's get this voyage underway, gentlemen. The sooner I get you both across this river, the sooner I can go back to old number seven."

Harris looked at Buddy who grinned at him.

"Seagrams Seven, son," the old man winked.

"You da man," Harris mouthed so that the boat's owner, who was busying himself around the cabin now, did not hear.

Buddy pointed to himself and mouthed back, "Me?" Then he made an exaggerated face and shook his head slowly, like *naaaah*.

"Okay, listen to me you two," The old man was in his element. "If I'm going to pilot this craft then you two are going to help me out."

"Whatever you need," Buddy said.

"First off, where are my pants? Someone needs to help me find my goddamn pants."

"Shiver me timbers and all that shit, Harris, those pants are all you," said Buddy. "I'm a be outside, pitching masts and whatnot."

"Yeah, you better get a harpoon ready in case a shark attacks the boat."

Harris shook his head and helped the old man find and get into his pants.

The old man, Harris and Buddy stood atop the cabin at the steering birth. Although he was coming off a drunk, the grizzled old man was able to manage a pretty clear course through the river. At least he looked like someone who knew what he was doing.

As they drew closer to the Manhattan shoreline, the reverberations of helicopter rotors challenged the occasional boom of thunder for dominance. They didn't see any helicopters and it was getting too dark again to see clearly, the dawn occluded by black rain clouds.

"Harris, you see that? People!"

Buddy pointed at the far shore. Harris could make them out, little specs, human beings, gathering along the pier and the side of the highway. He couldn't hear them, but he knew they all wanted to get out of Manhattan.

Lightning flashed and lit everything up for an instant.

"Whirlybirds," the old man announced. Harris and Buddy looked up to see first one, then a second and a third helicopter lifting off from between the skyscrapers and tall buildings, hovering in the sky and making a beeline for the west side of the island.

"Those are military," said Buddy.

Dozens of them were about, a crescendo of rotor blades.

"They were flying those around in the streets of the city?" Harris asked, trying to imagine it.

"Yeah."

The helicopters became distant specs in the sky and disappeared over the horizon.

"Looks like they're heading over to Jersey," Harris noted.

"Yeah, looks," agreed Buddy.

"Wonder why they're leaving?"

The people on the shore became clearer.

"Here, look at this." Buddy handed Harris the binoculars.

It took his eyes a moment to adjust, then Harris could see them well enough. People, men and women in business clothes, construction workers, women in dresses, jeans, too numerous to count, massed on the lip of the highway along the docks. Many of them waving at their boat as it came closer. Even more had their backs to them and were fighting.

They were being attacked. Harris saw between the heads and shoulders of the desperate people. Those human beings who somehow weren't anymore, the zombies, they attacked the people, and the people fought back. Harris watched a police officer firing a service revolver, a longshoreman bashing a head in with a hammer, a uniformed female soldier firing an M-16 on full auto.

"Here, let me see," Buddy took back the binoculars.

Harris thought about he people over their fighting for their lives, waiting to be rescued. But the helicopters had flown off. Why had they flown off? Were they full? Couldn't they have taken some more people with them? Had this been going on all day? Couldn't they have fired a missile or something into the zombies? His brain was jumbled with questions and fears and exhaustion and he couldn't think straight.

Buddy was saying something to him.

"What?"

"We can't dock there."

"Why the fuck not?" He rarely cursed, and when he did the emotion was up in him.

"They'll swarm the boat." Buddy was talking about the screaming and gesticulating people and the things running and tottering after them. Dozens of the living had already jumped into the water and were swimming for the boat. Their faces were clear when the lighting flashed but they still seemed so far away.

"So what? Let them," Harris was disgusted. He only cared about one thing. "Let as many of them as they can get on this boat and let the captain take them the fuck out of here."

"You don't get it, do you?" Buddy looked at Harris. He did his best to keep calm. "It ain't like we're gonna get over there and there's gonna be a nice straight fucking line, like in the fucking post office, everyone waiting their goddamn turn. You ever seen people in desperate situations? Look at them now. Everyone's out for selves."

Harris looked and saw and heard people screaming at the boat, droves of them jumping into the water, some surfacing and starting to swim, others surfacing then floundering, going under, appearing again once or twice, many not again.

"Listen, Harris," said Buddy. "We're gonna get there, alright? But not here. Even if we do manage to get ashore in *that* spot, you do see they're bein' attacked, right? So after we claw our way through *that* crowd all coming in the opposite direction, we still gonna have to battle it out with those things, man. Think about it."

Harris counted to ten in his head. He pictured her struggling through the crowd, screaming his name, leaping into the river, swimming for the boat, for him.

Buddy was right. He was overreacting. For a moment there all he could think about was Raquel and getting to her, and it had seemed the big man was axing that plan. But Buddy was right.

"Hear that?" the old man barked.

They listened and as they did so there was something from the sky in the distance, not thunder. Some artifact of man drew nigh.

The lightening flashed and Buddy saw clearly and gave them name, "Jets!"

Little dots on the horizon, coming in over the island from the north, growing larger and more discernable with each bolt of lightning. The thunder boomed but was soon lost in the roar of their engines.

Buddy watched the people on the ground with his binoculars as best he could in the dark. Muzzle flashes lit up the gloom there. Fighting for their lives, staring at the sky, the looks on the faces of the ones he could see were not looks of relief.

"Oh my god," breathed Harris.

As the jets came in over mid-town, Buddy counted at least eight of them. They fired missiles from under their wings that screamed down into the city, disappearing from view between the buildings, lightning illuminating their vapor trails.

"No-no-no-no—" Harris steadied himself for the coming blasts, wondering why in the hell the United States military would be bombing New York City. How bad had things gotten down on the ground?

But there were no explosions.

The jets headed south past the island and wound their way back for another run, firing a second volley of missiles as they passed.

Harris followed the trail of one missile streaking down from the sky, over the heads of the people below, smashing into the side of a building. He had seen enough movies and watched enough History Channel to know that there should have been some mammoth explosions then as high explosive or incendiary rounds detonated. The missile disappeared into the side of the building traveling as fast as it was but there was no visible detonation. The building continued to stand.

Matter of fact, the sky line hadn't changed at all.

"What the..." Buddy's words trailed off.

The jets left, banked and disappeared north from where they'd come. Harris squinted through the darkness at the people but didn't understand at first what he was witnessing.

Buddy had lowered the binoculars. Harris reached over and took them from him.

"You might not want to see this, Harris."

When the lightening came Harris focused in on a man on the street, ignoring all others. The man stood tall, shirt ripped, his tie hanging undone from his shoulders. A gash on his forehead. He wielded what looked like a support for the portable railings found in banks and government buildings, bludgeoning an attacker with the flat weighted end.

Thunder and darkness and shadows. When the lightning came again the thing—*the zombie*, Harris thought—was down.

Three successive bolts from the sky and Harris watched as the man dropped his improvised club, took a step back, and twisted to face the water. His silhouette struggled, grabbing at his tie, tearing it off his shoulders, clutching at his neck.

Lightning, and Harris saw that the guy couldn't breathe. He watched the man reel forward, choking, gasping, his face going from pink to purple to bright red in succeeding flashes. The man down on one knee, gripping his throat, eyes bulging out of his head.

The thunder was over them and Harris felt little spatters of rain start to pelt his hands and face but still he watched through the binoculars.

The man was on his knees and one hand, clawing at the sidewalk with his other, foamy slobber trailing from his mouth. Harris watched as a zombie in a blood-stained brown delivery uniform with one arm pounced on the man from behind, dragged him up by his hair, back to his knees, jerking his head back.

Lightning rent the sky in time for Harris to view the zombie, severely burned on the one half of its face and missing an ear, as it reached around from behind, sinking its teeth into the choking man's neck, tearing free his throat amidst a crimson torrent. The lightning did not discharge again for some time and the man's end came to him in the dark.

Harris panned with the binoculars. They were perishing, all of them. Those that had fought off the zombies collapsed, apparently unable to breath. Some, already dying, faces bloated and discolored, fell prey to the approaching zombies. Others writhed and twisted by themselves or in twos and threes on the streets, some pitching desperately into the water.

The men and women swimming towards the boat went under, choking and gurgling, grasping at their faces and throats, cries in the darkness.

In time, Harris became aware that their boat was moving away from Manhattan, back towards Queens.

"What's going on over there, Buddy?"

"I don't know. Neutron bomb maybe?"

"Gas," said the old man, and he sounded like he knew what he was talking about.

"Poison gas?" Harris asked no one in particular and no one said anything.

As their boat headed back towards the Queens side of the city only the undead moved on the streets and docks they'd left behind, feasting on the fallen.

The jets returned once, firing another salvo of missiles into the shadows and canyons of downtown Manhattan.

HARRIS GRIMACED AS the fire shot up through his abdomen. Hunkered low on the toilet bowl, he felt the liquid expelled from him spatter the sides of the bowl. The bloody runs, one of the signs, a symptom someone'd been bitten. He refused to look down and see what he knew would be there.

The porta-potty door closed, Harris was thankful no one could see him. When his stomach started getting queasy he had thought about using the bathroom in his and Julie's house, but it didn't flush any longer and he wouldn't leave that mess there. For two reasons. One, Julie might find the bowl full of it and that would tip her right off as to what was happening to her boyfriend and he wouldn't get his chance to kill Thompson. Two, even if his plan went off without a hitch, Julie'd still be left with that mess to clean from their commode.

There were only a few situations in which Harris felt vulnerable. Sitting on a toilet had always been one of them. He thought it stemmed from his elementary school days. Harris remembered using the toilet as a first or second grader, sitting there in a stall in his parochial school's bathroom. He'd heard laughter and looked up at three older boys, sixth graders, looking down on him. They'd pulled themselves up the sides of the stalls sandwiching his and giggled as they hung there and the little boy inside went potty.

Maybe that was the reason. Or maybe it was the fact that in Catholic school Harris had been taught God watched them all the time. Normally this was a very comforting thought for the little Harris, like when he'd lay in bed at night next to his brother James and fear what was in their closet and then think *God has it covered* so they were okay. But to think that God could see *everything*, that God was watching him as he did number two and wiped his hiney, *that*, well that was just terrible. God didn't need to see *that*.

His other boyhood bathroom phobia did not spring from his religious elementary schooling. Up until he was thirteen or fourteen Harris wouldn't bring a magazine or newspaper into the bathroom with him. He knew the people in the pictures couldn't see him going to the bathroom, but some part of him thought they might be able to. He'd known then that it was an unreasonable supposition, but that didn't make him feel any better.

As a married man he always closed the door when he did "number two." Raquel used to joke with him that they shared everything but he wouldn't leave the door open when he took a shit. She did, but since she usually used the bathroom in their master bedroom he wasn't in the room when she was going. For himself, he was too embarrassed by his sounds and smell, he didn't want *her* to hear that.

The basic fact that he shit just like everyone else proved he was an animal just like everyone else. Not that he ever thought he was some transcendent entity. Like most people who spent a good part of their lives overlooking their mortality, for some reason taking a dump was just another reminder for Harris that he too was like everyone else, and as such, fated to an end.

He thought about all this as he farted and shot blood about the inside of the bowl. He frowned and a light, clammy sweat was starting to break on his forehead. He'd seen enough people bitten to know that this—the shits—wouldn't last much longer, that he'd be able to walk out of here and go about his business. He was also aware that this presaged the beginning of a quick end. Maybe a couple hours were left to him.

Harris wondered if there was a God watching him now, figured it wasn't worth mulling over, that he'd know soon enough, and thought about something else.

The *Love Boat*. One of his favorite shows as a kid. It used to come on at nine Saturday nights. Harris loved to watch that show. Thing was, his brother James wanted to be doing whatever his older brother did. However, there was a three year difference in their ages and James' bed time was eight o'clock. Harris's mother used to cut a deal with him. Lay down in bed with your little brother and when he falls asleep you can come downstairs and watch *Love Boat*.

Harris would get in bed next to James and lay there faking it, listening to his brother's breathing, waiting. Sometimes James fell asleep and Harris was downstairs at nine watching Isaak and Captain Steubing and Goffer and then Mr. Rourke and Tattoo on *Fantasy Island* after. Other times Harris fell asleep waiting for James to fall asleep, and then he woke up the next morning briefly mad at himself but not too long because his dad had picked up bagels which were still warm and he wanted to read the comics in the fat Sunday newspaper.

His parents had been good people, hard working people. They'd given him and James better lives than they'd had. Harris lost both his parents when he was in his thirties. First his mother, then his father. It had been tough, but he was glad they went when they did and didn't have to survive to see all this, to know the fate of their world. In a way now he was glad that he and Raquel had not been able to have children.

Harris realized he'd been sitting there for awhile and nothing was happening. His legs were getting cold and numb. He leaned forward and wiped and it was all mess and muck on the tissue. He had to mop up with what seemed half a roll of toilet paper but when he was good and clean enough he stood and pulled up his draws and jeans.

The sun would be going down soon. Around Eden people were cooking on their grills, lounging around in small groups. There was a volleyball game going on at the net and Julie was there.

Harris wondered what it would have been like to have known her in the regular world, before this. Of course, he'd been happily married to Raquel then, so he wouldn't have given Julie a second look. Well, that was a lie. After all, he was a man, and he might have spared a second look, but that's all it'd ever be. Just an admiring look, maybe thinking back to when they were younger and he'd first started dating Raquel.

Considering the things he had to do he took comfort in that most everything was pretty much in place. Maybe he should go over to Julie and say something, hold her. He'd already held her, held her close to him after this morning and smelled her head. She all the time not realizing he'd been fatally wounded, his flesh violated by the undead, his own body turning into one of them.

If he went over to her at this moment he thought he might get all mawkish and break down and cry, bawl like a child, beg her for things beyond her power to grant, ask her not to leave him, not to let him die. It would be a humiliating spectacle that would place a God-awful and undeserved stress on her.

Instead, he concentrated on focusing his anger. Though her back was to him and she was serving, he smiled in Julie's direction, then walked to the house Thompson shared with Diaz.

"Where's your roommate?" Harris asked the Dominican.

Diaz was stretched in a hammock he'd tied between a tree on the sidewalk and the railing of the porch. He'd just gone and strung it up there like that, blocking the whole sidewalk for anyone who wanted to walk past. *Thoughtless son of a bitch*, Harris condemned him silently.

Diaz took the joint out of his mouth long enough to say, "He's inside."

Harris called in through the open window, "Hey, Thompson," trying his best to sound his usual, polite self, when what he thought inside was come out here and die mother—

"Yeah? Hey, Harris, what's up?"

"I was wondering if maybe you could give me a hand?"

"Why? What's going on?"

"Over at my house, some stuff I need help moving."

Thompson looked at Harris through the window and Harris thought the other suspicious, just had to be. After all, Thompson had set it up so Harris and Julie would die violent, horrific deaths, but it hadn't worked. The kid was probably quaking in his boots, waiting to be found out, but he didn't want to act strange so as not to tip his hand. Harris believed this. He had to believe this.

"Would have asked someone else," Harris nodded his head towards an oblivious Diaz, a confidential gesture meant to disarm Thompson. "And Julie's kind of freaked about going back in the house after this morning."

"Give me a second," Thompson said, disappearing from the window.

"Sure. No problem."

But Harris immediately started wondering if there was a problem? Was Thompson suspicious? Had he gone to get a gun? Harris took a few steps back, angled his body and leaned on the top of the hammock, made it look like he was talking with Diaz. Instead he had turned his body to give Thompson as little a target as possible, hoping if the kid came out firing he'd hesitate just a moment, seeing Diaz in the way like that. A second being time enough for Harris to clear the .45 at his waist, even in the state he was in.

I don't want it to end that way though, thought Harris.

Diaz opened an eye, saw Harris standing there above him, gave off something between a laugh and a giggle.

"What's so funny, Diaz?"

"You, man. You just don't get it, do you?"

Who knew what the zonked out Diaz meant. Harris wasn't about to try to figure him out, nor did he want to engage the man in conversation. If Thompson burst out of the house firing Harris figured he could flip the hammock, overturn Diaz into the line of fire. Nobody would miss the man.

Harris was still sweating.

He wondered if Diaz would step up when he was gone, try and flex his muscles around Eden. Who would stand up to him? Bobby Evers might try, but Harris worried about Bobby being tough enough. Bobby Evers might be too good to be tough enough, a gentleman and a gentle man. But Bear could keep Diaz in line. The thought gave Harris reassurance.

"What do I need?" Thompson came down the steps, catching Harris unawares, his pistol in his belt on his hip, fastening a button down shirt.

"Nothing," Harris said. "Come on."

Thompson walked beside Harris. As they passed the volleyball game Julie looked up and smiled. Whether the smile was for Harris alone or Harris and Thompson because he was walking with Thompson, Harris did not know, but he smiled back and gave a little wave.

Harris felt he had to say something to Thompson so he said, "Hope you're ready for a little heavy lifting."

WILLIAM RICHARDSON STOOD outside the door to Janis' room. His little girl was asleep under the sheets, Maggy on the bed next to her, stroking her hair.

Janis had been worsening throughout the day. His little girl was hurt, possibly dying, and there didn't seem to be a whole lot William could do about it. He considered trying to get her to a hospital again. Hospitals must still be safe. At a time like this hospitals would be getting a lot of use, they'd be well guarded, people coming in all the time.

Flushing General was only a mile from his house.

Maggy's car was still in the garage, and the garage could be accessed from the basement.

"William," Harris called from the bottom of the stairs.

Richardson looked again at his wife and daughter, turned, and went downstairs.

Harris appeared better than he had when he'd come in. Less bedraggled. William's jeans and flannel shirt fit the man well. He looked more alert too, having slept a few hours in the spare bedroom.

"I'll have to be leaving, William. I want to thank you and your family for your hospitality."

"It's fine, it's okay." William didn't want Harris to leave. He felt safer with him around.

"I also want to ask you, do you think you have a spare kitchen knife or something you can lend me?" Harris felt funny asking, as the man had given him his own clothes already, but the warm look on William Richardson's face dispelled any discomfort.

"Yeah, let's take a look."

Billy and Sarah sat around the TV in the living room, watching a DVD. Some Disney animated movie they'd seen a dozen times before.

The Richardson's had a fine array of cutlery in their kitchen drawers.

"Help yourself."

Harris picked up and weighed several knives.

"You know what you're doing with those things?" asked William.

"Not really. I am pretty mean carving a turkey though."

He settled on one of the larger utensils, looked like something a killer in a slasher movie might wield.

"Thing is, about those things outside," Harris explained, stowing the knife away in his duffel bag with the spare rounds for the revolver and some food he had, "the only thing that puts them down for good it seems are blows to the head."

"Yeah, they said that on the TV."

"Listen, Harris. I know what I said before, but you're free to stay for as long as you want. Even until this thing blows over."

Harris looked at William and William worried he was going to say something like, *until this thing blows over? You've got to be kidding me Will. This thing isn't just blowing over.* But Harris didn't and the thought never crossed his mind and he hoped beyond hope that this thing *would* just blow over, that he'd get into Manhattan and find Raquel.

Reaching out, Harris put a hand on Richardson's shoulder. "I can never thank you enough for what you've done for me, William. If you'd left me out there, they'd have gotten me. They were chasing me. They'd have found me."

"I don't know Harris, you made it up to this point. I don't know how you crossed into Queens. That alone is pretty amazing."

"Luck."

"Well, I hope it continues for you. But I've got to ask you, you think it's a good idea going out there?"

"No. It's not a good idea. But my wife is out there somewhere, William."

Thinking of Maggy and the kids, William Richardson could understand and appreciate the sentiment. Sarah laughed at the movie in the living room.

"Truth is, Harris, *I* feel better here with you with us. Safer."

Harris smiled, "You're okay, William. You've got this place boarded up pretty good. When I run into people out there—" he would have said "rescue teams" but last Harris had seen some of the rescue teams needed rescuing—"I'll let them know you guys are here."

"Thanks. I bet we're not the only ones like this."

"Yeah, but you know, you're the only ones that let me in. Thank you."

"You're welcome," William said. He thought of running the idea of taking Janis to the hospital past Harris then thought better of it. The man was on a mission and had to be moving before the sun went down.

"You don't mind, I'll make my exit the same way I came in."

Harris followed William from the kitchen to the living room, stopping briefly to say goodbye to Billy and Sarah. The revolver was snug against his belly in the jeans.

William stuck his head in Janis' door, said something quietly, and Maggy joined them in the hall.

Harris looked as far as he could in all directions, craning his neck. He slid the window up as quietly as possible though nothing appeared near enough to hear it, then leaned out the window and looked some more.

"Okay," he came back into the hallway, facing the Richardsons. "I already thanked your husband Maggy, and I'd like to thank you too."

"You're welcome," she said. "You can't stay?"

"Believe me," Harris said and William and Maggy both knew he meant it, "If I could, I would. But no, I can't."

"Okay then."

William ducked and followed Harris out the window onto the roof of the first floor. The Richardson's roof, like all of their neighbors's, was sloped such that the view from the street and their view of it was obstructed.

Harris lowered the ladder slowly and carefully with the minimum amount of noise.

He looked up at William, who said "Luck," and then he was down, trotting across the back yard, reaching the fence separating William's property from the home in the rear. Without looking back Harris scaled the fence, dropping noiselessly to the other side.

William pulled the ladder up, resting it as Harris had on the roof. As he climbed back in his window he caught sight of Harris emerging from between the properties of the house behind his and the one on its right, reaching the street and disappearing in a slow jog.

The window locked, William looked in on Maggy with Janis. He stood in the doorway for a minute, wondering if Harris would survive, hoping the man would make it. He went downstairs and sat on the couch next to Billy and Sarah.

Sarah got up and moved over on her father's other side, where he could wrap an arm around her. Billy was in his early teens, getting too cool for mom and dad, but these were trying times and William didn't give a good goddamn, he put his other arm around his son's shoulders and held them both there as they watched their movie.

It was an old one, one of his favorites from when he was younger. *The Wind in the Willows.* Mr. Toad. *Damn shame they closed that ride in Disneyworld*, William thought. It had been one of their best, and his kids had never gotten the chance to ride it.

After a few minutes Sarah went upstairs to "check on Mommy."

William didn't remove his arm from around Billy and the boy didn't seem to mind.

Mr. Toad was jumping rope on the top of his horse with his buddy whip, saying, "We'll go for a jolly ride!" when Sarah's crying voice called to her father atop the stairs, "Daddy, come up, daddy. Janis…"

William sprang up, his son looking, wondering if he should follow, his father already up the stairs.

Maggy was sobbing, cradling Janis' head, the girls eyes closed.

William Richardson knew his youngest child was dead.

He nearly reeled but he looked at Maggy, then at Sarah and Billy in the doorway, and he knew somebody needed to be strong for them. He sat down next to his wife and held her tight.

"Oh Maggy, I'm so-so-so sorry," he said. "Shhh-shhh-shhh, it's okay, it's okay."

She cried, her face a mess, and suddenly, inexplicably, William just wanted to get away from all this. He had to get out of the room where his dead daughter lay or else…

He stood and walked out, saying to Billy, "Go sit with your mom a minute."

The lights in the bathroom went on when he flicked the switch and the water came from the spigot on the sink. William lay the Glock 40mm on the vanity and cupped both hands, let them fill with water which he splashed on his face.

It's not right, it's just not right. His throat tightened up on him.

William stood there, bent over the sink, on the brink of tears himself, his breath short—

"Dad!" panic in Billy's voice, then Maggy screaming for him, "Will! Will!" and the snarl of some animal.

William Richardson lunged from the bathroom, forgetting the pistol on the sink, making it down the hall to Janis' room in seconds. He didn't know what to make of what he saw there at first.

His Janis was alive! She was up and on top of Maggy and they looked like they were play wrestling but Billy was trying to pull Janis off their mother and Sarah was in a corner frantically crying, her face flushed red.

It only took him a second to understand. Blood all over Janis' face, her mouth and chin, blood from Maggy's right shoulder, his wife's gasps as she struggled with their daughter. The look in Janis' eyes, a look that told William Richardson in no uncertain terms that this *was not* his daughter any longer. Her bloody mouth, teeth gnashing, snapping for Maggy's face.

"Dad!" Billy cried hysterically.

William took Janis by the shoulders and tore her from Maggy, pressing her up ainst the wall. His daughter a small girl, six years old, and not fifty pounds but she was twisting and slippery and he dropped her. She hit the ground on her feet and immediately surged forward, sinking her teeth into his hand, the pain unreal. Without thinking William backhanded her with his other, sending her spinning away, a chunk of him in her mouth.

His daughter staggered against the wall and regained her balance. She looked at them through half lidded eyes as she chewed, a low growl emanating from her.

"Janis honey," Maggy cried, clutching her own shoulder.

Janis swallowed what was in her mouth and bared her teeth.

"Shit!" William cursed in front of his kids and didn't think anything of it because Janis or whatever the hell the thing was came back at him, the look in its eyes demented and gone.

When she was a foot away from her father, Janis launched herself at him, aiming for his throat but William got both arms up in time to defend himself. He lost his footing when she collided with him, the both of them going down, Maggy staring at them in shock, Sarah crying tearless sobs, Billy lunging back and forth in one spot wondering what he could do. William used his superior bodyweight to roll his daughter over and wrestle her to a position where he sat astride her chest, pinning her arms at her sides under his legs. He incurred several deep bites in the process, blood flowing freely from his hands and forearms, the thing beneath him finally secured.

"Billy," said William. "Go downstairs to the basement. Get me the rope we keep down there. You know what I'm talking about?"

"Y-Y-Yes dad."

"Good. Now go."

The boy did.

"Maggy? Maggy, are you okay?" William couldn't risk turning around to see. He feared losing grip of his daughter and having to wrestle her down again and deal with those teeth.

"Yeah, yeah, I'll be okay, William," came her reply, and William felt some measure of relief to hear that his wife sounded like she was holding herself together even as waves of agony coursed through his own hands and arms.

"Daddy, what's wrong with Janis? Why did she hurt you and mommy?" Sarah asked, sounding so much like a little girl it made William want to bawl but the thing under him thrashed, howled, and gnashed its teeth, trying to get at his legs. He had it by the hair and had the head pulled back.

"Sarah, okay…mommy and daddy need you to go into the bathroom and get as many clean towels from under the sink as you can carry, okay?"

"Yes, daddy."

William stared down into a face that had been his daughter's. Blood masked it and pink spit bubbles frothed from the sides of its mouth. The thing snarled at him and there was a chunk of his bloody red meat between the two front teeth.

Sarah returned with the towels.

Maggy took one and pressed it to her shoulder, staunching her wound. She felt dizzy and nauseous.

"Okay, here's what we're going to do," William said after Billy came back into the room with the rope.

"Sarah, take mommy…downstairs to the garage. Wait for me and Billy…in the car. Open the trunk for us, okay?"

"Yes, daddy."

"Okay, go on now."

The girl led her mother out of the room by hand.

"Billy, listen to me, we're going to tie your sister up and take her to the hospital."

Billy thought it was a crazy idea but was too scared to say anything. Everything was crazy about the last two days.

"Okay…help me…first you're going to bind her feet," William explained how he wanted it done and Billy did as his dad said, tying his sister's feet together tightly, struggling at first because she was kicking with her legs until his dad leaned forward a bit and then back really quick, digging the tops of his feet into Janis' little thighs, further pinning her to the floor. The carpet in his daughter's room was a coagulated morass.

Billy worked his way up and bound his sister tight as his father instructed. The arms and hands were the trickiest part and she got free for a second and bit her father again, the meaty part of his left hand between the thumb and forefinger disappearing in her mouth, and Billy watched his father punch his sister in the face like he would punch a man.

The blow bounced Janis' head off the floor and stunned her long enough for them to finish the job of securing her.

"Give me a pillow case…please," asked William, taking it from his son and unceremoniously stuffing as much of it as he could in Janis' mouth without losing any fingers, her teeth gnawing at the cotton.

He used another pillow case to tie in place the one in her mouth, looping it around her head and tightening it as best he could.

"Don't make it too tight, dad," offered Billy. "Janis won't be able to breathe."

"Okay," disoriented, William stood and had to reach out to the dresser to steady himself, Billy coming to him with fresh towels Sarah had left.

He wiped at the worst bites on his hands and forearms. The thing had torn a mouthful from the underside of his left forearm. The wound gaped back at him bloody and meaty-looking, nasty.

"Goddamn," he said and winced, the pain unreal, a fire burning its way up his arms.

William folded the smaller hand towels and pressed them to the ugliest wounds, Billy helping him secure them by knotting blood-soaked pillow cases in place. When they were finished William looked like some kind of half-assed mummy.

"Okay, here's what we're going to do," he told his son to go and get the gun out of the bathroom and to be very careful with it, to point the barrel at the floor. He met Billy in the hallway a few seconds after, the thing bound and slung over his shoulder, a pulsing, squirming cocoon driveling blood.

"Let's go." William went first, afraid he might black out and come crashing down the stairs on top of his boy. He wasn't doing so hot and he knew it. He had to get his family to the goddamn hospital fast and hope for the best.

Maggy wasn't looking too good either. She had a dreamy look in her eyes in the front passenger seat, staring at the ceiling of the car. Sarah watched from the back as her father and brother stowed Janis in the trunk and slammed it shut.

William leaned against the door, letting Billy climb into the back next to his sister. He felt lightheaded and for a moment felt like he wasn't standing at all. He imagined he was floating, then snapped out of it, the burning sensation seizing his shoulders and chest, bringing him back to his senses.

"The gun, dad," Billy handed it up to William. The pistol was hard for him to hold, with his hands all bandaged up with pillow cases and wash clothes, the blood, and the sting from his wounds. He used thumb and forefinger to place the weapon on the seat between his legs.

"Okay." He reached up to the visor and fumbled with it for a few seconds, coughing now, finding the automatic garage door opener and, out of habit, enjoined his kids to put on their seat belts.

The garage door started up with a mechanical hum and they could see legs outside on the street turning towards them.

Billy looked to his mother. She was breathing shallowly as she focused on the ceiling. His father was a disgusting mess as he put the car into drive and eased it slowly from the garage.

The things on the street wheeled, some limping, clumsy steps towards them, one pitching over beside the car and plunging to the driveway, out of view.

Billy looked and made sure the locks on all the doors were closed, then grabbed his sister Sarah and pressed her face to his chest so she wouldn't have to see this.

William Richardson steered around one slow-moving thing, got the car out onto the street, and passed out. The vehicle rolled forward in drive and stopped when it rammed a parked car on the opposite side of the street.

"Billy…" said William, coming back to consciousness, a heavy feeling in his throat, something welling up there, something his body wanted to vomit out, "Billy…" Fumbling with the pistol between his legs, he dropped it somewhere on the floorboard at his feet, passing out again.

Billy clutched his sister close. Sarah started each time one of the things outside thumped on their car. They'd encircled the vehicle, some of them mangled and chewed up, shot to pieces, others more natural-looking, as though this was just some crazy spoof: an elaborate hoax done to shock the Richardson family.

Mrs. Lynch, the cat lady from down the block, was trying to get through the windshield. She clutched the severed tail of one of her felines.

Billy hyperventilated, not knowing what to do. His father slumped forward. His mother looked like she had stopped breathing but her eyes still gazed upwards. Neither moved. Sarah sobbed noiselessly against his chest as he sat there. The things outside seemed unable to crack the glass and get to them, incessantly banging at their car. Mrs. Lynch squalled at him.

Paralyzed by fear, Billy closed his eyes and listened, and felt as though he were on the inside of a drum.

JULIE WAS IN their bedroom getting ready for sleep .Harris went about his evening routine in the bathroom. Routines, that's what it was all about. Habits and schedules helped keep one's sanity within the four walls of Eden, within this dead world.

He flossed, working the floss between his teeth, pulling up and out, tooth by tooth, checking them in the mirror. Listerine followed. Original flavor, which burned his mouth, really let him know it was in there working, doing something.

He gargled, spat into the bucket, squeezed paste onto a toothbrush, his mouth still stinging, and went to work on his uppers and then his lowers, back of his mouth, up under the fronts and then the bottoms. Spat into the bucket, used a coffee mug to draw water from another bucket, rinsed out his mouth and spat. He put the spit bucket in the shower they didn't use. He'd empty it in the morning, like he did every morning.

Teeth are important, thought Harris. Since he'd been living here, a couple of people in Eden had come down with infections from abscessed teeth. One had actually died. The other had to be held down while Bobby Evers—no dentist—went to work with a pair of pliers.

Harris dropped his drawers, squeezed a weak stream of urine out into a third bucket and was glad he did so, not wanting to wake up in the middle of the night to go again. He shook himself, pulled his boxers back on and looked at himself in the mirror. His beard had lost the disheveled look, no longer shaggy and messy looking, like "the wild man of the forest" as Julie liked to quip. He hadn't shaved since this whole thing had begun, which would mean he hadn't shaved… for a long time.

Some people in Eden were obsessed with time, with the keeping of it, even arguing as to what day of the week it was. Harris paid it little mind. He changed clothes with each new day and the coming of the seasons.

He flicked the switch, killing the light in the bathroom and stepped into the master bedroom. After fluffing the goose down pillows, Julie had drawn the blinds, shutting out any light from Eden's street, people still awake outside.

Summer was gone and there was no need for the window-mounted air conditioner which would lull him to sleep, so Harris grabbed his ear plugs, rolled them up one at a time, and popped them into place.

He could still hear Julie.

He closed the door to their bedroom, slipped out of his shoulder holster and rested the dual nines on the chair at the foot of their bed.

Julie checked the load on the Mossberg as he had taught her and passed him the 12-guage with the muzzle and bayonet pointing away from them. He thanked her and propped it up against the wall on his side of the bed. Julie did the same with the AR on hers.

Harris pulled his t-shirt off and put it in the hamper, killed the light in the bedroom, and got into bed. He leaned over to the nightstand, flicked the indicator on the clock radio setting the alarm, and rolled back over onto his back.

Julie turned over, put her head on his shoulder and wrapped an arm around his chest. Harris brushed her hair out of his nose where it tickled him, cradled her with one arm.

He lay there staring into the dark.

Mr. Vittles appeared from the shadows and nested himself on the bed at their feet.

Julie said something to him but it was muffled by the ear plugs.

"What's that, sweetie?" He popped out the one in his right ear, the side closest to her.

"Good night Harris," said Julie.

"Good night."

Maybe he should tell her he loved her?

She said it before he could.

He told her he loved her as well and she nuzzled a bit closer, relaxed, and lay still.

Harris felt her breathing, the rise and fall of her chest next to his torso.

After about ten minutes he was pretty sure she was asleep, just like he was pretty sure James was asleep in the bed next to him when they were little.

Harris couldn't sleep. He moved his big toe and felt Vittles go for it, batting it with a paw.

Night time was always the worst. All the dead people, the memories, they all came back. Funny thing, Harris didn't think so much of Raquel, of his brother James, of Daffy, of people and loved ones he couldn't be sure were gone forever. He found himself haunted by the same ghosts that visited him before all this.

His Uncle Pete, a big Ukrainian mug of a man. Harris remembered the holiday dinners at his Aunt Edna's apartment on Jackson Avenue in Brooklyn. Uncle Pete always talked with a lisp and Harris grew up assuming his old uncle had a speech impediment. It took him awhile to figure out that the man's speech was slurred from holiday drinking. Uncle Pete dropped dead from a heart attack when he was in the seventh grade.

He was the first person close to Harris to go.

Max died next, their family dog. His parents adopted Max when Harris was five years old and he grew up with Max a permanent part of their family. A spunky little jack terrier. One day in his junior year of high school Harris had come home from his after-school job and Max was in his father's arms, on his way to the vet, his old legs out on him for the last time.

Max licked Harris' hand before his parents got in the car, his mother asking Harris to look after James. They took his dog and had it put down.

Others, many others, after that. Aunts, uncles, a grandmother, distant cousins he'd only met once or twice when he was too young to remember them. When he got into his thirties, people his age, friends from college, people he had worked with, high school chums, started dropping dead from heart attacks, cancer, car accidents, one with AIDS, another a suicide.

Max's death bothered him more than all of those. Max had been more than a dog to Harris, to his brother James and their family. Max was like the third son, another brother, a little hairy sibling who sometimes yapped too much. Some people could never understand, never decipher how other people felt so close to an animal.

Max had been there when James and he had dragged blankets over the sofas in the living room and called them forts, when they beat each other silly in improvised battles with the cardboard rolls in the middle of wrapping paper. Max there to give him a look when he snuck girls into his room with his parents out for the night. Max had been a permanent fixture, a seminal figure in his emotional life. Aunts, uncles, even his grandparents, they weren't around all the time, so when they died Harris didn't feel it like he did the day the nine pound terrier never returned from the vet.

He'd had pets since. Other dogs, Daffy, Mr. Vittles here. They were all cool in their own way, but Max had left something within him that loomed forever large, something inexplicable and indelible. Maybe it was the little guy's unconditional love and the wag of his stumpy little tail. Maybe it was because he'd been there with Harris from an early age, his constant companion. Harris thought it was a little bit of both.

He wondered what had become of Daffy doggy, and decided thinking about her wasn't a good thing because it drew up a whole host of other thoughts, of others missing, probably dead, they *had to* be dead. Maybe walking around out there somewhere.

He prodded Julie and she rolled over. Each night started out with her head on his shoulder and him flat on his back, but ended up with his leg wrapped around her, their torsos molded together, his nose above the top of her head, feet entwined. Their nightly routine. Routines and habits were important in Eden.

Harris breathed her in and lay still.

The ear plugs muffled sounds. He couldn't hear the purr machine at his feet. Not everyone went to bed at a decent hour in Eden, and if the windows were open he'd be able to hear them outside. That and the occasional wail and moan, the lament of the undead reaching them from beyond the wall, it all added up to reasons he gladly wore the ear plugs.

Harris wondered if he loved Julie enough. He told her he loved her and he meant it and he thought she knew he did. But sometimes he felt like he wasn't capable of loving her the way he'd been able to love Raquel. The way he still loved Raquel.

Did he love Raquel? If asked, he wouldn't hesitate to say yes. But his feelings were fading in some way, like they belonged to another person somewhere else some time since past.

He didn't want to be unfair to Julie, had told her from the start that given their situation he wasn't looking to start a relationship. He'd been very blunt that he had seen a lot of people, some very close to him, die very badly. She'd reminded him she had also.

He was glad she was in his life. What he'd have done once Buddy disappeared, what he'd have done without her, he honestly didn't know. Harris hoped the big man was okay somewhere, yet, like Daffy, he decided it best not to dwell on Buddy's fate.

Harris kissed the back of Julie's head, pulled her close and closed his eyes.

Mr. Vittles smacked his big toe and was still.

"**GLAD YOU GUYS** can stay awhile," Dom said, and smiled.

"Thanks for having us," replied Harris.

"Yeah, it's not like we're going anyplace," added Buddy.

They were on Dom's roof. Dom was a tall, obese man, though he didn't seem as tall on account of his extra weight.

Dom's house stood out on his block because it was detached on both sides. His roof and his neighbor's on either side were separated by five foot gaps of air, empty space above little cement walkways dividing the homes. The walkways led to backyards and the yards were separated from one another with wooden fences.

Dom fixed filet mignons on a Viking Grill. Harris had no idea how the big sweaty man got the grill up here on his roof, or the porta-potty for that matter. Maybe he'd brought them up before everything? But then surely he'd be in violation of a city code of some sort and some department or other would come and issue him a summons.

Harris couldn't figure it.

Sheb Wooley was singing on the combination compact disc player/radio about a one-eyed one-horned flying purple people eater. Harris remembered the song from when he was a kid. *Sha-na-na* covered it on their old show.

"Where are you guys coming from?"

"Manhattan," Buddy said kind of quiet like.

"Mmmm," nodded Dom. "I sorta saw what happened there."

From the roof he had a clear view of Manhattan's skyline. A long way off, but there were no signs of life on the island. Buddy confirmed as much with his binoculars.

Harris wondered what'd become of the old man and his boat.

"My wife worked in the city," noted Dom. Sensing he might have made it awkward for the two men he'd spotted in the street and invited up twenty minutes earlier, added, "She got out. Of the city, that is."

"Thank God for that." Buddy thought of Harris and Harris' wife and the probable fate that had befallen her, of all those people they'd seen die with their own eyes, of the things roaming the city streets beneath them.

"You've got a generator here?" Harris had heard a dull hum from behind a closed door after Dom opened the front door to them.

"Yeah. Generator, bottled water, enough meat for a couple weeks." Dom looked proud of himself. "Gonna ride this storm out."

"You think this will pass?" asked Buddy, not a challenge. He wished the other man had some information for them, some way of knowing when and how this whole situation was going to cease, when things would go back to the ways they'd been beforehand. *But not exactly as they'd been*, thought Buddy.

"Doesn't everything?"

Harris put Dom's age somewhere between his own and Buddy's, but closer to Buddy's. *Could be wrong though.* The man didn't take very good care of himself —he was smoking another cigarette—so maybe he was one of those people who looked older than he was.

"What if it goes longer than a couple of weeks?" Again not challenging, Buddy just wanted to see what the other man would say.

"Shit. My doctor is always getting on my ass to lose weight as it is. And quit smoking too. Food will run out in two weeks," Dom took the smoke out of his mouth and looked at it contemplatively. "Cigarettes before that."

Harris had never been into smoking cigarettes. When he was younger, when he would go to the bars and have a few drinks, maybe he'd have a cigarette then. When he'd met Raquel she'd smoked. She quit when they were getting ready to try and have a kid. The baby never came and she never went back to the habit. Still, they made it a point, every country they visited on vacation, buy a pack of the local smokes, see what they were about.

The moon would be coming out soon, the skyline behind them slowly disappearing into the evening. Allan Sherman was singing a letter home to his parents from Camp Ranata.

"I been up here a week already," explained Dom. "First few days, lots of people out in the street, just wandering. Then the dead. Until you guys came."

"What about your neighbors?" asked Harris.

Dom pointed. "Jack next door, he packed the wife and kids in the minivan and got out just as soon as shit went sour. Riley, over there, well he and his family holed up for a few days, nailed themselves in like I done here."

"Heard from them lately?" Buddy wanted to know.

"No." Dom shook his head sadly. "Two days ago a group of them things were pounding on the doors of the houses on this block. 'Course, they couldn't get in here."

'*Course*, thought Harris. It had taken Dom ten minutes to pry the boards from the inside of the door after he's seen them on the street below and called them to him. Those ten minutes had been unnerving ones for Harris, standing around with Buddy, waiting for the man to let them in, waiting for a zombie to come wandering down the street. Wondering which would happen first.

"But Riley," huffed Dom, "They got into his place. I heard them carrying on there. Wasn't much I could do. I shot down on them, killed twelve or fifteen of them. They were going at it in there for a long time. Had to listen to Riley and his kids screaming and fighting. Sounded like they were throwing everything that wasn't nailed down at them too. Riley didn't keep a gun in the house."

Dom, on the other hand, did, and lots of them. Three of his rifles and a shotgun were resting against the lip of the roof. He had a pistol on the side of the Grill. He had boxes of ammunition stacked neatly next to the rifles.

"Noise brings them," observed Buddy.

The radio only loud enough for their ears.

"Yeah. When I shot the first five down, fifty more came. Some runnin', too. Those are the ones bothers me most. The slow ones, they aren't so bad. But those fast ones..."

Harris thought of the zombies he had been forced to outrun in the last several days. God, how long was it now? How many times had he sprinted for his life? How long could he keep running? He'd met Buddy when he stopped running, but that was just plain dumb luck.

Like happening on Dom here.

"You think there's more people in their houses down around here?" Buddy asked.

"Yeah. I watched those things on the street. They couldn't get into all the houses. If you look you can see two houses over there across from us with the windows all boarded up. There's people inside there."

The steaks sizzled on the grill and Dom turned them.

"How about you?" asked Harris. "Why you up here?"

"I got everything I need," said Dom, motioning to the grill, his portable toilet, two thirty six quart red Igloo coolers he'd pulled beer and soda out of when Harris and Buddy first arrived.

"Some of them make a lot of noise," Buddy said of the undead. "Doesn't it get to you, you being up here, them being down there screaming and carrying on?"

"Yeah, it'd go to my head if I let it, but it beats being locked up inside a cage. And so long as they're down there and I'm up here, it's not all bad."

The sweaty man had a point there, thought Harris.

"And there's one more thing, something I'll tell you about after we eat. Hope you boys like your steaks medium well."

They ate their steaks and the thawed-out corn on the cob. Dom and Buddy drank beer and caught a slight buzz, and for the first time in what seemed like forever Harris was able to relax somewhat and did not feel he had to fear letting his guard down.

"That hit the spot," pronounced Buddy.

Something dead down on the street beckoned in the dark and they stiffened.

It didn't do it again right away, but Johnny Preston's song about Little White Dove and Running Bear somehow didn't sound the same.

"Christ I hate when they do that," Dom murmured and Buddy agreed.

The zombie howled again soon thereafter.

"Think they're trying to communicate?" Harris asked.

"Not with each other," said Dom. "Not with us. They don't seem organized. Lucky for us."

Another time and Harris was visibly agitated now.

"Bastard," he spat. "Damn things going to do that all night, right?"

"Maybe it smelled our steaks," offered Buddy.

Dom got up from where he sat in his folding chair, selected one of the hunting rifles from the three next to the shotgun, leaned over the lip of the roof and remained motionless for a moment.

Down below the dead thing screamed a fourth time as Dom sighted along the barrel of his rifle. Harris and Buddy joined him on the edge of the roof, Harris staying a good three feet from the lip, ruing the drop. The zombie looked up at them with its hands out at its sides. In life it had been a Roman Catholic nun and it still wore the traditional habit. It stared at Dom like it expected to be invited up.

Before a fifth shriek came the echoing crack from the rifle.

"She won't be bothering us anymore." With satisfaction in his voice, Dom put the rifle down and popped open a fresh beer.

"Won't that just attract a whole lot more of 'em?" asked Buddy.

"Yeah, but if we keep low up here they'll just wander past eventually. They're not that bright, you know. Nothing to see, ain't no reason for them to hang around."

The moon came up full in the sky as they talked into the night and listened to the things come and pass in the streets.

The witch doctor said, "Ooh-eeh, ooh-ah-ah, ching-chang walla-walla bing-bang, ooh-eeh, ooh-ah-ah, ching-chang-walla-walla bing-bang."

"What are we listening to here?" Harris asked.

"Some CDs I lugged up from downstairs," explained Dom. "Novelty hits. They don't make many of them anymore."

"Yeah, I remember this stuff from when I was a kid," said Harris.

"You guys never heard of Afro Man?" Buddy asked.

They both looked at him.

"'Because I Got High'?"

Neither had.

"Big song with some of the younger brothers inside. Forget it."

After awhile Dom said to them, "You guys must be pretty tired by now."

Harris had circles under his eyes. Buddy nodded.

"Well, help yourselves to some sleeping blankets. This roof's not the most comfortable in the world, but it's not the worst, either."

"Thanks, Dom," said Buddy, "for everything."

"Yeah," seconded Harris.

"Listen, before you fellas get to bed. There's something I need to talk to you about."

"Go ahead," Buddy sat down in front of the man and Harris did likewise.

"My wife, remember I told you about her? She made it out of Manhattan on the first day you know."

Harris watched Buddy from the corner of his eye. Buddy was quiet, with a calm look to him, a reassuring look, one prompting the heavy man to keep talking.

Whatever was coming, Harris *knew* it couldn't be good. He kept quiet and let Dom tell it.

"I was so happy to see her. I mean, you guys... we all have loved ones who didn't make it...."

"Take your time," said Buddy.

After awhile Dom sighed and got himself together.

"She made it home, she crossed the fifty ninth street bridge on foot because there weren't any buses or trains running. My Lenore made it home but she was hurt. I swear the bite wasn't too bad. I'd heard what they said on TV."

Oh brother, thought Harris, hyper-vigilant again, eyes scanning the rooftop. *Where was the wife?*

"I put her downstairs. In the basement. We finished it years ago, made it into a family room. I looked after her as best I could. But she faded. She didn't understand what was happening to her. I couldn't tell her. I didn't know what to say. I didn't have the heart."

What a horrible, terrible situation, thought Harris.

"When she was asleep, almost like in a coma, I knew it was too late for her. She was barely breathing and she'd been soiling herself, but it was all blood and... So... so I locked her down there in the basement and boarded up the door.

"She's down there now...like one of them things on the street. Don't worry. She can't get out. She's not Lenore no more. I know that. But I won't go down there. I can't. Nothing I need is down in that basement anyway."

They sat around for some time, looking at each other and out into the night-time, none feeling the need to speak.

And then Harris said, "Dom, my wife was in Manhattan too. That's where me and Buddy were coming from, just trying to stay alive up until now. For all I know she's still over there."

"It's a rotten situation, isn't it?" asked Dom.

Harris wondered which was worse, to know or not to know the fate of the one you loved? Was Raquel alive or dead? Dead and walking around? Nerve gassed by his own country? Would it be worse if she was dead to know where she was and *what* she had become?

"Yeah, it's bad," he agreed several minutes later. "It is."

"You know," Buddy chose his words carefully. "You know Lenore isn't going to get better, don't you Dom?"

"Yeah, that I do. I just couldn't bring myself... I know what needs doing. I just thought maybe, maybe I'd ask you guys..."

"Let's talk about this tomorrow, Dom," Buddy said in a soothing tone, and Harris could imagine the older man talking to his children or grandchildren this way, and thinking so made him realize just how little he actually knew about his traveling companion.

"You said she's locked up good and tight right now?"

"*It's* locked up good and tight," corrected Dom. "That thing in the basement, that's not my Lenore."

Buddy nodded.

They sat around a few more minutes until Dom said, "Aww shit, you guys get to bed. We're okay up here. I been up here a long time."

Buddy and Harris retrieved sleeping blankets from the other end of the roof and spread them out opposite the grill.

Harris took off his shirt and jeans, folded them and set them under his head as a pillow. He could use a change of clothes and a shower. Dom had electricity and Harris wondered if that generator could power a washing machine. Water couldn't be running any longer though. The washing machine was probably down in the basement, with what had been Dom's wife.

He couldn't sleep. The zombies protested off in the distance, not close, but close enough to hear. They sounded by turns angry and sorrowful. Harris thought about it and decided it must really suck to be dead.

Dom sat in his lawn chair in the dark, an unmoving shadowy hulk against the sky, the glowing tip of a cigarette his only giveaway.

A car alarm went off a block over and didn't stop for three minutes, and when it did it soon kicked back on, the siren piercing.

Harris looked over at Buddy who was dead asleep, oblivious to all.

The alarm blared again. Harris could imagine some undead standing next to the car, thwacking it with its hand, setting off the alarm over and over again.

He got back up, pulled on his jeans and went over to sit by Dom. The man wasn't asleep and smoked a fresh Marlboro, tapping the ashes out into an empty beer can. He was listening to the Beach Boys and had the volume turned so only he could hear them.

"Can't sleep?"

"They're loud."

"If you want, you can go downstairs and sleep in a bed. Two bedrooms down there."

"No, that's okay." Harris resigned himself to another sleepless night. He didn't really want to be any closer to Lenore, to whatever that thing in the basement was.

"I got a package of ear plus down in the bathroom medicine closet. You can help yourself to those."

Harris thought about it and it sounded good.

Dom told him where they were and told him to take them all, that he had no need for them.

Harris descended the ladder into the linen closet and emerged in the upstairs hall. He passed the bedroom doors and went down to the first floor. The door Dom let them in by was boarded and sealed.

He flicked a switch and fluorescent light flooded the room. *Gotta love that generator.*

Harris was in a large open area, part kitchen, part dining room. A bay window on the other side of a dining room table was planked over completely. A small window above the kitchen sink was similarly encumbered. Nothing outside was getting in.

Harris spied the open door to the bathroom. Another door, which must have led downstairs, was crisscrossed with wooden boards, the contents of Dom's tool box strewn around the floor.

A thin beam of light from beneath the basement door. *The basement light must be on*, he realized. Harris did his best to avert his eyes from the door as he made his way into the bathroom, opened the medicine cabinet behind the mirror, found the ear plugs. The box was still sealed.

What had his mother told him and James she was looking for when she took the cotton swabs to their ears when they were kids? *Peas and carrots.*

He closed the bathroom cabinet and looked himself over in the mirror. A mess stared back at him. The stubble on his face had started to sprout into a full-on beard, and there was no more itching. Big dark circles ringed his eyes and his hair was matted.

Harris checked out the fridge freezer combo in the kitchen. Dom had it stocked. So long as the generator held out, he'd have enough food just like he said.

On one wall were framed family photos, and Harris couldn't explain why but he walked over and checked them out. Pictures of Dom and his family. A younger and thinner Dom in a tux, his wife in her wedding gown, a pleasant-looking woman. Dom and Lenore, and Dom with his arm around a young girl, the three of them standing at the Grand Canyon. The same girl at her first communion ceremony. Dom with three other rough and handy-looking men, all with beards and flannels and potbellies in bright orange hunting vests, cradling rifles in the woods.

Harris felt something watching him.

He turned about slowly, eyeing the two doors he hadn't paid much attention to when he'd come down. They led into other parts of the house but were closed. The generator hummed behind one of them.

No, not there. The basement steps.

A shadow interrupted the light from the crack. Something was on the other side of the door, something that knew he was there, that could hear him in the kitchen.

Harris wondered why he'd left the .357 on the roof and tried to calm himself, the door to the basement sealed.

He took a tentative step towards it, keeping his eyes on the shadow there. The outline shifted and the tips of three mottled fingers squeezed through underneath the door, grey and swollen, one nail black.

"Jesus!"

There wasn't much room for the fingers and they just fluttered a little, searching the linoleum. Noises from the other side of the door, grunts and shuffling, sounded like a pig in a trough.

Harris thought about the fingers, considered crushing them, stomping them into the kitchen floor. The notion soon passed. Crushing its fingers wouldn't hurt the thing on the other side of the door, not in any way that could meaningfully incapacitate it. And it wouldn't do for Dom to come down and find his dead wife's severed swollen digits smeared on the kitchen linoleum.

Harris held himself and his revulsion back and exited the kitchen slowly, watching the drumming fingers the whole time, shutting the kitchen light off behind himself.

Back on the roof he thanked Dom, made no mention of what he'd seen, took his clothes off and folded them up into a pillow again. He lay down flat on his back and looked to the sky, but there were no answers coming.

These earplugs weren't his favorites. They were made of wax. He placed one in each ear and pushed them into position. He preferred the ones you rolled up and stuck in your ear canal. Then again, he'd prefer being in bed at home with Raquel and he wasn't going to get that either.

The car alarm had ceased but Harris lay there with his heart going a mile a minute waiting for it, the .357 beside him, a hand resting on it, thinking he'd never be able to doze off. As he lay waiting for the car alarm to resume he passed over into a world of nightmares he could wake from.

The sunlight woke Buddy. He blinked and sat up, yawned, and scratched himself.

"Morning." Dom squatted beside the grill.

"How do," replied Buddy, seeing Harris was still asleep. The man had his head buried in his clothes, covered up.

Buddy stood and stretched, shook his leg, cracked his elbows and fingers, and pulled on his clothes. It was past sunrise and he felt good, finally a solid night's sleep.

Dom cracked eggs in a pan, mixing them.

"Hope you like scrambled," he said and Buddy said that he did.

While the eggs cooked, Buddy surveyed the neighborhood. The streets below were deserted. There were no people coming out of their houses to get in their cars and head for work, to wait on the corner for the bus.

"Let's eat," invited Dom. He had a thermos full of fresh coffee and it was strong and good. The eggs went down and they were the best eggs Buddy had ever had. Dom said they'd cook some up for Harris when he woke, to let him sleep some more.

"Yeah, he's been needing a good night's sleep," Buddy agreed.

"How'd you two hook up?"

Buddy told him, starting his story from their initial meeting at the school building, leaving out where he'd come from, what he'd seen, what he'd done.

"Your kids?" Dom nodded.

Buddy looked down at the tattoos on his upper arms. The sleeves on his t-shirt had ridden up so his ink was showing. On his left arm a little girl angel with the name Monique in fancy script. On his right a cherub-like boy with the name Henry.

"Yeah."

Dom saw how his question made the big man falter. He apologized and said he wasn't trying to be nosy.

"No, it's okay," Buddy said and meant it, said how he just didn't want to talk about them.

Dom sipped his coffee and lit another cigarette, thought how he'd like to ask Buddy if that's where he was going, if his ultimate destination was to find his kids. But he didn't, because a man's business is his own and Dom had the feeling that there was more to Buddy than the man let on, and it might not all be worth resurrecting.

Instead, Dom said to the man seated across from him, "You know, I was wondering. That little situation I was telling you about downstairs…"

Buddy knew what Dom was getting at and spared the man the necessity of asking.

"I can help you with that."

"Thanks." relief washed over Dom's face.

He finished his cigarette and stubbed it out on the roof.

"If it's any consolation," offered Dom. "I know that thing down there… that's not Lenore."

"It's hard, Dom, I know. You couldn't imagine how many people I seen didn't make it. They broke down, just couldn't go on anymore. Not like you could hang around with them, wait for them to snap out of it. Not if you want to live yourself."

"Yeah. I've been spared most of that up here," Dom said, indicating the roof.

"If it's okay by you, I'll go down there, take care of it myself. Leave Harris asleep."

"That's fine," Dom said and poured himself another cup of coffee.

When Buddy stood outside the door to the basement the only sound was the low hum of the generator from the next room.

The crack under the door was dark but Buddy spied the scratches on the linoleum. He put his ear to the boards nailed in place and listened but there was nothing to listen to.

The thing was down there, maybe waiting right behind the door. Buddy knew if she was a fast one she could pop right out on him the minute he got the door unfastened.

Buddy considered the nine millimeter in his left hand. He had the silencer threaded on, figured it best Dom didn't hear. He lay the pistol on the floor next to the electric lantern and started pulling nails out of boards with the back of a hammer.

He worked silently, listening for noise from the other side of the door, hearing nothing, depositing the nails on the kitchen floor, figuring he'd have to pick them up later. It'd be a real bitch if someone stepped on one and needed to get a tetanus shot.

When the last board had half its nails pried free, Buddy picked up the pistol, steadying it at the door, using one hand to pull the remaining nails out. The board gave with one nail left, the plank falling, swinging once and then hanging.

Buddy kept an eye on the door and put the hammer down, reached out with his free hand and grasped the knob. He listened. Nothing at all.

The door opened inwards at the top of a set of stairs. Buddy peered at the short landing. The light from the kitchen spilled over into the stairwell, casting its light all the way down to the bottom where the stairs let out into a little passageway.

Buddy picked up the electric torch, flicked it on and cast its beam down the stairs, around the exposed side of the stairwell beyond the banister.

He stepped down onto the landing to the top step. Checked to see if there were spaces between the steps where someone or something could reach through, trip him up and drag him down.

Four steps down Buddy heard something from behind and spun.

"Don't shoot," Harris said. He looked like he had just risen.

"Nice of you to join me," said Buddy.

"I would have been here earlier, but I woke with morning wood and didn't want to parade it around Dom."

"The old tent pole," laughed Buddy, but not too loud. "Well, you here now."

"And you in the dark," said Harris reaching out along the side of the wall, finding a light switch and flicking it on. Buddy wondered why he hadn't done that himself.

"This light was on last night when I came down here," Harris told him, the Colt Python in his hand.

"Let's do this," said Buddy, and Harris followed him down the stairs.

The stairway let out onto a passageway into a main room. Like Dom had said, it was completely finished and furnished, walls and ceiling added. Carpeting. A big sectional couch. Entertainment center with an enormous flat screen plasma television, DVD/VCR home theater, stereo system, speakers everywhere, more framed photos. Buddy and Harris looked around the room, but there was nothing behind the couch or the recliner.

Buddy nodded towards the sole door at the end of the family room. It was closed.

Harris motioned to himself, indicating that he'd open it. Buddy set himself in front of the door, braced the nine millimeter in one hand with the other. Harris pulled the door open to reveal an empty hallway.

"Damn, Buddy."

"You're starting to sweat like Dom now."

"I've always sweat a lot."

"I've noticed."

"Maybe we should just call her, wait for her to come out?"

Buddy shook his head.

Four doors off the hallway and they took them one at a time, Buddy opening, Harris watching the others to make certain Lenore didn't emerge.

The first door led into a boiler room. It looked like the pilot light was still burning and nothing was out of place amidst the dusty pipes.

The second door let into a laundry room. Washer, drier, a shelf to fold laundry. There was a laundry basket half full of folded clothes. Buddy pulled out a pair of enormous men's underwear. They had to be Dom's. He showed them to Harris and they both smiled. Buddy put them back.

Behind door number three there was a room where Dom kept all his tools.

Harris and Buddy stood looking at the fourth door, knowing this was it.

"Can we just call her out?" Harris asked.

"Shit, okay, go ahead."

Harris spoke to the door, "Lenore."

They waited expectantly but there was no reply.

"Lenore." Again, louder.

"Hey Lenore!" Buddy shouted.

"This isn't cool," said Harris.

"Ah, fuck it," Buddy pushed the door open and there was the thing that had been Lenore.

She didn't look up at them from where she knelt on the floor. Around her photo albums and shoe boxes, their contents—mostly pictures and papers—scattered around the room. The dead thing was looking at an upside down photo album, trying to turn a page, not having much luck, just going through the motions.

Harris was glad then that he hadn't mashed its fingers last night.

"Lenore," Buddy said, voice low, firm.

She ignored him.

Harris and Buddy looked at one another.

"Lenore," Buddy said again. This time it looked up at them but it was like it didn't see them and went back to its photo album.

"I know this is going to sound stupid," Harris said little louder than a whisper, "but do you think anything can be done for them?"

Lenore looked up at them, as if noticing them for the first time. Her mouth cracked open and she hissed, slobber spilling over her chin.

"No, Harris. I don't think anything can be done for them."

Harris raised the revolver.

"Nuh," Buddy brushed his arm aside, gesturing with the silenced nine. Harris nodded.

Buddy took a step into the room. The dead woman went back to her photo album, not in the least interested in his existence. He didn't get too close to her, extended the pistol, and squeezed the trigger.

"We should clean this up," Harris said. "I'll go see if I can find some paper towels."

They cleaned up the room as best they could, wrapping Lenore's body in giant black plastic garbage bags meant for leaves, picking up the photos and papers, putting them back in shoe boxes, unsure what belonged where. Harris got down and scrubbed at the fluid and gray matter splattered on the floor and wall and didn't stop till he was satisfied that everything was as clean as it was going to get. They stacked the shoe boxes and photo albums on the shelves they'd been pulled from.

Later that day Harris and Buddy carried the remains of Dom's wife out into the backyard. Dom smoked a cigarette on the other side of the roof, keeping watch on the street. He refused to see Lenore before the two men buried her, didn't want to. He'd remember her the way she'd been.

"HO-HO-HO!" The National Guardsman waved the barrel of his M-16 at the approaching Ford pickup truck. Behind him the survivors from his regiment, a handful of their original number, fanned out in a line on the avenue, covering the Ford, the silent stores on either side of the block and the deserted road behind them.

Buddy stopped the truck several yards from them.

"Let's play this cool," he said, noting Harris with his hand on the grip of that big old revolver he was lugging around.

Harris nodded, taking his hand from the Python.

Just to be safe, Buddy had the sawed-off shotgun next to him on the seat and a Smith and Wesson nine millimeter on his lap within easy reach.

The lead Guardsman trotted up to the pickup, lowering the assault rifle as he came, a reassuring signal to the two men seated inside.

"Hello there," Buddy said, the man leaning down outside the driver's side.

"Yeah, hi," he said, gruff but not unfriendly.

"Where you guys coming from?" Harris asked.

The Guardsman pointed back down the avenue towards the Queensboro Bridge into Manhattan.

"The city," he said.

"Shit, nobody getting off that island," murmured Buddy. He and Harris had seen what went down there with the boat captain.

"They bombed it, didn't they? That's what they did."

"You're asking us? They sure as hell did," Buddy affirmed. "How'd you guys survive?"

"Most of us didn't," he explained. "We were at the Mid-Town library, attached to a Marine heavy armor unit. We got overrun. Tanks can't fight those fucking things."

"It's true then?" Harris asked, knowing it to be, having seen it with his own eyes. "They are eating people?"

"They're eating people and then some of them people are getting up and eating more people," the Guardsman replied. "We hoofed it down into the subway tunnels—trains weren't running by then—and we hauled ass to the next station."

202

"Grand Central and 42nd?" Buddy asked, the first inkling Harris had that the big man knew about the Big Apple, that he might have been from around here. Up until this point he'd had this image of Buddy passing through on a motorcycle, and not some crotch rocket. Definitely a Harley. Maybe it was the saddle bags.

"Right," the guardsman continued. Three of his men were standing near the truck, their weapons poking down towards the macadam, and Harris didn't think they were going to try anything. "We came up onto the street from there and they were all over the place. Fucking everywhere."

One of the other guardsman, sad eyes on this one, nodded and turned.

"Anyway, we got back into the tunnel just about the time we heard the jets coming in and we hauled ass. Now here we are."

"You guys need a ride?" Buddy asked.

"Yeah, that would help," the man said,nodding. "Name's Edmond, and these here are Gill, Brophy, Shapiro, Annunziata, Hernan, Burdett—"

"What's up with that guy?"

"Koster's injured."

"Well get him in back then," said Buddy. "All you guys pile in. Where we headed?"

Harris moved over on the bucket seat, allowing Edmond to slide onto the front bench with them. The other guardsmen clambered into the bed and settled down, alert. They had ditched a good deal of their equipment and were laden only with their weaponry and ammunition. The one named Brophy carried an M-60 machine gun and Harris couldn't imagine towing that thing on an underground tunnel run.

"Just drive," suggested Edmond. "I think the best thing right now is to try and just get out of here."

Buddy put the pickup in gear and started down the avenue, veering from it at the first corner.

"I had a hell of a time getting in here from the Bronx," Harris said. "And that was a couple days ago. I doubt they're letting anyone over the bridges."

"You guys haven't heard have you?" Edmond shook his head. "Of course you haven't. Television and cable are out, and most of the radio stations are done."

"Heard what?" asked Buddy.

"The whole city is gone," Edmond sighed. "It's fallen. Done. Pretty crazy right now.

"It happened so goddamned fast," he said, his voice sad. "Containment didn't work."

The streets were deserted save for some abandoned cars scattered at random.

"So this crap is going on everywhere, right?" asked Buddy.

"Whole fucking world from what we hear."

"Sarge, 2 o'clock!" came the call from the back of the flat bed.

"Slow down," Edmond cautioned and Buddy brought the Ford to a halt.

A woman rushed down the street at them, dressed in a bathrobe which was untied and trailed open behind her. Her flesh was filthy and ensanguined and she cried as she came, a look of sheer terror in her eyes and a swaddled infant clutched to her bosom.

"Hey lady, wait!" A couple of the Guardsmen were standing in the back of the Ford looking to make room where there already was not enough, but the woman rushed past them in her bare bloody feet, never looking at them.

"Here they come!" cried Brophy.

A zombie lurched into view at the end of the block. This one wore the uniform of a bank security guard. It turned slowly and took first one step and then another, heading in their direction.

After the first came three more like it, one dragging behind itself a limp foot from an ankle that had been nearly chewed through.

"How you wanna play this, Sarge?" Gill asked, anxious.

"Fuck them, we engage when we gotta," yelled Edmond. To Buddy and Harris he explained, "Noise attracts them." To his men in the back he called, "Settle in there, guys." To Buddy, "Get us the hell out of here."

Buddy put the truck in reverse and made a three point turn, aiming them in the opposite direction. He drove carefully through the streets though there were no other cars coming or going.

"Can't everyone be dead already," he said.

"No," answered Edmond. "Figure a lot of them got out, got out of the city early on. Figure a whole bunch more are holed up inside their homes, waiting it out."

"Waiting it out," Harris muttered. Whatever this nightmare was, it didn't seem to be letting up.

"That's what they were told to do," said Edmond. "Government came on the TV and radio stations and said stay in your house, we're taking care of it. Now look at us. We ain't taking care of shit."

"Any idea what Uncle Sam's planning next?" asked Harris.

"There is no government anymore."

As they talked Buddy drove the truck up and down streets and avenues, avoiding arteries and drags where the homes and stores and buildings were engulfed in raging conflagrations.

"What about the evacuation centers?" Harris wanted to know.

"Ah, Christ," Edmond said, a hand to his forehead. "Sure, people flocked there early on. Before they sent us over to Mid-town, we were stationed at one. Then we started receiving reports that they were being overrun by those friggin' things. People were showing up at the refugee stations and just walking into warehouses full of them."

"Listen, guys," said Buddy. "Here's what I'm thinking we should do."

"Let's hear it," Edmond invited. "I'm open to suggestions at this point."

"One of two things. One, we drive this thing to a highway and see if we can't get out onto Long Island. Manhattan isn't an option and I have a feeling the other crossings won't be cake walks."

"Yeah, last we heard the Throgs Neck Bridge was swarmed with them," said Edmond. "And they blew the Whitestone and Verrazano."

"Damn," said Harris. "They blew the Whitestone."

"Thing is," Buddy continued, "we've got about half a tank of gas left in this truck so eventually we're going to have to find a gas station and hope the electricity isn't turned off so we can pump some gas, or we're going to have to go and get ourselves another vehicle."

"You mean this isn't your own ride?" Edmond was kidding.

"Or two, we find a place for ourselves to hole up. Wait it out. See what happens. You said these things eat people, right?"

"Fuckin' A," said Edmond. "I seen it myself, thirteen of our men including the lieutenant, in front of my very own eyes. When we shot those fuckers around McGillicutty, there wasn't much left to him."

"So eventually these things are going to run out of a food source and starve to death, right?" Buddy glanced at Edmond and Harris, hoping for confirmation.

"I sure as shit hope so," he said, but the sergeant didn't sound like that was likely.

"So we find ourselves a place to chill," Buddy decided. "That sound okay with you fellas?"

"Fine by me," said Edmond.

"How's that gonna fly with your boys in back?" Harris asked.

"At this point, they're just feeling lucky to be alive," explained Edmond. "Sure everyone wants to get back to their families, but first we gotta look after ourselves. Get Koster someplace he can rest."

"Okay," Buddy said. "It's settled then."

"So what kind of place you thinking we can find? House? Apartment building?" Edmond asked.

"Supermarket," said Harris. "Let's find a supermarket. Hang there."

"Sounds like a plan," Buddy said.

FROM TWO BLOCKS away the zombie spied Harris and took off after him running, arms pumping. He considered letting it get close enough to shoot its head off, but the noise would attract more of the things and his Colt only had six shots before he'd have to reload it.

Harris ran. It was almost completely dark out and he didn't bother to stop at any houses where lights burned inside. As he ran, he thought it no small wonder that there was electricity still, street lamps burning. He kept to the wider avenues and boulevards, skirting the slower moving monsters he came upon. When he passed them they would hobble forward after him cawing and gawking.

The booker was still on his tail, about a block away. It ran with its arms and legs splayed and a demented bellowing, a spastic beast let loose from the blackest hell.

Harris started to think he could outrun the freak. All he needed was a straight-away wide enough so he could get up some speed and not run headlong into another one staggering about, but narrow enough that he could make a quick turn here and there and shake the thing. In the meantime, he monitored his breathing and kept an eye open. His nasal passages loosened, he hocked and expelled a gob of mucous in the road. The sun had mostly bowed out, only residual light left, and this was not good.

He hoped he wouldn't encounter another of the running ones.

Seven more blocks of running pretty much flat-out and Harris was getting tired, his throat dry and his lungs raw, a throb in his side he did his best to ignore. When he saw the school he decided he'd do his thing there. Schools were places he'd spent a lot of his life. He felt comfortable in them.

The running aberration in hot pursuit was half a block behind when Harris crashed through the front doors, relieved to find them open, wondering for half a second what he would do if he was heading right into a hallway or building crowded with the things, a warren or haven for the monstrosities. He was relieved to find the corridor empty. He skidded to a stop on the slick floor about ten feet inside the entrance, reaching into his duffle bag and pulling out the big ass kitchen knife William Richardson had given him.

"Come on," he breathed.

It took a few seconds more and then the thing was up the steps after him, the front door booming against the wall behind it, the freak loping for Harris with a baneful perseverance in its eyes, its arms extended as it came for him, teeth flashing, spittle—

Thwack!

The knife made a wet sound as Harris buried it in the creature's face, the blade disappearing up to the haft just to the side of its nose. The thing drooping to the floor, down for the count.

Harris breathed heavily.

He went to the front door and found it easy to lock. Just a twist of a screw located under the bar pushed to open it. Similar to the door at Hillcrest. He used a penny in his pocket to turn it, wondering why people didn't save their pennies anymore. He'd seen people—mostly younger ones—toss their pennies into the street or leave the register without gathering their change when it was less than a nickel.

See a penny pick it up, his father used to say.

Satisfied the door was as secure as it was going to be, Harris moved away from it, not wanting any of the slow-moving things outside working their way towards it to see him. He retrieved his knife from where it was implanted, stepped on the body's neck and yanked the blade free. The knife had gone all the way through so that it poked out the other side.

It was a big knife.

Harris kept his noise to a minimum as he traversed the halls. The lights off, there was enough natural illumination from the faded day outside to see by. That, and the red glow of the illuminated EXIT signs.

He looked into the classrooms and offices he passed, not seeing anyone or anything. There might be people hiding in some of them, maybe huddled in a coat closet or under a desk and he thought about calling out as he went his way, but decided against it.

There could be more of those things in there, too.

The hallway branched off to the left and the right and Harris went right, making sure nothing was behind him down the left first.

All the classrooms appeared vacant.

He passed a set of doors behind which the gloom of a darkened stairwell beckoned, and dared tread not near it.

Harris proceeded cautiously, paranoid, turning to look back the way he'd come every few seconds. He had this feeling that they'd come pouring out of the classrooms all at once, surround him, bring him down, denude him to the bone.

Another hallway branching off from this one, unlit. Harris peered into the inky depths with their daunting shadows and baleful promises and moved on.

At the end of the hall he reached a set of double doors with another illuminated EXIT sign above them.

This would be a gym or assembly hall or something of the like. He'd been in enough schools to be familiar with their layouts.

Opening the door and smelling the wax from the hardwood floor he knew it to be a gymnasium.

There was a light switch aside the door and Harris flicked it, immediately wishing he hadn't.

At the far end of the gym one of those undead things looked up from where it knelt, chewing on the bowels of some teenage girl in what had once been a pristine green and white basketball uniform. The undead moaned at Harris and worked its way, slowly, almost arthritically, to its feet, a loop of intestine still clutched in its hand, trailing from the girl.

From the way it was dressed it looked like it had been the basketball team coach. The nightmare staggered towards him, arms akimbo, like some spasticated inebriate.

Not today, thought Harris, turning and pushing through the double doors to the hallway, disturbed to find the passage barred by a trio of undead that hadn't been there before. They gasped and cawed when they saw him and started his way.

"Right." Harris closed the doors and made a beeline for the other side of the gymnasium, keeping well clear of the basketball coach, spying another set of double doors, figuring them to probably let out onto the schoolyard or street. He hadn't been paying much attention as he'd run up to the building.

Harris reached the doors as two more of the undead emerged from the boys' locker room.

He pushed against the double doors but, they didn't budge.

Great.

Harris put his shoulder to them, to no avail.

He looked around, thinking fast, six shots in the pistol in one hand, the knife in his other, loose rounds in his bag and pockets. Bleachers. The locker rooms. The basketball hoops on fiberglass backboards attached to the wall via metal tubing. Maybe he could climb up onto one of them, get above these things.

Instead he jetted over to three soda and snack machines set side by side. He tossed the knife on top of one and hauled himself up after, rolling atop two of them. He sat there, his feet drawn up as far away from the edge as possible, the .357 aimed between his legs, and waited for the first of the undead to reach the machines. It stared up at him and emitted an apoplectic screech.

There were eight undead in the gymnasium and one by one they circled the vending machines, staring up at Harris expectantly. Some moaned and others rasped incoherently, but most stood silently in place, staring, waiting. The basketball coach walked bent over, still holding four feet of bowels, craning its neck to see the man on top of the soda machine. A woman in a dress with both hands chewed off thumped her stubs against the display window, streaking the plastic red.

Marvelous. The zombies didn't seem able to climb, and although a few punched and pawed weakly at the vending machines and tried to shake them, that didn't seem like it was going to work for them either. Harris knew he was relatively safe where he was, barely out of their reach.

They couldn't get to him and he could pick them off one by one anytime he wanted.

Thing was, they weren't going anywhere.

And neither was he.

His sweat and clothes had dried on him, leaving a sour smell at which he wrinkled his nose. In time, Harris drifted off.

"Yo boss, whatta ya guarding them things for?"

Harris and the fifteen dead things circling the vending machines on which he drowsed all looked as one as a large black man with a pair of worn black leather saddle bags over his shoulders and a sawed-off shotgun in his hand strode into the gym as Harris had hours prior.

The guy didn't wait for an answer.

"Let me do this," he explained, making eye contact with Harris, fiddling around in his saddle bags. "We want to keep this quiet. Noise brings them."

The stranger had set the sawed-off aside on the bleachers and had a pistol with a silencer attached in his hands. The things surrounding the vending machines sauntered away from them in his direction.

"Be my guest," said Harris.

Harris had never heard a silenced shot in real life before but he thought they sounded much like the ones heard in movies. *Thhhp! Thhhp!* Muffled, not silent, but still much quieter compared to the crack an unsilenced shot made and he'd heard a lot of those reverberating through the streets he'd trekked.

The things dropped one by one. After downing eight of them, the man reloaded and put the gun on the bleachers next to his saddle bags. He moved into the nearest ones with some kind of military blade, coaxing the zombies towards him, circling around each and taking it down with quick thrusts through their skulls.

"Gotta conserve ammo," he offered by way of explanation, wiping the blade off on the skirt of the thing with no hands.

The undead hadn't even gotten close to the guy and he was a damn good shot too. Harris was impressed. Eight rounds, eight of these things dead.

Still, Harris wondered, *what next?* and he kept the Colt Python close.

"Come on off of there," said the big man, sheathing the knife and putting the scabbard in the saddle bags.

"My legs are asleep on me." Harris let himself down off the vending machines, which meant turning his back on the other man, and when he put his full body weight down he nearly crumpled but managed to keep his balance. He had the .357 in one hand and made sure to keep it down, not threatening with it, knowing the other man was a better shot than he.

"How long you been up there?" the black guy was sitting on the bleachers, one elbow on his knee, relaxing.

"Few hours. Tried massaging them as much as I could up there, didn't really want to stand up and stretch them out."

"I'd come over here if I were you, get away from them doors."

"Why's that?"

"I was being followed, that's why I came in here. Some of these things, whatever they are, they're not sneaky."

Harris walked over to the bleachers, avoiding the carcasses, careful not to get between the door and the man with the silenced pistol.

"Call me Buddy," the man said and extended his free hand. Harris took it, noting that it encircled his own like his was a kids'. Harris was a hair under six foot himself and not a slight man, but this guy was a bruiser. He noted the saddle bags in which the man had stored the sawed-off and he had the guy pegged for a biker or some other roughneck.

"Harris," he said.

"So, Harris, just how long were you going to chill out up there?"

Harris couldn't help himself. He broke into a smile. He liked this guy Buddy who had probably saved his life. "I was waiting for them to take the Pepsi challenge," he said back.

Buddy laughed and his laugh was deep and throaty. Harris thought he detected a slight southern accent but couldn't tell. He knew a lot of black folk with accents that sounded slightly southern to his white ears and a lot of them weren't southerners at all, so what did he know.

"I saw the lights in the gym from outside. Figured I'd check this place out. No kids in here?"

"Didn't see any living ones. But I didn't really look into any of the rooms too closely."

Harris was rank and his clothes damp, and he could smell himself.

"It's gotten worse out there?" he asked.

Buddy shook his head. "It's bad, man, it's bad. More and more of them things, less and less soldiers and cops. The curfew. No one supposed to be outside on the street."

The big man paused.

"Wait a second, Harris. You hear that?"

"Hear what?"

The doors to the gym opened from the other side and a Marine in fatigues burst in, screeching and bee-lining it for Harris and Buddy.

Thhhp! a geyser of blood burst from the man's upper chest, unbalancing it momentarily but it rushed on—*Thhhp*!—its head snapped back, the side of it fragmenting, and yet the creature still—*Thhhp*!—the head jerked back again and it collapsed to its knees, then ignominiously pitched forward onto the mess that was left of its face and was still.

"Damn," said Harris. "You think it was alone?"

"It was when it was tailing me in the streets."

"Right." Harris cinched his knapsack tighter. "Buddy, thanks man. I think you saved my life. But I gotta be going."

"Hold up a second," Buddy held up a hand. "What's the hurry?"

"Manhattan."

"Manhattan?"

It was the way Buddy said it. He didn't say it like *Manhattan?*, like *what-are-you-some-kind-of-asshole?* He said it as if it was a perfectly legitimate destination given the circumstances, just not one he'd expected to hear.

"Yeah, Manhattan."

"Ohh, you got someone there, huh?"

"Yeap."

"I hate to sound like that goddamn donkey from Shrek," said Buddy, and Harris sensed the man was working something over in his mind. "But mind if I tag along?"

Buddy was planning something and Harris wondered what it was. If he'd wanted Harris dead he could have just left him for the things, or he could have killed him himself by now.

"Just so long as you don't slow me down," he said, realizing as he said it just how stupid it sounded, breaking into a short self-conscious laugh himself.

The big man must have had a good sense of humor, because he was chuckling himself. "Yeah," he observed. "You looked like you were going places when I waltzed in here. I'll try not to get under your feet."

Harris waited while Buddy searched the body of the dead Marine.

"You ever handled one of these before?" Harris caught what Buddy tossed him. "This is a hand grenade, isn't it?"

"Mmm-hmm."

"No, man, I've only seen them used in movies. Here, I might blow us both us."

Harris opened the doors, pistol up. The coast appeared clear.

"Hey, what you got there? That big ol' hog leg?" Buddy was referring to Harris's revolver.

"This is a Colt Python, a three fifty-seven magnum."

"Mighty fine-looking weapon. How's it shoot?"

"Devastating. And if I can learn to handle it like you do that silenced pistol of yours, I'll be dangerous."

"You're going to get your chance out there on that street in about two seconds Harris. Ventilated rib on that thing. Nice.

"So why are we going to Manhattan again?"

Harris looked away.

"She got a sister?"

"Mister," sighed Harris, "You are kind of like that donkey with all that noise you make."

"Oh yeah," noted Buddy. "Right."

Then he let out his best Eddie Murphy laugh.

NIGHT TIME WAS proving an increasingly treacherous time to move about in. During the day Harris or Buddy could usually spot the undead before they ran into them. That is, if they stayed to wide open streets and avenues. Even then, there were other undead that seemed adept at hiding, waiting for one to get close or—worse yet—*pass* their hiding spot, and then they'd attack from behind.

Harris hadn't been a religious man in a long time, but he considered it nothing short of a minor miracle that he'd made it this far. Hillcrest seemed so long ago. Had it really been less than a week? He and the big man who called himself Buddy moved through the night, a full moon lighting their route. Armed soldiers in personnel carriers came and they hid when they heard them, neither man trusting that the militia and the hardcore troops would be casting a discerning eye at potential targets. In the distance they heard the sounds of machine guns.

More than once they passed areas where battles had been waged. There would be dozens of inert bodies, some in soldier's gear, many others obviously civilian. Several of the bodies were blown to pieces, the ones that weren't were all head-shot. Then there were the wholly and partially eaten bodies, various chewed-through limbs, unidentifiable innards and remnants, the lower half of a man here, the upper portion of a woman there. Thousands of shell casings littered the streets.

They walked by buildings with whole sides blown out, charred and rubbled, looking like some devastated town from the European theater in the Second World War.

Once they saw five living human beings ahead of them. Harris yelled out to them but they ran off. When he and Buddy reached where the group had been the people were long gone, with no indication of where that might be.

Eventually Buddy suggested they find a place to hunker down.

Harris wanted to keep going, but he knew Buddy was right. They weren't getting into Manhattan tonight. Raquel was either okay or she was… He refused the alternative.

They found a six story building of condominiums on a residential block. The door to the entrance hallway and elevator yawned open. Buddy led their way up the stairs, a flashlight taped to the barrel of the sawed-off shotgun. Harris had a second flashlight the man had produced from the saddle bags. The electricity had gone down all around and the gloom in the stairwell was deep.

On the first landing Buddy cracked the door to the hallway and listened.

"You hear that?" he mouthed to Harris, and Harris leaned forward. Banging, somewhere down the murky passage in one of the apartments.

Up, Buddy motioned and they mounted the stairs again, deciding against the second floor as well, only stopping when they reached the landing for the third. Again the big man cracked the door and listened but there wasn't anything to hear.

Harris followed Buddy's lead, trying the knobs on the doors they passed, each door numbered. The first few locked, and Harris wondered where the people had gone. Were they inside, hiding? Was something else inside? A building this size shouldn't be so silent.

They could knock but that didn't mean anyone would let them in, and it might bring out something worse.

The shadows in the hallway seemed to play tricks before Harris' fatigued eyes when a door opened for Buddy.

Buddy held up his index finger, Harris sidling closer with the flashlight in one hand, revolver in the other. He knew what they were going to have to do next: check the condo, make sure it was clear.

Buddy moved in first, the sawed-off held at shoulder level, the beam of light splaying across a short hallway that let onto an eat-in kitchen on the right, a living area straight ahead. He swiveled into the kitchen, panning the light back and forth over the counter and cabinets, under the table, around the chairs. Harris closed the door behind them and slipped the chain into place but didn't secure the deadbolt. They would get out fast if they had to.

The living room was empty save for some furniture: a sectional, coffee table, entertainment center. Two short halls led off it.

Harris motioned to one passage, indicating he'd check it, but Buddy shook his head. *Together*, he mouthed.

They investigated the corridor on the left first. A full bathroom and a bedroom, no people, living or otherwise. They checked the closets, under the bed, anyplace something nasty could be lurking, waiting.

The hall on the right had three doors. An empty closet. Master bedroom with another full bath attached. Harris drew back the shower curtain and checked the tub. A wash cloth draped on the hot water spigot. The third door opened into an office, a desk and computer, bookshelves and filing cabinet.

"I always knew I should have invested in a condo."

"Yeah," said Harris. "They're all right, but then you gotta follow the rules of the co-op."

"That a bad thing?"

"Well, not necessarily, but some people might have a problem if you want to leave your shoes in the hallway outside your door, something like that."

"Uh-huh." Buddy nodded and they returned to the living room. Harris secured the front door with the dead bolt.

"Give me a hand," he said to Buddy and together they moved a piece of the sectional, the table from the kitchen and a recliner, and piled them against the entry.

Reasonably assured that they were safe, Harris finally started to calm down. He noticed then how weary he was, thinking he hadn't sleep in days, just those few hours at Richardson's house. *The hell had happened to William and his family anyway?* Outrunning those things all day, hiding like a trapped animal. His face was stubbled, it itched him something awful.

Buddy rummaged through the fridge.

"See if you can find some candles," he said, pulling Tupperware containers out of the refrigerator, checking their contents, smelling them. He withdrew a half gallon of orange juice, felt it was still somewhat cold—the power must have gone out earlier that day then—and drank from it, offering it to Harris when he was done.

Harris took it and drank without wiping the top.

"We've got some candles." Harris had found a package of fifteen six-inch white candles.

Several of the candles glowed, shedding their iridescence over the framed family portraits adorning the living room walls. Harris thought about the Richardsons again, about their daughter being bitten and how now he knew if you got bit you died and then you came back.

Buddy sprawled out on another part of the sectional.

"So. Manhattan, huh?"

Harris was tired, not much in a talking mood. But felt he owed the other man something.

"Yeah, Raquel's there. My wife."

"Um-hmm."

"And you? You got anybody?"

"In this city, no." The sawed-off was propped up against the cushion within easy reach. "No, my people moved away from here long time ago."

"You lose anybody?" asked Harris, wondering if there was a better way to put it.

Buddy contemplative for a few seconds. "Yeah, guess I have."

Harris wondered about Daffy. Was the dog okay? He had left her out in the backyard. She could hide under the deck in inclement weather but food would be a problem for her and she was probably hungry and lonely. Was all of Westchester County also like this place?

"When was the last time you got some sleep?" Buddy asked.

"Oh, while ago."

"Here's how we're gonna do. We sleep in shifts, okay. Why don't you go first, catch yourself some z's. I wake you in a few hours, then you keep an eye and an ear out while I do likewise."

"Sounds good. But how about you sleep first?"

"Nah, I'm cool. I got some thinking I want to do anyway. And you look like you could use it a lot worse than me."

Harris stood, taking his flashlight and gun, deciding he'd sleep in the master bedroom.

"Hey, Buddy." He stopped on his way. "Thanks."

"You're welcome."

Buddy listened to Harris enter the master bedroom and settle down. He sat alone in the dark listening to the sounds of the condominium.

After awhile he pulled a chair over to the screened window. The moon was still full, so he had a good view of the street below. There was a glow in the distance as a mammoth fire raged. Buddy figured it for a block or two of houses, hell, maybe even a whole neighborhood. How would such a fire start? People setting fire to those things? The military burning homes? A couple hours before he'd met Harris he'd watched a tank spew flame from its turret, lighting up a group of stores where the dead attacked the living, burning all.

He watched the street and listened. In the distance he heard sporadic gunfire. Several minutes would pass between bursts. Once a treaded military vehicle rumbled by at the end of the block.

Motion below caught his eye. Across the street a figure emerged from an alley, bent forward, moving slowly, looking both ways. It was followed by another, then a third. In all ten people scampered down the block like wet rats looking to get out of a storm.

Buddy considered calling out to them but wondered what he would say. What he could say. Instead he remained silent and watched them until they rounded a corner.

He wondered where they were going. Probably the same place everybody else was.

"YELL AND I'LL kill you right here."

"Harris, What the—"

"Shut up."

The nine millimeter pressed roughly in Thompson's neck.

"Harris, I don't—"

"I said *shut up.*"

Thompson had no idea what was going on, but he was frightened because he knew Harris wasn't kidding and he had never seen the man like this. As soon as they'd descended the stairs to the basement of Harris and Julie's house and turned on the lights alarm bells had started to sound in the back of Thompson's skull. But instead of reacting to them immediately he chose to ignore them, doubting himself, telling himself he'd no reason to fear Harris. Why would the other man want to harm him?

He thought he was helping Harris move some stuff. Things Julie couldn't help with either because they were too heavy or because she was still freaked out by the attack that morning, maybe she didn't even want to venture into the house. He cursed himself for being naïve enough to think that Harris' asking him was Harris' way of letting Thompson know all was copasetic between them. That all was okay after what'd happened that night those weeks back. That maybe they could be friends again.

Nothing in the basement needed to be moved. A solitary lightbulb hanging from the ceiling revealed the basement was bare except for two iron poles cemented into the floor, chains strewn around the poles.

"You know what Markowski used those poles for Thompson? You know. Used to tie zombies to them, shoot them, cut them up, probably did other stuff to them too. You used to do that stuff with him, huh?"

Thompson didn't say anything—Harris had told him to shut up— concentrating on the pressure from the pistol bore. Harris' hand reached around him and took the pistol Thompson kept at his waist. Thompson heard it clatter against the floor somewhere in the stygian depths beyond the light and feared with it lost as well his last chance. But Thompson told himself Harris could be reasoned with.

"Move," Harris commanded, herding him forward to one of the iron posts.

Mr. Vittles came into the light.

The poles both waist high, embedded in the cement of the basement floor, a few feet apart each from the other.

The blow to the back of his head knocked Thompson down and he reeled, saw stars, gasped, the skin under his hair opened, the side of his face wet.

The cat gave Harris a look.

"Sit with your back against that pole."

"Harris—Harris, p-please—" Thompson begged from his hands and knees. Harris kicked him savagely, like he was trying to score a field goal, and Thompson flopped over onto his back.

"How's that feel? That feel good?"

Thompson got his breath back, wincing from the pain in his trunk. "Harris, please, I don't want to die like this—"

"You don't want to die like this. Like this. Back up against the pole. Put your back against the pole."

Thompson cringed from the agony in his midsection as he hauled himself up onto his elbows then his rear. Harris stood over him with the nine millimeter aimed at his head.

Harris moved around behind him where Thompson couldn't see him and this terrified him further, and he thought this his chance, act now or never, but before he could make a move a wallop from the pistol butt opened yet another fissure in his scalp. He buckled forward and Harris had him from behind, took one of his hands then the other, securing them with plastic restraints.

Mr. Vittles made a noise deep down in his throat and slouched away from the men.

"Then go on then," Harris yelled after the cat.

"…help… Help! Help!" Thompson started to shriek but Harris began kicking him viciously about the head and face, pummeling him into the stake, snarling "Shut up-shut up-shut up."

Thompson was barely aware of it when Harris threaded one of the 3/8ths inch chains through his arms, around his lap.

"Try to move," Harris commanded a couple minutes later when it looked like Thompson wasn't going to black out. Petrified, Thompson said nothing.

Harris kicked him in the shoulder and Thompson fell forward, his sprawl arrested by the chains between his arms.

"H-Harris—Harris," he managed between split lips and broken teeth. "Wh-what's going on, man?"

"You tell me, Thompson," Harris said and there was spite in his voice, spite and malice.

Harris went around and squatted down across from Thompson, placing the nine millimeter on the basement floor.

"Ha-Harris, look, look, ho-honestly man, I-I-I do-don't know what the fuck, I don't know what the fuck you're talking about, man. Just tell me."

Harris looked at him and smirked, shaking his head derisively.

"Then just shut up." He stuffed a wadded cloth into Thompson's mouth while Thompson protested futilely.

Harris stood none too steadily, leaving the nine millimeter on the floor. He ignored Thompson, unbuttoned his shirt and pulled it off. Thompson saw his upper arm was bandaged, the skin around it black and dead, the veins pronounced, varicose, Harris' entire upper body discolored.

Thompson shook his head in bewilderment, his eyes tearing.

"I'm going to want to take that rag out of your mouth. Talk to you. But when I do I don't need you screaming for help. Okay? So, if you scream like that, this is what you're going to get."

Harris kicked Thompson's arm repeatedly until he was satisfied it was broken.

"Don't pass out on me, Thompson. We're just getting started," Harris had the second skein of chain from the floor, a metal collar attached at one end. The other end already secured to the second pole.

"Harris, Jaysis, what's got in ya?"

Bobby Evers stood at the bottom of the stairs, his hunting rifle slung around his back.

"Bobby," Harris muttered to himself.

"Thompson, oh Christ almighty lad, what's the man done to ya?"

"Bobby, listen to me—"

"You better bleedin' well get started mate because I am listen' to ya. What the fook is the meanin' a'this?"

"Bobby. Bobby. This morning, the gate. It was Thompson, Bobby," Thompson was shaking his head vehemently, seated on the floor, "Thompson opened the gate, Thompson let them into Eden. Thompson broke into my house and Thompson left the door open so they could get in."

"Jesus Christ, Harris, what's a matta' with ya', your skin, man."

"Oh," realized Bobby, "Ya been bit."

While they were talking, Bobby had moved forward closer to Harris and Thompson. Spying the bandage on Harris' shoulder, a sad look crossed his face and he brought his lower lip up over his upper. The rifle was still slung across his back.

"Harris, first things we gotta get Thompson here untied, get him some—" Bobby stepped towards Thompson seated on the floor, ignoring Harris, meaning to unbind the young man.

The metal collar attached to the end of the chain caught Bobby in the side of the face and he went down. Evers hit his knees and held out a hand, unable to see from one eye, the collar hitting his hand as Harris jerked it back and forward like a wet towel, three of Bobby's fingers snapping back. Evers let out a final "Jaysis" and rolled onto his left side, shrugging out of the thirty-thirty but Harris was upon him from behind, wrapping a forearm around his neck and pulling back on it with everything he had.

"Just fucking don't move, Bobby," spat Harris, straining. "Just be still, damn you."

Bobby flailed, trying to reach around and pry Harris from his neck, the hunting rifle gone across the floor somewhere in their struggle.

"Damn you, Bobby, damn you," Harris growled between barred teeth.

The last thing Bobby saw was Thompson straining at the pole, trying to scream through the gag in his mouth.

Harris choked Bobby out but kept the Irishman locked like that for some time thereafter because he needed to be certain. He felt incredibly weak and worried that if Bobby was bluffing and got up when he let go he might not be able to take him down again.

Sweating profusely, Harris wobbled when he stood and had to hold out a hand to the pole to steady himself.

"Yeah, Thompson, I got bit. Surprised?" Harris took up the metal collar again from the floor and placed it around his own ankle, snapping it shut.

"So you want to tell me what happened now Thompson, or do I gotta tell you?"

Crying silently, Thompson looked away from Harris.

"Okay. I tell you. But we gotta make this quick, before someone else comes looking."

Before Bobby woke up.

Harris made sure the fit was snug, that his foot could not slip out of the restraint.

"So this morning I wake up and I'm being chewed on by some dead Rastafarian motherfucker, right? So the zombies come into my house and up into my bedroom and they bite me and they almost eat my girlfriend, Thompson, they *almost eat my girlfriend*. But we wake up and manage to blast hell out of them. They almost got my girlfriend, Thompson. Think about that. My *girlfriend*, Thompson. Julie. Is that what you were hoping? Sick fuck."

Harris tugged on the chain, checking its connection to the stake. He left enough slack in it so he could easily reach Thompson's position. Satisfied, he sat down across from the other, resting his back against the cold pole.

"You know Thompson, when she first came to Eden, you wouldn't leave Julie alone. How'd it go—let me guess. Oh yeah, first the initial attraction, that puppy dog crush. Then the friendly-guy, let-me-help-you-out-there, that whole act, seeing if maybe she'd take to this nice guy, this kind fellow looking out for her."

Thompson whimpered.

"But she doesn't show any romantic interest in Mr. Nice Guy, so Mr. Nice Guy starts obsessing in his mind, and all he can do is think about the leggy supermodel woman, the one who wants nothing to do with him romantically. So Mr. Nice Guy—that's you, isn't it, Thompson? Mr. Nice Guy goes and gets drunk off his ass one night and—in front of everyone else—declares his love for this girl who doesn't care one whit about him the way he thinks she should. And what's worse—you know what's worse, Thompson?"

Harris picked up his nine and waved it in Thompson's direction.

"What's worse is she's got a boyfriend by then, and he's there that night and her boyfriend tries to calm *you* down, because by now you're yelling and making a scene and you're yelling at the girl and making her feel uncomfortable. And you get stupid enough to take a swing at the boyfriend and he has to lay you out like the punk motherfucking faggot that you are. And that's humiliating, isn't it Thompson? That's frustrating, right?

"Oh yeah, you can't answer."

Harris dropped the clip and started popping nine millimeter rounds out of the magazine, tossing them over his shoulders.

"She loves you, she loves you not, she loves you…Well guess what, Thompson." Harris held the final bullet up between his index finger and thumb and apprised it. "She doesn't love *you* motherfucker. So next morning, you apologize to all involved, say it was the drink.

"But you know what, Thompson? I never bought that excuse. I been drunk before and done stuff I regretted later, but the drink didn't make me do it. I did it because I *wanted* to do it, Thompson, that's how I felt. All the drink did was lower my inhibitions.

"But *you*, Thompson, *you* wake up, and you're convinced Julie will never be yours because, well, because she doesn't like you, matter of fact she's probably feeling pretty repulsed by you.

"Uh, let me finish, we're almost done here."

Harris thumbed the last round back into the magazine.

"So you apologize and everyone says it's okay, but truth is, it's not okay, not least of all by your way, and you can't get her out of your mind, but you don't want to be a stalker and you know how the community wouldn't take too kindly to that kind of garbage. You start to scheme and plot in your head, thinking *maybe*, maybe if you can get the boyfriend out of the way, then you'd have a chance. Right?"

Thompson was saying something through the gag.

"And maybe you'd be the one leading the charge, leading the rescue, come guns blazing into the house."

Harris popped the magazine back into the pistol. He pulled back on the receiver and let it snap forward, chambering the round. He hit the release button and dumped the magazine again, tossing it away.

"Girl's boyfriend is dead now, right, and what's she gonna remember? She's gonna remember *you* saving her ass from the same fate, and *maybe* she'd lighten up and in time, as she got over the dead boyfriend, *maybe* she'd start to feel differently about you, maybe you two could have a future together, right?"

Thompson was protesting violently, shaking his head back and forth, pleading through the gag.

"Or maybe, just *maybe* Thompson, maybe you're so goddamn sick in your fucking head that you figure, if I can't have her, no one can, and you expect she'd be killed along with the boyfriend. Are you that sick, Thompson? Are you? Because anyone who opens the front fucking door and let's those things into Eden, he's gotta be."

Harris looked at the pistol in his hand.

"No, Thompson. I hate you. I fucking hate you. And you know what I hate the most about you? I hate the fact that I'm going to spend my last moments with you. With *you* of all people. That fact makes me sick. I hate that you make me feel this way."

Harris shook his head and a tear streaked down his cheek.

"That because of you, I see that I can be this way to another human being. That I have this in me."

Harris ignored whatever Thompson was babbling about, reaching into his pocket calmly, finding the lighter, sliding the Zippo across the small amount of floor that separated them.

"I found that outside this morning," said Harris, "By the gate."

Thompson looked at his Zippo and the look of disbelief on his face broke as more tears and bawls came and he sobbed and his face turned all red and he begged Harris through the cloth to listen to him, to talk to him.

Harris ignored him, thought about Julie and then Raquel, flicked the safety off the pistol, pushed it against his own chest and fired.

It was like getting hit harder than he could ever imagine being hit and it burned, it burned very badly.

The gun shot sobered Thompson up. He watched in shock as Harris collapsed from a seated position onto his side. The hand under Harris still clutched the pistol. His other arm was traipsed over his head, stretched out, the fingers of that hand twitching spasmodically.

Harris's mouth opened as he gasped for breath, his hand letting go of the pistol as he rolled onto his back, both hands going to his chest where blood flowed.

He heard the muffled protests coming from Thompson as if from a distance. He couldn't breath. It was like someone had knocked the breath from him, like when he got hit in the chest with the dodge ball back in gym class in fifth grade. The floor felt hard and cold under him and it wasn't a bad feeling.

The chain around Harris's ankle lay slack, a loop of it running to the pole.

Harris lolled his head to one side, staring at an empty wall, staring into the illimitable void. Someone was saying something somewhere but he couldn't make out the words.

The basement was still and Thompson watched as Harris's panting lessened, subsided, ceased. Harris was facing away from him so Thompson couldn't see the glassy look steal over his eyes.

Thompson beheld his lighter and wept. Harris was dead. Bobby wasn't moving and looked dead as well. Thompson's nose was running and he couldn't wipe it, he was heaving with his sobs. He strained against the chains that were looped through his wrists and arms and lap but they wouldn't give and his arms, his ribs, most of his body all screamed at him.

Stuck tight to the pole, Thompson cried until there were no tears left.

Harris was dead.

Thompson sat there, alone in the basement, chained to a pole, unable to move, a dead man chained to a pole not two feet from him. He could reach out with his foot and prod Harris's body if he wanted, but what was the use?

Every time he moved even just the slightest bit, his midsection sent searing jolts of pain through his core. Thompson figured his ribs were broken. His one arm was useless and blood oozed from the splits in his scalp.

As Thompson sat wondering how long it would take someone to find him down in the basement Harris's body shuddered and sat up. The zombie turned its head and watched Thompson begin to shriek through the gag.

JOHN TURNER BRUSHED the back of his hand across his forehead, wiping the perspiration away and pushing his glasses back up his nose. Not a hot day, but the sun was out. Working outdoors, mixing concrete, fixing sidewalks and curbs with his father Fred, with Panas and Thompson, the sun high in the sky, it all brought out the sweat. The leather from the holstered .38 on his side chafed him.

"Let's take a break, guys," announced his father, "How's about it?"

Things vastly different in Eden since Graham's ouster. Decisions were argued over and reached by everyone, not disseminated from on high. There were no leaders, though most tended to defer or at least listen very carefully to what certain people like Buddy or Harris, even Bobby Evers, had to say. People also tended to esteem John's father, as he was a hard worker and one of the older men in Eden.

"Sounds good," said Panas, an American flag do-ragged on his head.

Not everyone in Eden accorded respect to his father and the other older men and women. Guys like Diaz were pretty much selfish bastards. The only thing that seemed to keep them in line was the approval or disdain of everyone else, and some days that wasn't even enough. Not that Diaz was disrespectful towards John's father—if he was, John would have had to do something about that—the guy just had a certain attitude that made him unpleasant to be around.

Diaz wouldn't have been someone John would have hung out with before all this happened, before Eden. And John would have flipped if either of his sisters had brought a guy like Diaz home.

"Hey John," called Laurie from down the block.

Laurie was a cute girl, a couple years younger than John at eighteen. She'd been in Eden when John and his father had arrived, but she was alone, no boyfriend or parents.

John waved to her, holding up a finger, letting her know he'd be there in a sec, looked over at his dad.

"Want to grab some lunch?" Fred Turner gestured towards the mess tent up the block. They labored repairing the cracks and fissures in the cement while another group pulled kitchen duty, prepping meals for the day. These days everyone shared responsibility in Eden and all were expected to pull their weight to the extent that they could.

"In a few, pop. Let me go talk to Laurie for a minute, see what's up."

His father nodded and John walked over to Laurie.

Bobby Evers nudged the elder Turner's arm, smiled in the direction of John and Laurie. Fred smiled back.

"Hey, how you doing?" John asked Laurie. She an attractive kid and maybe John would have been too nervous and shy to talk to her in the real world, but after all the crap he and his father had been through since all this, from what happened to his mom and his sisters, his kid brother Kyle, after all that he didn't give a crap and he wasn't nervous, not expecting anything much out of life anymore anyway. His main goal these days was to keep his father out of harm's way.

"Come here and look at this." Laurie grabbed his arm and led him off down an alleyway. It was the same alleyway in which John had come across Isabel a few nights earlier. His father referred to Isabel as a Jezebel and a vamp and other names he was not familiar with, but John understood their import and his father told him to leave her alone, that she was no good. That night she'd been kneeling between Palmer and Diaz, servicing the two of them. The whole thing had kind of turned John on and disgusted him at the same time. He'd walked away before they'd seen him. Gone home and whacked off, felt strangely guilty about it afterwards.

The alleyway let out onto a community drive behind the row of homes. Most of the fences dividing the yards behind each house had been uprooted, allowing for the creation of a single long track of land where vegetables and fruit were grown. There were three or four people in a backyard a few houses over, pulling weeds.

Laurie led John up the stairs and into a backyard where tomatoes flourished on their stakes. He walked a step behind admiring her form, the way her hips swayed slightly as she moved. They watched their steps as they made their way to the back of the yard and the bulwark. This wall a part of the original yard when the block had been designed decades ago, flush now with the greater wall that had been erected to guard them from that without.

Laurie beckoned him up a small ladder onto the scaffolding next to her and he climbed, enjoying their proximity, his arm and side brushing hers. Then she pulled herself up and atop the wall itself, the lip of it wide enough for her to sit safely on looking over into the yards beyond.

John didn't feel a need to go and see the zombies that were probably standing around down there. He detested the undead for what they had done to his mother, to his sisters and Kyle. For what they had done to all those other people he and his father had had to watch die. He hated them, but he feared them more.

Eden's walls kept the undead at bay, but they visited John in his nightmares.

"Come on," Laurie summoned. "It's safe."

He shrugged, stepped up the remaining rungs to the scaffold, got his grip, and hauled himself up the wall beside her, smiling at her as he did so, self-conscious of the sweat beading his brow, wiping at it, forefinger pushing his eye glasses up the bridge of his nose.

"Look," she almost whispered.

Past the wall atop which they sat a backyard, another row of houses parallel to their own, much like Eden's, complete with community drive and individual yards.

The fences in these yards still stood, no one had torn them down. This particular yard was ringed on three sides by a wooden fence eight feet tall, a separate wire fence at the front overlooking the stairs leading down into the drive.

A zombie stood on the stairs, looking at the ground, seemingly oblivious to their presence. John had seen this particular corpse before. Some of the undead were transient, others stood around for days and even weeks on end in the same old spot, like they had nowhere to go, which, he figured, they did not.

This one had been a man, as attested by its nakedness from the waist down. No pants, shoes, or socks, its mottled cock hanging limp between its legs. The thing had sustained some kind of damage down there and its penis hung lower than normal, attached to its groin by a strand of skin that had been stretched out. From the waist up it wore a collared shirt, stained and bloodied, ripped in places. Most of the epidermis on its face peeled away and from the nose down the white of the skull shone, lips gnawed off revealing decayed gums, the muscles of the neck and cheeks clinging to the bone.

Not a pleasant sight.

"I don't think it knows we're here," said John.

"No, not that," Laurie whispered back, pointing. "*That.*"

There were two sheds in the yard. One was large, with a boarded up window. Its entrance was around the front, which they couldn't see. Behind this shed, closer to them, stood a smaller, corrugated shed, like the one John's father had had at home to store their lawn mower.

Laurie pointed to the space—three feet if that—between this second smaller shed and the wall that ringed Eden. A calico cat stared up at them, watching them intently, not sure whether they meant her harm or not. The cat had three kittens nursing her teats, and from the looks of it John figured the kittens were only five or six weeks old if that. His family had had cats since he was a little boy.

The sight made him smile. Somehow, someway, this feline had survived to birth her brood. No small accomplishment given the zombies devoured every animal and bird and living thing they could get their hands on. John knew. He had seen a zombie eat his family's dog and then his little brother Kyle before his father brained it with a pry bar.

"Aren't they cute?" Laurie beamed.

God, she's lovely. John's smile filled his face.

"How old do you think they are?" she asked him, still keeping her voice low, the half naked zombie on the steps immobile, occasionally shifting its weight from one leg to another, its wang dangling.

He told her what he thought and she sighed.

"Shoot," he said. "We can't just leave them there, can we?"

Laurie cast a wary glance towards the half-naked zombie. It hadn't changed position.

"They've made it this far okay," she noted. "And as long as they stay where they are, maybe they'll be okay."

John thought about it. Holding on to where he was, making sure his perch atop the wall stable, he turned and looked behind him. The gardeners were still doing their thing, an occasional laugh or snippet of conversation floating his and Laurie's way.

Buddy was up on his roof. The big man had on shades, an unbuttoned Hawaiian shirt, and shorts. He was sitting in a little lawn chair ridiculously small for his frame, low to the ground. He saw John and waved, and John reciprocated.

"What are you thinking?" Laurie asked him.

John was thinking that if he could lower himself down onto the roof of the smaller shed that from there he could easily drop to the ground between it and the wall, keep out of sight of the lone zombie, pass the kittens back up to Laurie, something like that. He wondered if the mother cat would stick around or if she would run away and he wished he could assure her that he didn't want to harm her or her babies.

He told Laurie all this but left out the other strand of his thought, the one that hoped should he rescue the cat and her kittens Laurie might be impressed. And that couldn't be a bad thing. No siree.

"I don't know John" she warned. "It's risky."

"Yeah, but not too much," persuaded John. "I drop in, you keep an eye on that thing. It'll take a minute tops."

The wooden fence abutting the sheds stirred as if from a breeze.

"I've got an idea," Laurie said. "Let me go and get a basket and a rope. One of us will climb over and the other will lower the basket."

John understood where she was going with this and agreed. He looked one more time at the solo zombie—it had its back to them- and then climbed down the ladder onto the scaffold, holding out his hand as Laurie followed, marveling at the warmth of her touch. Laurie squeezed his arm and went off in search of a basket.

He leaned back on the wall and looked around. From this vantage he could no longer see Buddy, but he could see the gardeners. Julie was talking with them.

Julie was *friggin' hot*. No two ways about it. Laurie was attractive in her own way too, kind of a younger Julie maybe, John thought, though Julie didn't look that much older than Laurie.

His buddy Thompson liked Julie, but she wasn't giving him the time of day. Matter of fact, Julie hadn't shown an interest in any of the men in Eden since she'd arrived. Maybe watching all her companions die in front of her on the way in had killed her romantic drive. Possible. Then again, maybe aggressive assholes like Diaz—who had Shannon, for Christ's sake—had a way of putting a girl off men in general.

He thought about Laurie. John never really considered himself in the running, hadn't even thought about sex or a relationship at all until recently when he'd started to spend more time around her. And Thompson, well Thompson was a nice enough guy in his own way, but he was also young, a year older than John, which made him younger than Julie, and Julie seemed like the type of woman who would go for a different kind of man, a more mature man.

Laurie was cute though, and how. *Oh man*. She didn't dress provocatively like Isabel or anything but she looked great to him. Those jeans.

Eden had been a much better place since Buddy and Harris had arrived. The two men had come in together, seemed like they'd known each other for a long time, but John realized this might not be the case. This situation had thrust friendship upon many. One night when he was drunk Diaz had wondered aloud if Harris and Buddy were "fruity for one another" and John's father had told the man to shut the hell up, that he was drunk and wasn't saying anything other than garbage that would wind up provoking a confrontation and that he'd get his "ass handed to" him.

John thought about that. Harris and Buddy weren't gay. They'd just been through a lot together. It wouldn't bother him if they were. Larry Chen was. That was cool.

Diaz was tall and wiry, a scrappy type, could probably hold his own in a fight. Could Diaz take Harris? John wasn't so sure. Harris seemed tough enough even though he was mostly low key. John would be willing to bet money that Diaz couldn't take Buddy out in a fair fight. Buddy had to be in his fifties and he was affable and talkative, which might put people at ease, but John knew there was also a tough as nails son of a bitch under all that.

The whole thing with Graham had proven it, the way Buddy'd just executed the man. Hadn't even hesitated, went and blew the fat man away. And John had heard about the thing with Markowski. Not that the big prick didn't have it coming to him.

Before Eden, before all this, John would have thought all that wrong. But morality had changed since then. Which was why he also couldn't just dismiss Isabel as a promiscuous slut as his father could, though he knew for a fact that she had slept with at least six men in Eden. Isabel'd even made eyes at him, which had been confidence-boosting at the time, because she was an older woman and all with great tits and he hadn't known about her banging seemingly everyone at the time. He'd thought he was special.

After a time, he understood that the way she was looking at him was the way you look at a piece of meat you're sizing up. Nothing exceptional. Just today's meal. He did his best to steer clear of her from then on, and had done a good job until he'd come across her blowing those guys the other night right out in the open.

John was trying not to pass judgment on people anymore but he still thought it wrong that Diaz was in that alley with Isabel, what with Shannon and all.

Laurie came back his way grinning, a big old wicker picnic basket in her hands. "Think this'll work?"

John looked it over. She had coiled a length of clothesline cord inside.

"Yeah, it'll do." He tied one end of the clothesline to the handles, leaving the knot loose so he could undo it when he had to. "Want to give this a try?"

John ascended the scaffold first, looking over the wall. The single zombie alone there stood still, ignorant of their presence. John reached down and took the basket from Laurie, setting it on the lip of the wall, taking her hand and pulling her up next to him, aware again of how close they were and how good that felt and how good she looked and smelled, of how she made him feel inside.

"Okay," he said and shimmied a few feet off to the right, putting himself out of view of the single zombie should it look, placing him in a position where he'd be between the small shed and their wall. John reached down and checked the .38 in his holster, the speed loaders on his belt. Just in case.

He looked over at Laurie. She looked back at him and he liked how she looked at him. Admiration, in a woman-man way, not the way he admired his father or Harris or Buddy. In a way that carried hints of future possibilities with it. *Yeah, boy!* He felt invincible.

From where he sat on the wall he had something of a view of the houses and alley below. The zombie was out of his line of sight, the roof of the large shed blocking one from the other. Julie could see it from where she sat and John knew she'd keep an eye on the thing. Aside from the one zombie he could detect no others. Nothing in the community drive, nothing in the alley he could see. Of course that didn't mean they weren't down there, but if they were he figured Laurie would let him know and he'd get back up over the wall before even the fast ones could make the yard.

The wooden fence separating the yard below from the one next to him creaked in the wind. *What wind?* But he dismissed the thought from his mind.

John reached out a foot tentatively, finding the roof of the smaller corrugated shed, wondering if it could hold his weight. He shifted more weight to that foot, pushed with it, testing to see if the shed would sway, but it held tight, steady.

Okay. John pushed off with his other leg, over the gap, coming to rest firmly on the roof of the little shed. It creaked a bit under him but didn't collapse as he'd half feared.

From this position he could see the cats below, the mother looking up with interest. The roof of the larger shed within reach, puddles of water from the last downpour pooled atop it.

He turned to Laurie and saw the concern on her face disappear when she saw the look of confidence on his. Saw Buddy up on his roof, standing, watching him intently with brow furrowed, probably wondering what the hell he was doing.

He'd show the big man when he was done. Maybe even give him one of the kittens. John was a big believer that everyone could benefit from a pet in their life.

The drop to the yard below was shorter than he was tall, so he figured he'd be able to pull himself up when the time came. He dropped down and got his bearings.

John noticed that the lock on the shed was absent, that the shed itself had seen better days, all rusty and dented as it was, and then he scanned his eyes about, a little uneasy outside the relative safety of Eden.

The mother cat hissed at him as he approached.

He motioned to Laurie and she let down the basket.

"Hey mommy," John soothed, trying to sound as least threatening as he could. "I'm not going to hurt you or your babies."

The mother cat wasn't going anywhere, even with this larger human animal looming over it. John figured if he tried to snatch a kitten its mom would claw the crap out of his hand. He decided to snag the mother first.

The basket hung at waist level. John got the mother cats attention with his left hand, snapping his fingers and waving it a foot from the cat's face, her kittens mewing, frightened, and he reached in quick with his right, gripping her by the scruff of her neck, the mother hissing and going for his hand but he'd already twisted her up and away from him, pulling her from her babies, gripping her tight.

John flipped a lid on top of the picnic basket and unceremoniously dumped the struggling mother cat inside before she could draw blood. He slipped the lock into place and listened to her muffled growling from within.

Laurie smiled down at him.

Phew! That was the hard part, and it had gone off without a hitch. John paused to slide his glasses back up his nose then reached down to the first of the kittens, an adorable black and white, took it by the neck like he knew he could without hurting it. The kitten went limp in his grasp as it did for its mother whenever she took it so.

He opened the other side of the picnic basket, placed the kitten gently inside with its mother, keeping one hand on the lid in case the mom tried to barge out, reached down for a second kitten, this one all white, put it in the basket, and was reaching for the third kitten when a zombie that had been hiding in the little shed burst out and tackled him from behind.

John fell, surprised, twisting as he did so to avoid collapsing on the last kitten, Laurie screaming his name above, the zombie regaining its balance, a fast one. In the enclosed space between the shed and the wall its speed lethal.

John was up, fumbling with the clasp on his holster at the same time that the zombie rushed him again, his hand going up to protect his neck, pushing at the zombie's face as it grabbed him and bodily lifted him off the ground and ran the five steps between the shed and the wall, slamming John against the wooden fence fronting the yard, the fence giving way slightly, undead hands reaching for him from that yard, clawing at his back.

John screamed as the hand he blocked with was bitten, the attacking creature tearing through his pinky and ring fingers, severing them, John clearing the .38 at the same time, firing into the zombie, one crack, two, the shots loosening its grip on him, sending it back a couple of steps, just enough for him to fire a third round directly into its head, the bullet ricocheting inside the cranial cavity and blowing out its jaw.

"Aw, shit!" John looked down at his bloody hand as he pulled back against the hands seizing him from the other yard and fell forward onto his knees, striking his wounded hand on the dirt.

He'd lost his glasses somewhere in the struggle and all was a blur.

Laurie was screaming on top of the wall, crying hysterically, clutching the clothesline attached to the picnic basket.

"Pull them up," John yelled at her, turning at the sound of splintering wood, a gaggle of zombies tearing their way through the wooden fence behind which they had been massed waiting.

Bam! Bam! Bam! John emptied the revolver into the fence and the zombies behind it but he was starting to panic and his aim was shaky and he couldn't see and couldn't tell if he had shot any in the head.

Laurie pulled the basket up as John fumbled with a speedloader, cracking open the revolver, dumping the six empty shells, trying to fit the new ones, the gun and his hands bloody and slick.

Buddy tore ass from his roof down into the house, stopping only to grab the weapon closest at hand, the flamethrower in his living room.

Harris came charging through the yards, unmindful of the crops he trampled under foot, hearing the commotion, the gunshots, Laurie on the wall with a picnic basket face red, tears bursting from her eyes, pointing and screaming.

The fence behind him giving way, John extended the .38 and fired once, right into a zombie's face below its nose.

Sweating like a pig, he reached out and took the third kitten in his wounded hand, never once considering throwing it up to Laurie, scrabbling for the roof of the corrugated shed, placing the .38 there, setting the kitten aside it, propping himself between the wall and the shed, trying to climb up, his hand slick and bolts of agony shooting through it, but somehow he made it, pulling himself to the top of the shed, the kitten mewing, his .38 back in his hand, Laurie hysterical, the lid off the picnic basket, the mother cat looking out at them and hissing, Harris on the wall next to Laurie, people inside Eden yelling and calling out to each other and to John.

"Dad!"

The shed gave under John's weight, collapsing inward, pitching the whole structure against the wall surrounding Eden. John banged his head against the barricade on the way down, seeing lights, shaking it out, somehow managing to keep the .38 in his good hand but the kitten had slipped away from him and was taking a few tentative steps on the ground.

More slats of the wooden fence parted and tore free and the zombies came through the gap, John on his back on the ground, firing the .38, punching a hole through the first thing's chest, his second shot coring through its mouth and dropping it, the corpse collapsing on the corrugated roof crumpled in the small space. John fired repeatedly, missing once, scoring a neck shot with his next round, the zombie twisted around ninety degrees, righting itself, propelled forward by the others behind it, a wall of them in the enclosed space overcoming the kitten, overwhelming John.

"No!" Fred Turner cried from atop the wall, firing a shotgun down into the horde blindly. Harris, his face grim, selected targets and fired first one nine millimeter out, then the second, felling zombies where they stood. Bobby Evers eschewed his .30-.30 in favor of a pistol, capping zombies. All of them fired and reloaded and fired but for all that, their efforts were to no avail.

In the huddle beneath John screamed, the zombies burying him, some of them dead, most not. There was one on his stomach and he fired a round into its head, but it was already dead. He felt them biting his legs and the pain was incredible. He did his best to sit up, but their weight pressed down upon him, and his last shot discharged blindly, not knowing if he hit anything. He reached for another speed loader with his good hand, wanting to live, to survive, scared shitless and in agony, and zombies wrestled his hand away from his belt with the extra loads and bit into his other forearm, teeth sinking into his hand between his thumb and fingers.

The mother cat leaped out of the picnic basket and stood atop the fence, back arched, hair on end, hissing down at the zombies eating the fallen man, the zombies that were dying as other humans shot them in the head, her kitten down there somewhere. The cat jumped from the fence into the fray, caught in mid air by dead hands, passed around for a second above them all, her bites and scratching going unnoticed, finally pulled down to a waiting mouth which rent her belly as she screamed.

An undead mouth bobbed down and when it reared back, John's other hand was shorn three digits to the palm and he stared in disbelief at the deformed crimson club at the end of his wrist, as if it belonged to another.

"Get him off the fucking wall," Harris shouted to the gathered, indicating Fred Turner. John's father trying to reload his gun, unable to do so as his tears blinded him

Worse, John was still down there, screaming in agony, calling for his dad. The zombies had torn his left hand free and were digging into his stomach.

Palmer and Kate Truman pulled Fred from the wall, but the older man struggled, wanting to get back up and save his doomed son.

Laurie had stopped screaming and just shook, watching the scene unfold.

It looked like dozens of zombies had gathered in the adjacent yard, and once the trap had been sprung by the one in the shed they'd all surged forward.

Many of them were dead but others were reaching into John's belly as Julie looked, rending his flesh, exposing the organs inside. He was still screaming when they yanked handfuls of steaming entrails free, Julie reaching up and pulling Laurie off the wall, pressing the younger woman to her.

"Move!" Buddy made it to the wall, knowing it too late. What the fuck had the Turner boy and that girl been doing on the wall to begin with? Shannon had the picnic basket and was crying, looking down at two little kittens.

People made way as Buddy, lugging the flame thrower, clambered up onto the wall with Harris and Evers.

There was a low moaning from the Turner boy. The sight of him. Disemboweled. A leg chewed through and detached as Buddy watched. And the kid, Buddy saw, the kid was still alive, dying but holding on, the look in his eyes somehow still coherent, he *knew*.

Buddy brought the muzzle of the flame thrower up, triggered it, a stream of fire belching forth, filling the gap below between the wall and the space where the corrugated shed had once stood. The undead went up like dry kindling, staggering around aflame, bouncing off the walls, howling. Buddy worked the spray around, jetting it into the others massed in the yard beyond, the ones waiting to get in and pick over the scraps.

Fuck them all to hell.

John Turner's eyes were open but he wasn't seeing anything.

Harris had left the wall, was helping Mickey and Bear and Palmer restrain John's dad.

Evers was next to Buddy with his thirty-thirty, firing into the burning zombies.

"No," Buddy told him. "Let them burn. Fuck 'em."

The noxious funk of burning flesh and fur. A few of the immolated zombies wailed, obviously in some kind of pain and it brought Buddy some satisfaction to know they could feel pain. He *wanted* them to feel pain, as much of it as they could and as much of it as he could visit upon them, because no amount would ever be enough for what they had done and for what the world had become.

He doused them with the flame and watched them burn.

He surveyed it all, angry with himself. Why hadn't he gotten up earlier and gone and seen what those stupid fucking kids were up to? What was left of John Turner was unrecognizable, steaming and blistering, conjoined with the molten remnants of the undead.

Harris approached the wicker picnic basket that lay discarded. When he opened it he shook his head, reached in, pulled the kitten there out by its scruff.

"What are we going to do with you then?"

The kitten looked at him and mewed.

The lone zombie sans pants stood where it had been at the front of the yard, watching its enkindled brethren, watching Buddy and Evers until the potency of the heat and stink drove them from their roost.

DIAZ THOUGHT HE heard a gunshot, but, *naah*, it couldn't have been, so he took another long drag from the spliff, shifted in his hammock and closed his eyes.

Voices behind him but he ignored them.

"Bobby?" The concern for her husband in Gwen's voice was bordering on hysteria.

Bear picked up a length of steel pipe and was the next person inside Harris' house after Julie.

Screaming down in the basement and a woman crying and Bear rushed down the stairs, nearly tripping over his own feet, Harris' cat hissing and bounding up the steps past him.

He stalked into the basement with the pipe in his hand, one eye staring off into space.

Thompson let out a last scream, a bloodied rag hanging half out of his mouth, his cry petering into a strangled gargle. He lay on the floor, jackknifed with his arms bound behind his back secured to a pole. The zombie was atop him, had chewed through his leg at the calf and ripped a couple ribs from him. It reached within Thompson to pull what was inside out then turned and faced a weeping Julie with Bear behind her.

"Harris," said Bear.

Naked from the waist up, blood leaking from a chest wound, the zombie looked over at him and Julie, gave them both a look like they weren't important and resumed its consumption. Bear saw where the bandage on the upper arm had been loosed, flapping over a discolored bite.

Julie shuddered as she cried and Bear wrapped an enormous arm around her, pulling her a step back. People were on the stairs behind them.

Thompson looked dead but his one foot that hadn't been chewed off moved.

"Oh, Harris," Bear sighed. He lay the pipe aside and took the .357 from its holster on Julie's hip.

"Oh, Harris," he said again.

Bear fired once, the round entering the back of the zombie's head, exiting the front, depositing the contents of its skull across the basement.

"Bobby!" Gwen in the basement, crying. "My Bobby!"

Larry Chen looked up from where Evers lay, shook his head.

Gwen went berserk, screaming and wailing and had to be carried back up the stairs.

"Get her out of here too," Bear said of Julie and they took her from the place, leaving the bald man with the dead.

Bear squatted down onto the soles of his feet and cried. When he was done crying, he prayed.

A moan ended his supplication and he looked up. Thompson had rolled over onto his side to face him, the remainder of his stomach cavity slipping out onto the basement floor.

Bear stood and stuffed the Colt Python in his pants and took up the pipe. He went and stood over the thing that had been Thompson, the thing that was clawing towards him and moaning. Bear raised the pipe and brought it down, and then he brought it down again, and he continued to bring it down even when he needn't have until he was good and tired and flecked with gore.

THE MANHOLE COVER slid back and everyone immediately ceased what they were doing. The muzzles of a dozen pistols, shotguns, and assault rifles brought to bear on the dark hole in the street.

With a grunt a pair of saddle bags heaved up out of the opening, landing on the street.

"No fucking way," breathed Mickey, lowering the barrel of his AR-15.

A man climbed out of the earth, an older man, a big man with hair gone grey, but still one tough-looking and very-much-alive motherfucker.

"Buddy?" someone asked as if it could be anyone but him.

Buddy stood up and looked around and saw mostly faces he knew and some he didn't.

"Boo!" he said but no one laughed.

A small crowd encircled him, incredulity, awe etched on faces.

"Bear." Buddy greeted those he knew by name. Some of them were reaching out to touch him, to verify his corporeality.

"Glad—glad to have you back, Buddy." The biker, with eye red-rimmed, turned and walked away.

Buddy looked them over, every one of them, hugged some of the women, with the men he shook hands or a pound or an elbow-to-chest-hand-on-the-back half-hug to Mickey and Larry.

Isabel's UGGs were the extent of her winter weather garb. Her shirt riding up showed belly and she had a baby in her arms, a little boy.

Buddy spied Julie sort of hanging back towards the rear of them all and he waved to her, and she gave a little smile. Like Bear she turned away, and he knew with certainty then something had happened to his boy Harris.

"Mickey, where is he? Where's Harris?" With the question most everyone else began to file away, going back to their mid-afternoon business.

"We should talk, Buddy."

Buddy felt like he'd been hit in the stomach. He bowed his head and licked his upper lip. He'd come this far, survived, come to take Harris and Julie and Bobby and Gwen and all of them who wanted to go to a better place, a safer place.

He wanted to scream at Mickey, to grab him by the shoulders and shake the fate of his only true friend from him but he did not.

"Okay," his throat tightening.

"Buddy," said Fred Turner, the only other man standing there with them. "What about the others?"

"We all made it," Buddy said looking around Eden. It wasn't any different, just another change in seasons, banks of shoveled dirty snow.

"Except Sal," he added somewhat quietly, looking around for the man's wife. "Where's his wife?"

"Camille didn't make it either," said Mickey.

"Shit," breathed Buddy, but that made it so much easier. He'd been dreading running into Bianaculli's wife and having to tell her the fate that had befallen her husband. He had so much to tell them all, but he needed to know what had become of Harris and Bobby. Mickey tried to take Buddy's arm, "Let's go sit down somewhere and talk."

"Give me a minute." Buddy brushed him aside and went after Julie.

"Julie. Julie!"

She looked at him and gave a weak wave and entered her house and he could tell she was crying. Buddy swallowed hard and knew Harris was gone. At the same time he looked up and thought he saw someone—was it Diaz?—staring down at him from a window but as soon as he looked, the guy drew back out of sight.

Buddy didn't knock. He walked into Harris's house and found Julie sitting on the couch.

"Julie."

"Hi, Buddy." She sniffled and wiped her hand across her nose.

Julie stood up and Buddy saw that as thin as she was, her belly protruded.

"Do you mind?" he asked.

"No, go ahead," she said, not making eye contact.

He went to one knee and reached out and lay a big palm on her stomach, imaging the warmth under the sweater there, the life.

"My boy Harris," he whispered.

Julie fell onto her own knees, weeping, and Buddy held her tight and felt the tears in his own eyes.. He let them come and they cried together like that.

After awhile he placed his palm back on Julie's tummy and felt the life inside kick and that made him smile through his tears.

"Yeah, Harris, you da man."

Late that night Buddy decamped from the house where Julie lived alone.

The snow fell under a full moon and it would have been an otherwise beautiful night if not for the wailing and the stench.

The plans had been made. Those who needed to know *knew* and would be waiting on him. They were going to a better place, a place Buddy and the others had found. A place Sal Bianaculli had seen before he'd died and wished only that Camille spend the rest of her days there.

Those who didn't need to know, the ones Buddy could care less about, they'd no idea. They'd wake up in the morning and a few more people would be gone and they'd go about their lives in Eden living off their stores, harvesting the next paltry crop in the spring and hanging on as best they could.

Buddy moved fast and light without the saddle bags. He wore black jeans, black combat boots and a black turtleneck sweater over a long-sleeve black t-shirt. His only weapons were the silenced nine millimeter in his right hand and the knife sheathed on his left ankle.

He passed through the night like a wraith, and Fred Turner on watch seemed unaware as Buddy crossed the street behind him towards the houses. People inside were sleeping, only one or two shaded windows had some light filtering through.

Buddy was a different man than he had once been, a *better* man, but he knew enough of his old self co-existed within him that should Fred Turner or anyone else in Eden try to stop him from what he needed to do he *wouldn't* let them. He had no truck with most of the people in Eden but he would not hesitate tonight to kill any one of them and all of them if he must if they got in the way of his doing what was *right*.

Much like Fred after John's death, Diaz's had been a downhill path since Shannon's end. Where the elder Turner turned to silence with a glazed look, Diaz literally went to pot. He smoked day and night, drank like a fish and, in the opinion of most, was slowly but surely killing himself. Julie had told Buddy all this.

A fresh covering of snow fell about him and when people awoke his boot prints would be long gone.

Buddy reached Diaz's house, went right up to the front door. No lights on in the house that he could discern. Buddy aimed the silenced nine at the doorknob but reconsidered, reached out and grasped the handle, turned, and it was open.

He entered Diaz's house and pushed the door closed behind him, but not all the way. Silent and dark in the vestibule, he let himself into a living room that appeared unlived-in. Buddy figured Diaz for upstairs in his room.

The front door being left open could have been a warning signal. Diaz might be expecting him. He had seen Buddy with Mickey and he'd seen Buddy go after Julie. No matter how stoned he was he must have thought they would talk to Buddy.

If it was a trap, if Diaz was waiting somewhere in the house, Buddy wished he'd bring it on. He knew only rage.

"Hello, Buddy."

Diaz didn't look surprised to see him. He was lying on his bed on the second floor, atop the blankets in his boxer shorts like he had been waiting there all eternity for this moment to arrive and unfold. Diaz had a big paunch and a couple of chins which hadn't been shaved in some time, a lethargic, resigned look to his face and eyes.

Candles burned on the furniture beside the bed. An assault rifle leaned against the far wall, well out of reach of his sprawl. The Dominican didn't look like he'd the inclination to go for it anytime soon.

Diaz took a pull from his blunt, breathed in deep and held it, and exhaled. He looked lazily at the silenced pistol staring at him.

"Want some?" Diaz gestured with the joint. Buddy stood there.

"I know why you're here, Buddy."

The house creaked in the cold.

"Come on man, say *something*," Diaz pled lamely. "You're bugging me out here, man."

Buddy considered the knife or the gun.

"You ain't afraid to die, are you?" Buddy asked, venom in his voice.

"This?" Diaz motioned to encompass much more than the room. "This ain't life, what we got going on around here, man."

The blunt burned down as they looked one at the other, Buddy with contempt, Diaz listless.

"We never thought you'd come back, man. I told Mickey 'cause I'd hoped he'd be the one, do me the favor."

Diaz took a last pull on the cigar, killing it, held it in for as long as he could and exhaled.

"I just want to be with Shannon, man," he sighed almost to himself.

Buddy stepped up to the foot of the bed, extended his arm with the nine millimeter.

"You want me to go for my gun, will that make it easier for you?" Diaz inquired languidly.

"Fuck you. I don't need an excuse."

"Just one favor—" Diaz was animated for a moment, propping himself up with his hands on the bed, his stomach spilling over the elastic of his boxers. "Not in the face, okay?"

Buddy fired and blood spurted from a puncture next to Diaz's bellybutton. Diaz looked down in disbelief and his face spattered with blood as a second and then a third pock erupted in his abdomen and chest. He collapsed on his back staring at the ceiling, breathless.

The only noise the music from the iPod speaker docking station beside him on the bed.

Buddy walked over, pressed the silencer between Diaz's eyes. They bugged out—

"That's right."

—and Buddy pulled the trigger until the slide locked open on an empty chamber.

He swabbed the silencer with Diaz's blankets and wiped the blood from his own hands. He reloaded the pistol and went around and blew out all the candles in the room. He was calm again, and there was no need to leave them burning. Might have an accident, burn down Eden.

Outside the street was empty and silent. He moved rapidly, a sense of release flooding over him.

"Buddy," a voice hissed, but it was Bear's and he didn't start. Bear materialized in the night, chainsaw strapped blade-down across his enormous back, Julie and Gwen and Mickey were behind him. All dressed for the weather: boots, jeans, sweaters under jackets, hats, and gloves. All loaded, backpacks bulging with weapons and provisions, whatever they'd considered worth bringing with them. Bear had Buddy's leather jacket and saddle bags.

Buddy nodded, hugged the two women quickly, squatted down with Bear and slid the man hole cover out of the way.

Bear squeezed down first, a flashlight dangling from a lanyard around his neck. Buddy handed down the man's pack, his saw and submachine gun, then Julie and Gwen's gear. Gwen went down and then Mickey. Julie took one last look around Eden as she tugged the strap of the AR-15, the weapon across her back. She looked at the wall she'd come in over, then at the house she'd shared with the man she loved.

Julie shrugged and disappeared down the hole.

A lone, piercing cry from over the wall made him look up.

Fred Turner was awake on the north wall, rocking back and forth slowly where he sat. He watched as Buddy handed his saddle bags down into the earth.

Buddy slipped his right arm into the sleeve of his jacket, then his left. He didn't look around as Julie had. There was nothing for him here.

Instead he looked up at Turner on the wall and he waved and the other man nodded and waved back.

Buddy stepped onto the ladder, climbed down a few rungs, reached up and heaved the manhole cover back into place.

DIAZ TOOK A long pull from the water bong, held it in, closed his eyes, and let it go.

"This is some good shit," he said for anyone who might be listening, "You want a hit off this?"

They weren't really ignoring him, they were just talking about pop culture again and he wasn't really in on the discussion, opting to get zooted instead.

"No, no, no, you're thinking 'Dukes of Hazard,' Harris," explained Mickey. "Denver Pyle was Uncle Jesse."

"Yeah, I'm not arguing that with you," said Harris, "But Denver Pyle was also on Grizzly Adams."

"Grizzly Adams? That was what's his name, that guy who looked like one of them shaggy seventies singers," said Isabel. She sat between Diaz and Thompson and every time she tried to make eye contact with Harris he evaded it. Julie saw it and she knew him to be a man good and true.

"Dan Haggerty," Mickey named the actor. "Wonder whatever happened to that guy?"

Thompson cast a thumb over his shoulder at the wall as a deathly moan floated up and over.

"No, I think he died before all this crap," Mickey tried to recall, not remembering which celebrities died when and how, always wondering if he was going to look over the wall one day and see someone he knew. A celebrity wouldn't be so bad, but a family member or a friend, Christ.

"Pyle was Mad Jack on Grizzly Adams," said Harris.

"Shit, I remember that show," said Diaz. "What was the name of the bear?"

"Ben," answered Harris, who usually ignored Diaz.

"Nah, Ben was that nerdy guy's rat."

"No," said Mickey, "The bear's name was Ben, too."

Thompson reached into his flannel pocket, tapped on the bottom of a pack of Newports and popped one out. Put it in his mouth, flicked his Zippo and put flame to the stoge.

"Let me get one of those," Diaz murmured and Thompson handed him one along with the lighter.

"Wasn't Denver Pyle on that old show Ritchie Cunningham used to be on?" asked Julie, remembering her *Nick at Night*.

Mickey laughed, "Ritchie Cunningham. That was—"

"Ron Howard," finished Isabel.

"Yeah, that's him. He was a kid on the *Andy Griffith Show*. But no, the character's name on the show was Gomer Pyle. But what was that actor's name?" Mickey scrunched up his forehead and bit his tongue.

"You foos are ruining my high man." Diaz handed the lighter back to Thompson, the other absent-mindedly placing it atop the pack of cigarettes besides his leg.

"Okay, Harris, you've got a good memory," said Mickey, and Harris saw it coming, the friendly challenge. Mickey loved his movies, and since he'd lifted the portable DVD from a corner drugstore on a foraging mission some time ago everyone else had seen less and less of him as he spent his time with his obscure films.

"Hit me," said Harris, wondering if it sounded funny with Thompson sitting there. Thompson didn't seem to notice and he sat and smoked his Newport.

"Does the name Forrest Tucker ring a bell?" Mickey clasped his hands in front of his body like a small child.

"Forrest Tucker…Forrest Tucker." Harris mulled it over. The name did sound like one he knew. Mickey was familiar with all these old movies and TV shows Harris had grown up watching, shows Mickey and the others, except maybe Isabel, were all too young to have seen outside of re-runs. Mickey was a true cineophile and pop-culture maniac, had rented thousands of films in his life, watched as reruns a lot of the stuff Harris had seen coming up.

"Want a hint?" Mickey looked like he wanted to give Harris one.

"You don't have to tell me. I got it. *F-Troop!*"

"*F-Troop?*" Julie knew that one from syndication. They used to play reruns eleven o'clock at night when she was in high school.

"Larry Storch," said Isabel.

"Right, Larry Storch was Corporal Agarn," said Mickey, "And Forrest Tucker was—"

"Sgt. O'Rourke," said Harris.

"Shit, didn't none of you watch any shows with a brother in it?" asked Diaz, killing the blunt.

"Does *Good Times* count?" asked Julie.

"Shee-it, Jimmy Walker, bobolon," sighed Diaz, laughing to himself thinking of how Jimmy used to argue with Bookman the super. After awhile he realized he was laughing alone and everyone else was looking at him, that Shannon wasn't with him and would never be again.

You motherfuckers could ruin a wet dream, he thought to himself but then realized he had said it out loud, which caused another fit of laughter.

"Ever seen *Abominable Snowman*, Harris?" asked Mickey.

"Oh man, you're going waaaay back there. Even I didn't catch that one on the first go. Saw it on a Saturday morning channel eleven horror festival or something."

"The *Abominable Snowman*," said Julie, "Isn't that the Sasqwach?"

"Sasqwach, Yeti, all the same," affirmed Mickey.

Shannon was a hairy bitch, thought Diaz, *had a bush like one of those seventies porn stars.* He missed his Shannon.

"I seen a picture of one of them things once," Thompson added favorably.

Harris asked, "Was it out of focus, big, man-like hairy thing walking along swinging an arm at its side?"

Diaz said something that no one understood and while he laughed to himself the others paid him no mind.

"That's the one," said Thompson, and Harris noted that whatever had been between them, if anything, it seemed to have gone, and he felt better that it had. Thompson wasn't a bad kid. Just this place, these circumstances, it all had a way of bringing out the worst in them if they weren't careful. Diaz, for instance. Diaz was cracked.

"I hate to tell you this honey," said Isabel, "But those photos were doctored."

"Damn, looked real enough to me," shrugged Thompson.

"What's *Abominable Snowman*?" asked Julie.

Diaz kept looking over at Isabel's tits. They were huge beneath her sweater. Shannon had had pretty big ones herself, and Diaz had forgotten what color Isabel's areolas were, pink or brown.

"Forrest Tucker was in that, wasn't he?" asked Harris.

"Right!" said Mickey enthused.

"And Peter Cushing." The film was coming back to Harris.

"Peter Cushing was that British guy starred in all them horror movies, right?" asked Bear.

"Yeah," nodded Mickey. "Peter Cushing, Christopher Lee, Vincent Price, between them they must have starred in hundreds of horror films."

"Pink or brown?" Diaz cackled but no one understood one word of what he said.

"I remember it," said Harris. "Peter Cushing is a scientist up in the Himalayas, living in a Tibetan monastery with the Dalai Lama—" he laughed, thinking of the actor playing the Lama.

Mickey continued for him, "Yeah, and Forrest Tucker plays an American adventurer, comes looking for the Abominable Snowman, takes Cushing along with him, way up into the mountains."

"I bet I can guess what happens next," said Julie. "Abominable Snowman gets them?"

"Not exactly," said Mickey.

"Yeah, they find the Yeti, and there's a whole bunch of them," said Harris. "Matter of fact, they shoot one of them and kill it, take the body, planning to bring it back down to civilization with them, prove its existence. But then things start to happen—"

"They're hearing voices and stuff," Mickey took over. "Drives them insane. Their guide runs off. One of them goes climbing a mountain chasing voices, falls off. Another gets a close encounter with the snowmen and dies of shock."

"What, the Yeti didn't kill them?" asked Bear.

"That's the thing," said Harris. "The abominable snowmen never lay a hand on the humans. It's the humans who go and screw things up, killing a Yeti. Forrest Tucker freaks out, starts firing off his revolver, gets himself buried in an avalanche."

"What happens to my boy Cushing?"

Mickey looked at Harris and Harris nodded and let him tell it.

"Peter Cushing's been hiding out in this cave where Tucker and the other guy had stashed the dead Yeti, right?" Mickey reveled in telling the story. "He comes back to the cave and is confronted with two Yeti. They're in there carting their dead Yeti-brother off."

"I know Cushing goes out like a *g*," growled Bear.

"No, he doesn't. Well, yes he does, kind of. One of the Yeti approaches Cushing, gets up in his face real close like. Cushing is terrified, thinks the thing is going to tear him limb from limb. He looks up into its face, sees an intelligence there. A sadness. Like the thing knows something he don't."

"What's it know?" Isabel asked sounding bored by the conversation because she had never seen the movie and was a fan of neither Peter Cushing nor Forrest Tucker.

"Harris?"

"Cushing figures it out. The snowmen aren't so abominable. It's the humans who are. They'd capture one of the snowmen if they could, bring it back with them, set off the beginning of the end of the Yeti race, and for what? Cushing realizes it's the humans who are really the monsters in the film, and that snowman doesn't harm him, doesn't lay a finger on him."

Bear nodded, "It doesn't have to."

"That's it? That's how it ends?"

"No," said Mickey. "Cushing goes back to the monastery, where he and his wife and his colleague live and work. Tells the Lama he's going back to the west. And the lama asks him if he found what he was looking for. Cushing lies, says there is no abominable snowman. And the Lama knows he's lying, and he knows *why* he's lying."

"That Dalai Lama is one bright huevon," said Diaz.

"Some *horror* movie," grunted Bear.

"Yeah," admitted Mickey, "more *sci-fi* if you ask me."

Julie gave Harris *the look,* and he knew it was time to turn in.

"Well, ladies and gentlemen," he said, "gonna head back to the little ranch."

"Always a pleasure, Harris," said Mickey, "Julie."

Thompson nodded, didn't say anything. His ego was still bruised from when Harris had laid him out. He knew he'd deserved it, knew as well that he'd have to start being a man and take his lumps when he had them coming to him. Still, he didn't watch Harris walk off with Julie.

"What's on your agenda tonight?" Isabel asked Diaz. He was sitting chewing something over.

"Nada," Diaz said. "Bear, you got any more of that weed man?"

"Shoot, got a whole LB back in the crib." Bear loved him his occasional smoke. "Cop some off you?"

"We cool enough, Diaz, but you need to slow down with that stuff and stop mixing it with that Devil's dust." Bear stood and stretched. "Give me five. Meet me back at my place."

"Gotta drain the vein," said Emery. He looked at Isabel. "You don't suppose you want to help a brother out now, do you?"

Isabel laughed. She'd helped Emery once or twice before with his "vein." The man wasn't even average and to boot he was a two-minute brother. "I'll pass."

She looked over at Thompson. "Want to take a walk?"

Thompson shocked she would ask *him*, him being probably almost twenty years younger than her and all, but he didn't show it. *Be a man. Go for a walk. Hit that shit.* Didn't matter if most every other guy in Eden had done it before. Isabel was cool like that.

"Yeah." He smiled, lost in her eyes. "Let's go."

When they were all gone, Mickey looked over at Diaz and thought about trying to start a conversation with the guy, then thought better of it. Mickey said "good night" to Diaz and headed towards his house.

"Good night," said Diaz two minutes after.

He sat there a bit afterwards, looking straight ahead at the wall. It ate him up, the whole thing, having to sit with Harris, having to watch the man who'd killed his Shannon, watch him sit there with Julie. Life was no way fucking fair.

He'd find the time, the place. Harris was gonna get what he had coming to him. He'd killed Shannon.

Bear was waiting for him, wasn't he? Diaz got up, folded his chair, took it with him, thinking he'd better keep how he felt about Harris to himself, no way he could say anything about it to Bear, Bear would—

Something glinted in the moonlight catching his eye. Diaz bent over and checked it out.

Thompson's lighter.

"Dumb fuck."

He picked it up, pocketed it. He'd give it to Thompson later. *No, fuck that shit.* He'd always wanted a Zippo himself. If Thompson was thinking with his dick and left his property behind, well then, finders fucking keepers, losers fucking weepers, sticks and stones and all that shit.

As he walked to Bear's place he toyed with the lighter in his pocket, thought how Harris had gone and popped Thompson in the mouth like that when he did. Harris was probably in his forties. Still tough though. Diaz wondered if he could take him out. Well, maybe not fair, but what the fuck was fair about a fight?

He was right about to walk on through Bear's door when a thought occurred to him. He fingered the lighter and stood on the porch. Looked down the block at Harris's house, right next to the wall.

Diaz pulled the lighter out of his pocket, flicked it, watched the flame burn. He had an idea. It might just work. Even if it didn't, Thompson wasn't none of his business anyway. Diaz had the clearest and most vivid thought he'd had in some time. He'd drop the lighter when he did it and if Harris survived, and there was the off chance that tough motherfucker just might, he'd find the lighter. Yeah, maybe, just maybe, it might work that way.

Of course, once he opened the gate the zombies might come storming in killing and eating everyone in Eden like they'd done over in Jericho. Diaz tried to give a fuck but couldn't, and didn't feel bad about it. Since Shannon was gone... Since Harris had killed her...

"I want to go to bed, Diaz," Bear called through the screened window. "You gonna stand out there on that porch all damn night or you gonna come in here get some of this Dona Juanita?"

Diaz smirked, put Thompson's lighter back in his pocket for a later date and went inside to get some to take home and smoke.

ACKNOWLEDGEMENTS

ZOMBIES HAVE ALWAYS scared the crap out of me. My earliest memories of a zombie movie were the exploding head/watermelon in the original *Dawn of the Dead*. I saw this movie as a kid and Tom Savini's special effects wizardry left an indelible impact on my vulnerable psyche. Goddamn you, Tom! That means: thanks brother. George Romero is the undisputed king of zombie cinema and the highest accolades aren't high enough for this man, a guy who directly influenced some of my other favorite zombie horror directors, including Lucio Fulci and Dario Argento.

Danny Boyle gave us *28 Days Later*, which technically isn't a zombie movie, but I'm not looking to pick nits here, I'm looking to give props and shouts outs. Boyle and Zack Synder between them lent us the conceit that the homicidal monster—be he a Rage-virus infectoid or a cannibalistic zombie—can, like the Pink Floyd song, "run like hell," a conceit I adopt openly (brazenly steal, if you will) herein. I wish I could say I love all the new slew of zombie movies that have been coming out. Alas, it isn't so. I enjoyed the *Resident Evil* games but hated the films; I prefer listening to Milla Jovovich screaming her lungs out affixed to a burning stake as *The Messenger*, Joan of Arc, rather than battling the evil Umbrella Corporation.

We need more good undead literature. Right now I put Robert Kirkman and his *Walking Dead* comic book in the top spot. Keep on keeping on brother! I don't buy the supernatural channeling aspect or zombies who can speak, but mad props to Brian Keene and what he's accomplished. Richard Matheson—what can I say? Again, *I Am Legend* isn't a zombie novella (despite what the third filmed version tries to make it appear to be), but it might as well be. I'm just wondering when someone in Hollywood is going to come correct with the cinematic version. Maybe it'll have to happen outside of Hollywood.

Finally, I need to thank you, dear reader. If you read this book and liked it, help spread the word. Whether you liked it or not I'd like to hear why, so if you have the time and the inclination give me a holla' at TommyArlin@gmail.com. Peace!

Tommy Arlin,
Parts Unknown
2005

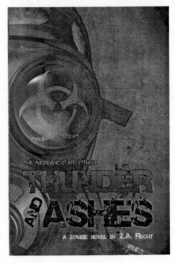

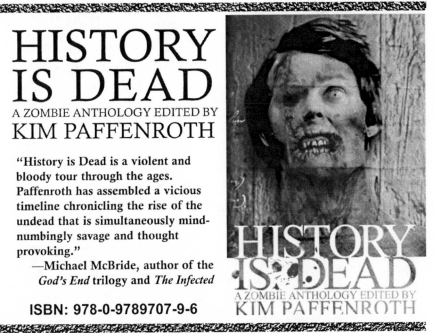

THE
UNDEAD
ZOMBIE ANTHOLOGY
ISBN: 978-0-9765559-4-0

"Dark, disturbing and hilarious."
—Dave Dreher, *Creature-Corner.com*

THE
UNDEAD
VOLUME 2
SKIN AND BONES

ISBN: 978-0-9789707-4-1

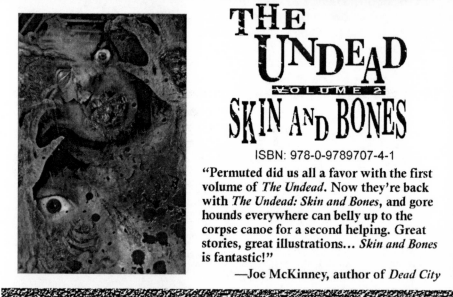

"Permuted did us all a favor with the first volume of *The Undead*. Now they're back with *The Undead: Skin and Bones*, and gore hounds everywhere can belly up to the corpse canoe for a second helping. Great stories, great illustrations... *Skin and Bones* is fantastic!"
—Joe McKinney, author of *Dead City*

The Undead ⚡ volume three
FLESH
FEAST

ISBN: 978-0-9789707-5-8

"Fantastic stories! The zombies are fresh... well, er, they're actually moldy, festering wrecks... but these stories are great takes on the zombie genre. You're gonna like *The Undead: Flesh Feast*... just make sure you have a toothpick handy."
—Joe McKinney, author of *Dead City*

Printed in the United States
210230BV00002B/105/P

9 781934 861172